Pavlov's Bell

Terry Kerr

*For Prue and Hattie.
I didn't forget.
Hell, I'll never forget.*

The following is a work of fiction. Any resemblance to actual persons living or dead is unintentional and should not be inferred. Though real locations are used, I have taken many geographical liberties, particularly with Ealing Broadway station.

This work is copyright and must not be reproduced in any way without the author's permission.

Before

She could have killed him, right there and then. Even though she loved him, she could have killed him.

It was August, 2009, and she was shivering. It wasn't a hot summer, but she wasn't shivering because she was cold. In fact, she wasn't shivering at all. She was spasming.

This must be why they call it 'kicking the habit,' she thought, and while that wasn't funny, it almost made her laugh. Her legs were uncontrollable, jittering and jiving as if bolts of electricity were being passed through her.

It was the legs that were the worst somehow. The ill temper, she'd expected that (even if she hated it) The foggy, not-quite-headachy *head, ditto. But this? Lying in her bed on a* should be hotter *August night with her legs doing the Cha-Cha-Cha was just so ...well, embarrassing.*

Hang on, *he said.* It's okay. Keep it together. Then, soft; hard times pass. *He kissed her on the forehead, whispered it over and over, and dear God if there'd been a gun in the house at that point she'd have run for it (dancing legs or not) and shot him through the head. What did* he *care? How many cigarettes had he smoked in* his *life? None. What did* he *know about what she was going through? Nothing.*

Eve Wilson (known to many as Eve Rogers) lay in her bed in August 2009, going cold turkey, in the purest agony of nicotine withdrawal, and listened to the man she loved, her husband Carl, patronise her and it took every inch of her self-control not to punch him or scream at him or just turn over and bite into his shoulder. Hard times pass, *he said, over and over.*

Hard times pass.

Chapter One

Standing in the church, looking at the coffin, Eve Wilson would have cheerfully sold her soul for a smoke.

Come on hon, said her husband from the only place he could be these days, *did we go through all that for nothing?*

Yes babe, she thought back, *looks like we did.*

The priest was talking, but about what Eve had no idea. Her listening skills had gone on vacation. He could have been saying that her dead husband was Jimmy Saville's pimp, that he buggered sheep and bit the heads off babies for all she knew or cared. All she could think of was a Silk Cut, so round, so beautifully packed, so dangerous, so sexy. Rip off the cellophane, pull the paper from under the lid, pop one of those bastards in the mouth and light it up and…oh! The only thing that ever came near it was an orgasm. A shudder ran through her, and on her left her sister Sarah took it as a sign that finally Eve was ready to collapse and bawl and holler. She reached out an arm which enfolded Eve's shoulders. On her right, Jon, Carl's brother, did the same thing – out of duty or concern or both she knew not and cared less.

She accepted the comfort in the way it was expected. Would they hate her if they knew what had just happened? Would they hate her if they knew she had been racked with a physical craving for nicotine that had bucked her thighs like the most intense come she'd ever experienced? Would they hate her if they knew all she could think was not *goodbye my darling* or *what do I do now* but *please God, let there be a cigarette machine behind that font. Let it have sixteen Silk Cut for a tenner. Frig that, I'll take Lambert and Butler. Jesus, right now I'd smoke Marlboro Lights. Smoke all sixteen in one go, all shoved up in my mouth in a big circle and lit with a blowtorch, and you know something? That might actually make up for this shit. Please and thank you God, okay?*

But there was no cigarette machine behind the font, and so she thought of the week just under four years past now, the week when she shivered in the not hot at all August night as he held her. All for nothing. Hard times pass.

Dear God, don't let that be a lie.

Chapter Two

Eve flushed as quietly as possible, acutely aware that Sarah and her husband Steve were asleep across the landing, trying to catch as many Zs before their long trip back to Manchester. *Maybe something will come of all this,* Sarah had said, holding her. *Maybe …you know …*

She knew. *Maybe you and I can put it all behind us. You reckon? Maybe. Stranger things have happened. Carl could have sat up with me every night for a week as I grew out of my dependency, and then he could have gone and caught himself pancreatic cancer and wasted away in less time than it takes to tell. Him no smoker, him get cancer, you got to love the irony.*

Still, it might be possible. There just might be some sort of reconciliation between Eve and her sister. Maybe Carl's death might act as some sort of glue to finally cement them together, to bridge that odd, silent distance that existed ever since …well, forever really.

Yeah, maybe. Stranger things have happened. Though I'm not sure what.

She opened her bedroom door (*her* bedroom, not *their* bedroom, and that hurt, oh yes), and there was Carl at the window, looking at her with that strange little half-smile thing he did.

She didn't cry out or faint – not for consideration of her guests' sleep, but simply because there was no need. Carl wasn't a ghost, there were no such things as ghosts, this was just her mind calling him back to her, her mind trying to take the edge off the day, her mind trying to help.

"Did you buy smokes?" he asked.

"Nope," she said, climbing under the duvet. Even with twenty togs above her, the February night was bastard cruel. She made herself as small as she could, like a hedgehog, trying to be warm.

"Good deal," he said, staying by the window. Eve closed her eyes, listening to his voice. She'd loved his voice. *How long will it be until I forget how he spoke? What will my vision do then, poor thing?* "I didn't go through all that for nothing."

"Yes you did," she said, burrowing her head into her pillow. "We both did. We all do."

*

Sarah and Steve went back early the next morning. Eve and Sarah shared another awkward hug at the doorstep while Steve sat in the car, trying not to rev the engine impatiently. He had, after all, been away from his company for two days. Grief was all very well, but it didn't pay bills. Still, he'd done his best to cover it, and for that Eve supposed she could find something in her heart for him. Though what exactly she couldn't say.

"You need anything, call," said Sarah. "I mean it. Anything."

"You bet," Eve replied, and bit her bottom lip to avoid braying a huge peal of laughter at the thought of calling her only sibling two hundred or so miles up the country and saying, *Hey Sarah, can you nip to Boots? I'm out of Always Ultra and I just can't be frigged going myself. Hey, come on …you* did *say anything!*

They held each other for another second or two, and Eve could see it all over the older woman's face, the way she'd been able to see it since she'd been a little girl. *Who are you,* it said. *Where do you come from? I don't know you, you're nothing like me or Mum and Dad. Where I come from two and two make four and there are three hundred and sixty degrees in a circle, but you …you still see the Man in the Moon, don't you, little Eve? You still think the toys come to life when you go to sleep, you still think the wardrobe leads to Narnia.* But she said nothing, she kept her counsel, and that must've hurt her sister the way not revving the Beamer was hurting Steve, so Eve gave her another quick squeeze. "Give me a ring when you get home, let me know you're safe."

"I will," said Sarah, then they were gone.

Jon, Carl's brother, rang that afternoon, asking how she was, telling her that if there was anything he could do ...she liked Jon, he was very much like Carl (in fact Jon was four years Carl's junior, but much to her late husband's annoyance they had often been mistaken for twins), but she did wonder how he'd respond to being told that he'd just interrupted a conversation between herself and his dead brother about whether Charles Dickens was a more important literary figure than William Shakespeare. She'd just been telling Carl how the vividness of Dickens' characters made for rich human drama when the phone had rung, and yes, she liked Jon, and he was really the only thing in the real world close to being Carl ...but when the phone had rung her dead husband had vanished, and it took many hours to call him back again.

Chapter Three

"You need to work," said Tom, two months later.

Eve was sitting in his office, just off Wardour Street, and wondered if she should punch him. On reflection she decided it would be counterproductive, so she sat there and kept her face steady. "No I don't," she said.

"I'm not turning this into a pantomime," said Tom as he shifted a pile of papers from one side of his desk to another. He was a fidgeter when things got sticky with his clients. She'd seen it plenty over the years. Once, when she'd turned down a lead in a BBC medical series that would have made them a lot of money, he'd practically made a Tower of Babel out of the odds and ends that sat before his computer. But she'd won. Eve Wilson could be a stubborn cow at times.

"And I don't blame you," she said, and made to stand. "Well, lovely to see you again, Tom. We must do this again."

"Sit down, Eve," he said, and the tone of his voice made her obey. It was implacable – a sort of pitiless exasperation. Eve didn't think she'd ever heard him speak like that before. "I was talking to your accountant. Alwyn," he added, just in case she'd forgotten his name.

"Really," said Eve, perplexed. Why would her agent and her accountant be talking?

"He's been looking at your numbers," Tom went on, answering that unspoken question, "and they're looking thin. Not anorexic yet, but thin."

Looking thin, Eve thought. She suppressed the image that brought to mind and kept a straight face. "So? Surely there are some residuals due in soon."

"From what?" asked Tom, twiddling a pen through his fingers like the world's oldest gay majorette. "You've been in the theatre for the last three years. Exclusively. Do plays pay actors residuals, Eve?"

"Don't patronise me," she said, losing her straight face. If there was one thing she hated …

"Then don't behave like an idiot," snapped Tom.

This is going well, thought Eve. *I'm really glad I picked up the phone and took this call. I was having a fine old imaginary conversation with Carl. Thanks for ruining my day, Tom.* On the heels of that, *Okay kid, keep it together. Please.* Digging her nails into her palms, she said – as calmly as she could – "I'm sorry. So, what's the story?"

The pen went back to its resting place next to the phone. "I'm sorry too. The story is you need a job. Especially since …Carl." *Isn't it odd how few people can use the word* died? "Before he …well, your joint money could bring you that nice standard of living you have. But now …you need work. And fast."

A weight dropped on her. The thought of it. So soon. "Tom, c'mon," she said, "I only …I mean, it was only February when we buried him. I don't think I could …"

"I know hon, I know," said Tom. He wasn't a bad bloke, really. He was doing what was best for her. But she felt as she did back in 2009 as the nicotine had worked its way out of her system. She could have killed him. *Hard times pass,* Carl had said. *Any idea when?* "But the fact remains that you haven't worked since …he was diagnosed …and there just isn't a lot left. Ask Alwyn if you don't believe me."

"I do," she said, and did. He wouldn't lie. But *Jesus!* The thought of actually *working* again …

"And look," Tom continued, back to the fidgeting, "I don't like to say this, but …"

"Then maybe you shouldn't."

"But I *have* to," he went on. "You're coming up to forty, Eve. Dangerous time for an actress."

"Actor."

"Oh, for *fuck's* sake, Eve, I'm trying to *help* you here! Can you please cut me a bit of frigging *slack?*"

There was a very dark part of her that really didn't want to cut him any slack – in fact, that very dark part of her wanted to rip his head off and drink the blood. But she kept quiet. Just.

"Hell, you're still a good looking woman," Tom went on, "and don't start on that *looks shouldn't count* bollocks, because they do, you know they do, but you're hitting a point where you're too old for Mary Warren and too young for the Scottish Play, with me?"

That prissiness almost made her smile. But still, she was becoming frightened. *Yeah, he's right. Damn him.*

"I think …I think we may have to think about changing your career path …"

"No," she said. That slight niggle of fear evaporated. In its place was her default setting. Stubbornness.

"Look, come on," pleaded Tom, "even Judi and Diana do telly, or film. Even they have to buy coffee."

"Don't care," Eve said. "No telly, no film, no adverts. Just *no*. How many times have we had this discussion?"

"Counting this? Twice."

Once again, he almost made her smile. But the key word was *almost*.

The office went silent, Tom staring at her, trying his best puppy dog *please make me happy* face. She was having none of it. She refused to have any of it. She could hold her breath longer than him. Longer than anyone.

"Here's what I'll do then," said Tom eventually, sighing, accepting defeat. "I'll put the feelers out, see who's scouting for what. Nothing too heavy. Just enough to bring your balance up. How's that?" Then, seeing the look on her face, he leaned forward, quickly. "Yeah, quality work, with you, something of value. But will you *please* bend a little? Value is a relative term." *You want me to list the names who've done* Coronation Street, *was the unspoken subtext. Knights of the realm, hon.*

Don't care, was her unspoken counter argument. *I'm not them, I don't sell out.*

Softer, because he was a good agent, Tom said, "I'm only looking out for you, you know."

More unspoken subtext: *because there's no one else looking out for you. I'm all you've got now your husband's in the ground.* "I know," she said. *God, how many more years have I got left like this?* "Okay," she said. "Do it."

*

She managed to get home before the tears exploded out of her, but it was close. Her breath was hitching as she parked up, and her lip was trembling as she slotted her front door key home, but it wasn't until she fell onto her sofa (*hers*, not *theirs*) that the dam burst. *A million years of crying already,* she thought, *and a million more to come! In between learning lines and crossing out moves, that is!*

After half an hour, with the storm just about passed, she heard the living room door close behind Carl. She raised her blurred eyes to the clock. 6.25. *Yeah, that's his time. Rehearsals done, now he's home.*

Except he's not rehearsing anything, unless it's an experimental piece called 'How to be Eaten by Worms.' He's dead, remember?

Hey really? That must be why we went to the Church that day and I wore my best black dress! I know he's dead, arsehole! I'm just not ready to let him go yet! Okay?

"Hey …what's all this, Evie?" Ah, that voice – how she loved it! Come to think of it, there wasn't much she didn't (*hadn't*) love (*loved*) about him. She told him about her day as his arms enfolded her and rocked her back and forth. "That's the problem with agents," said Carl, and she could tell he was half-smirking, half-scowling. "They're nearly always right. Which is why we hate them. You know he made sense, don't you?"

She told him she did, which is why she'd nearly lost her temper.

"How much of a stubborn pain in the arse were you?"

Eve told him she might have been a little …well, *intractable*.

"And the sky is blue and the world is turning," he said, and she knew he was grinning. Then, "Hey, c'mon Evie," he said, switching to that infuriating *lets-get-to-business* tone he (*used to*) use just to annoy her. "Something'll turn up, to paraphrase Mr McCawber. I'll ask around, see who's after what."

"What can you do?" asked Eve, speaking aloud for the first time in the conversation. "You're dead." But Carl had gone.

Not that he was ever there, of course.

*

That night she was huddled on the sofa, flicking through her photograph album. Of course, the more recent ones were on the PC, but the thought of turning the bloody thing on and scanning through her desktop icons was too much of a trial – besides, the Dell was upstairs in what they called "The Office" and she didn't want to move. So there she was, flipping pages. Carl directing *An Uncommon Pursuit* at the Lyric, Hammersmith, taken from the programme. Tall, thin (though not as thin as he'd become), intelligent, soft brown eyes scanning the stage …

Another tear, a huge one, ran down her cheek. She waited to see if it would bring a friend, but it didn't. So she turned the page.

Here she was in Pisa, one of the few holidays they'd managed together. She was sitting outside a café, foaming cappuccino in her hand, milk moustache on her top lip, forming the words *don't you fucking DARE!* She was laughing though. They'd laughed a lot, and mostly together, and when you came down to it, wasn't that the secret of a good marriage?

How long ago had that trip been? Five years? Seven? Was that possible? Was she really now thirty-eight (a dangerous age for an actress …or actor)? Was she then, back in Italy, already adding that rinse to her ash blonde hair? She tried to remember if it had sat on the bathroom shelf in that hotel, but all she could remember were the times he'd chased her round that bedroom, or when they'd traipsed through the ninth art gallery on their itinerary and she'd whispered in his ear, "If I see one more painting of some bastard nailed to some sticks I'll scream," she couldn't get past the memories of the fun they'd had, and then there was that blockage in her throat, the one she'd grown so accustomed to over the past few months.

So she turned the page.

Frowning, she turned back, the blockage gone.

Then she turned forward again, sitting up.

The photo that should have been there was missing.

What the ...she thought, flipping the pages back and forth, as if this would somehow make the missing photo appear. It didn't. Before, Pisa with the cappuccino. After, blank page. After that, she and Carl outside the Fortune where he was due to begin previews for *The Woman in Black*. So ...where was the photo that should have been in its place? And more importantly, *what was it?*

Eve tried to call it to mind, but couldn't – after all, who the hell could remember all the photos they had stored about the place?

So she couldn't remember what it was, she had no idea where it was ...which meant only one thing. It didn't matter. If it mattered, she'd not only be able to recall what the image was but also what they'd done with it. And if things didn't matter, the only sane thing to do would be to forget about them.

Which meant, of course, that Eve tore the house apart looking for it.

First she examined the carpet, in case the photo had fallen out of its corner mounts on the way from the bookcase to the sofa. Nothing. So she pulled the sofa out in case it had floated underneath.

Which it hadn't. So then she pulled the cushions off the sofa. She found a pound coin and a button, but no photo.

Eve stood in the centre of the room, starting to pant a little – not from exertion, from frustration. She then pulled the armchair from the wall and removed its cushions. Nothing. Then she went to the bookcase and pulled every book from the shelves. No photo. She then flipped through every page of every book, just in case. And since there was no photo found, she rifled through the drawers – bills, bank statements, pizza menus – to find nothing but bills, bank statements and pizza menus.

'For *fuck's* sake!'

She stood in the living room (*hers,* not *theirs*), practically dancing with frustration, the way she'd practically danced with nicotine withdrawal, acutely aware that a full blown tantrum wasn't far away, aware of how stupid she must look with her grey eyes wide and bloodshot, her ash blonde (rinsed) hair pulled into sweaty clumps, and wished to God that none of this was happening, wished to God with all her aching heart that it was 2009 again, and never mind about how hard it had been to pack up the cigs, she just wanted it to be the past again so there would be none of this, no standing alone in an empty house one room of which had a detritus covered floor simply because she couldn't find a photograph she couldn't even remember.

"Hey Carl," she said through a hissing in breath as she desperately attempted to keep calm, "I got me some hard times here. So …when do they pass, hey? *When?*"

But the room kept quiet, and that just made things worse. "I *mean* it, Carl." She was on the verge now. "*When?* You're so clever, so *when?*"

Nothing but the traffic on Ealing Road.

"*WHEN DO THEY FUCKING PASS?*"

Nothing bar a diesel engine and a motorbike for an answer.

Incensed beyond all human reason by being ignored by the world, Eve threw herself on the sofa and kicked her legs like a two year old, screaming inarticulate threats at nobody, howling at the unfairness of everything.

There went another night as Eve Wilson learned how to be a widow. In the months to come, she'd look back on it all and consider it a bit of a holiday, really.

*

She tried to sleep the morning away, but couldn't. She was awake, and that was that. That was the way she'd always been – once up, she was up, she'd never been able to turn over and go back to sleep. A look at her watch told her it was just after seven. She made a noise that wasn't a sigh or a moan, but sounded like a bit of both. *What's the point?* that noise said. *Why bother? What will I actually do if I get up?*

Well eat, her stomach growled in answer, and she supposed that was good enough. She *schlepped* downstairs to the kitchen, poured some cereal into a bowl and made her way into the living room to watch something while she exercised her digestive system.

It was right in her line of sight as she opened the door, away from the pile of papers she'd pulled from the drawer, on its own, lying on the carpet where it *absolutely* hadn't been the night before, where it *absolutely* had to be seen.

A photograph.

No, not just *a* photograph, *the* photograph.

Very carefully, Eve placed the bowl of muesli on the coffee table and took four very unsteady steps to the middle of the room. *How did I miss this?* was her first thought, but even before it had formed properly she dismissed it. *I didn't miss this. I couldn't have missed this. It* wasn't here.

Her hands trembling, she picked it up. A glossy 6x5 of her husband with another woman, taken at a party somewhere …Enfield? Yes, Enfield. At *her* house. At Laura's house.

"Christ," Eve heard herself say. She wanted to sit down, but didn't trust her legs to carry her that far, so instead she stayed on her haunches, gazing at this impossible thing in front of her. Carl and Laura. At that party …well, *one* of her parties anyhow. Taken by Eve herself, if memory served.

Out of focus at the back of frame was a Christmas tree, and both people looking into the lens had that slightly bleary-eyed *it's half eleven and I'm not drunk yet but I'm on the way* look about them ...and yes, that photo had been Laura's idea, her odd Scots/Italian voice had hectored Eve into taking it ..."C'mon, c'mon, get one of me and your man," she'd said, "get one of us – Christ knows it's the only time you'll get us to pose together!" Yes, that's what she'd said – or something near enough – and it was true, because they didn't really like each other, did they, but they were at that party, Eve and Carl (*why?* she couldn't remember) and they'd done a good enough job of pretending to get along and the wine had flowed so when Laura had started badgering, Eve had raised the camera and they'd both smiled a slightly *not quite drunk* smile, and when Eve had lowered the lens Laura had said something like, "There, that was painless, wasn't it?" and when the roll had been developed (because that's what you did in those days), Eve had *insisted* it went in the album, because even though you loved your husband sometimes you just *had* to piss him off a bit.

But it wasn't in the album last night. It wasn't in this *room last night. In fact, I'd put money on it not being in this* house *last night. But hey presto! Here it is this morning, large as life and twice as ugly. What does that mean? Does it mean anything?*

Just then, the phone rang. Without thinking, Eve picked it up, photo still in one hand.

"Hello?"

"Hi Eve," said an odd Scots/Italian voice in her ear. "It's Laura. Just wondering how you were."

"Oh ...you know," said Eve somehow, looking down at the photo which wasn't so much trembling now as bucking like a dinghy in a tsunami.

"Aye," said the woman down the line. "Well, no I don't, but still ...anyway, I've got a job for you, if it's not too soon."

Chapter Four

'"It took many men to bring him down,'" read Eve into the mic, "'but eventually down he went, and down he stayed. Fernack wiped his forehead, beckoned the wagon, and prayed Duke would never, ever get up again.'" She raised her cup of water and looked through the glass. "How was that?"

"Perfect," said Laura, her voice crackling through the talkback, making her sound like a Scots/Italian Dalek. She turned to the engineer, who flinched visibly. Eve grinned despite herself and sympathised with the poor bastard. He couldn't be much over nineteen and Laura Rossi had eaten many a boy like him for breakfast – in all sorts of ways. "How was it for you, Barry?"

"Fine Ms Rossi. Good read, Miss Rogers."

"Eve," said Eve, swigging more water, knowing that to this boy she'd never be "Eve", knowing that just making that gesture would piss Laura off to the max. Not that Eve disliked the woman (much) she just enjoyed mucking up her power games. "Should we try the next?"

"You ready?" Asked Laura.

"As I'll ever be," said Eve, shuffling the sides. "Just give me the nod."

"I'm copying over the card," said Barry. "Give me a second."

Eve scanned the first page while things were busy elsewhere, hoping to God it looked like she was calm and professional. Inside ...well that, as the Saxon had said encountering the dark haired Viking, was truly a Norse of a different colour.

The photo goes missing, then turns up again – not in the album, but right on the floor, where she can't miss it. As she picks it up, the phone rings. It's the woman in the photo – the *only* photo Eve possesses of this woman. Twenty-four hours after her agent tells her she needs a job, this woman offers her one – and a nice, easy one, three books (one a short story anthology) on tape recorded over a five day stretch in a studio in Soho. Good money for reading aloud.

A "nice, easy job," the sort her agent had advised her to take ...but it wasn't Tom's voice she heard, it was Carl's.

"I'll ask around, see who's after what," he'd said.

"What can you do, you're dead," she'd replied. But that night the photo was gone from the album, then it was back, and Laura rang with a job. Maybe not the greatest job in the world – or even the greatest *books* in the world - but it had more value than a frigging advert, and what had Tom asked her to do? Bend a little? Okay then. This far. But no further.

Of course, Eve *knew* it was just a coincidence. Eve *knew* that Carl wasn't a ghost. Eve knew both of those things. But still, what had she said as she'd put the receiver down after telling Laura to call her agent and talk money?

"Thanks, Carl." *That's* what she had said.

He said he'd ask around …he said he'd see who was after what …and maybe …maybe he *had*.

Even though he was dead, maybe he had.

"Okay, clear. Ready to roll," said Barry.

"Right," added Laura, a slight edge to her voice. Had that boy next to her attempted to *start the session?* Oh, he'd get that knocked out of him, Eve was sure of that. Laura nodded through the glass.

"*Mr Harrison's Afternoon,* by Stephen Vaughn," said Eve, her clear, trained voice cutting through the air like crystal. "Chapter One. 'It was a Wednesday on which it all happened, a Wednesday in June, but it seemed like a Sunday in September.'"

*

"I was sorry to hear about Carl," said Laura as she ordered the coffees. "Sorrier still that I couldn't get to the funeral. I was in Bolton, doing that show at the Octagon." She looked at Eve as though Eve would know – *should* know – what that show at the Octagon was.

Of course, Eve had no idea. Of course, she nodded in an *I understand completely* sort of way. "I sent a sympathy card. You did get it, didn't you?" Some form of mild rebuke there, a 'you didn't acknowledge it' tone.

"Yes, I did," said Eve, and had she? Maybe. There'd been a ton of the damn things, and she'd no idea where they were. Stuck in a drawer somewhere, probably. Most of them unopened. "And thank you, it was very kind. I haven't got round to …you know."

This time it was Laura's turn to nod *I understand completely,* and the words dried up a bit. She was a hard woman, Laura. Hard, but fair – that had been Carl's assessment of her. *She's a bitch, but a* fair *bitch. She's a bitch to everybody. And a credit grabber. No one has a good idea but her. Still, she puts on a decent enough show, I'll give her that much.* That was as close to a compliment as Carl would allow himself. *I don't mind her,* Eve had said, and that was true, she didn't – but couldn't really understand *why.* Laura was pretty much her complete opposite, the 'anti Eve' as Carl had once said – tall, dark hair, dark skin, dark eyes and a tendency to have sex with any man she wanted. Not to get ahead, just because she could. Just because that gave her the power.

Every man? Except Carl. Eve thought Laura might have tried, all the same. Why? Just because she could. Maybe before she and Carl had got together, maybe later …after all, *something* had to account for the way they were together, for that spark, that energy that Eve couldn't quite place. The only time she'd ever brought it up, Carl had put it down to pure mutual dislike, the fact they were similar sized fish in a similar sized pond …but *had* it been? *Really?* The way they'd almost baited each other on the rare times they'd met was almost like …well, Beatrice and Benedik, really.

The waitress brought the Americanos over, and Eve took the opportunity to look about her. Two days into the gig and it still seemed incredible to be out in the world again. Less than four months since her man had died, only half a year since he'd been diagnosed, yet it seemed like everything had changed, it seemed like she'd been on the moon. Everything seemed brighter, sharper, louder …it was like when she'd been at RADA and that guy she'd been sleeping with (Brendan? Bernard? Barney?) had brought the coke, and she'd done a bit – just a touch, half a sniff – and *whap!* It was like she'd slipped on 3D glasses, the whole world just leaped out at her. In truth, it had scared her a little, so she never did the coke again (oh, that she could say the same about the dope, or the speed, or the booze …)

"How're you finding it?" Laura asked, jolting her.

"Finding what?"

"The job. Because if you don't mind me saying, this is the best book reading I've ever produced."

I've ever produced. Not I've ever heard, *but I've ever* produced, spoke Carl in her head. *Credit grabbing bitch.* "It's all right; I'll fuck it up this afternoon."

"'No you won't. Remember, we're out of this studio Friday, and if we're not finished you don't get paid," said Laura, smiling. A smile from Laura was a rare thing, something to treasure. *Something inside that woman sure went sour,* Carl had once said. *She wouldn't laugh if she saw a table walk.* "I mean it though, Eve. Not many takes, no hanging around and – if you don't mind me saying this – there's a quality to your voice I haven't heard before. There's some *fragility,* I suppose you'd call it. It's haunting."

"Do I take that as a compliment?" *Hey, you hear that Carl? Maybe she's maturing. Or mellowing. Or whichever.*

"You certainly can." *You get that, Carl? Y'know, maybe that ...whatever it was ...between you two clouded your judgement.* Then Laura leaned forward, and if she wasn't actually concerned then she did a damned good impression. "Look, are you sure I can't get you something to eat? Sandwich? Doughnut? You're too fucking skinny."

Eve managed to keep her face arranged a hell of a lot better than she did in Tom's office. Hence, when Laura had leaned forward and said "You're too fucking skinny," the other woman would never have noticed that not only did a goose walk over Eve's grave; it stopped off and did The Hustle.

You're too fucking skinny, Carl, she'd said as she watched him towel himself dry. He'd climbed out of the shower – Jesus God, not ten months ago – while she was cleaning her teeth and there were ribs and a collarbone where before there'd been skin. Oh, sure, she'd known a bit of weight was dropping off him – hey she saw him practically every night without clothes, didn't she? – but this was in the day, with the sun crashing through their bathroom window, and there it was, something that gnawed at her as she rinsed and spat MacLean's Ice and Shine into the bowl, something that said *hey, look at him ...was he* ever *that thin, even when you first met? Jesus, why did I never notice those* cheekbones *before?*

"You're too fucking skinny," she said, still loving him, still fancying him, still wanting him inside her no matter how skinny he was. "Don't you get fed at the Court?"

"With a cast like mine," he said, rubbing his neck with the towel, (and oh look here, sister, but doesn't what's stirring down there mean he still fancies you as well? After all these years! Wasn't lust supposed to fail?) "you can't afford to take breaks. You just have to hit them and hit them and hit them some more until they begin to understand what Brecht was all about. Jesus, I don't know what they teach in schools anymore."

"They teach directors to be bastards and actors to be dummies ...its symbiosis.' But did she care about symbiosis? Not then, not that morning, she cared about how hard his cock was, to be truthful, about what it could do and where it went, and so what if he dropped a couple of pounds from his face or his chest? As long at his prick stayed more or less the same, she'd be a very happy bunny indeed.

Yes, she told herself later on those nights where she lay in her cold bed alone as her husband was wired up to monitors and tubes ran up his arse, she *should* have paid closer attention, she should have *noticed,* but come on, really, who noticed *erosion?* Who stood on a shoreline daily and said, "Yep, we lost a good three millimetres overnight?" No one. You just couldn't tell when it was right in front of you, not until it was too late.

And of course, he'd hidden it from himself ...he must've been so scared ...

All of that ran through Eve's head in a very short time indeed, which was something else which made her sad. Almost a year to live through, ten seconds to remember ...that's got to say something. "I'm going to get you a BLT," Laura said, "and you can stick whatever fucking diet you're on up your arse. But take your time chewing, I'm not having you ruining takes by burping." But before attracting the waitress's attention, Laura softened her eyes and looked over at Eve. *Something sour,* Carl had said. *Table walking* ...but there had been *something* between them, hadn't there, something that wasn't much, but *something* ...

"How hard *is* it for you right now?" Laura asked, and that sudden switch of topics startled Eve into telling the truth.

"Hard."

"It'll pass," said Laura. Then she looked away and found the waitress with a gesture. "Always does."

*

"I did good work today hon," said Eve as she lay in bed. It was coming up on April now, but she was cold in her bed. She'd been cold in her bed for a long time. "Two down, got halfway through the third. Laura was proud of me. Even gave me a compliment, even shared a bit of credit around. You would have been proud. What do you mean, you were? How could you ..." But before she heard the answer, she was asleep.

*

Eve pretty much raced through the job, minimum of fuss, minimum of retakes, shook Laura's hand, kissed Barry on the cheek (such a young kid, and was Laura mounting him night after night? Carl seemed to think so, and in truth so did she, but neither of them knew for sure), and as she left the studio for the last time Laura mentioned that there may be more work later that year, was it okay to call, and Eve had said it was.

That night she'd sat in front of her television and watched a quiz show or something with the sound down and listened to Carl talk about Chekhov and Dickens and Shakespeare and Mamet and Friel and Eve nodded when she thought he was right and argued when she thought he was wrong, and there went the evening.

But the following morning she came down to her living room (*hers*, not *theirs*) and that photo was back on the floor, dead centre of the living room carpet. She stood looking at it for a moment, feeling a slight slide in the world (though nowhere near the titanic lurch she'd felt a few weeks previously) and she made it to the bookcase and took down the photo album. Sure enough, the requisite page was blank. So she bent down to place the photo back and *that's* when it hit her.

The photo was ripped in half. There was only Laura. Of her husband (her *late* husband), there was no sign.

Eve stood there and had no idea what to do next.

*

Do you think he's really still here? she thought as she flushed and started to wash her hands. It was three in the morning, and at three in the morning there's no room to lie. Three in the morning is the time for truth. *When you talk to him? You see him, you hear him – but do you think he's* really *here? You do* know *it's just your grief talking?*

What about the photo, she asked herself. *The reason I've not slept tonight? That frigging* here-today-gone-tomorrow-*self-ripping photo? Is that my grief talking?*

Could be, in a way, she argued back. *Some form of memory blanking …maybe even a touch of somnambulism. You know, shock can do funny things to a person. Shock and grief.*

She turned that over as she plodded back to bed. Yeah, shock and grief were awful things, shock and grief really messed with your head …but *how long* had Carl been dead now? Months, wasn't it? Okay, so she could still be grieving …but still in *shock? Unlikely. I mean, how long does shock last, anyway? Shock's a debilitating emotional state. It dumps all sorts into your body – adrenaline and all that other happy stuff. Shock wears you out. You can't be in shock for months, it'd kill you.*

You're evading my question, the rational part of her brain said, the part that she made talk in her sister Sarah's voice. *I want to know whether you* really *think your dead husband's in the room with you when you talk to him.*

"I'm frigged if I know," she mumbled. She knew she was talking aloud, but she didn't care. She had no one to keep awake these days beyond herself, and no work in the diary. "And *who cares* anyhow? *Who cares* if I'm just thinking aloud? *Who cares* if I vandalise photos in my sleep?"

I do, said Sarah Voice. *I care, and so do Jon and Steve and everyone else in the world. Laura too, probably.*

"You don't know Laura, you've never *met* Laura."

Come on, I'm you. I know everything you know.

"Then you know what I know about Carl."

That's why I'm asking.

"Sarah," Eve said with an incredibly heavy sigh. "You *so* piss me off."

Some things you got to say out loud, Sis. Some things you –

But Eve finally, mercifully, fell asleep, and never heard the end of that statement.

*

"Hard times pass," Carl had said from the middle of the pain. He'd been drifting in and out by then, morphined up to fuck as his brother Jon had put it, and there wasn't long left, he was on his countdown. The doctors and the specialists and the consultants had stopped talking about procedures and treatments and had simply talked about making him as comfortable as possible, and yeah, that's how you knew. That's how they told you without telling you that your husband, your lover, your man, the shining centre of your earth wasn't going to get up and rip those drips out, he wasn't going to hear the new Katherine Jenkins album, that he would never find out what was going down with the folk on **Borgen**, that he was going to get put in a box, that one day and one day pretty soon he was going to be finished with that whole breathing thing, oh yeah he was going to put that aside in a file marked DONE, Mrs Eve Wilson was going to be a widow at the age of thirty-eight, don't buy him Christmas presents, they're just a waste of money. She'd sat by him, head lying on his chest, her hand across his, and there'd been beeps and boops from monitors as he pissed in one bag and he shat in another and his breath was **steel** somehow, it stank of **steel**, but he was her man and God she loved him, and that one night, even though his eyes were shut and he was drifting in some drug encased sky, he'd said, "Hard times pass."

"That's right baby," she'd said, was she crying? Oh yeah, back then she was **always** crying. "Hard times pass, love."

He hadn't spoken again that night. She'd sat there as long as she could, but eventually the nurses moved her along. They indulged her as much as they could – not because they knew her, but because they understood – but sometimes they just had to get her to go home. That was cool. She understood.

Hard times pass, *he'd said. On the way home she marvelled at the connection he'd made, the way he'd taken the memory of her suffering and put it to himself, his hard time would be over soon.*

Chapter Five

"Think you can face going back on stage?" Tom said four months later. August, the time her mind always went back to the week or ten days or however long it had been with the restless legs and the cloudy *not quite* headache. *Four whole years off the fags, baby,* she thought. *Hard times pass.*

Once again, she was back in his office, once again he was offering her work. He'd rung that morning, interrupted her shower, interrupted Carl as he soaped her back and ran his fingers down her thighs, and she'd not been happy, but how do you tell someone that? So when Tom had asked her to come and see him, was twelve thirty okay, she'd said yeah, fine, and she'd run back to the bathroom as soon as she could, but Carl, wouldn't you know it, was gone.

"Depends," said Eve, and sniffed. She was coming down with a cold, and the one thing she hated was a summer cold. Summer colds were a bitch to shift. Summer colds were the pits. Still, she understood why Tom phrased the question the way he had. She'd been signed on to play in *Ghosts* at the Arcadia when Carl's test results had come through, and Mr Chopra had run through the list of options, none of which sounded good, none of which were fun, all of which were futile, and she'd had to *bow out* as they called it.

"Depends on what?"

"The play, the director, the theatre, how long, stuff like that." Carl had tried to talk her out of *bowing out* – "You've made the commitment, Eve, they're promoting you – and work will keep you occupied," but Eve was having none of *that*, thank you very much. She was staying by his side, that was it, *shut up Carl, you've no way of changing my mind, Jesus, don't you know me by now?*

"And how much they offer."

"That's for you to haggle, but get me what you can. Who's the crew, what's the play?"

"Sir Peter's the producer, director's a new guy I don't know …um,' he fished around on his desk and brought out a sheaf of paper, "Mike Hughes, he's developing a reputation for challenging work. Got good notices for some play about the '84 miner's strike he did in Bradford. Play's a new one too, *Pavlov's Bell*, written by Barry somebody or other. He's done some radio, the odd Fringe piece. Anyway, he's a prospect I'm told – but he doesn't have a name yet, so they need a star. Especially if they're going to try and fill the Dagmar."

"They're taking some unknown kids to the *Dagmar?*" Eve's eyes popped from their sockets. The Dagmar was less a theatre, more a cannibal. It ate things. Plays, mostly. Carl had hated it. *It's a draughty barn and it's not soundproofed and it hates plays. It wants them to fail. It's a spook that place.* Still, he'd kept the one and only piece he'd directed there afloat – barely – but every night he'd come home in a sweat, even if it had gone well. Hell, *especially* if it'd gone well. "I tell you, hon, somewhere in its past an old actor or director topped themselves after a bad review or something and just before they checked out they cursed the fucking place." He'd said that after the final night party, maybe five o'clock in the morning, after they'd rolled off each other, as he was still drying on her thighs. "It's like acting into a blanket."

That had been years ago. Too many years ago. "Sir Peter developing a death wish?"

"Could be," said Tom. "Or he's confident about these kids' abilities. Or every other theatre was booked. Anyway, they're hot for you."

"They want me to audition?"

"Nope," said Tom, "they're just asking you to take a look at it."

"So? What's the piece like?"

"Ah," her agent replied, then started absently to move objects around on his desk. His stapler swapped places with the hole punch. "You know, I meant to, but ..." the box of treasury tags moved to where a second ago the mouse had rested and he shrugged his tiny shoulders. "You know how it is."

"Tom," Eve said, leaning forward, "have you *ever* actually read anything you've sent a client up for?"

The keyboard was raised in the air and given a shake. Five paperclips and a drawing pin fell out. All but one of the paperclips had been opened into an elongated S. "Well ...not the whole thing. Agents don't need to read it all. We have instinctive abilities regarding what material would suit our clients. And the director sounds like someone you should work with. Sounds a lot like ..."

"Like Carl," she finished for him. Nine months after his death, and oh boy, there was still the rip. Didn't that ever heal? *Ever?*

"Yes, like Carl. He sounds like he doesn't like the easy way round things, like he wants to do things that are important."

It was a no brainer. "Email it through," said Eve. "I'll take a look. Can't hurt."

But it did.

*

Do things that are important ...doesn't like the easy way round things ...Yeah, didn't that *just* sound like Carl?

He'd been a man she'd been aware of for some time before actually meeting him. He came with some reputation. Carl was The Next Big Thing in Name Directors; it was rumoured that even Trevor Nunn was wary of him, and some gossip had Carl linked with a future artistic directorship at the National, and if not there then the Royal Court, and if not there then the RSC ...and *blah* and *blah de blah*. It was a small, incestuous world theirs, vampiric, everyone knew everyone else, six degrees of Kevin Bacon, that's just how it was. And one night she'd finished a performance of *Gothik* at the Arcadia, and had nipped into the pub across the road for a swift gin and cigarette, and the tall broad man with the intelligent brown eyes walked up to her, smiled and introduced himself as Carl Wilson, and bang bang, out went her lights.

It wasn't love at first sight, no – that never happened. But it *was* more than infatuation. There was just something *about* this man. Not just that he'd seen the show, not just how flattering he was about her performance, or how informed he was ...but just something ...well, *something* ...

Something so *fierce,* that when he invited the young woman he'd been accompanied by to join them (Eve hadn't even noticed her) a tall, stunningly beautiful blonde called Grace someone, his ASM on the play he was directing in Ealing, Eve had felt a completely unexpected and utterly miserable stab of jealousy. She didn't want this Grace person to sit with them, she didn't want their even number to become odd, she wanted this man to herself, she wanted to look at him and listen to him, because he was not only handsome he was clever and he had a very dry wit, he was softly spoken and polite (and what kind of director was either of those?) and even though this Grace person turned out to be very personable and pleasant, Eve wasn't happy with the closeness between them, she didn't like the way they stood hip to hip, she didn't like the casual way they touched.

And she'd really *hated* the way he'd offered that Grace person a lift home. She'd *really* hated the fact that outside the pub only an hour later, Carl had simply shaken her hand, told her again what a talent he thought she was, and had then linked arms with this Grace person and the two of them had wandered into the night, leaving her alone to scour the streets for a cab.

Still, she could've called her boyfriend to pick her up.

But she didn't. She didn't because ...well, because Chris and Eve were nearly over. Back then the thought had made her a little sad, the way that she would feel as a little girl, gazing from her Chorlton window as Spring turned to Autumn. She would make her way home from performances of *Gothik* (where she'd ripped the place apart as Mary Shelley), and there would be Chris, sitting in front of the TV, not acting, just occasionally pulling shifts at a newsagents, and she'd think, *the leaves are turning brown on this. I can feel it. Can he?*

If he did, he never mentioned it. He held her and kissed her and was genuinely delighted for her success. But sometimes she could see the fright in his eyes, a glint of desperation that said, *why her and why not me?*

If he'd asked, she'd have told him – gently, but truthfully. "Chris," she'd have said, "you're a bloody good actor, and you're a handsome guy, but you just don't want it enough. I do. I always have."

*

Eve Wilson was determined and stubborn. She decided she wanted to act when she saw a pantomime at the Royal Exchange when she was six – *Snow White*, to be exact. All of a sudden when that curtain had risen to reveal a painted backcloth, Eve's imagination (that so frustrated and infuriated her *two-and-two-make-four* sister) found a focus. The theatre, it seemed, was a world where the impossible happened daily. With occasional matinees.

From that point on, it was a matter of *when*, not how or if. There was no mucking about from Eve, no Am Dram or school plays. She had an instinct about such things – she knew, without being told (or even without seeing them) that these things were not good enough for her. She immersed herself instead in the world of TV and cinema – and, of course, the professional stage. She began to learn what was good and what wasn't, what was worthwhile and what was pap – and, more importantly, who could act and who couldn't. She sat in her seat (whether that seat be in her front room, or the cinema or any theatre she could get to), and made a whole series of mental notes. This person made that move, it was good – this person said something that way, and it was bad.

She sat in her seat (whether that seat be in her front room, or the cinema or any theatre she could get to), and made a whole series of mental notes. She joined the local library (ironically enough, the one her sister Sarah would work in many years later) and checked out play after play, reading the words aloud in her bedroom, or actor biography after actor biography, checking for words of advice.

When the time came for her to leave school, she told her parents she wanted to go to London, to study at RADA. Nowhere else, just there, because it was the best.

They stared back at her, but by this time they'd lived with her for sixteen years and were well aware of their strange daughter's personality. In fact (though they would never admit it, not even to themselves) they'd pretty much written Eve off by then, and had concentrated all their efforts on Sarah, Sarah who was practical, Sarah who was sensible. "Okay Eve," they said. "Do what you want."

So Eve had.

So Eve became a star.

Not in the *stop-in-the-street-and-stare* sort of way, but she became a star all right.

She was a star at RADA – and of course she passed her audition, first time, no call-back; this was, after all, what she'd been working toward for ten years – she was the student who within the first weeks of her first term was being singled out for praise, was being admired by her peers.

Oh, she loved it. Not in an arrogant way (or at least she didn't think so) but because she had *found* it, found what it was that made her special, and was working it to her advantage. She was in the right place, doing the right thing, and everybody knew it. Granted, it led to a few boyfriends, and granted those few boyfriends introduced her to tobacco and dope and booze and the odd bit of speed, but these things were secondary to the fact that she had been *right all along*. And when the time came to leave RADA some three years later, it was gratifying (but unsurprising) that she was given the Gold Award for Best Performance, it was gratifying (but unsurprising) that an agent should approach her at the mixer afterwards and offer to represent her, and it was gratifying (but unsurprising), that at nineteen she was offered a role in the potboiler to end all potboilers, *Random Harvest*, at Equity minimum with no subsistence.

But still …she thought about it before saying yes.

Granted, it was a job offer (and her tutors had banged on and on, *endlessly*, about the need to *keep working*, that an actor who wasn't acting wasn't actually an actor) but it wasn't what she wanted to do. It was a crap play in a crap theatre. It wasn't *important*. It wouldn't *change* anything.

No, she'd thought in that Acton bedsit with the communal phone receiver in her hand, *this isn't what I want. And maybe the next one won't be either. But if I take this and do well, then I may be noticed. Who knows where this will lead?*

But as she accepted the offer, she found herself thinking, *I do. I know where it'll lead, eventually. Where I* want *it to lead.*

So she took the job, and met Chris (and that alone made it worthwhile, sort of) and then …well …she just didn't stop working.

Random Harvest led to an audition for *Butterflies are Free* in Primrose Hill – another crap play, but (as Eve had thought), she'd been noticed, and this was a much showier part – it was, in fact, the female lead.

"A lead," Chris had said, overjoyed (but maybe a little panicky, there'd been nothing for him since *Random Harvest* had ended) "that's *brilliant!* You must be ecstatic."

"Well, I've not got it yet," said Eve as he held her, but (a) she knew she would, and (b) no she wasn't. It was just the way she was determined things would go.

Of course, she got the part, a part that got her noticed some more. In some ways, she was unsurprised by this since Act One ended and Act Two began with her stripped to her underwear (in a non farcical, *I-was-about-to-have-sex* way) but what *actually* mattered was the fact that just about every critic more or less ignored the fact she was half naked, and instead said extremely flattering things about her. They used words like *radiant* and *explosive* and *magnetic*. After the First Night and those reviews, the director (a burly Welshman named John, a good man) had enfolded her in his arms and told her that she was on her way now, that nothing but good things would happen to her, and in the future she should give him as much fucking work as she could, and he'd laughed and she'd laughed back, but a look into his watery blue eyes had told her he didn't think he was joking, not on either count.

And he'd been right.

Despite the good reviews (well, for her anyway), *Butterflies* had folded in six weeks. *Goodnight baby and farewell,* Eve had thought as she took the phone call. As she'd hung up Chris had held her, and had there been any bitter joy in his heart that his girlfriend was back on the scrapheap alongside him he didn't say anything.

Okay Eve, she'd thought, *what're you going to do now? I mean, hey – those reviews have got to have raised your profile, surely? I mean, any minute now, that phone'll ring –*

In a story, that's where the phone would have rung with an offer. But in reality it was a week later, and when it did, it was a beauty.

Less than two years after leaving RADA, Eve Rogers was in Stratford, doing a season with the RSC, working with Peter Hall and Judi Dench and Patrick Stewart and a whole slew of brilliant people with huge reputations. But the most incredible thing of all? None of it fazed her. She was Eve Rogers, doing her job, doing it well, and fitting in with the people who'd been doing it much, much longer than she had. *This,* she thought as she waited for the house lights to dim before walking on stage as Desdemona, *is the place I was meant to be. This is the work I was meant to do. From now on, it's this standard or nothing.*

Compromise, from that moment on, was never an option.

Just before her season with the RSC was up, she took a phone call from Tom Millar. *Saw your work, it was good, I think you're on the way up, how's about I represent you?*

She'd heard of him – he was a major player – and for a second or two she'd thought to herself, *why's he asking me?* But a second or two was all it took for her to think, *I suppose it's because he thinks I'm good,* and she'd said *okay, thank you, that would be lovely,* and then she'd rung her now ex-agent, who'd been well fucked off at her and slammed the phone down.

This was the first decision she ever made without first including Chris, and looking back she could see that was the point where she became a grown up, twenty-one years old, time to think for herself.

As for Chris, well …he tried. He eventually picked up a pantomime in Southampton. "It'll mean being away from you for Christmas," he'd said, "but work's work."

"Of course it is, no problem at all, honey," she'd said (and was there just the *faintest* touch of condescension in her voice? Surely not!) "and hey, you won't be working Christmas Day, will you? I'll travel down the night before, see the show, and we can *still* have our Christmas!" She really *had* been thrilled for him though, genuinely happy. He was her man, and she did love him, and he was good at his job…but still, as she sat and watched from the stalls that Christmas Eve and saw Chris being funny and touching as Buttons, she found herself thinking, *you've found your level. This is what you have, what you will always have. Shame, really.*

So Eve found herself working steadily in the theatre for the next three years, good years and good plays, and she a low budget film for Channel 4 – directed by Ken Loach - which paid her almost nothing, but by God the reviews were incredible …

She never became a star - except she *did* become a star. She became a star within The Theatre World. She worked on Classics and Brave New Works and people in the business knew her. She developed a reputation. Offers kept coming in, tumbling over themselves, and some of them were telly or big films, and she turned every one of them down.

"Why *not?*" Tom had asked, exasperated as she instructed him to turn that BBC medical series down, no doubt thinking of the commission he'd lose on the frankly insane salary they were offering.

"Because it's shit," she'd responded.

"*Of course* it's shit, it's Saturday night BBC One, *of course* it's shit – but it's *well paid* shit, it'll subsidise the theatre, and it'll bring you exposure and …"

"And I'm not doing it," she'd said, in that odd, implacable tone that had arisen over the years. "I'm not, no argument. I'm building something here, Tom. I'm building a *reputation* – surely you can see that? I'm going to keep working in the theatre doing stuff that's worthwhile, okay?"

"But if you take this..." he'd started.

Once more, she'd finished. "But I'm not. So what else is there?"

Tom sighed, kissed his huge commission goodbye, and said *"Three Sisters.* At the National. Six months with options for three and three."

"Audition?"

"No, straight offer. But it's *peanuts* ..."

"When do I start?"

She never stopped working.

And she knew why.

It was because, in all modesty, she was very good at her job. Okay, she was considered attractive by some and that didn't hurt, but Eve knew looks alone couldn't fill theatres or guarantee funding for small projects. You had to be able to deliver, and she knew she could. She'd found that out a long time ago, back in Stratford, when she'd played Desdemona and had picked the play up, put it in her pocket and danced away with it.

*

That had been the first time she'd *burned,* the first time she'd felt as if she was out of herself, the first time she'd felt herself a channel, a vessel through which other forces worked, a conduit. She stopped being Eve and *became* Desdemona, that was it, simple, and others in that cast were brilliantly talented, oh yes they were, but none of them *burned* like she did, very few people *ever* did, that's what Carl had said all those years later, but *she* could, and that's why the phone kept ringing. She was just very, very good.

She *burned.*

And on one of the nights she'd burned, she'd nipped into the Lion for a few drinks and smokes before heading home, and there had been Carl and Grace someone, and by the time they'd said goodbye on Fitzroy Street she'd known one thing for sure; she'd met the only *other* human who burned.

Chapter Six

A woman can think many thoughts as she did a bit of shopping and then drove home.

Eve let herself in, Waitrose bags rattling and shaking, and even though Carl had been in the ground for nearly ten months now, she still wanted to call his name, she still looked for the note by the phone that would tell her he was out, that he'd be late, that he loved her and always would. *Thinking muchly of him today, Eve old Eve,* she decided as she put the fruit into a basket and the milk in the fridge, *but still, when are you ever not? When will you ever* be *not?*

Then she coughed and a whole load of phlegm hit the back of her throat. *Bastard summer cold. I mean, you're just not welcome, mate. Okay, you're* never *welcome, but at least I expect you in January. Turning up in August is just taking the piss, got me?*

Even if the cold *did* get her, it made no comment. It just made her cough again. *To Hell with you, I got me a cure.*

She poured a huge gin, waved a bottle of tonic at it, and sat on the sofa, the sofa upon which her husband had frequently ravished her (that was his word and how she loved it, *ravished,* that's how she always felt when his hands fell on her body), and she raised her glass to him, she told him she loved him, she told him about her day, told him about the cold she was starting with, about the job offer (of sorts) that had come her way, that it was at the Dagmar, what a riot, and after a while heard the door close behind him, she felt him beside her, heard him agree and disagree when he should.

He's not really *here though,* said the Sarah Voice who lived in her head. *You know that, right? You just make him up and it comforts you and that's all it is.*

*

"Have you *read* this?" Eve barked down the phone the following day. Her head hurt, her throat hurt, and not all of it was a hangover. Enough, but not all.

"I told you," said Tom in her ear, "not all of it. Why?"

She didn't reply at that second, unsure of what to say, how to put it …how to express *exactly* what she'd felt as she'd staggered to her computer and opened her emails, starting with the one from Tom. She'd really overindulged the night before and she had a head full of elephants all of whom were fighting with each other over the last Jaffa Cake. On top of that she'd dreamed heavily in the dark, heavily and ominously …something she could only half remember …and on top of that the summer cold had decided that it might just hang around for a while and worsen, so consequently the first ten pages of *Pavlov's Bell* had been little more than a blur.

It was only slowly that she realised *Pavlov's Bell* appeared to be a play about a recently widowed actress who was terrorised by a mad fan.

Shock had cleared her hangover like nobody's business, cleared it right up. Shock was a bucket of black coffee and a slap in the face. *They're asking* me …*to do* this …and oh it may have been four years but by God what did she want right now, besides her husband to hold her and kiss her and tell her it would be all right? A smoke. A packet of smokes. They'd help, they'd make it okay, they'd chill her out; they'd take the edge off.

Jesus Christ, does this craving never *end?*

Shaking, frightened somehow, she'd picked up the phone and called Tom, fully intending to tell him he could stuff this fucking play up either his arse or his boyfriend's, that they could set fire to it and roll it down the Thames to Valhalla, they could recycle it as bird cage liner.

"*Why?*" she said, and her throat really hurt, that cold was landing, that cold was going to take her, that cold was the boss now. "*Why?* Because it's about a recent *widow*, that's why. It's some fucking piece of *torture porn* on stage, that's why! It's some ..." but she was cut off then by a bout of coughing, a hacking, awful cough, of the sort she'd never had back in the day of Nicotine, how strange.

"Okay, okay," said Tom, and how far away was he? Six miles or so, ten minutes on the Tube, so why did he sound like he'd moved to Australia? Was there a storm outside, messing with the lines? Was that why the room was growing dark? "I'll call them up, tell them you're not interested, no sweat. Listen Eve, I'm sorry. Really."

"Forget it," she said, but only just. Someone appeared to be taking the walls away on a long track, her voice was fading like the end of a record, a single they'd called them when she'd been a kid, a 45, they played at 45 rpm in those days, but hey, when she'd been nine years old they'd invented compact discs, but now even they were, "it's okay, yeah, sorry I didn't mean to shout, but," obsolete, just iPods and downloads and not even a *Top of the Pops* anymore, did the kids today know what they were missing, "just a bit of a shock."

"You okay Eve? You sound a bit rough."

"Cold, got a cold," the first single she'd ever bought? *Do You Really Wanna Hurt Me* by Culture Club, what a classic, a rave from the grave, still around in a box somewhere, along with scrapbooks and her old teddy bears.

"Get yourself to bed, call if you need anything," said miniature Major Tom in her head, "*anything,* got me? And I'm sorry about the play. Leave it to me."

Is that a boy or a girl? her Dad had asked, looking at Boy George on *Top of the Pops*. "Will do, thanks. Sorry."

Tom was saying something, but she put the receiver down and switched off the computer, then lurched to her bed because somehow her house (not *their* house) was a ship now, and the ship was in a storm, a tropical storm, must be, it was dark, and she lay on her bunk and even though it was August she shivered, just like she'd shivered in August all those years ago, and the cold dark wave rolled over her and she was in her parents' house in Chorlton, it was Christmas Day, and they were watching *Top of the Pops*.

Eve was lying on the floor, the way she had when she'd been little, hands propping her chin, her parents were sat on the sofa behind her and Sarah was at the table with a crossword puzzle book, the one she'd got for Christmas 1982 from Aunt Samantha in Liverpool, a crossword puzzle book – not a colouring book or a join-the-dots book – a crossword puzzle book, full of grids and white blocks and "Little Orphan Annie? Not Quite! (5, 9)", and there she was at the table, frowning, concentrating, pen in hand, she was thirteen, she had a pen, she was at Big School, Eve was eight, she had Teddy and Sindy, and it was Christmas Day, but they weren't cold, they had central heating, one of the first families here to have it, their dad knew about accounts, he was a success, it was Christmas Day and they were warm and Sarah had her book, but Eve had *Top of the Pops*.

"Is that a boy or a girl?" said her Dad from behind her, and then Eve noticed that she was watching Tom on her TV, Tom in his office making a call.

"Oh Dad," Eve said, heavily, heavily the way only eight year olds can say it. Tom was her favourite band.

"You're out of touch, Kevin," said her Mum, and oh, by that tone of voice Eve could tell (how? She was only eight) that Mum had found the gin and the gin had found her and that in years to come the gin would find her Mum earlier and earlier and one day the doctors would try to find Mum's liver but there'd only be a walnut.

"What's this?" said Sarah to Carl, who was sitting next to her, "four down, 'Barking clappers? Almost!' (7, 4)," and that was wrong for many reasons, one because she didn't know Carl yet, it'd be many a long year before she'd meet him, and by that time her parents would be dead, and two because Sarah *never* asked for help. Sarah would no more ask for help than she'd walk through Stretford Arndale naked.

"Dunno," said Carl, who had a thin moustache, something he'd never grown ever, not while Eve had loved him, not in photos she'd seen.

"What use are *you* then," said Sarah, and there was no arguing with that tone of voice, she really didn't think he was use, and there was no point in Eve speaking up, her sister had spoken, and wasn't that the truth, what she said went.

"None," said Carl. His moustache had gone and he was as Eve had first seen him, and she was only eight but she loved him and it broke her heart that he was dead. "But I will be. Soon."

You can't be any help, never again, Eve wanted to say, but she didn't. Her sister had the floor. "You can't even solve this puzzle."

"Puzzle hasn't started yet," said Carl, tipping a wink to Eve. She blushed, giggled and hid her face. If Sarah thought she was being laughed at …"And you're not the one to play, little lady," Carl went on, looking at her sister. "Not yet. Not at first. Your time ain't come. But it will." *That's not Carl,* Eve thought, and that made her turn cold despite the central heating. *That's someone else …the words are wrong …the voice is wrong …* "But whatever the piece is, darlin', you gotta do it."

Piece? Piece? There's no piece. That's a crossword, *not a jigsaw puzzle,* thought Eve, but her husband (if it had been him) had gone, and Sarah was no longer a child, she was a woman, she was like she'd been when Eve had last seen her, and she did indeed have a jigsaw, and she was shovelling the pieces into her mouth as if she were eating cereal, and huge tears ran down her cheeks like rivers.

"What's wrong?" Eve asked her.

"I have to because you won't," said Sarah, and she held the jigsaw box outward in a warding off gesture, and the picture was of Carl as he lay in his coffin, arms folded across his chest, face waxy and dead and never to be alive again, and then Sarah screamed, and she ran towards Eve holding the box in front of her, and the picture of Carl grew larger and larger until it filled the world.

*

The dream broke up then and became black, and Eve knew no more until the following morning when she woke thirsty, starved and with a slight tickle in her throat, but besides that, quite well.

Chapter Seven

Few would call Eve unimaginative, but when it came to the whole notion of dreams, she was virtually her sister. Ordinarily at least. There was little in the way of omens or visions that she ascribed to them. She'd learned to be pretty much dismissive of the whole after dark picture show since she'd been five years old and dreamed she'd had a cat, then woken up all excited at the prospect of playing with Kitty, only to discover there was no Kitty to play with.

Which made the whole fever dream even more irritating, largely because it wouldn't go away.

It hung around like a bad smell, like the time she'd accidentally eaten anchovies in a restaurant in Stratford and they'd repeated on her very badly and her backside had made the most appalling smells all through playing Ariel, smells that appeared to be tethered to her by invisible cords.

Barking clappers? Almost! (7,4)

She tried watching television, but it was the morning and through eighty odd channels she could only find people talking about soap operas, or children in hospital, or people selling fake jewelry at the LOW!LOW!PRICE! of £3.99, operators Are Standing By.

Puzzle hasn't started yet.

Eve tried to read, but she couldn't even pick a book from the shelves. She stood impotent before them, hand reaching out then rejecting, almost mewling in frustration.

Whatever the piece is, you gotta do it.
Whatever the piece is…
That was what unlocked it.

"What's the piece?" they would say, but they didn't mean *pieces*. They meant *plays*.

It was common enough among their community. That tended to be how people in their world referred to their work. "Got a piece through," "My agent's sent me for a piece," "Got an offer." "Really? What's the piece?"

Whatever the piece is, you gotta do it.

He hadn't looked like Carl at first – not with that moustache – and he hadn't sounded like him at the end (in fact, hadn't she been sure that it wasn't him?) but he'd known that *piece* meant *play* …

No, Sarah Voice spoke up, *you knew that. You know that. Carl's dead and a dream's a dream. You bring him home in your mind and you talk to him and he holds you, but he's dead. It's all you.*

Okay, granted …so what then?
Barking clappers? Almost! (7, 4)
The piece.
The *play*.
Barking clappers.
Something …something almost there, like an itch that couldn't be scratched.

She ran to the phone table, picked up the notebook and pen that lay there, then sat on the sofa and wrote BARKING CLAPPERS.

What's barking? Okay, it's a place in London, it's mad people, it's the stuff on the outside of trees – sort of – it's the sound that dogs make.

Eve hated puzzles, couldn't stand them, it wasn't the way her brain worked. She stared at the page for a good five minutes, at those two words, then stood and tried to remember where she'd last put her mobile. Somebody else could sort this for her.

*

"Hey," said the voice on the other end. Sarah never said *hello* anymore. She said *hey. She watches those hip teenage American shows,* Carl had said, just before the door had closed and the hard news given, when he'd been ill but no one knew it. *She's down with the kids, she knows* One Tree Hill *and* The O.C. *Which is curious, considering she's the eldest.* Eve had kept her counsel, but she knew it wasn't curious at all. Sarah had hit and passed the Big Four O, but she wasn't going down without a fight. She was going to prove she wasn't ready for the Knackers' Yard yet. "What's up? You okay?"

How you going to answer this one? Eve asked herself. She hadn't really set up a story ...so she fell back on a mostly unused and slightly rusty skill. She improvised. "Yeah, fine ...just, you know, bored. So bored I'm doing that puzzle magazine you left behind."

"I left a puzzle magazine behind?"

"Yeah. Don't you remember?"

The silence on the other end indicated all too well that (a) Sarah didn't remember having a puzzle magazine when she'd been down for the funeral, (b) that – if she'd had one – it was extremely unlikely she'd have left it behind, and finally, (c) that if she had been in possession of a puzzle magazine and had left it behind, what in the name of all that was holy was her sister doing with it?

Eve allowed herself a small smile. It wasn't often she got to wrong foot her sister in any way, shape or form, and when it happened she felt a sort of delight. Strange to say, considering that Eve was a well-paid and well respected actress and Sarah worked in a library in Stretford, but something about Sarah really did make her feel like the less successful sister. If she ever went to therapy Eve would have to give that one a workout.

"No, I don't. Still, you know, stressful time and all that, wasn't it? So, what you stuck with?" *You strange imaginative child.*

"Barking Clappers? Almost! Seven and four."

"Any letters?"

"Nah, total blank."

"Hard one for me to come straight up with. Still, in a rush?"

"Not especially."

"If I get it, I'll text you. Or email. Might even phone if you get lucky." *You need me,* Sarah's voice was saying, only she didn't know it, *and I love it.*

"Or if it comes to me, I'll do the same."

"Sure." *Like that'll happen.* "You doing okay?" she went on, and that oddly triumphal tone of voice was gone, and there was real concern there, real love. It was hard love, always had been between them, but love was love and that was all that mattered, Eve supposed. They may not talk for months but when things got rough they were there for each other; definition of a family, if ever one was needed.

As she thought those things, the landline rang. "I'm doing fine, Sarah. Listen, got to rush, other line."

"I know. Busy girl." *And I just work at a Stretford library – but who do you turn to for help?* "You get on. I'll let you know when I get the answer." *When, not if.*

"Thanks Sis."

Eve's left hand ended the call on her iPhone, and her right picked up the Princess cordless. "Hello?"

"Hi Eve." It was Tom. An extremely contrite Tom. In two words she could tell how he looked, mousy and upset. He was a brilliant agent, a bear of an agent, a terrier, an absolute bastard when it came to wringing the best for his clients …but his clients had become like an extended family and he hated to upset them. After all (she thought unkindly) they may decide to run off and give their commission to someone else.

"Hey Tom." *And now I'm impersonating my sister, how strange.*

"Look, I'm sorry. Really didn't mean to upset you. I even read through that script. You were right, totally inappropriate. I called them up, rejected it on your behalf. They were disappointed but understood. We still friends?"

"Yeah, course we are." And they were. Eve was a woman who didn't fall out with people easily. What had struck her most about their conversation was Tom admitting to reading a script. "And I'm sorry if I was off with you. I really wasn't feeling too good."

"Better now?"

"Much thanks." She was, too – and ravenous. Had she a horse in the cupboards she may well be thinking about trying to get Neddy between two slices of bread.

"Okay, you rest up. And next time I'll try and match the material better. Deal?"

"Deal."

They knocked pleasantries back and forth for a minute, then hung up. *That's that then,* thought Eve, and wandered to the kitchen where there was no horse, but there was Sun Pat Crunchy Peanut Butter and an unsliced white loaf, which she inelegantly hacked into doorstops and smeared with maybe half the jar. *Fuck the figure, apparently I'm too skinny anyway.* She walked into the conservatory, pulled the blinds, and waited for Carl to come and stare in disbelief at what she was eating.

And after a while, he did.

*

At about nine that evening, while Eve was watching Lean's *Oliver Twist* for the six millionth time her mobile rang. SARAH CALLING, the display said.

"Hi, Sarah."

"It's got me stumped," said her sister with no preamble. There was irritation in her voice. If there was one thing she hated, it was being stuck on a puzzle.

"Forget it then, it's not important."

"No, I'll get it. Eventually. I just wanted you to know how badly it's pissed me off."

"Much appreciated."

"Listen, Steve and I were wondering if you fancied coming up here for a bit, take a break, see what the old home town's up to. What do you reckon?"

What Eve reckoned was that she could be knocked over with something lighter and thinner than a feather. Sarah had *never* offered anything like this before ...and, in truth, Eve hadn't especially wanted to go back home. Last time she'd been there had been five years ago for her Dad's funeral, the week before she'd opened in *Gothik,* a month before she met Carl, and what had she found? A town that was just a bit smaller than she remembered, a bit smellier and a bit greyer. A bit more developed and a bit more soulless. There'd been sort of a pang of nostalgia connected to nipping into the Bowling Green for a pint, sitting in the snug and remembering first the times she'd sneaked in before her eighteenth and necked the occasional half of Stella, and then the times when she'd found work behind the bar during the summer breaks ...but beyond that ...

"She's trying," muttered Carl – and was this a first? He hadn't gone away when the phone had rung. "Doing her best. Looking out for her baby sister."

Yeah, but ...

"Yeah but *what,*" he persisted. "Come on, you've got to give Sarah her due."

I know, I know ...

"Eve," said her sister. "You there?"

"Yeah, sorry Sis. Woolgathering, whatever that means. There's a possibility of a job coming up, nothing definite but I could do with hanging around just in case. If it doesn't come up, I'll make use of your spare room. How's that?"

"That's good enough. You take it easy, got me?"

She makes it sound like an order. "As easy as I can. Say hi to Steve."

"You bet. And I'll get that puzzle. You know I will! Goodnight, Eve."

She said goodnight, hung up, looked at her dead husband and shrugged. "I know, I know, fault's as much mine as hers, there's many a bridge to be built as has been burned, I got it …but not just yet, hey?"

Carl just shrugged back, enveloped her with his arms, and she set the movie running again.

There went another night.

*

Ain't me yet, said Carl in the dark. It could have been a dream – and next morning Eve would tell herself it certainly *had* been a dream – but in the dark it really did seem as if he was talking to her from the door. Though why he was using that stupid Mockney voice she really couldn't say. *It will be, but it ain't yet. My time ain't come. That's someone else.*

Who is? Eve thought, and tried to say, but she was tired, it was dark, it was night, so all she did was turn over.

Whatever the piece is, you gotta do it, he went on.

So you said, Eve thought, and turned onto her other side. *Carl, I love you, but this cryptic shit is seriously pissing me off. Can you just* tell *me what you mean?*

Barking clappers? Almost! 7, 4.

What part of "Tell me what you …" but then she really did fall asleep. She fell asleep in the middle of a lot of nocturnal conversations these days.

*

Eve's text message alert woke her the following morning. Squinting at her watch she somehow made out the figures seven and zero and five. *Dear God, who hates me so much they'd wake me up at this time?* Then, fumbling around her dressing table and moving the iPhone to eye level she found out. *1 New Message from Sarah.*

You know something? I am *going to stay at yours. And every morning before you get up I'm going to –*

Thoughts of her revenge dried on the cortex as Eve pressed the "Read" button with her thumb and the words took shape, the answer that her sister had obviously worked on all night.

That's my Sarah all right, Eve thought, kind of numbed. *That's her. That's what she'd do. So. What do I do with this? What does it* mean?

The message on the phone said "Pavlovs Bell!"

Chapter Eight

In the shower, Eve decided it was all a coincidence. She'd read the play whilst coming down with a fever, had the dream, nice and easy lemon squeezy.

That's right, coincidence. Like the Talking Books gig. You needed a job. That night, Laura's photo does a magic act, she rings the next day with a job. Just a coincidence.

Whatever the piece is, do it.

Carl can't have had anything to do with it, because he's a stiff. No matter what he said about asking around.

"Barking clappers" equals "Pavlov's Bell."

So you have a fever dream with Carl in it – or sometimes Carl in it – and he tells you to do the piece.

Do it.

And that's just a coincidence, too. Because the dead are dead and anyway – even if they're not, whoever heard of a ghost finding you work? And you read the play, didn't you, and hated it.

Coincidence. Like the Talking Books gig. *Nothing supernatural about any of this. (Then how did the photo get torn ...what's all* that *about, unless it really* was *somnambulistic vandalism?)*

But so *what* if it was nothing but coincidence …the last gig had worked out okay, hadn't it? And what had Tom said about the people behind it? They sound like people who don't take the easy way out, people who like a fight …they sound like …

"Like Carl," Eve said aloud as she towelled dry, unable to shake the whole thing off.

Okay, this thing has got in your head, and you can't let it go. Not that it matters, Tom's told them I'm not interested, so the whole thing's academic, right?

Still, she found herself wandering to the computer in the upstairs office. *Did I delete the damned thing?*

As she booted the computer, she looked about her. Posters, playbills, framed programmes. Carl had been a big Simon and Garfunkel fan – one of his few faults, there were fewer tunes more likely to induce suicide than their repertoire, in Eve's humble opinion – and the line he loved more than any other was the one about preserving your memories, they're all that's left you. *Got that right if nothing else, Mr Simon …or are you Garfunkel?*

There were their memories, stacked up on the walls, their history, their ghosts. Their *memento mori*. There was everything they had ever done – not together, never together – but there was their professional life, lined up like soldiers; and *more* horrible solid reality hit her – one regiment was never going to grow. It had been hit by governmental defence cuts. The Fifteenth Regiment Eve Wilson Cavalry was left to forge on solo.

Eve Wilson loved her husband; she'd loved him more than life itself, but at that moment, as she stood there looking at the mementoes of their years together, she felt the same hatred she'd felt in the *not hot at all* summer of 2009. Had he turned up in front of her she'd have ripped his fucking throat out.

You cunt! You fucking useless twatting CUNT!! Why? Why do it to me? Why did you have to fucking well DIE? Why did you have to fuck off and leave me on my own you selfish miserable TWAT? It's okay for you, your job's done! I've got to STAY! It's painful and hard and loud and I DON'T LIKE IT HERE!

The computer flashed its startup screen, but Eve hardly noticed it. For the first time since that moment when she'd sat alongside her husband in a consulting room and heard the doctor say "Well Mr Wilson, I'm afraid I've some bad news," Eve found herself raging at the stand up, falling down *unfairness* of the world. The sheer *lunacy* of it all. The desperate *uselessness* of existence – the fights, the effort, the strain. The studying, the hard work, the industry and application, the lines learned, the plays studied or the machines operated. Long nights where sleep was impossible to find and Pro Plus and coffee were your best friends the following day. The months of arguing pointless moves in pointless plays written by pointless writers, the months of dreading the pointless reviews, the months waiting for the pointless response of the pointless audiences, the months wasted *in all that pointless effort!*

And for *what?* Why *bother?* All that endeavour, all that struggle – all that pointless struggle – and what *happened?* Sooner or later you just fell down dead and got stuck in a box and either burned to powder or turned into food for maggots and worms, so why do *any* of this? Why waste the energy?

There was, of course, no blinding flash of revelation – it was unlikely that in a one second sitting before a Dell monitor Eve Wilson would be granted an insight into the mysteries of the universe that had baffled philosophers since the dawn of mankind. There was only a sense of astonishing weariness, a weight, a crushing blackness as for the first time she actually realised that this *really was* her life now, that Carl really was nothing but photos and worm fodder and a headstone that gave name and dates in white on a black surround and told the world he was a BELOVED HUSBAND.

He's really not coming through that door anytime soon, he's really not going to watch a DVD or shower with me, he's really not going to direct another play, he's really not ever going to cough or belch or fart again. No matter what goes on in my brain, no matter what movies I make up and dialogue I give him, it's me and not Carl. Carl's been cancelled. He's not on hiatus, he's not coming back in the autumn with new episodes, he's off the air, the run's over, that box office doesn't take tickets anymore.

With an arm that weighed sixteen stone, Eve opened her email folder, scrolled around a bit, and found the attachment from Tom. *I'm not crying though,* she half thought. *But that's okay, I've got Sarah to do it for me.*

Not knowing why she thought that or what it meant, she opened *Pavlov's Bell* and started to read. Because whatever the piece was, she had to do it …didn't she?

*

Two hours later she rang Tom and asked if he'd turned the play down on her behalf. He said he had. Eve then asked if there was any way she could get put back in the frame, any way at all – but not without a very serious meeting first. Puzzled, Tom said he'd see what he could do.

He rang back at noon the next day, saying – if she wanted – he could arrange a meeting between her, the writer, the producer and the director. Eve said that would be fine, she'd like that very much. So Tom did.

Chapter Nine

"Nice to meet you again, Miss Rogers," said Barry Mackie. He left it a beat, then – obviously interpreting her silence for a failure of memory – "I engineered your recording sessions back in March."

"Yes," Eve said eventually. For the first time in quite a few years her face had let her down, the control had gone, and unsurprisingly she found it difficult to figure out how the muscles were supposed to work. It took a while, but at last her features seemed to arrange themselves in a semblance of pleasant recognition. "I knew that. It's just, I didn't expect ..."

"Two things people never expect," he finished for her, "the Spanish Inquisition and engineers who can string two words together."

"Sorry," Eve replied. "I must seem very patronising."

"Nah, the engineering was just to earn some money. Though not a whole lot. Writing's really what I do."

"And do well, if I may say."

"Thank you, you may indeed." He turned to the second man seated at that almost empty pub table and gestured. "This is Mike Hughes, he's the director."

But Eve wasn't really listening to what Barry was saying. For the second time in less than two minutes she was struggling to keep her face normal. Mike Hughes, a man with a developing reputation for challenging work, a man who apparently liked a fight, was tall, powerful looking ...and had a thin moustache. As she shook his hand and heard him say how pleased he was to meet her in his slight Mockney twang, Eve wondered how he'd feel if she'd replied with, *Don't you remember, we've met before, in a fever dream a week or so back.*

Mike Hughes was the man she'd seen sitting next to her sister at the kitchen table working at a crossword puzzle.

Somehow, she didn't fall apart. Somehow she kept up with the small talk, somehow she managed to accept Mike's condolences ("I never met Carl, but I saw enough of his shows – the man was a genius, darlin',") and somehow she managed to keep smiling. *But oh dear God, what's with this? More coincidences? C'mon, haven't I had my share now? Isn't it time to pack them in? I must have used up my ration until 2025.*

But she managed somehow, and eventually the small talk died, and Mike said, "So. Are you going to come aboard?"

"Maybe," said Eve. "Though maybe you won't want me to after you've heard me out."

"Well, get talking and let's see. If its money I'm sure Sir Peter can find some down his sofa."

"That's for him and my agent," said Eve, feeling more like herself now. For the first time since the words *I'm afraid I have some bad news, Mr Wilson* had been uttered, she had something she could deal with on her hands, something practical – and she was utterly unsurprised to find she liked it. She dug into her handbag and retrieved the script she'd printed off. "This is a good piece," she said, and out of the corner of her eye she saw the way Barry visibly grew. "It's frightening and it's intelligent and more than that, it's *honest*. It'll make a big splash, generate a lot of publicity – probably even controversy – and it'll make your names."

"All of which I like so far," said Mike. "But there's a *but*, isn't there darlin'?"

That darlin' is so going to piss me off. "Yes, there's a *but*. It's good. It's just not *great*. Though it could be."

*

Both Eve and Carl had received many scripts over the years – they were, after all, names in their respective fields, and names brought in punters, and punters brought in money – and the majority of them were just shit.

Not appalling, not illiterate (though there was the odd one that came through that was purely and simply unreadable and they had to wonder who was sleeping with whom in order for the damned, wretched thing to see the light of day) but mostly they were just ...*meh,* like overcooked vegetables (or hospital food), harmless but forgettable, lacking anything that made you feel like turning the page, lying there like Frankenstein's Monster on the slab before the lightning struck. To the howls of anguish of their respective agents they had turned every one of those bland scripts down. "You've got to think of our reputations," Carl had once said. "We put our names to *important* projects, not these seat fillers. What'd it do to us if we turn up working on shit like this?"

The reason those scripts weren't up to much was that they weren't *honest.* They were packaged, pre-planned, written to be commercial hits, nothing more edifying than episodes of a soap opera, nothing but moving wallpaper.

But every so often one would come through that *meant* something. It mightn't always be the most professionally written; it might well be a bit rough round the edges, but it had *it,* the *nugget,* the thing they were looking for, and the cry would go up from one or the other of them – "Eureka!"

Reading *Pavlov's Bell* in her study that night, this time all the way through and with a clear head, Eve had called out "Eureka!" Almost. There was just that one tweak. And a few cuts.

*

Out of the corner of her eye, Eve saw Barry about to sit forward like a lion protecting his young. She placed her feet squarely on the floor and prepared to stand her corner.

But it was Mike who spoke. "Okay, *how* can it be great?"

"In your opinion," she heard Barry mutter, but Mike didn't glance to him, so neither did she.

"What we have here," Eve said, hoping they noticed the inclusive *we*, "is a potentially *brilliant* piece. But at the moment, the actress – Joanna – is just a victim. All she does is sit in a chair and beg until she caves in and admits how brilliant and wonderful her fan is."

"That's the *story*," said Barry hurriedly. "*That's* what it's about."

Eve saw the impatient glance Mike gave him and relaxed. This wasn't going to be as hard as she'd thought. The director wanted her; he wanted her name, the validity she'd bring. Any objections would be taken care of.

"Yeah, I get that," she said. "And it's a good story, I've already said that. But how much *better* would it be if the piece was about the objectification of women? Their vulnerability, how the fan has got reality and fantasy all warped in his head?" She leaned forward, putting everything she'd ever used on stage into her voice. Her eyes occasionally flicked to Barry, but mostly they were centred on Mike – he, after all, was the man who *really* had the power here.

After her, of course.

"What if Joanna gets him to *see* that? What if the final scene is completely turned on its head and it's *Joanna* who gets the upper hand? What if she makes him see how misguided he's been, what if she forces him to back down and set her free?" She was in full flow now, she was *burning*, she was magnetism personified. She could see the slightly stunned look in Mike's face, the expression of a man who'd just seen a dog dance on a table. The background noise had dialled down to just a mild murmur, there was no one in that bar but the two of them – not even Barry. "We could have, instead of a good piece about a psychotic, a *great* piece about not *only* the relationship between a star and her fan but *also* the interdependence of men and women, the inherent violence it encapsulates, and how that can be transcended and *bettered*. That way we have a story with a real, definite and *important* point."

She sat back then, breaking the spell. And did a part of her enjoy the look on Mike's face as he shook his head and blinked his way back into reality? Yes, a part of her did, and she didn't deny it. It was what made her *her*, after all.

"Oh …kay," said Mike after a second, absently stroking his moustache. "I see your point. It could take us to a whole new dimension." He turned to the writer. "Barry? What d'you reckon, mate?"

Eve looked at him too, and saw that most common expression on a writer's face – a vague kind of sulky resentment at having his ideas challenged. "I don't know," he said. Then, with a shrug, "Yeah, I could get it to work. If I had to. Take a lot of rewriting though." *Which he clearly doesn't want to do,* Eve thought. *And almost certainly won't. Look at him; he's so* invested *in this piece. He probably wouldn't change a comma without a fight.* She sighed, though not too heavily, and prepared to leave without a job. *Hey, me and Mr McCawber – something will turn up.*

But still, with her suggestions on board, this really *could* be a great play.

"Maybe not as much as you think," said Mike, and his voice was fuzzy as he continued stroking his face fungus. Oh, there was an expression she recognised, and it broke her heart for the millionth time (though today it seemed fresh, as if for the first time, and *that* was odd) ...it was one she'd seen on Carl's face often enough in the morning as he prepared to set off, or at night as he reflected on the day's work. Mike was *visualising*, seeing the whole play in front of him as it would be on the first night. His pupils darted left to right as he tracked the actors' moves, his brows furrowed or lifted as he encountered problems and overcame them. *Hold on there, Mr McCawber. Maybe something has turned up.*

"Yeah," Mike went on, "I *see* it. I see how it could work." Then he brought himself back into the present, and smiled, the first real smile he'd given since the meeting started, and this time it was Eve who rocked back a little. Not much, but enough. *He's got some charisma of his own, this one ...despite the moustache.* "Okay, thanks for coming to see us, Miss Rogers."

"Eve," she said, blinking.

"Eve then. You've posed us an interesting problem, and I think Barry and I need to have a meeting to discuss it." He stood and extended his hand. Eve did likewise and took it. His clasp was dry and strong. "We'll be in touch."

Before she knew it, Eve heard herself say, "I'll look forward to it." Then she turned to Barry, who had left his seat but wasn't exactly standing – more crouching, eyes sullen. "Nice to see you again," she said and shook his hand. His hand was damp and loose.

"Yeah," he said, as he clearly didn't feel the same. But still, as she left the bar and made her way out into the late August sun, Eve Wilson had some things to mull over.

*

That night, for the first time since the monitors had flatlined and Eve had begun her descent into widowhood, she could not raise the memory of her dead husband.

Well no, that wasn't quite right. She could *remember* him all right – after all, it had hardly been a year, after all, nobody forgot somebody that quickly – but she couldn't *call* him to her the way she had before.

She tried; she tried so hard she thought she'd make her nose bleed. She closed her eyes and remembered him as he had been, tall, confident, articulate, witty, infuriating, and those memories were fine, they were clear as crystal, they were clear as a bell (as clear as *Pavlov's* bell), they were as clear as any cliché in the vocabulary ...but those memories weren't what she'd *had* up until that point. She didn't hear him, didn't feel him, and couldn't smell his aftershave. No, she wasn't a stupid woman, and she knew, deep down in the most important part of herself, that he'd never *really* been with her (and never mind ripped photos and coincidental job offers), she *knew* that it'd only been her grief talking ...but still, as she'd thought often enough, who really cared? The phantom Carl she'd created had comforted her, had taken the edge off, the way the fags and the dope once had, and now ...

Maybe you don't need him anymore, the part of her mind that was Sarah said.

Oh fuck off, big Sarah, Eve answered. *Of course I do. I'll always need him. He was my –*

Yeah. Was, Sarah interrupted, which was just *typical* of her. *You were going to say 'support', little Eve, but what you meant was 'crutch', the way the fags once were, the way the dope and the speed once were, and you just don't keep the crutch once the leg has healed, do you?*

What do you mean?

Jesus, no wonder you keep me in here! Without me you couldn't even figure out a lousy crossword puzzle, could you? I'm saying the Phantom Carl has done his job, the way that fags and the rest had done theirs. He's a past tense now, the way they are. He got you through the rough bit, and well done to him, he did his job well, but now your system just doesn't need him anymore.

Eve sat up on the sofa, scared. *Really* scared, for the first time since the Doctor had sat opposite them with the grave look on his face. *NO!* She screamed. *NO! I DO need him, I DO! I CAN'T go through this alone, I CAN'T live the rest of my life without him!*

Yes you can, Sarah went on, that old implacable voice simply stating the facts, ma'am. *Remember when you gave up on the coffin nails? You thought you'd never get along without them. But you did. And two years before that when you snuffed out your last spliff? You thought you'd never cope without some good old Acapulco Gold either. And the speed? But you did. What was that crap Carl kept spouting when you had your jiving legs on? "Hard times pass," wasn't it? Well, looks like he was right. This hard time has passed, this addiction's been kicked. Well done, little Eve. Never said it to your face, but I'll say it in your mind – I'm proud of you. You're in the real world again. How does it feel?*

Eve kept silent for a long time, then heard herself say 'Terrible. It feels terrible.'

From her sister, no reply. No reply from anyone.

After a while of no replies, Eve decided there was one crutch she hadn't really jettisoned after all. So she went into the kitchen to pour herself a drink.

As she stood there, pouring Tanqueray into a glass (and thinking idly of her mother, who had practically worshipped at this particular altar, wondering about acorns and trees and how far one fell from the other) Eve realised something that had happened at the meeting.

He – Mike – had started to visualise my idea, seen it happen before his eyes, and he'd reminded me of Carl so much that it'd broken my heart again. But this time it'd seemed fresh. Sharp. Real, not the memory of pain, but pain itself. Why?

She put the bottle down and retrieved a can of Schweppes from the fridge. As she added half of it to the alcohol, the answer came.

Why? Because that was the first time I'd thought of Carl all day, that's why. I had something else to focus on. Even back when I was doing the talking books with Laura – and the engineer who turns out to be a writer – Carl was in my head like tinnitus. But not today. So when Mike got that look on his face, that Carl *look, it broke my heart all over again.*

She took her first sip of the night standing at the kitchen counter. *Does that confirm everything Sarah said? Is she, God help me,* right? *Am I over that part? Has that hard time passed?*

Nobody said a word, but above her the bedroom door slammed. No, *banged.*

She almost dropped the glass, but just at the last second her fingers tightened and she managed to save it. She stood in her well-lit kitchen and looked at the ceiling, unable to move. There was no doubting what she heard. That had been her bedroom door. Had she been in that room since returning from the meeting? Yes, to change her clothes, maybe three hours ago. Since then? No. Had she left the door open or closed? No idea.

But somebody had closed it, all right. Had banged it shut so hard it was a wonder the damned thing hadn't fallen through the floor.

I've an intruder, Eve thought, and that was a cold thought, a terrible thought, but the only logical thought. *A burglar. Or worse. And I'm here, all alone. Any minute now I'll hear his footsteps on the stairs …coming down …coming for* me.

That broke her cold paralysis. No way was she just going to stand here and play the screaming victim. *That's not me, remember,* she thought, very nearly breaking into hysterical laughter. *I never* play the victim. I get the fucking play rewritten *rather than play victim.*

So instead of quaking in her boots like a little girl frightened of the bogeyman, Eve Wilson – known to the theatrical world as Eve Rogers – left her kitchen and made her way up the stairs.

After selecting a very sharp knife.

I'm no fucking victim. Just wait and see, mate.

My, my, said Sarah Voice as Eve mounted the first step, *aren't you courageous? Off to stab the Big Bad Man with your Big Bad Knife?*

Maybe. Or maybe stupid. Or maybe this has nothing to do with courage at all. Maybe courage is simply carrying on after your husband rots and dies. Maybe compared to that, a little walking up some stairs is just exercise.

Except that was crap, and she knew it. If any dictionary defined 'courage' in any other way than ascending stairs in an empty house at night in order to determine the cause of a phantom sound, she'd cook the thing and eat it. With HP sauce.

Whoever you are, whatever you're doing, I will find you and make you run. I do not play your game, you play mine.

She was, after all, a stubborn old cow at times.

No noise, bar her soft footsteps as she approached the landing. Yes, her heartbeat was a little faster, her breathing a touch more rapid …but noise there was none. *Houses are silent,* she found herself thinking as she stared at the four doors ahead of her, branching out in a half fan; bathroom, master bedroom, office, guest room. *Houses are silent when occupancy numbers are cut in half.*

The bedroom? The bedroom first? That's the door, after all, that banged. If there's anyone here, he'll be there, rummaging through the underwear drawer to see what he can sniff.

Yeah, the bedroom. I've finished counting. I'm coming, ready or not.

So thinking, Eve ran up the last four steps, knife clutched in her right hand, and threw the door open.

To find nothing but her empty bedroom (*hers*, not *theirs*) just as it was when she'd last stood inside it, her day clothes piled up on the chair, the duvet still ruffled ...but nothing touched, nothing moved, nothing disturbed.

Under the bed then, she thought, *he's under the –*

Then Sarah Voice broke in, urgent. *Jesus, girl – you're standing in the open doorway! He can run up from behind and strangle you!*

Eve twitched, then flattened herself against the wall, giving her clear sight through the door. Nothing. No shadow of movement at all.

Under the bed. Check under the bed. And be ready ...

She sank slowly onto ground level and peered under. There was dust, a forgotten copy of Simon Callow's *Being an Actor,* and absolutely nothing else.

Which left only the wardrobe. In this room, anyway.

Which, once opened, revealed some clothes. Only hers. Carl's had long since been sent to a charity shop.

Nobody here but us girls, said Sarah Voice. *What now?*

"The other rooms, of course," whispered Eve, and set off for the bathroom, intending to check every inch of every room regardless of what she may find.

There was no intruder anywhere.

*

You can still invent conversations with your sister, but not with your dead husband. What's up with that?

No idea, she answered herself as she picked up the glass from the kitchen table some half an hour later and took it into the living room, *how about you?*

Maybe, that other voice said. *But I'm not saying yet.*

'Fuck you very much then,' Eve said aloud, and drank. *So, no intruder. So what then? What made that noise – always supposing I did hear a noise and it wasn't imagination.*

She took another sip of gin and considered that. *Had* she, in fact, heard the bedroom door slam? Yes, she decided, she had. A good hard slam, like someone in a blazing temper trying to make a point. She *had* heard that.

So, if no person made it, Sarah Voice piped up again, *what? Draft? Nope, we got us a windless night. And last time I was there, I saw no dog or cat - or even a gerbil – to get up to didoes. So, we rule out person, animal, wind ...what does that leave us with?*

Ghosts, Eve thought, and laughed. *The things you don't believe in, the things you say are coincidences. Maybe Carl's pissed off I can't call him into my head anymore, and decided to take it out on the woodwork. What do you reckon?*

Sarah said nothing, but in her imagination Eve could see her sister screw her face up and wave her hands in irritation. This made Eve laugh all the more. *Still, big Sarah, I agree with you. No ghosts. No ghosts, no intruder, no wind, no animals. So ...you want to know what banged the door? Well, SO DO I! And I haven't a clue. So what say we forget it, have a drink and go to sleep?*

Which is exactly what she did.

It was a deep, cavernous slumber that permitted no dreams. So deep was it that when the phone rang at a little after three in the morning she didn't even twitch. Maybe if it had rung longer it might have woken her up, but after four muted warbles whoever was on the other end gave up, and the silence was undisturbed until eight o'clock the following morning when Eve awoke mid snore.

Chapter Ten

"Hi," said the voice down the line two days later, "is that Eve?"

"Yes," half-questioning. She knew this voice, just not too well.

"Mike Hughes. We met the other day, remember? Sorry to call you at home – and if you want to berate anyone for giving me your number, darlin', you'd better get on to your agent."

"Don't worry; I'm going to bite his nose off."

"Yeah? Don't blame you." Except Eve wasn't going to do anything of the sort. She could tell by the laughing tone in Mike's voice that she'd won. The play was going to be rewritten her way. No director found your home number and called out of the blue with bad news. Bad news they left to others. Good news they delivered in person. "Anyway, reason I called – I managed to convince Barry that you were right. He's at work now, reckons he can get the new scene to us next week. So – are you on board?"

"I'm on the gangplank, certainly. Not quite on board yet. I want to see those pages first. Okay with you?"

"Fine by me, darlin'. Frankly, I want you attached to this project – you'll not only act the arse off it, but you'll be good box office. However, if you repeat that to Sir Peter or your agent I'll deny it while the cock crows in the background. Sir Peter hates getting screwed over a fee!"

"I know. Look if the new scene's what it should be, then I'm in. By the way, how much persuading did he need?"

Then the chuckle dropped, and Mike became professional. *He's not going to badmouth anyone,* Eve thought, and the director stepped up a notch on her Respect-O-Meter. "A little, he's committed to his vision – one of the things I like about him – but once he saw the value of getting you on side and that your view of the piece could really make his name, he agreed. Believe me, I've had bigger fights with writers."

"Okay then. Get me the new scene as soon as you can, and I'll give you my answer straight away."

"I'd appreciate that; these rewrites are cutting into our rehearsal time. We'll only have three weeks till previews."

"Three weeks will be plenty, trust me. It's virtually a two hander, after all."

"Granted. But I want you to know I'm taking a big chance here. No pressure, but if you still decide not to sign up, I could well be screwed."

Yeah ...he could be, couldn't he? A sudden, almost alien thought engulfed her. *How selfish am I being? I'm putting myself ahead of everyone else here. Mike ...Barry ...Sir Peter ...not to mention the SM, the ASM ...the theatre box office staff ...Uncle Tom Cobbley ...every one of them waiting for Eve Wilson (known to some as Eve Rogers) to deign to come down from On High and participate. What's happened to you? Have you ever done this before –* anything *like this before?*

No, not once. *But still ...this is* different. *This could be an* exceptional *play, if Barry gets it right. This could say lots of important things. This could be a phenomenon, an actual by-God* play, *a proper* play, *that sets the West End alight. And in a world of jukebox musicals and Lloyd-Webber revivals, how good – how* vital *would that be?*

"Eve," said Mike, "you still there?"

"Yeah, sorry. Woolgathering, whatever that means. And I wouldn't go worrying too much, Mike. If this goes the way I think it will, all you'll have to do is light the blue touch paper and watch the rocket take off. Oh, and clean your mantelpiece for the Olivier. Maybe even the Tony."

"You know how to dangle bait, I'll give you that," said Mike, and that chuckle was back. "Okay, deal. As soon as *I* get the pages, *you* get them."

"And as soon as *I* get them, you get an answer. A straight one."

"Then that's how we'll leave it," still chuckling. "Have a good one, Eve."

"And you, Mike."

She hung up then and trotted into her kitchen to make a sandwich – Weight Watchers bread and low fat cheese. Hey, if she was going to work again she needed to look her best. She thought about what might be about to happen to her, about her possible return to the stage, about how she may be able to have influenced a promising young playwright into producing something explosive.

At no point did she talk it over with Carl, either internally or externally.

That seemed to be over with after all.

*

Five days later, there it was; an email from Mike, with attachment. *Here we are,* Mike's email read. *He's worked like a demon – or at the very least, a man possessed. So what d'you reckon? In or out? M. PS: Say you're in.*

Eve's mouse hovered over the attachment icon before double clicking, for some reason unaccountably afraid. *What* do *I reckon?* she found herself wondering. *I reckon that somehow I feel the way I did when I heard that door slam above my head – and I did hear it, even though I've heard nothing since. I reckon that my heart's beating a little too fast and my breath's just a little too shallow. That's what I reckon. Of course, I've no idea why.*

Yes you do, said the Sarah Voice, *it's because you're coming up to the anniversary of your husband's death and you're getting ready to go back to work again – proper work, real by God out there work, not stuck behind a microphone in a recording studio, but work that'll be seen and heard by real people again. And it's been a while. So that's why you feel a little bit apprehensive. Plus, you used every inch of your charisma to turn this play into a star vehicle, which means you've invested a lot of your ego in this already. I'd be – to put it crudely – shitting myself as well.*

Still she didn't double click. Still she sat there with the mouse shaking slightly under her palm. *Is that what I did,* she asked her imaginary sister. *Is it?*

You bet you did, and you know it. Yeah, I'm sure you did it with the best intentions – let's make this important, let's say blah *about* blah de blah *and won't we all look like little tin gods up on our hill for you mortals to worship and digest our words of wisdom – but let's play our cards face up here, shall we? You also made damned sure you got the best stuff; you made damned sure you got to say all that you deem vital. You took a virtual two hander and weighted the whole damn thing in your favour. None of which makes you a bad person – everyone's got an ego – but what if your suggestions made it* worse? *What then?*

Then I turn around and walk away, thought Eve, trying to be hard and logical ...but coming up just a little bit short. *Something else will turn up.*

Yeah? Well, for you maybe. Certainly for Sir Peter, and I daresay for Mike. But Barry, our heroic author? This could be his one big shot and you waded in with your size fours and tell him it's just not *good enough for the great Eve Rogers. And if you don't like what he's done to accommodate you, you're just going to turn tail and walk away? That's nice of you.*

"Fuck off, big Sarah," said Eve, righteous anger blowing away everything that had clouded her mind for the past few minutes. "I did what's best for everybody – *especially* the play itself."

With her sister thus silenced, Eve double clicked the mouse and read.

*

Two hours later; "Mike? Eve Rogers. I'm in. Get Sir Peter to call my agent and fight like crazy over money. And tell Barry he's done a hell of a job. The rewrites are just about perfect."

*

She went back to her computer after leaving the message on Mike's Voicemail – and wasn't *that* typical, good news was always given to the Orange robot woman – meaning to paste the rewrites into the original text and run a copy off. Okay, so no deal was actually done yet, but despite the inevitable haggling she'd no doubt something would be worked out, and it could do no harm to start to learn the thing, would it?

The computer, however, decided it didn't want to boot up. She sat looking at the blue screen with the legend WINDOWS IS STARTING UP for ten minutes before realising nothing was happening. 'Come on,' she muttered, mildly irritated. But *nothing* came on. The screen said the same for another five minutes. Eve blew a quick, hot breath from between her teeth. She drummed her fingers on the desk, a rapid tattoo. Still WINDOWS IS STARTING UP and nothing else.

"But you're *not* starting up," Eve said. "Why lie to me?" Her patience – paper thin with technology at the best of times – was starting to give, and she reached out and depressed the power button. Then for good measure she pulled the plugs – all of them, monitor, computer, printer, speakers. Then she rubbed at the headache that was forming at her temples and slotted them all back in again and pressed the power button. Clicks, whirrs …then WINDOWS IS STARTING UP …

"Like hell you will," she whispered …but this time it did. "Thank you, you tin piece of shit. Now no more fuckery, okay?"

The computer heard her, and obeyed. It even allowed her to CUT and PASTE as desired. The printer, however, had other ideas. First of all it insisted that it was out of ink, which was a pure piece of fiction as it hadn't been used in over twelve months, not since Eve had run off some pages about pancreatic cancer treatments the night after Carl's diagnosis. And those tanks – all of them, the colour and the black – had been nice and fresh. So *bollocks* to it's *The following ink tanks are empty: Color. Black.*

And bollocks to your Yank programmer, Eve thought as she flipped the printer lid, ripped the cartridges out and them slammed them back, a little harder than was perhaps necessary. *Colour has a 'u' in it. Right. Print.*

This time the cartridges were all fine and dandy, there was a PAPER OUT! PLACE PAPER IN PAPER TRAY, THEN PRESS RESUME.

This Eve took in while staring at the stack of white A4 that was lined up in the paper tray. "It's *there*," she said, aware she was speaking aloud but unable to stop herself. "There. *Look!* Look, you stupid bastard! Paper!" She even found herself grabbing a handful and waving it at the monitor, as though it had eyes. "There! See? Paper!" She rammed them back in the tray, almost shaking with aggravation. Thumbing the RESUME button, she yelled "Right. Now. *Print*, arsehole!"

But it didn't, mostly because she'd hit OFF and not RESUME. With an inarticulate cry of rage she switched the unit back ON and hit the PRINT icon again. This time, finally and thankfully, the pages slotted out with words on them. Unwilling to move – unwilling, really, to breathe – in case that broke the spell, Eve sat there for twenty-five minutes as the script grew before her.

The thought that maybe someone didn't want her to learn it never entered her head.

*

Eight o'clock that night, as Eve sat in her living room, sipping herbal tea (no gin, not on a weeknight – that was the rule when she was working ...and she *was* working again now, wasn't she?) and making notes on the script as she mouthed the words aloud, the phone rang. *That's either Mike calling back to tell me how great it is that I'm on board or Sarah seeing how the land's lying,* she thought as she picked up the receiver. But it was neither.

It was Jon who answered her "Hello." *Jesus,* she thought as she heard him say "Evie, how you doing?" *Carl's brother. His only family. My only link to the man I loved with all my heart, soul and ninety-five per cent of my body. And when did I last speak to him? A week ago? Two? Four?*

She tried to remember and couldn't. Since the funeral, yes – a few times. They'd gone out for lunch at least twice – painful, slow, hesitant but necessary lunches as they worked through their pain together – and, sure, on the phone quite a bit since …but when last? *When?* When had she stopped thinking about him? "I'm not doing so bad, Jon," she said, hiding the terrible flare of shame that coloured her face. "You? How's life in Shepherd's Bush?" *All those miles away …all twenty or so. No wonder I can't get to see you too often. You're on the other side of the moon.*

"All the wild excitement a man can get with an empty Television Centre out of one window and a full Loftus Road out of the other. Listen, I hope I didn't interrupt – I just got to thinking about you. Haven't spoken in a while."

"I know, I'm sorry. I really am. I just …" *Just what? Forgot you existed?* "I've been negotiating a play. It kind of took up too much time."

"Ah, hey wow – *brilliant!*" Eve couldn't help but smile. *Everything's brilliant to Jon,* Carl had once said. *You could set his hair alight and put it out with paraffin and he'd not only thank you but he'd phone up all this friends and tell them how excited he was.* "That's a good deal! Big part?"

"The biggest."

"Brilliant," he said again. 'Let me know the dates, I gotta come and see this. I love my pretend sister on the stage." *Pretend sister*; Jon thought *sister-in-law* had far too many syllables. It hurt her heart for some reason. Then, as serious as he could be; "You coping? Y'know …it's not far off …"

"Carl's anniversary. Believe me, I know." *Now the tears will flow again, now my nose will clog, now my heart will break for roughly the nine millionth time this calendar year.* But it didn't. *Why not?* "And I'm coping. The work …it'll help."

"Yeah. I bet it will."

They spoke on for a while, nothing much, chit chat, she asked after stuff and he asked after stuff and they hung on *good to talk to you again* and *you too, I won't leave it so long – we'll go for lunch soon, yeah?* - but as the silence fell and Eve went to the kitchen to nuke her by now cold cup of Camomile in the microwave, she was troubled. Troubled that she'd forgotten Jon. Troubled she wasn't missing Carl so much as she once was.

Troubled, but at the same time …the *Pavlov's Bell* rewrites really *were* something exceptional. Whatever the reasons for her doing what she'd done – noble or self-aggrandising – she'd pushed Barry into really good work, really *important* work. So yes, she was troubled …but she was excited, too.

Excited, and maybe just a little self-satisfied. No, that was wrong ...*vindicated*. That was it. Vindicated.

But for all that, as she lay in bed that night, she found herself talking to the ceiling for the first time in a month or so. "Hey Carl? Looks like I'm back on the stage again. What do think? Did you read the play? It's better now, isn't it? Isn't it? Hey? Carl?"

The dark held its secrets, if it had any to keep. She was on her own in the room, and after a while she slept.

*

The next week passed in a bit of a blur. It was a week of phone calls – ones from Mike, thanking her for joining the play; ones to Tom, telling him to get cracking on the contract; ones to Sarah, telling her she was going back to work properly; ones from Tom, telling her Sir Peter was being pissy over fee and billing, but not to worry because he'd get his way all right (and, of course, he did).

It was a week of lunches, two with Mike to work out the final rehearsal schedule (three weeks, called from ten till five each day, Monday to Friday with an option on the weekends) and one with Jon in which they chatted about everything and nothing …but it was good to see him again, good to see those alive blue eyes of his which had dulled so much during his bother's illness dance once again. Once more though, as they spoke about things that didn't matter, Eve felt that sharp rush of grief, painful like a gas attack. Talking to Jon, who was so like but so different from Carl, it hit her over and over, every time like the first time. And as Jon had brought her second Americano, she once more found herself thinking that this grief was different. This grief was fresh again, like ripping the scab from a nearly healed wound.

It's painful because it's new – new and old simultaneously, she thought as she sipped the liquid and heard Jon talk about his shambles of a love life with reckless good humour. *It's painful because it's nearly over. It's painful because I'm moving on.*

It was a week of line learning, evenings where she sat from six till ten with Dido on the CD, making sure she had more than just a working knowledge of the script before she walked through the door on that first Monday …a Monday that as the week ticked by began to be more than a metaphysical concept but an actual, breathing thing that almost seemed to be rushing toward her.

It was a week in which – lunch with Jon aside – everything was to do with the work. Yes, of course, she thought about Carl, she thought about his anniversary, she thought about what she'd do for it (it fell on the Sunday during the first rehearsal week), but mostly, she thought of herself.

She really didn't think Carl would mind. And even if he did – even if he was somewhere up On High, looking down on it all - what of it? She was no longer able to call him to her, after all – her nights and days were truly now spent alone. Eve made her way through that week without a single imagined contact from him. He no longer spoke in her head, she no longer felt his arms around her.

Yes, moving on, she thought on the Thursday night as she clicked off the bedside lamp. *My hard grieving over. Thank you, whoever's responsible. All of that was tough. Maybe I didn't show it, maybe I didn't even admit it to myself, but it was tough. If this is how my life is to be from now on, then okay, I can live with it. Yes, I loved Carl and will miss him and think of him all the rest of my life – every day – but, frankly, I'm not sure it's entirely healthy to imagine him around all the time. That grief was a hard time, and the hard time (thank you) has passed.*

So she thought then, as Eve Rogers turned over and sank into sleep.

Chapter Eleven

One thing had never really changed throughout her professional life – Eve never slept well before starting a new project. There was just too much to think about. Had the contract issues been resolved to everybody's satisfaction? (Nearly, there was still a bit of fuss over billing, but nothing that wouldn't come out in the wash.) Had she done her homework properly? (Yes, as much as she could do without grafting in the rehearsal space.) Had she gone over the call time until it rang in her head like a mantra? (You bet, ten o'clock start at the Dagmar rehearsal rooms, above the theatre stage, Curzon Street. Up at seven thirty, out of the house by nine, Tube station by nine fifteen, Curzon Street by nine forty-five, time aplenty.)

But most of all, it was that Christmas Eve (no pun intended) feeling that kept her awake; that sense of things about to happen, gifts to be unwrapped, the anticipation of the unknown. What would the next day have to offer? Or the day after that? Or the previews? Or the run?

It was at times like that that she really pitied those who had their nine-to-five lives, people who knew exactly what their days would bring. Oh sure, both she and Carl had done their fair share of bitching over their careers – about difficult *this* and obstructive *that* and they'd both finish each moan session with the phrase "I'm giving this up to work in a bank, I swear I am," but they both knew that was just crap. They loved their lives. They loved the unknown.

So Eve had never slept well before starting her first day at a new job. Until Sunday 26th August, that is. She took to her bed at eleven, read for a while, then turned out the light – after making *absolutely sure* the alarm was set – and expected to lie there until at least one o'clock.

Instead, she went straight to the land of Nod. And didn't wake until half past eight.

"Shit fucking *fire!*" She screamed as she blurrily made out the time. The alarm had made no noise whatsoever – she hadn't been pulled from her sleep from anything bar opening her eyes and wondering why the light seemed a bit wrong. *Half eight! I'm an hour late already!*

No you're not, hang fire, Sarah Voice tried to say, but there was no time to listen. She was busy running through her morning schedule to see what she could jettison. *Breakfast, that can go,* she thought as she ran to the bathroom. *I'll get a big lunch – or maybe see if the ASM will get me a sandwich, there's a Garfunkel's round the corner. Shower, yeah - that had better stay. Tube? No, probably no time. If I'm quick enough washing there may be time to drive it.*

Drive? asked Sarah Voice, *from Ealing to the West End? In morning traffic? You'd be quicker walking.*

Do one, dickhead, answered Eve as she urinated. *I am not getting on a packed train feeling like this. I've got to* focus, *and I focus best behind the wheel of my Focus.*

Laughing a little at that, Eve raced through her ablutions as quickly as was humanly possible. Had the Guinness World Record people been on hand, she may have made the next edition.

It's okay, it's okay, she thought as she closed the front door behind her, script tucked under her left arm. *Five past nine. Fifty-five minutes. I can do this. I can* do *this.*

She would've, too, if the Focus had started. Instead, all she got when she turned the key was a click. *C'mon, c'mon…don't fuck me about.* She turned the key again. Nothing. Not even a row of lights on the dashboard, not even a *rrrr-rrr-rrr* that translated as machine speak for *please, it's a cold and frosty morning, I'd rather not bother if it's all the same to you.*

But it *wasn't* cold and it *wasn't* frosty. It was perfectly pleasant late summer, and there was nothing from her car at all. Rage was building up inside Eve, ready to pop like a boil, and before turning the key for a third time she battered the steering wheel with her fists, tears welling up in her eyes. *Damn you, you motherfucking whore! Start! START!*

Even mental swearing in a fake American accent wouldn't do it. There was nothing at all happening. *Bastard shit thing was* fine *yesterday,* she thought savagely as she stepped back out onto her drive and slammed the door behind her. *Got me to Waitrose and back, not a problem, somewhere I could've actually* walked, *yeah, that was okay for you, wasn't it? But now, today, when I actually,* really *need you, you decide to pack in. Thanks for that, God. Thanks a fucking bunch!*

Right, spoke up Sarah Voice, and for two pins Eve would have reached up into her brain and pulled the lobes that controlled that Voice from her brain and stamped them into pink mulch on the tarmac. *Time to stop being a brat, Eve, and do something practical. First up, phone Mike and warn him you might just be a touch late – transport issues. Say nothing about oversleeping, okay?*

Yeah, yeah, sure, goodish plan I suppose. She checked her watch before rummaging in her bag for the iPhone. Nine fifteen. Not much chance of getting there dead on time, but …

The phone was dead. No battery life at all. *Oh you are fucking SHITTING ME!*

You could go inside, use the landline …

No time, Sis. I'm off and running.

She was, too. Down Ealing Broadway, looking for a black cab, hoping desperately she had enough in her purse to cover it.

It seemed her luck was at last in. A Hackney was just turning the corner before she'd gone ten yards and – give thanks and praise – its light was on. Eve flagged it down and practically leaped into the back seat. "Curzon Street, please. Quick as possible."

The cabbie flicked the meter on. "Any way you'd prefer to go, love?" He asked, the two way speaker system making him sound like a Cockney Dalek (as opposed to a Scots/Italian one, something in her memory said, but Eve couldn't find context for it right at that moment so she shut it off.)

"Any way that'll get us there in -" she looked at her Omega – "forty minutes."

"Only way that'll happen is by helicopter, sorry. And I left my helicopter in Monte Carlo last night."

"Whatever you can do, I'd be grateful." Then, as they pulled up at a red light (eliciting a small whimper of irritation of which she was totally unaware), she said, "Hey, you wouldn't have a mobile I could borrow, have you? It's only a quick call, and I'd add the price to the fare."

"Sorry love," said the cabbie. "Won't have one. Those things give you cancer, you know."

No they don't, Eve thought, and the panic she'd felt since opening her eyes vanished in a second to be replaced by a terrible weight over her heart. *Phones don't give you cancer. Nor do fags, or radiation or anything else.* Life *gives you cancer.* Life gives everyone *cancer in the end.*

But she said nothing, and kept quiet for the rest of the trip.

*

Dusk of a late summer's day.

Eve sat in her living room and watched the light fade, script in hand, empty cup of camomile tea on the table, wishing to God that it was a weekend, because truly she felt like getting so drunk she'd fall over.

"Hey Carl," she spoke into the night, "you want to know something? For the first time since it happened, I'm almost glad you're dead. Because you missed just how badly I stank today. I honestly *stank*. Had you been there, you'd have divorced me. No question."

This was the first time she had ever felt that way after any rehearsal. Ever. Even back at RADA, when she'd been in her first ever speech class, she'd known she was good. She'd known she had it – whatever *it* may be. Okay, granted, she could occasionally make the wrong choice, and she'd sometimes needed steering *there* instead of *here,* but that's why God made directors. But even if she'd offered something up only to have it turned down, it hadn't mattered. She'd known she was doing what she was *made* to do, that she had a *right* to be there.

Until today.

She hadn't been able to find *it* – whatever it may be - at all. From the moment she'd practically burst into the rehearsal room at just after twenty past ten (and, of course, there'd been roadworks at Tottenham Court Road, meaning a lovely further delay), all apologies and lightly coated in perspiration, she'd been …well, *disconnected* was as good a way of putting it as any other. She couldn't centre, couldn't concentrate. It didn't help that they were rehearsing in the attic space and the perfectly pleasant temperature of the outside world seemed to thicken, producing an atmosphere like treacle. It *certainly* didn't help that the actor she was playing opposite – a youngish man with the impossible sounding name of Hedliegh Turner – had nailed just about everything he was required to do, giving an intense …hell, why lie …giving a *burning* interpretation of a psychotic. He'd just obliterated her. It didn't help one bit that Barry the playwright had sat at the back of the room, glowering at her, listening as she delivered every one of his lines – especially the ones she'd insisted he rewrite – with all the dramatic intensity of the Orange robot woman stating that the person she'd called was unavailable, but she could leave a message after the tone. (And if she'd like to re-record said message, she could press Option One at any time.) Every time she'd caught his gaze he'd curled his lip slightly as if to say, *go on then – you made me do this. Let's see why. Let's see what you're made of.*

The answer, it seemed, was she was made of Not Very Much At All.

The thing that hurt most of all, though, was the look on Mike's face every time he stopped the rehearsal to offer a note. There was an almost *why should I be saying this* expression on his face. *Aren't you Eve Rogers? Aren't you Dame Judi and Dame Diana and Dame Maggie all rolled into one? Why am I asking you to "try it like this" or "have you thought of maybe …?" You should* know *this. Everybody* told *me you knew this. Why* don't *you know this?*

At some stage as that long, awful day had dragged on, Eve had realised that Mike had looked at her the way she'd looked at her car when it wouldn't start – just before she'd taken to beating the steering wheel, that is. It was the way you looked at an object that just flatly refused to do the one thing it should.

He was looking at her like she was useless.

Not intentionally, of course. He wouldn't do that, not if he was a director of any sensitivity – and she sensed he was, somehow – but still …he looked like a man who thought he'd bought a pedigree and ended up with a mongrel.

"I'm sorry," she'd said to him as he'd called a halt to the work. "Couldn't get my head round it today – couldn't shake the bad start."

"No worries, darlin'," he smiled back – but did that smile entirely reach his eyes? "Everyone has an off day now and then. Hey, I'm lucky if I get an *on* day! Just go home, rest up, come back tomorrow and knock me out of the fucking room. Got me?"

"Okay. Thanks."

But as she'd made her way home on the Tube, Eve replayed that last conversation in her head over and over. She wasn't a stupid woman. She knew a threat when she'd heard one. Even one made in a smiley Mockney tone.

Okay, that day is done, as the old song says. Put it behind you, ignore it, do like your director says – rest up, come back tomorrow –

"DANGER!" Blared a voice from the television, making her jump, making her heart block her throat, making her throw her script across the room. *"YOU'RE IN DANGER, CAN'T YOU SEE THAT? ARE YOU BLIND?"*

The television had been off – on standby, sure, but off – and now it was on, the glare from the screen illuminating the room. There in forty inch HD finery was some old film or other – a black and white science fiction piece from the look of it. Some men in parkas were cowering from a white coated scientist who appeared to be glowing with some badly aligned special effect. The sound was deafening.

"*I HAVE IT IN MY POWER TO DESTROY YOU. ALL OF YOU!*" Eve's wide eyes saw this man point at the token woman in the group – a small, pretty, vulnerable, blonde. "*YOU ESPECIALLY! AND I WILL! SO DESTROY ME BEFORE I DESTROY YOU ALL! ACT! ACT NOW!*"

The set clicked off, the dark descended and the silence engulfed her. Rooted to the sofa by shock, Eve looked to the coffee table. There was the remote control, some three feet from her hand. She couldn't have touched it without knowing. She hadn't touched it. So how the hell …

Abruptly, an explanation of sorts offered itself, and she fell on it gratefully. *There's something wrong with the electrics in this place. Obviously. The alarm clock, the telly …hell, the computer the other week. Better get someone in to give them the once over. Don't want any fires, do we? The way things are now the smoke alarm wouldn't go off. Yeah, I'll call someone tomorrow, maybe get Jon to sit in and wait for him, if he would. Yeah, the electrics. What else could it be?*

What else indeed?

So, with that explanation offered and accepted, Eve managed to control her heartbeat and returned her attention to her script, taking in the pencil annotations, hoping that if she stared at them hard enough they'd unlock the treasure chest and a huge piercing streak of EUREKA light would come spilling out.

Before switching off the light some hours later, she took the precaution of booking a seven thirty alarm call with the operator. *Things to do tomorrow. One: call the electrician. Two: Be less shite.*

She managed one out of the two anyway.

Chapter Twelve

Three things happened before she visited Carl's grave on his anniversary and found the perplexing piece of paper that Sunday – well, no; to be accurate, one thing *actually* happened and two things *failed* to happen.

The thing which *actually* happened was that Jon was, indeed, available to house sit on Wednesday (he was up for a camera operator's job on a reality show based in Leeds, and said, amiably enough, that he could wait anywhere for his mobile not to ring), and the electrician Eve had found in the Yellow Pages had walked about the place, prodded meters at walls, flicked switches and had pronounced (so Jon told her over a meal that night) that everything was just ticketty-boo, that'll be £75, please. "The little prick even managed to look magnanimous about charging you that much to wave what looked suspiciously like a light meter about the place. 'I'll just charge you the call out,' he said, all puffed up. Jesus! £75 for half an hour's work! If I charged that I'd never work again!'

"You *do* charge that," Eve had told him, ladling up some spaghetti. "In fact, you charge more."

"Yeah,' said Jon, his face dropping into what Carl had called "his patent Bassett Hound look," "that's why I'm unemployed so often. Still, should give you peace of mind."

Eve agreed that it should, and they ate and had a fine old chat about this and that, about how neither of them could really believe it'd been a year since Carl had died, and how pleased Jon was that she was picking up her life. So that was the thing that happened, and even that was a negative. Electricity fine. So why should the TV and the computer have decided to play up? Well, who knew?

The *first* thing that failed to happen was that there was no recurrence of the problems that had dogged her first day's arrival to rehearsal. The alarm clock blared out when it was set (though she kept the alarm calls as a backup – there was no way she'd be caught out twice), the car started when the key was turned, London Underground didn't go on strike ...no, from the Tuesday onwards, everything in her morning routine was (to use Jon's phrase) ticketty-boo.

She'd have wondered a lot more about that, about why for *just one day* everything had decided to conspire against her, and why the television set had suddenly erupted into life for no apparent reason, if it hadn't been for the *second* thing that failed to happen that week.

She didn't improve.

Eve just couldn't *get* it, she couldn't find her way in, she sat there (or walked about, but since for most of the second act she was bound to a chair she was mostly sitting), floundering. The lines came out, and in the right order, and she contorted her face into parodies of emotion and shouted when the lines had she shouts in parenthesis, and cried (well, hitched her breath) when required ...but it wasn't *enough*. She was going through the motions – what Carl had called Taking Care of Business. He'd been talking about an actor he'd once worked with – someone who'd gone on to, ironically enough, take a lead in the medical drama that Eve had turned down. "He's okay," Carl had said. "Reliable. Turns up on time, knows his lines, hits his marks – never lets you down. And he's not *bad*. Does the job, takes care of business. I can see why people employ him. But that's *all* he does. And it's not enough. It doesn't *flow* through him, he doesn't transcend. There's no power there, no charisma. He just takes care of business. He'll work, but nobody will remember him in ten years time."

That was Eve in the first week of rehearsal for *Pavlov's Bell*. She took care of business. After that first day she was on time, dead letter perfect, utterly reliable and professional ...but nothing *flowed* through her. She didn't transcend.

What made it worse was that Hedliegh Turner, the young lad not long out of Webber Douglas, was wiping the floor with her.

As a rule, Eve had never been bitter about other people's talent. Sure, she was human, and there'd been the odd conversation with Carl (and sometimes with fellow actors) where she'd offered the opinion that this actor should be tripped up or that actor should have his throat cut, but there'd been nothing malicious about it. She'd actually preferred to work with really talented people, as they could carry her along in their wake, force her to raise her game so she could compete. She'd never really wanted to be The Big Star, surrounded by people who just served her needs and whims, she wanted to *collaborate,* to join in – and if their talent made hers shine too …well then, everybody gained, didn't they?

But young Hedliegh – what, nineteen? Twenty? - was crucifying her. If he'd *burned* on that first day then by the time the week was over he was virtually supernova. Anything more – and Eve feared he had a lot more – and she'd be melted to the bone, like one of the bad guys at the end of *Raiders of the Lost Ark.* She was okay with the other two, Richard Coats and Rachael Spruce, she could cope with them, but they had little to do in the piece, all they did was set up the mystery at the beginning of Act One. But Hedliegh…

He darted and dived around her, twitching, a bag of energy. He made the transition from fan to madman seamless – even during his early scenes he managed to imbue his character with a *too straight* back, eyes that were just *too* alive. Nothing much, this wasn't Jack Nicholson in *The Shining,* but just enough so that when he peeled off the black hood he wore for the first ten minutes in Act Two (and one he insisted on rehearsing in), the audience wouldn't feel cheated.

Eve just couldn't keep up, and had no idea why.

It came to a head (sort of) on the Wednesday of that first week. They were working their way though the last four pages, the ones Eve had insisted had been rewritten, the ones where she'd finally freed herself from the ropes he'd tied her to the chair with and had wrested the knife from his grasp. She was holding it to his throat, saying, "It wasn't. But you know something? I think it is now. I think you showed me that. When you sliced me. When you tried to rape me. When you abused me," when Mike had called out;

"Just hold it a minute, will you?"

Eve had looked over, and there was the expression she'd seen far too many times that week. A sort of bemused bewilderment on Mike's face (and was there just a little anger on those features now? A touch of exasperation?) and – worse – more barely concealed sardonic laughter behind Barry's eyes.

"Hedliegh," Mike went on, "why are you on the floor right now?"

Hedliegh chuckled a bit. "Because Eve's got a knife and she'll cut me if I get up."

"Uh huh. And Eve, why have you got a knife?"

"Because I've just escaped from the chair and I'm torn between revenge for my torture and behaving like a decent person."

"Good," Mike smiled. "That proves you've both read the script! And I'm pleased! But, frankly, I don't believe a word of this."

That was the worst thing that had ever been said to Eve in her professional life, and it felt like a kick to the guts.

"The trouble is," Mike went on, standing, pacing a bit, stroking his moustache, "at the moment you're doing what the script says. You're doing things *because* the script says. You move because the script says you move, or because I've told you to move. It's all *external.* Okay, it's our third day. Okay, things will improve. But if you don't start to internalise everything *now,* it'll never happen. What we have here is a powerful story – an *important* story – about obsession, desire, dominance, ego, about how *deadly* these things are. A story about Man's objectification of Woman. What I'm *seeing* is two actors moving about a bit. Eve," he continued, and that's when she really realised he was only talking to her, that he may be throwing this note out generally, but it was, in actual fact, specific, "when you stand up and take that knife from behind your back, when you confront Hedliegh, I don't want him hitting the deck just because the script *says* he's to hit the deck. I want you to force him to the floor; I want him to have *no alternative* but to hit the floor. If *I* don't see that then the audience won't see that. And if *they* don't see that, then they'll laugh. Because look at him, he's six inches bigger than you and about two stone heavier. Knife or no knife, he'll punch you into the fuckin' Stone Age."

Eve had never had a note like that. *Ever.* Not even in her first job, back in that tour of *Random Harvest*. She hadn't fallen in love with the lead in that play because the script *said* she did that, she'd burrowed inside her character Kitty and found the bit of her that *did* love this man – and when she'd had to leave him because she realised he didn't love her back (no matter how much he said he did), she didn't cry because the script had *she cries* written on it, she'd cried because that bit of her that was Kitty had been genuinely broken hearted. And now, here she was, all those years later, with all that experience behind her, being given a note that would humble an amateur.

But she'd nodded, assured Mike she'd get it, and went back to the top of the scene.

She didn't get it though. Not then.

And the worst humiliation? The very lowest point of everything? The following afternoon when the understudy, a pretty dark haired pixie-faced woman called Kathryn had *her* rehearsal. And she blew Eve away. Kathryn got it. Eve hadn't. Eve could only sit at the back of the room and watch as finally, suddenly, the play sprang to life. And Eve wasn't blind. She saw the look on Mike's face. And on Barry's. *Okay, okay,* she'd thought. *Tomorrow. Friday. Tomorrow I take the role back and claim it.*

But she didn't.

Instead, the Friday dragged on and the work got no better, and for the life of her Eve couldn't figure out why. She was doing everything she thought she should do, she was dragging every bitter scintilla of experience she could, she even (in utter desperation) resorted to copying what Kathryn had done the day before ...but it wasn't translating. At five o'clock Mike had called the day to a halt, wished them all a happy weekend, and then added, "Let's start afresh on Monday, shall we?" (Subtext: *what a waste of time all that was.*) On his way through the door she'd seen him mouth to Barry, "I'm going to get shitfaced tonight."

Hedliegh had smiled at her and wished her a good weekend before trotting into the daylight – even Richard and Rachael, who had that look of a couple who were either lovers or were just about to be – had said something positive. But Barry? He'd gathered his script up, glanced at her, and said, "Happy now?" as he left.

There she was, alone. No one asked her for a drink. No one asked her what she was up to. No one invited her for a coffee, even. They just left her, the way you'd leave an elderly relative in a nursing home, one you didn't know very well. They left her the way you'd leave a pariah.

That night she'd returned home in a foul mood, thrown her script across the hallway, and found a large gin with a small tonic, and practically drowned in it. It saved the night, but ruined the Saturday. That's crutches for you.

Chapter Thirteen

That Sunday, she woke with tears on her cheeks and had no need to ask why.

A year. A whole twelve months.

Impossible it may have seemed, but she had indeed aged an entire three hundred and sixty-five days more than her husband ever would. There he was, still dead, while there she was, still living. Twelve entire months since the last monitor had stopped bleeping. Twelve entire months since her husband had taken his last breath. *Time, it goes so fast when you're having fun.*

She lay in her bed, bleary and miserable, reliving the moment as the nurse had walked slowly and professionally across the room to her, had taken her hand and said, "I'm so sorry, Mrs Wilson. I'm so sorry," and Eve had – incredibly – tried to smile back at her, as if to say *it's not your fault, don't apologise,* or *I know you all did your best or it's okay, I know he's at peace now,* but the smile hadn't made it past that bizarre intent, she had broken down and howled (*howl, howl, howl*) at the stupidity of it all, the simple crass finality, the brutal simplicity that lay at the centre of it all; her husband, her lover, her friend, her inspiration, was just a lump of clay on a bed, with no more use to her or anyone than an empty packet of Silk Cut Ultra.

The nurse had led her away to some small, private ante room and had sat with her as she'd bawled her eyes out, holding her hand, saying nothing, and back in the room there were doubtless porters and God knows what loading Carl onto a trolley to wheel him to the morgue so they could stack him with the rest of the stiffs like some macabre supermarket, and what had she thought then? *Hard times pass.* That's what he'd said to her two nights before as he'd slipped in and out of consciousness, as she'd smelled his steel breath, *hard times pass.* She'd tried to say that to the nurse, to reassure her somehow that Eve Wilson was going to be okay, that she understood the parade of life and death that made up the workings of the world, but she couldn't form the words.

All she could do was howl. Howl, howl, howl.

*

She placed the flowers on the grave and said, with no self-consciousness whatsoever, "I miss you."

CARL WILSON, the headstone said, gold leaf on black granite. BELOVED HUSBAND.

He had been, too – though once he'd been BELOVED BOYFRIEND. Once he'd actually called her up, that was. Okay, yes, she had been living with Chris – but Carl didn't know that, did he? He didn't *have* to wait roughly a month after that first meeting in the pub after the show, did he? He could have rung the next day – and, horribly, she'd really wanted him to.

She'd gone back home that night and Chris had been up (and judging by the smell he'd rolled a couple of his jazz cigarettes to pass the time), and he'd asked how the show had gone and she'd told him and they had a bit of a chat (with Chris savagely – and hysterically – lampooning the acting on some drama or other he'd watched that night) and they'd eventually tripped off to bed and that had all been mighty fine, but Eve just couldn't seem to shake Carl's face from her mind. Even when she looked at Chris, she seemed to see *Carl* – like a badly aligned special effect. (And something about that phrase seemed to trip her thoughts as she stood at the grave, remembering, but she couldn't tie it down so she let it run off.) Even on that one short meeting, that hour or so, she'd started to fall for him.

Leave it, she'd thought, *it'll pass. Just one of those mild infatuations you get from time to time – "crushes," people call them. Two weeks from now, it'll be Carl Who?*

It wasn't, but she'd resigned herself to never seeing him again when the phone rang. It was a Sunday, and Chris was working a shift at a newsagent's - hey, it beat signing on - while she was sat in their old front room preparing for a revival of *Brand* at the Lyric, to start rehearsing the Monday after her run in *Gothik* ended. Not a huge part, but one she could make work, and her head was deep in religious fervour and poverty as she answered "Hello?"

"Hi," said that smooth, quick confident voice she would get to know so well in her ear, "Eve Rogers?"

She didn't need to ask who it was. She'd kept that voice in her head. "Certainly is," and though her voice was level, was there a skip in her heart? "Hi Carl, nice to hear from you."

If she'd wrong footed him, he didn't show it. "Nice to be talking to you. You'll probably think this is terribly forward of me, but I bullied your number from your agent." (Once again, by the grave, this struck a distant chord in her head, but once again she couldn't quite place it.)

"If you're offering me a job, no. I don't think it's forward at all. But I should warn you, I'm contracted for the next five months."

"Actually, I'm not. I'm phoning up to see if you'd like to have dinner with me one night."

The answer that immediately sprang to her mouth? *Yes, I'd love to. When?* But, to give her credit, what she actually said was, "Ah. As pleasant as I'm sure that would be, I'm not sure my boyfriend would approve."

Once more, if there was an emotion on the other end of the line, the voice didn't show it. "Oh well, worth a try. Although, if you ever change your mind, you can reach me through London Management."

Eve didn't want to let this conversation end, even though she knew she really should. "Is it likely I'll change my mind?"

"Anything's possible," said Carl. "Life is infinite in its possibilities, a beautiful and talented young woman can change her mind. I live in hope; I'm an optimist. I even think I may win a Critic's Choice award some day."

Beautiful. He called you beautiful. And talented. "Does Grace know you're phoning up strange women and asking them out?"

"Grace?" Honest puzzlement. "What would she care? She's my ASM. Nice woman, like her a lot, but married with three kids. As a matter of fact, it was her who convinced me to find your number – got fed up with me talking about you."

He thinks you're beautiful and talented and *can't stop talking about you. Also, apparently, single.*

Yes, said her Sarah Voice, *but* you're *not. So stop this, ring off, and wait for your boyfriend to come home.*

"Anyway," he went on, "looks like my timing's off, which is why I'm a director and not an actor. Never mind. Nice talking to you. And like I say, should you change your mind …"

"London Management," she said, smiling. "You never know."

"No. You don't, do you? Goodnight, Eve."

She'd wished him the same and put the phone down, gone back to her studies and three hours later Chris had returned, grumpy and out of sorts. But she'd cheered him up. Did she think about Carl while she did so?

Maybe. It had, after all, been a long time ago.

*

So she stood there by the headstone of her dead husband on the early September Sunday and wiped a tear or sixty from her eyes, said once again, "I miss you, Carl," and turned to go.

It was then she noticed the other flowers.

God almighty, what's happening to me, she thought without any real trace of alarm. She knew perfectly well – grief, that was what was happening to her. Grief dulls your senses. Grief takes away your clarity of vision. Even scabbed over grief did that – but today the grief wasn't scabbed much, today that grief was as raw as it had been a year ago. There were three other bouquets. The card on the first said, *I'll never forgive you for breaking my Action Man. Miss you, bro – Jon.* More tears, this time over a watery smile. He'd rung that morning just to say *hi, take care, call me if the day gets rough and I'll come over,* but he'd said nothing about stopping by the grave. Maybe he knew she wanted to be on her own. "You're a good man, Jon," she heard herself say. The second was from Sam Mendes. *It gets darker every day you don't light up the West End. Sam.*

You got that right, she thought, mentally making a note to call him up – or at least his people – and thank him. But when she got to the third, she froze.

Why, read the card, in plain back slanted script, an elegant hand. *Why did you have to go and do something as stupid as this? All my love, honey.* And a kiss. No name, but a kiss.

Eve didn't need a name. She knew that handwriting, she'd seen it on a contract back in March. So formal. So neat. So …teasing.

Laura. Laura had sent those flowers, had written that card. Laura Rossi, who her husband really couldn't get along with.

Why?

*

Eve never drank before going to work, but on that Sunday night she made an exception.

Why?

She called Jon, said she thought the flowers were lovely, thanked him, asked about the Action Man, and listened as he told her the tale about a particularly violent game of war that had sent a plastic leg flying into the long grass never to be seen again.

Why did you have to go and do something as stupid as this?

She rang Sam Mendes and left a message, thanking him, too. It was a lovely sentiment, she said, and she appreciated it. She said she knew Carl would, too.

All my love, honey.

She returned a message from Sarah, told her sister she was okay – well, sort of. You know how it was. Eve said she'd got through it, a statement she knew Sarah would appreciate, speaking as it did of pragmatism and practicality.

The one person she did not phone was Laura Rossi. Nor did she phone Eve.

No name, just a kiss.

Why?

All my love, honey.
Why did you go and do something as stupid as this?
Just a kiss.
All my love.
Why?
The sky grew dark through the windows, but Eve didn't turn on the light. She drank. She didn't look at her script or worry about the work. She just thought about that note, that bouquet, about the neat back slanted hand that had written it.

Thought, and worried. What did it mean? Why had she said that? They'd really not liked each other – a grudging respect (very grudging on Carl's part) – but that was that. So why send flowers? Why write that note? *That* note in particular?

Maybe she was …paying respect in some way. Maybe not so much for Carl, but for me. I mean, we always got on …

Sarah Voice had a thing or two to say about that. *Oh? If so, why bother with the expense? She could've rung you up – we know she's got your number – said "how you doing?" and all that happy crappy. But she didn't. She sends flowers to the grave – or drops them off, or whatever. And what about that note? I mean, weird enough what she actually said, but …why didn't she sign it? Put her initial on it, at the very least? Why leave it anonymous? What's the point of that?*

Interesting point, that. She must have known I was going to see it. She must have known I'd recognise her handwriting. But she leaves her name off it and writes something so bizarre and alien to her nature …I mean, did she do it just to fuck me off? If so, well done. Because I am seriously fucked off here. But then, Eve thought on, actually sitting forward on her sofa as if addressing her sister, who (she imagined) was sitting on the armchair at the far end of the room, *why bother with the bloody thing in the first place? They weren't close, hardly liked each other, I had to practically force them together for that damned photo.*

Yeah, just like Beatrice and Benedik, said Sarah Voice, and Eve ran cold.

No!

Maybe, Sarah Voice continued, *you've thought it yourself. Actually you're thinking it* now, *since I'm you. That spark, that tension …remember? The one you couldn't quite figure out …*

No! Eve's lips were clamped together, a hard, thin bloodless line. *Not Carl. He couldn't. He wouldn't.*

Why not, Sarah Voice maintained. *You did.*

I didn't! I NEVER did! I never so much as looked *at another man!*

Not with Carl, no. But with Chris?

Suddenly the Tanqueray didn't want to be in her stomach any longer. There was no time for the bathroom, but she made it to the kitchen sink. And as she vomited, she remembered.

*

It had taken a month, a month during which she'd tried to resist the beat that ran through her head, a month during which she'd attended rehearsals for *Brand* and learned lines and moves and made choices which were offered and sometimes accepted, a month during which she'd returned home each night to find Chris sitting glumly on the sofa after a day of sending out CVs and headshots and hearing nothing back, a month during which she'd seen him for maybe an hour a day before he trotted across the road to the corner shop to earn the measly pay packet that paid his share of the rent. A month in which she tried not to think that it'd been five years since she and Chris had got together (*Time, it goes so fast*), five years in which she was Becoming, where she'd never stopped working, and he …well …A month in which she'd tried her best not to think about Carl, about his voice, his eyes, his magnetism, the way he *burned*, the way he …

Oh come on, Eve found herself thinking as she bent over the sink, trying not to look at that thin pool of liquid she'd expelled and most definitely trying not to smell it, *it's Tell the Truth time here at casa Wilson. You spent a month trying not to think about the way Carl had* made it. *You spent a month trying not to think about how Chris* hadn't *made it, nor did it look as if he ever would.*

True. Unpalatable, but true. Eve Rogers was On The Way, she was being Talked About, she was The Next Big Thing on the London stage – already, even back then, people were talking about the way she was refusing to be commercial, refusing to Sell Out. Tom her agent had done a great job of leaking stories to the press about how Eve had been offered *this* film or *that* telly – no names, no pack drill, but enough hints so people In The Know could place a franchise spy movie or a Major TV Series. She was On The Up.

Her boyfriend, however, wasn't. He was just another grunt, another foot soldier in the endless actor's struggle against unemployment. She was already Someone, soon to be Someone Important, and he was an infantryman – no, worse; he was a spear carrier.

Did that matter? Did that matter if she loved him? No, of course it didn't.

But as that month wore on, as Eve tried to ignore the beat in her head and heart, the beat that went *CARL-Carl, CARL-Carl,* she wondered more and more if she *did* actually love Chris. At least, love him enough.

They just didn't talk, that seemed to be the problem – hardly surprising, since they hardly saw each other. If you only spent a couple of waking hours a day together, how much time was there for talk? Even worse was that he had nothing to talk *about*. His days, after all, were nothings – phoning his agent (sometimes), sending out his stuff (sometimes), watching daytime TV (always) and selling comestibles across the road. She had days of Ibsen, of immersing herself in the world of *all or nothing*, nights of studying and restudying text …nights on her own.

When they *did* talk, there seemed to be less and less that they had in common.

When they *did* talk, there seemed to be less and less spark within him.

When they *did* talk, there was no fire anymore.

Chris, it seemed, didn't burn. But she did. And so did someone else. Someone who'd called her up one night, someone who could be reached through London Management.

In the end, though (well, not quite the end), she hadn't needed to make that call. *Brand* had opened to raves and packed houses, and enough critics had noticed her (one calling her "unbelievably good," another "astonishingly mesmeric," a third lamenting "the only thing wrong about this production is we don't see enough of Eve Rogers, a true new star of the English stage") for Tom to call her at the First Night party and practically yell down the phone, "I'm upping your fee next time. We're never going to want for takeaway pizzas." People clustered round her, because she was Milton's rough beast, her time come round at last, slouching towards Bethlehem to be born.

What of Chris on that night? Oh, he wandered through that party – having managed to get shift cover - beaming, smiling, proud of her (and he *was* proud of her …and if there was a touch of envy, a touch of fright, he didn't speak of it), and he tried to network, he tried to slide his face and name in front of as many people as he could, people who could *do* something for him, people who could make things happen …but those people could smell his desperation, the way dogs smell fear, and they turned from him. They weren't nasty, they weren't stand offish, but their smiles were forced and awful, and the way they said they'd keep him in mind unnatural.

At that party, where Eve's potential – the potential she'd shown at the RSC and at the National – had become actual, she began to realise she'd outgrown Chris. There was a pang around her heart at this; it hurt … but not much.

Not enough, anyway.

It was the first Monday of the run as she was taking off her makeup in her dressing room (thunderous applause and cheers still ringing in her ears: If she could eat that noise she'd never need to shop again), when the knock came at her door.

"Come in," she called, having no idea who it'd be.

"Eve," said Carl as he walked in, his eyes wide and bright, his grin infectious. "My God …I read the reviews, but they did *not* do you justice! I watched you tonight, quite prepared to hate you for turning me down, but I just couldn't. Well done. You were incredible."

She should've just blushed a bit and thanked him, asked after him and what he was up to, said "Well, it was lovely to see you again" and ushered him out. But she didn't. Instead, she looked at him, saw him, saw how he burned, how alive he was, and couldn't help herself.

She ran to him and kissed him, kissed him hard, her body flush against his, and that was the start of it.

Eve cheated on Chris for the rest of the run – five months, in total. Each night she could, she'd sneak off after the show and spend a couple of hours in Carl's bed, and the easiest part of all was she didn't have to make up an excuse. Chris didn't finish his shift until two in the morning. As long as she was back under her own duvet by half one, he was none the wiser. The more time she spent with Carl, the more she loved him. It *was* love too, not just infatuation. She felt much more for Carl than she'd ever felt for Chris – she just felt *right* with him, somehow, like they were pieces of a jigsaw puzzle that had been snugly slotted together. He was the one, if such a thing existed, and Chris just wasn't.

She wasn't proud of herself, she knew what she was doing was wrong, was cowardly, but it was like the cigarettes she smoked in those days – wrong, but addictive. Wrong, but powerful. Wrong …but *right*.

It was on the penultimate night of *Brand* (and Tom had already lined up a Stoppard at the Royal Court to follow, at a much increased fee), that she made up her mind.

"I'm going to leave Chris tomorrow," she said, lying next to Carl.

"Okay," he'd said. "Good. And me and you?"

She'd shrugged. "I love you," she said, and it was out, plain and simple, no going back …and no doubt that it was the right thing to say. "I thought I loved him, but now I realise I didn't."

"Right then," he'd said. "That works out well, since I love you too. So let's do it then. Let's be a couple."

"Makes sense," she'd said, managing to sneak a look at the bedside clock – half past midnight, nearly time to go. "Any ideas where we go from here?"

"None whatsoever." He'd smiled as he'd said that. "Shall we look at it as the start of rehearsals for a brand new play by an exciting new writer? Shall we just see where each day takes us?"

She'd considered that for a second, then smiled back. "Yeah. I think that's a plan."

So *Brand* ended, and after the last night party she'd gone back to the flat, half pissed (well, maybe three quarters), and told Chris that it was all over, that she didn't love him anymore, that she was sorry, really sorry (and she was), that as soon as she found somewhere else to live she was gone.

There was no big scene, no great drama. Chris sat there as she told him and just sort of nodded along, as if he'd expected it. He looked as if he'd known she was pulling away. He didn't ask if there was anyone else. At the end of her speech he wished her well, even hugged her (but stiffly, as if she was an aunt he rarely saw), and slept on the sofa.

It took a week for her to find somewhere else – a tiny bedsit in Archway on a three month lease – and during that time things stayed cordial between her and Chris. But as soon as the work ended for the day, she went to Carl's and fell harder and harder for him every night. By the time the Stoppard opened two months later the tiny Archway bedsit (which had hardly been used, in truth) was history, and she and Carl were living together in Acton, already talking about marriage, already talking about buying a house together. Maybe in Ealing.

The last time she saw Chris, he didn't see her. He was in an episode of *The Bill,* being chased by a copper. He ran out in front of a car and was killed. His scenes were over before the first commercial and he didn't say a word.

*

All of this passed through Eve's mind the way the gin had passed through her throat and into the sink – quickly and painfully. She held onto the worktop and shivered and thought, *so what?*

Sew buttons, Sarah Voice came back.

Do NOT fuck me off here, big Sarah. I'm tired and confused and feel like shit, so do NOT fuck me off! I repeat; so what? Yeah, I cheated on Chris, that was a bad thing and I've always felt sorry about it. But what has that to do with anything?

You cheated on Chris; Carl cheats on you. Isn't that what the Buddhists call Karma?

Carl did not cheat on me! Carl would not cheat on me! He loved me!

Did he? Yeah, I suppose he did. The way you loved Chris, maybe.

It is not the same thing and you *know it!*

How? How do I know it? How did that old quote go, the one Carl used to trot out whenever he'd had a bit too much red? "Who knows what evil lurks," wasn't it? We don't *know people in this life, kid. We just* pretend *we do. If you could cheat on Chris, Carl could cheat on you. And if you think otherwise, what about that card Laura left on the flowers? What does that say? Is that something you write to a casual acquaintance?*

He did not *cheat on me! And especially not with* her!

Oh come on! It's almost a crushing inevitability *it would be with her! If you don't fancy someone you're easy around them. Not like the way she was with him.*

Okay, okay – she fancied him. That doesn't mean he fancied her back. Even if he did, it doesn't mean he did anything …

You child, Sarah Voice blasted back, and for the first time ever it was angry. No, more than that, it was *furious. You stupid, self obsessed child!* Of course *he'd do something, of course he would, he was a* man, *they all would, every one of them! You think Steve's kept it in his trousers for the last fifteen years? None of them can, they're all just* men, *and Carl was just a man too, not a God, not a gold-plated idol, just a* man. *If a woman* winks *at them, especially one as skilled as Laura in such things, she'll* nail him. *More accurately, he'll nail* her.

"I won't believe it," screamed Eve, throwing her head back, a thin streak of bile flicking from her lips and splatting the tiles. "Nothing happened! Nothing *EVER* happened between them!"

Suit yourself, said Sarah Voice, now back to its usual patronising level. *Nothing ever happened, Carl was a good boy, and Laura didn't write what she wrote. There. Happy now?*

"Fuck off," growled Eve as she filled a glass with water. "Just *fuck off.* I can believe what I like. It's my life, my choice, so fuck off."

Her decision made, Eve drank the water and went to bed, where she lay awake for hours, unhappy. Sarah Voice didn't speak up once in the dark, but Eve could feel her sister inside her head, and wanted to rip the smug smile she saw there right off the older woman's face.

Only she couldn't.

*

As the alarm clock blared into life at seven thirty the following morning, and Eve's hand slapped it back into silence, she realised that at some stage during the fitful doze she'd managed a little after two in the morning, she'd come to a sort of conclusion about the previous day's events.

I can't change anything, she found herself thinking. *What's done is over. And if – if – anything did happen between Laura and Carl, then what of it? What can it possibly* matter *now? Okay, it hurts. Just the thought of the possibility of it hurts. But so what? In time, it'll be like Carl's death itself, a dull ache, a small scar, nothing much to bother about, hardly noticeable. Things change, life goes on. Hard times, after all, pass.*

Fine words, broke in Sarah Voice as Eve thumped down the steps to the kitchen, *but we all know how many parsnips fine words butter. You really think you can let it go, the possibility of betrayal? You really think you won't just have to* know, *one way or the other?*

You know, big Sarah, Eve replied as she poured Alpen into a bowl and went in search of milk, *I have far more pressing problems than what my husband may or may not have got up to some time back. I have to deal with the fact that I may just not be very good at my job any longer. I have to work on getting it back.*

Sarah Voice had no answer for that, so Eve munched in silence and tried to concentrate on her acting, on what was wrong, and how it should be put right.

It was difficult, but she managed it. To concentrate, that is.

Chapter Fourteen

"Okay Eve," said Mike, placing the drinks on the table and sitting opposite, "What is it I'm not doing?"

It was Friday, the end of the second week of rehearsals, and things were no better. No worse, but no better – and in some ways, that was the bitterest pill for Eve to swallow; the fact that she'd resorted to considering *no regress* as progress.

"I'll only answer if you swear to whatever you hold dear that this conversation goes no further." She sipped her gin. She wanted to neck it down, but she sipped. Giving in and getting drunk in public would be a bad move.

"I'm not sure I can do that, darlin'," said Mike, the fingers of his right hand brushing his face fuzz again, as if searching for crumbs. *I was right, that "darlin'"* is *seriously pissing me off.* "I got Sir Peter on my back – you saw what he was like yesterday. And he's got the board of directors on *his* back. And these people are nervous, darlin'. And if they get nervous, I get nervous. Everyone's got a lot riding on this, you know."

"Me included."

"Yeah, I get that, I truly do. Maybe you especially. You're up there, you're out front, it's your …"

"Comeback?"

"I was going to say it's your show, but hell yeah, maybe it *is* your comeback. But whatever it is, darlin', it's not working. I'm sorry to be blunt, but it's not working. And we go to previews in eight days; we have our First Night in eleven."

"I can count." That came out sharper than she intended, but who was she kidding here? She wasn't angry at him. She was angry at herself, angry that she'd no one else to blame than herself for being put in this position for the first time in her professional life, the Private Talking To by the Director.

Mike's hands went up in a *whoa* gesture. "Okay, sorry. Didn't mean to patronise – except I know I do sometimes. Mostly it's an affectation, something I do to keep a barrier between me and the talent, but sometimes I fall into it when I'm out of my depth. Like I am now. I don't know what to do with you, Eve. I've tried supporting you, I've tried cajoling you, I've tried encouraging you and I've even shouted at you. And nothing's changing." Eve glanced at him, and once more he misinterpreted her look as an attack on him. "Go on, get angry with me. It's fine. In fact, if I could see some of that in the room I'd be happy. If that's what it takes, do it. Hate me. It's cool, I've got big shoulders – I've been hated before and I'll be hated again. I actually don't care."

"I'm not angry with you," she sighed, sipping a bit more, then gazing around at the crowd around them. Thank God he'd suggested somewhere anonymous and not an actors' hole like the Colony or the Zanzibar where they'd be surrounded by people they knew and who knew them, people who'd be able to tell what was going on. Here they could just be two colleagues from a bank after a rough week for all anyone knew. "I'm not angry with *anyone*. Except myself."

"So I'll ask you again; what do I do? I'm out of options here. My bag of tricks is empty."

"And I'll reply again – swear you'll keep it to yourself and I'll tell you."

She held his look with her own – back in the day she could use that stare to enchant just about anyone, it was one of the joys of grey eyes; people would look just to see their own face reflected back – but she was beginning to think her day was done, and her enchanting time was over. She saw him pause, reflect, and cast himself back over that troubling, awful week. Mike had, of course, been right. It hadn't got any better. She was still struggling, still an outsider, still badly forging every emotion she desperately needed to look genuine.

Barry hadn't returned to rehearsals after Monday lunchtime, and as he left Eve saw what was written on his face, *why bother? That silly diva bitch has wrecked my work, I don't get paid for being here, I'm off to do something else.* She saw Richard and Rachael (closer by the minute) huddle in corners and stare in disbelief at her. *That's Eve Rogers,* they goggled. That? *God, I was doing better than that in my first term play. I've seen better amateurs. In a Church Hall. On a Monday. A wet Monday.* She saw Hedliegh try his absolute best to quiver and cry as she stood over him at the dénouement, the dénouement rewritten at her request (demand?), and she knew he was faking it every bit as badly as she'd occasionally faked her orgasms. She saw the way they unconsciously pulled away from her when they broke for coffee or lunch, how they huddled close and left a space for her, as if they were survivors and she was the shipwreck. She saw the irritation on Mike's face and heard the exasperation in his voice as he'd tried the strategies he'd enumerated earlier. Most wounding of all, she'd seen Sir Peter, her old friend from years gone by, who had seen her burn and burn again in classics too many to mention, struggle to maintain a neutral face as he'd sat through an afternoon's work. She'd seen the glance that had passed between him and Mike. *What have you done,* asked Sir Peter. *Did you break her?* Mike's answer: *No, she was like that when I got here. Everything else is fine, you can see that for yourself. It's just her.*

"Okay," said Mike after everything had passed through his mind. "You got it, our secret. What do I do?"

"Mike," she said, and necked half the gin, "I haven't got a fucking clue."

"That's not funny, darlin'."

"I wasn't joking," she said, leaning back in her chair. "That's the truth. I'm as much in the dark as you are. And I'm scared. I am, to be crude, absolutely shitting myself with fear."

"So …what? You're telling me you've lost it? Is that what you're saying to me?"

"Who knows? Maybe. Maybe it's all over for me. Maybe I'll have to get a job in a soap – *Emmerdale* does a nice line in has beens, or so I'm told. All I know is I just can't seem to find it." She leaned forward, all the glibness out of her face now, the genuine fear spilling out. "And I'm trying. I'm trying *hard!* I'll tell you something, Mike, I've never worked this hard – yeah, no need to pull that face, I can see you don't believe it. But it's true. This has been the hardest two weeks of my working life, *and I still can't get it!* I don't have a clue about how to get it. I listen to you, and what you say makes sense, I can understand it, I can even *process* it, *but I can't translate it!* I look at Hedliegh and I see what he's giving me, and I can't ask for more, but it doesn't *spark* anything in me! It should, it used to, but it *doesn't* anymore! I think I'm saying, Mike," she went on, a little calmer now, but still terrified inside, "that it's over for me. That the only thing I *could* do I can't do anymore."

There was a long pause, and in it Mike demolished half his pint, and Eve sat there, trying not to cry, trying not to tremble. It was out now, out in the world, spoken and never to be retracted. Even if just this one man heard it, it was out there, and there was only one thing in the universe that could never be properly retracted, it was words. Loans could be given back, weight lost, property exchanged, but words that were spoken could never go back in the mouth.

"Okay," said Mike eventually. "Thanks for your honesty. Now here's mine; we're too far along now to back out. That's what Sir Peter said to me on the phone last night, and I agreed with him. Though if we're *going* to be honest – *completely* honest – I'll tell you it was a reluctant agreement on my part. The company's spent a lot on you, Eve, on your fee, on publicity, on posters which have your agent's stipulated billing on them. Even the bloody programme is set to print. They know that your name, your return, will bring people through the door. That's why I pushed your rewrite through in the first place – a fact Barry never stops reminding me of, by the way. That initial push will bring back a lot of what was invested; advance sales are pretty healthy, I'm told. But if it wasn't for those reasons, we'd have let you go and put the bloody understudy on. Sorry to be brutal, but we would."

Yes, of course they would. Eve had known that. But still, to hear it …

"We'll honour your contract for the first option phase – if we're still afloat by then – and then I do believe you're going to become ill and we will recast. We'll say nothing but express regret and we expect you to do the same. If a crisis hits very early on, we may offer to buy you out – that's up to the board, not me. But unless something significant happens next week, Eve, *this is what is going to happen.* Do you understand?"

I think I preferred it when you called me "darlin'" after all. "Yes," she said, and her voice was tiny.

Mike finished his pint. "I'm sorry," he said. "Genuinely. I so looked forward to working with you, I'm sorry I wasn't able to help you, I sincerely wish that whatever it is that's troubling you can be worked out. I honestly think that whatever you had is still inside you somewhere – it just needed something else, *someone* else maybe, to bring it out."

"Okay," she said, and the tone of her voice was maddeningly familiar, she just couldn't place it. "Thank you for all you've done. And thank you for your honesty."

"I somehow doubt you mean that," said Mike, standing. "Hey, how're you getting home? You need a lift?"

"No thanks," Eve said, and suddenly she realised when she'd last sounded like she did now, it was when Doctor Chapora had used the phrase *there has been no significant improvement, Mrs Wilson. The best we can do now is make him as comfortable as possible.* It was the tone of finality, acceptance, defeat. "The station's just across the street."

"Right then." He hesitated, wanting to go but not wanting to appear in a hurry. "See you Monday."

"Yes," said the small child who sat in Eve's body. "You certainly will."

*

"Hey, guess what Carl," Eve said to the empty hall three hours later as she let herself in, swaying a little. "I'm a bit drunk. And also, a bit fired. I'm working my notice. Got a month or so left." She couldn't be bothered walking into the living room, so she flopped down on the hallway carpet. "I'm broke and no one can fix me. My days are done. What do you say, Carl? What do you say?"

Carl, being dead, said nothing. So Eve sat in her hall, gave in, and cried.

*

The last week of rehearsals was no better. To her credit, though, Eve didn't stop trying.

She'd taken a furious phone call from Tom on the Saturday afternoon as she'd stared at an old Western on Film Four. He'd heard the plans from Sir Peter and was absolutely *outraged!* *Nobody* treated his clients like that, he didn't care *who* they were! He was going to sue the Dagmar, he was going to sue Mike, he was going to sue Sir Peter –

Eve cut in before Tom could suggest suing God Himself, and told him to shut up, she'd agreed, she was better off out of it, what's done is done, let's just take the hit and get on with it, shall we?

"You agreed?" Tom had asked, disbelieving.

"Yes, I agreed. Mike's right. Sir Peter's right. I stink the place out. I'd do the same thing in their position. Carl *had* done the same thing, more than once."

"Granted," he'd spluttered, "but not with someone like you!"

"Ah, Tom. There's the rub, you see. I'm *not* someone like me anymore."

"Hey, don't – this is just a temporary ..."

She spoke over him. "Maybe. Maybe not. Watch this space, as they say. Just say 'yes' to everything they say, old friend. It's for the best."

A pause. She could almost see him, shifting things around on his desk. Except it was a Saturday, so maybe he'd be shifting things around his coffee table. "If that's what you want."

"It is."

They'd hung up then, and Eve had gone back to her Western. When that finished, a war film came on. She watched that, too.

*

She tried and tried through the week, but nothing happened. As the days tripped past she could sense everyone around her just sort of shrugging their shoulders and getting on with it. Everybody knew it was a pup. As they filed out on the Friday before first preview, Rachael had asked Mike, "Tomorrow?" and he'd shaken his head, as if to say, *what's the point?*

Before all of this is over, Eve thought as she trudged to the station, *before I become ill, I will take them all out for a drink – no, a meal, and apologise. Even Barry. I will eat my humble pie and like it.*

She spent that weekend before the previews not doing much of anything really – she slept and woke and ate and eventually slept some more – but somewhere in the back of her mind, she knew she was counting down the days until she was no longer an actor, until the truth was out of the rehearsal space and into the public domain: Eve just couldn't cut it anymore, don't bother her agent with an offer, she might be able to do a murder mystery in a hotel somewhere but that's about it.

It was a similar sort of countdown, she realised on the Sunday as she trudged her way to bed (no need for the alarm clock, they weren't called at the theatre until midday) to the one she'd engaged in during the last weeks of Carl's life. Each time she'd awoken, an unconscious beat in her brain had chanted *one less day to go, one day nearer the time.* The only difference was, with Carl there'd been no deadline – at least, not one she'd been aware of. There was just one day less, she was just one day nearer. In this case, the countdown had a definite zero point; Thursday, 7.30 pm, when the curtain went up. And nothing was going to stop it. At that point, all that she had been for twenty-two years would end.

Chapter Fifteen

"What do you *mean*, nothing will stop it?" asked Carl.

Eve knew she was dreaming, but didn't care. It was *Carl* again, and she hadn't seen or heard from him for so long. She wanted to burst into tears, even though she knew she mustn't. It'd spoil the show.

They were in The Hen & Chicken Theatre Pub, near King's Cross, and it was – when? The Past, that's all she knew; she was fresh and young, vital, her breasts still pointing forwards, eyes unbagged, ash blonde hair in no need of a rinse. She was almost in her prime. She could feel that energy, that promise, that vitality surge through her. It felt good. It felt good to be young again, to be at the start again.

But she'd given up on being young, the way she'd given up on dope, speed and fags. The way she'd now given up on being talented. So why was she here, sitting on this stage? And why was Carl sitting opposite her? He wasn't an actor. He should be in the audience, not on the stage. Oh, and one final point – *what bloody play is this, anyway?*

No play I've ever read or seen, she found herself thinking. *Because this play is being written now, by me, in my head. It's anything I want it to be. And look, I've given Carl the male lead. Outré casting, but God hates a coward.*

He'd said, *what do you mean, nothing will stop it,* which meant her line – as she crossed behind him and poured a glass of watered down Pepsi which was supposed to be brandy – was, "I mean, beyond a certain point, inevitability takes over. Or Fate, if you want to be sentimental. You want to know what I think? Well, even if you don't, I'm going to tell you. I think the idea that we control our own destinies is a joke. Not a funny one, not one that starts with 'there were these two fellers,' but a joke nonetheless."

"Are you talking about God?" Carl asked, and oh dear, maybe casting him had been a mistake. He was trying far too hard. He was given a line with a question mark at the end and so thought it had to be given some gravitas. *Better to throw those away,* she thought in her dream. *Save the emphasis for where it really hits home.*

"I don't think so," she replied, and there she was, in the zone, feeling it but not feeling it, acting it but being it, in control and out of control at the same time. "I think I'm talking about *forces,* if you like. Natural ones, like magnetism. Stuff that just happens, that's just there, acting all around us – gravity – stuff over which we're powerless."

Carl stood and walked to her, stiff, unnatural. He took her hand, and his were cold. Of course they are, she thought. He's dead. "So *that's* what you think, is it? I'll tell you what *I* think then. I think I'm going to stop it. I think I've been trying to stop it for a long time – not that you noticed. And, in the end, I'm *going* to stop it. It wasn't me before, you see, but it's me *now*. It's been me for a while. I will do everything I *can* to stop it, and Heaven help anyone who gets in my way."

Oh for Christ's sake, he's gone off text. He's bloody improvising in the middle of a scene. Oh Carl, I do love you so much – or I will soon – but stop being a bloody amateur! "Big words, big man," Eve teased, her mind racing.

"Yeah, aren't they? That's because I'm so bloody heroic. One more thing though, don't believe everything you read."

Thanks for the help, that makes no sense in the context of this play. "I'll do my best."

"Yeah," said Carl and sighed. It was a heavy one, full of heartbreak and despair. "That's where you'll go wrong, damn you." But then, suddenly angry – "I mean it, Eve. *Heaven help anyone who gets in my way. And I will use anything and anyone I can* to keep you safe!"

Before she could come up with a suitable response, the dream broke up and span into darkness, and Eve knew no more until nine o'clock.

*

The cast assembled on stage at midday, as per the call, and Mike took them through the traditional first preview speech – this is no more than an extension of the rehearsal process, a chance to learn through the audience reaction, don't go too big just yet and *blah* and *blah de blah* – and all the time Eve could see him drowning vertically, like a brave man should. *Here dies my career before it ever really got started,* she could see him thinking. *Please God, let me work again.*

He took them through a move rehearsal - no lines, just the moves – then a speed rehearsal – no moves, no emoting, just gabble your lines as fast and you can and *pick up the bloody cues* – then, after returning from a tea break (during which everyone was courteous and lovely to Eve, in the way you'd be to your slightly senile and ever so incontinent grandmother) he took a very mild rehearsal from the top. "Give me seventy-five percent of what you'll give me tonight," he said, "which will be seventy-five percent of what I want on Thursday." After that, he proclaimed himself satisfied (which he clearly wasn't, and that was all *her* fault) and dismissed them till seven. "I leave you now to your own devices and salvation," and his smile was so forced Eve reckoned his moustache would shoot off if he kept it up for another second. "Piss off out of my sight and stay sober."

The cast began to disperse then, Richard and Rachael doubtless looking forward to a little alone time before curtain up, but Eve heard herself clearing her throat. "Hey guys," she said.

They turned and looked at her – young, all so young, all at the start of whatever it is they were at the start of, and the memory of her dream tripped through her head. Their energy. Their promise. "The pub across the road does great food," she said. "Who fancies something? I'm paying."

They all did.

How odd, she found herself thinking as she placed the order at the bar – nothing heavy, some sandwiches and soft drinks, no one wants a Four Seasons pizza sitting in their stomach while they're out there giving it their Not Quite All in front of an audience – *in three weeks working together, this is the first time we've sat down as a bunch, as a group. Why?*
Because a fish goes rotten from the top down. And you're the top, and you're rotten. It's up to you to set the tone, you know this – you've known it since you became the name that you are. And you were always a good company leader back in the old days. You led the lunches, you included everyone, you found out their histories and their fears and their ambitions, and even if you didn't like some people – in fact, even if

you positively hated *some people, you included them, you made them feel warm, you made them feel like they were family. You did that because, in Carl's words, you were "going to war," and warriors needed to feel like they belonged, like they had a cause worth fighting for. But you've been too self-absorbed, too invested in your own struggle to even* think *about connecting with anyone else. You set yourself apart. You didn't even think about getting to know anybody. How sad.*

It was, indeed, sad. But since this would be her last work as an actor, she would reclaim her title as company leader at the end. This bunch of actors would not remember her as a talent – at the very best they'd remember her as a broken lightbulb that had once shone brightly – but she was determined they would remember her as a decent human being, as a friend. She could do that at least.

She took the tray of mineral waters and Diet Cokes and lime and sodas to the table, dished them out, and before their food could be brought over, Eve looked at them all, smiled a tired sort of smile, and said, "You know what? I'm sorry."

There was a little murmuring, a slight attempt at demurral, but she went on over the top of it. "I mean it, I'm sorry. I've let you all down here, I know it, and I'm powerless to stop it. You – all of you – are going to do great things. I only wish I could be there alongside you. But I think those days are past, don't you? I remember," she went on, again overriding protestations that were only polite, "the first play I ever did, *Random Harvest*. We had an actor in it – can't even remember the poor bastard's name now – who'd lost it. Been working for thirty, forty years maybe. He'd had a good run, and he was a decent enough bloke, but he couldn't do it anymore. He only had one scene and even *that* was too much for him. He knew it, we knew it, but we liked him and kept supporting him as best we could. But I said to my then boyfriend, 'When I get like that, I hope I know enough to quit.' Well, seems like I've got like that, and I do know enough. I think this'll be it for me."

Hedliegh tried to speak then, but she wouldn't let him. "It's you I owe the biggest apology of all to, I think," she said, "because you've been acting into a blanket. I've given you nothing back. And I've tried, Christ how I've tried, but it looks like the well is dry, my friend. But let me tell you this; you're a very, very talented actor, and you'll survive this, and you'll continue to work. You'll get good notices for this, and deservedly so." Then, to them all, "So, what say we drink to the end of my road and the beginning of yours?"

That's what they did. Even though they did it sadly, they did it. But on top of that sadness, Eve felt their relief. The elephant in the room had finally been acknowledged, by the elephant itself. It wouldn't make the coming weeks (if they lasted that long) any easier, but at least everything was out in the open.

Closure, she thought as the waitress brought their sandwiches over. *This is closure; the beginning of the end. My life as a wife, over. My life as an actor, nearly over – but I'll tell you what's funny, I'm no longer scared. I think I've accepted it, I think I've made my peace with it. I think it's okay. I think I can let it go.*

On top of that, *Did Carl ever think that? At the end? Or was he too doped, too 'morphined up to fuck'? Did he manage that acceptance? Did he even* know *he was dying?*

But for the nine millionth time that year, there were no answers forthcoming.

Instead, they drank their drinks and ate their food, and indulged in a fine old gossip (led by Eve) about what they'd done in the past, where they'd come from, and what they would do in the future.

This'll do, Eve thought at one point. *This'll do as an ending.*

Except it wasn't an ending.

*

The preview went pretty much as expected. It was flat. Eve tried – even though this was her last hurrah, she tried not go out on a downer – but it just wasn't there to be found. There were odd gasps from the audience and applause at the end, but no one was fooling themselves, least of all Eve. It had just sort of *happened,* really, it was just something that filled in an evening. She had Taken Care of Business. As she wiped off her makeup and stared at her naked face in the dressing room mirror, there was a knock and Mike's voice called, "Eve, you decent?"

"I'm dressed, if that's what you mean."

He stepped in and regarded her sadly, fatalistically. "You all right?"

"I'm not ready to dance the Can-Can, but I guess I'm at the best place I can be."

"I wish …I wish it could have worked out better," he said eventually.

"Me too." Then, with a deep breath, she pulled herself together. "Notes?"

Incredibly, he laughed. "Would 'be less shit' help?"

Incredibly, she joined in. "No, not a bit."

"Well then," Mike replied. "Noon tomorrow."

"Noon tomorrow," she agreed. Mike hung around for a second, as if he had something else to say, but then he decided he didn't after all and left. Ten minutes later, so did Eve.

The following day they went through the whole sequence again – more runs, a few move adjustments, some notes (for everyone bar Eve) on volume levels, then a quick bite to eat in the pub and more chat, more gossip – then back to the theatre for another desultory preview. Not good, not awful, just *there*. And again the day after that, the same routine, the same outcome – nothing much to report, just more of the same with no breakthrough from Eve. *And why should there be?* she'd thought as she sat in the train going home, *there's nothing left anymore, I'm a dead circuit. I wonder how long it'll be before I'm "sick"?. Are they already auditioning my replacement? Would they just bump Kathryn up? Not a bad idea, that, she's talented enough, if a bit young. I may suggest it to Mike tomorrow after –*

After the First Night. After her last First Night.

Yeah, after that. She was perhaps a little surprised that the phrase *her last First Night* didn't paralyse her with fear, but hey – things were what they were, after all, and who had the power to change them? Well, Carl reckoned he did, but that was only in a dream – one he couldn't even stick to the script in. *We mere mortals in the Land of the Ephemera are as private parts to the Gods; they play with us for their sport.*

She stepped off the Tube and into the night, back straight, head held high, determined to exit doing her best work, but knowing that her best was no longer good enough.

*

One of Eve's odd peccadilloes about performing throughout her career was that she couldn't stand to share a dressing room. Over the years, she reckoned, some people had probably thought her as stand-offish because of that. *Look at her, the big star, won't join in with the likes of us, has to be pampered, has to be separate!* Others, more generous, had perhaps ascribed it to nerves on her part; *they say even Dame Judi gets stage fright before she goes on. Maybe Eve's the same. Has to be on her own so she can puke in the toilets and not be overheard.*

The truth was neither of those things, and the truth was much less interesting than either – she just needed quiet. She needed half an hour of calm to pull herself out of the real world and place herself into the world she was about to inhabit. Eve admired (and slightly envied) those who could stand around and chat and laugh and muck about before going on – even in the wings between entrances – but she couldn't manage that. She needed her time, her focus. Sure, she'd talk, she'd be polite, even swap a joke or two, but she needed her thirty minute focus. Even now, on her last ever First Night, she needed her focus.

She managed it, too. She arrived at the theatre early, dropped good luck cards off to Hedliegh and Richard, sent bouquets to Rachael and Kathryn, left some presents for Mike and even Barry at the stage door (God alone knew whether Barry would actually turn up, but hey – someone would know how to get that copy of Robert McKee's *Story* to him), and then she'd shut her dressing room door behind her, opened her own cards (all of which had some variation on *lovely to have worked with you* written on them), changed, made up, and then spent half an hour with her mind floating above her head, focusing, concentrating, finding her still point, at no point filling her head with *this is the last time I'll…* or *this is the end of …* just centering her mind, hearing the Stage Manager's calls over the PA but *not* hearing them …thirty minutes …twenty …fifteen …ten …and behind the SM's voice, the growing swell of an audience mutter, like the arrival of a swarm of bees. What had Mike said? The advances were good? And the Dagmar – a dog of a theatre that her husband had hated and which now looked set to bury her career - held about a thousand, which meant that at a rough estimate some nine hundred or so were going to watch the beginning of the end of her acting life.

Then, "beginners please. Beginners."

She stood up, back straight, head held high, murmuring the joke she'd used a million times before to herself, "I'm not a beginner, I've done this before," and put her hand on her dressing room doorknob.

Which refused to turn. Her hand slid straight off.

She rattled it back and forth, but it still didn't turn. She pulled the doorknob towards her, but the door stayed fast. She pushed it away from her. Still it filled the frame, unyielding. *Oh, for fuck's sake ...*

Eve took a deep breath, then tried again. Nothing. The knob didn't so much as twitch under her hand.

"Beginners," said the PA again. "Beginners to the stage please."

"I'm fucking *trying*," she gasped, her chest tightening as she tried to get the door open. She started pulling great gasps of air and gave up any pretence of turning the doorknob and simply tried to pull the thing off its hinges. *C'mon*, she begged, *shift, open, do something, it's beginners, the curtain's up in less than five minutes now and I'm on first, and if I'm not there then there isn't a show, even though I'm worse than useless I have to be there so for fuck's sake OPEN!*

As with her car, mental swearing at an inanimate object had no effect. There remained a solid wooden door in front of her, and not the gap that would enable her to start to finish her working life. *What's going on,* she wondered, panicked and angry and sweaty, all of her carefully prepared focus up in smoke, *how did this bloody thing jam? Or did it jam? Did somebody lock this fucker? Mike or Hedliegh or Barry – yeah, Barry, it'd be him if anybody, he's locked me in here to stop me from wrecking his fucking masterpiece and when I get out I'm going to find him, rip his head off and shit down his neck the lousy rotten fuckfaced –*

"Miss Rogers to the stage, please, Miss Rogers to the stage, curtain up in one minute," said the PA.

"*I FUCKING CAN'T!*" She screamed, and at that point any control she'd retained vanished in a second. "*I'm FUCKING LOCKED IN HERE!*" With that, she abandoned trying to wrench the doorknob loose and simply resorted to battering on the panelling. "Hey! Out there! *Anyone!*" She could feel her voice roughening as she ruined her vocal chords, "*I'm FUCKING STUCK IN HERE!*"

"Miss Rogers," came a timid voice from outside – the ASM, what was her name? Julie? "Is everything all right?"

"Does it fucking *SOUND* like I'm all right? This fucking door is ..."

But Julie (was it?) simply turned the knob and opened the door, concern and curiosity on her pretty freckled face. "It's just we're …"

"Yeah, yeah," said Eve, rushing past her, trying to keep it together, ignoring as best she could that the door had magically been opened, "we're going up, yeah, I heard." Then, over her shoulder, "fucking thing was *jammed*."

"Yes Miss Rogers," said the ASM, trailing after her, "I'll get a chippie to look at it later – do you want us to hold, so you can get yourself together?"

"Why bother," snapped Eve as she made her way through the wings, "I'm as ready as I'll ever be anyway. Why delay the fucking execution?"

With that, she stormed onto the stage – sweaty, her hair askew, shaking with adrenaline, sat down at her prop desk, picked up her prop pen, looked over at the SM at the prompt corner and nodded.

Let's get it over with then, she thought, and the curtain rose.

Whereupon, she froze. Eve Wilson, known to some as Rogers, simply did not have a clue where she was, what she was doing, or what she was going to say. Her throat completely dried, her head span, her heart went into overdrive. She could hear nothing bar the roar of blood in her ears. *I have absolutely no idea what's going to happen,* she thought. She remembered one winter – 1993 – not long after she'd passed her driving test. She was taking her first car – of course, an old Citroen 2CV, what other car would a drama student have – on a drive. Nowhere special, just driving, because that's what you did when you passed your test, you just drove, and on this November day she was *just driving* and had hit a patch of black ice. She wasn't speeding, just pootling along at twenty-five miles an hour or so, but regardless of her law abiding pace the Citroen's front wheels had lost traction and she found herself spinning – slowly, but spinning – out of control, utterly helpless, and through the windscreen she had seen the lamppost coming up to meet her, and 2CVs were just made out of tin, and it didn't matter how slowly she'd been travelling – when concrete and tin met at *any* speed, there was only going to be one winner.

With everything out of her control, she'd thought quite clearly *I could well end up dying here. And there's nothing I can do to save myself.*

That was how she felt in those terrifying seconds on that London stage on her last ever First Night. A flood of sweat ran into her eyes, stinging, blinding her, and with a shaking hand she wiped it away. *There's nothing I can do to save myself,* she thought. *I could well end up dying here. It's out of my control. Jesus, quick – please! You, stage manager woman! Look up! Look up from your desk and see I'm dying! Drop the curtain, throw me out with the garbage, give the audience a refund ...do SOMETHING! THERE'S NOTHING I CAN DO TO SAVE MYSELF!*

Nothing ...except maybe turn into the skid.

That's what had happened in the car on that winter's night all those years ago. Her first instinct had been to stamp on the brake and the clutch simultaneously – to perform an Emergency Stop. After all, this certainly constituted an Emergency, didn't it? And Stopping was most definitely required.

She'd actually tensed all the muscles in her legs to do this and was just about to lift her right foot off the accelerator when a memory had spoken up in her head. Her father. *You hit water or you hit ice when you're driving,* he'd said, not long after she'd started her lessons, *or get in any situation where you lose traction, the first thing you're going to want to do is stamp on the brake. Because you'll panic. It's natural, we all do. But all that'll do is lock up the drive wheels and you'll go skating along in a straight line. You won't lose any speed at all, because there's no friction to slow you down. So resist that, don't do it.*

Instead, ease the pressure on the go pedal slowly and turn the car into the skid, turn the wheel into the direction you're spinning. Again, slowly. Don't panic. Panic will get you killed, most like as not. Am I scaring you Evie? No? Well, I should be. I want you good and scared so you listen to me. Slowly off the accelerator, slowly turn the wheel the way you're skidding. That way the drive wheels will lose power and allow inertia to overtake momentum. You'll slow down – gradually, but you'll slow down. Do this early enough – and if you're not speeding – then it could well save your life.

It had that night – obviously, or she wouldn't now be sat on a stage in London in a panic so severe it felt like a heart attack. She'd eased her foot off what her Dad had called "the go pedal," she'd turned ever so gently into the skid, and as she looked the lamppost grew and grew through the windscreen, coming towards her (no, she was going towards it, but that's not how it seemed, it had seemed like she was still and the world was revolving towards her) …but then it had passed, it was out of her view, and her foot was right off the "go pedal" and the car was at a halt. Facing a hundred and eighty degrees in the wrong direction, granted, but stationary. And she was alive.

Some unimportant things had happened then – she'd hit the hazard lights, jumped out of the car and stood by the side of the road to warn oncoming traffic or somesuch – but the only thing that mattered *here,* now on *that stage,* were the words *turn into the skid. Don't panic. Panic will get you killed. Don't panic.*

I could have died that night, I didn't, Eve thought, as she brought that trembling hand from her face. *I could have died.*

I didn't.

I quit dope and speed and fags. Three things that could have killed me. But they didn't.

I turned into the skid.

My husband died of cancer. I didn't.

I turned into the skid.

When I was younger and knew less than I did now, I turned into the skid.

You know what, Eve old Eve? If you did it then, *you can do it* now.

Turn into the skid.

Hey, you know what I've just remembered, Eve old Eve? On top of that "turn into the skid"? I've remembered what a stubborn old cow you are. How you went your own way, how you made your own career, how you just wouldn't give in. *You're still here, still alive, and you remembered how to control an out of control car. How about you remember to control an out of control* life?

When she looked down at her hand, Eve saw it was completely still. More, it knew exactly what it was meant to be doing. It reached into the desk drawer and pulled out the prop chequebook and pen, and started scribbling gibberish – gibberish that to the audience, looked like a name and an amount.

"Joanna," asked Rachael, and Eve looked at her, surprised. How long had she been on stage? How long had Eve been sitting there? Then she saw the concern on the other woman's face, the concern that wasn't scripted, the concern that conveyed *are you okay, you looked like shite there for a second.*

And that's all it was, just a second. All of that in just a second. "Yes, Linda?" Eve responded, and the concern on Rachael's gave way to surprise – mild, not enough for the audience to notice, but enough for Eve to see. She supposed it was on her own face, too. For even though she had said those words hundreds of times before in the last three weeks, she had never said them like *that,* as if she was *there,* as if she was in command.

I've turned into the skid, Dad, she thought. Then on top of that, *I think I'm getting ready to burn again.*

"You've got that reporter at two," said Rachael.

"Oh," said Eve, a petulant child, "do I have to?"

"You do," said Rachael, an indulgent parent. From then Eve responded, and Rachael answered and the scene took off, it *flew,* it became something greater than the sum of its parts.

Eve Wilson – no, she was at work again now, she was Eve Rogers – brought the house down.

Chapter Sixteen

Hedliegh waved the blood drenched knife in front of her once again. "It's a pity," he said, genuinely regretful, "because you and I were going to have such fun."

Eve said nothing, just kept her huge, bugging eyes on the blade as it see-sawed before her. The silence around was absolute.

"And I wanted that. I *really* wanted that. I meant what I said, Joanna. I love you. I've loved you from the start. We could have been happy – truly, truly happy." He knelt down before her, eye level, but she never looked away from the blade. It was pointing upwards now. Pointing at her heart. "But you just ...*wouldn't*, would you? You just wouldn't ...*see things my way*, would you?" He was building up, winding himself to the point, breath coming faster, smile moving from wistful to manic, voice rising. "Because you don't understand – no, you *won't* understand – that without me, without *us*, you're nothing!" He stood, fast, whirling about her, and Eve tried to keep her eyes on him, but she was tied to that bloody chair, and he was moving so fast, so damned *fast*, like a snake; a snake that'd grown arms and legs and learned how to talk. He was everywhere at once!

"You'd be alone in your house without us!" Behind her.

"You'd be sitting in the dark!" On her left.

"You'd be crying in the night!" Back in front of her. He was ready now, she saw it in those wide, insane eyes. He brought the knife up high, ready to swing, and he roared; *"BECAUSE WE OWN YOU!"*

Screaming, he brought the knife down. He was going to pierce her heart, spew her blood on the floor, extinguish her like a used match, just because she didn't love him, because she didn't know him.

That's when she brought her right hand up – the hand she'd managed to free while his back was turned – and grabbed his wrist.

And the audience gasped in relief.

He's not faking this, Eve thought. *He's not doing this because it's in the script. He's doing this because I'm making him do this!*

They were struggling for control of the knife, except of course they weren't really struggling for control at all. He'd let his wrist grow slack, released all the tension, and Eve had control. She was the one who was twitching her muscles, making it look as if there was a struggle going on. *First rule of stage violence,* she thought without thinking, *the victim has all the power.*

Any minute now she'd raise his wrist to her mouth and bite down, bite down hard (except she'd just lower her head, covering her actions to the audience and Hedliegh would let out a huge scream and fall backwards). All of this was in the script, and that's what they were doing – following the text like any good professional would.

But they *weren't* just following the text. Not tonight. Tonight, she was *burning* again. Tonight, she was inside and outside of herself simultaneously for the first time since the whole process had started. She inhabited her body and looked down on herself. She was both Eve and Joanna Playton, big time movie star and victim, and though the things she said and did were preordained and she knew exactly what was coming next, it was all spontaneous and fresh, it was new, it was terrifying …and the audience recognised that.

From the moment she'd steered into the skid and taken control of herself and the play, she'd felt it. Since receiving her first laugh after five minutes with the line "And Linda, do me a favour and buzz me in ten with the news my father's died again, will you?" she knew she had the audience by the balls. *And that's nothing,* she'd thought. *Wait until Act Two. I am going to blow you all away.*

She had, of course, been right.

Now they were near the end, and for the first time *ever* she was genuinely fighting Hedliegh for the knife. She could feel the audience, they were a wall, a living pulse, willing her on.

She brought Hedliegh's wrist to her mouth, lowered her head, and pretended to bite down, hard. He screamed in agony and dropped away from her, the knife falling to her lap.

Someone in the audience cheered.

Panting, keeping an eye on Hedliegh – he was young, he was strong, he'd be back any second - Eve cut through the rope on her left leg. It was easy. They were, after all, pre-cut. In fact they were so thin she'd had to mime a lot of her struggling earlier on in case they fell apart and give the game away. Hedliegh sprang at her again, nursing his injured wrist. He took a half turn as he did, almost three quarters of his back to the audience. This meant she could kick a good three inches from his testicles and he could still fall and make it look convincing.

Which he did. He whooped in a great lungful of air and kept it inside, then crumpled spectacularly, convulsing. Still eyeing him warily she pretended to cut like a maniac at her still bound left wrist – again, ropes so thin one flick with the blunt prop knife was enough. But by then Hedliegh was starting to move again – *so young! So strong!*

She stood as best as she could, pretending but *not* pretending that her legs were numb and tried to get away – but she was, of course, dragging a chair with her. The rope on her right leg was a little more secure than the others, but not much – in fact, she could feel it starting to give. *Not now, for fuck's sake,* she almost prayed. *Another page, just wait another page.* But still, even if it did come loose, she could cope. She was *burning* tonight, and when she burnt, Eve could cope with anything.

Hedliegh was almost up to his knees by then, about to maybe spring at her, when she held the knife out in front of her and said – no, growled – "Don't you fucking move."

He stopped, terrified. Both because that's what he was supposed to do and because she *made* him stop. This was the bit Mike had called her on, the moment where he'd probably realised it wasn't going to go well for him, the second he'd resigned himself to making the best of it. *I want to see your face, Mike. I want to see it now.*

"Move," she went on, "and I'll cut you."

"You wouldn't," Hedliegh gasped. "It's not in you."

"It wasn't," she said, everything flowing through her. "But you know something? I think it is now. I think you showed me that. When you sliced me. When you tried to rape me. When you abused me."

"*I LOVED YOU,*" he screamed, with just the right level of cracking voice.

Eve both put the sneer on and sneered for real. "Love? You don't even *know* me. You thought you did, I'll give you that, you fucking psycho bastard – but *being* a fucking psycho bastard means you've no *idea* what love is."

Hedliegh struggled to one knee, still scared, but trying to gather himself for one final push. If he couldn't have her, he'd kill her – it was written on his face, clear as a cliché, it could be seen from Row Z. Eve admired him for that. So many young actors were only trained for television these days, they just couldn't cut it on stage, but he could. *You're going to keep working, kid.*

"Stay there," she growled, but allowed a tremour in her voice. *You're not out of the woods yet, Joanna old thing. He only took a kick to the nuts, not a bullet to the brain.* "I swear to God I'll …"

"What," he interrupted. "What can you do without lines? What can you do without a director? You're nothing, you're a blank, a wind-up toy. You don't *exist* without other people! You need us, you need your fans to validate you, to *create* you. Without us you're nothing but a fucking *void!*"

This was is, he was going to do it – he was going to jump. Eve knew it, Joanna knew it, everyone in the silent auditorium knew he was going to do it. And he was bigger than her, stronger than her – and she was disadvantaged by the bloody *chair* she was dragging around. She just couldn't move quickly enough. Yeah, she had the knife …but could she, actually, *really* use it? When push came to shove …*could* she?

No, but she was Joanna Playton, actor. And a *brilliant* actor at that. She was renowned, world famous, feted and adored by millions …and the knife? Just a prop. She could use props.

Most important of all, Joanna Playton could improvise like a bastard.

She lunged forward, dragging the chair behind her (praying once more that skinny pre-cut rope would hold, which thankfully it did) and sliced the air in front of his face. It was a blunt knife, of course, which meant she could swing it within a couple of inches of his nose, but Eve still had to be in control of it, in control of all of the muscles in her arm. She had never hurt another actor in her life and wasn't about to start now. Not at the moment of her greatest triumph.

Hedliegh fell back, onto the ground, his right leg underneath him. He flung his head back and slapped his upstage hand on the boards, producing a ringing *thwack* sound that drew gasps from the audience. She scuttled above him, where the audience could see her good and proper (even in the Dagmar, with its sometimes dodgy sightlines and questionable acoustics), dropped to her haunches and placed the knife at his throat. "If you sit up," she breathed, "you'll slit your own throat, and I won't have to do anything. I won't need a writer *or* a director – you'll do it all for me. So lie there, be a good boy, lie there and listen." A deep, raspy breath, then; "Somewhere along the line, you may have a point, you know. I do need things to help me work – just like a carpenter needs a hammer or a bricklayer needs a hod carrier. Writers, directors, other actors ...even fans, if you like ...are the tools and colleagues I need so I can do my job. It doesn't make me unique. It doesn't make me different. I just do a job. A job that you think is just for your benefit, you mad fucker. Just because you see me on telly or films or plays or whatever, it *doesn't mean you own me,* or that I owe you anymore than I owe the putty in my window frames that keeps the glass from falling out. But all of that's just a side issue, isn't it? None of that's what it's really been about, none of that was the reason you played out whatever sick, perverted fantasy was in your head, was it?

It was just because I was a woman."

Staring at her, bug eyed, Hedliegh started to shake his head. "Ah, ah," warned Eve/Joanna, 'I wouldn't, Arthur, me old son. Doing that just brings this knife a little closer to your Adam's apple. And you can deny it all you want, but it's true. *I* know that – deep down, I think even *you* know that. You can't get anywhere with what people would call 'a real woman', so you fixate on me, one who's on the screen. You think you know me, even that you love me, you think I'm sending you secret little signals whenever I'm on the screen. You build your world around an image, a fiction, because you're so fucked in the head that if you even so much as *spoke* to a woman in the pub or at the chemist's she'd run off screaming. So you build your little world, a world of smoke and mirrors, but it all gets out of hand, doesn't it? The pressure builds. And you can wank all you like to my photos or my DVD's but that's *just not enough* anymore, is it? You have to *posses* this object you've created in your head and bring her here, to dress her up, to be your dolly - because, after all, *she's just a woman!* The closest you'll ever *get* to a woman!

But, guess what? She *doesn't want to play!* She doesn't want to play because *she's a real person!* And because you can't control her, that means you can't control the world, can you? And what does poor Arthur do then, poor thing? He has to cut her, make her bleed, try and rape her – he has to feel her up as she's tied to a fucking chair. At that point it didn't even *matter* who I was, I could have been any poor random bitch off the street for all you cared, because it was only about power in the end. Just that. *Power.* Power over a woman. You stupid, pathetic, useless, fucking *waste of space.*"

She gave it a beat – no, she could sense an uprising of emotion in the audience and it was too soon for that – she gave it half a beat, then put her left hand on his throat, and tensed her muscles to make it look like she was squeezing. Hedliegh sucked air in and tensed his back. "I could keep squeezing," she said, an almost regretful tone in her voice, "I could *do* that easily. I work out three times a week, remember? Even though you've cut me, even though I've sat in that chair for four days in my own shit and piss, even though you've starved me, dehydrated me, I could still do that, still squeeze the life out of you. And who'd care? No one. No one would even come to your funeral. Fuck, I'd probably get a medal. And I'd like a medal. I really would." Eve jerked her left elbow, making it look as if more pressure were being applied. Hedliegh bucked underneath her. She felt the *audience-think* (that's what it was like when she was burning, as if there was telepathy at work here, as if the audience were a hive mind, a *gestalt,* sending its thoughts to her), and most of them wanted her to keep squeezing, to exact her revenge, which made her heart soar. That's what she *wanted* them to want her to do. The trick, of course, being *never* to give the audience what they wanted. Give them what they *needed,* whether they knew they needed it or not.

"But what I'm actually going to do is cut my right leg off this chair," she went on. "Twitch, and I will strangle you. Cough, and I will strangle you. But stay there nice and still, and I'll just cut myself free and walk out of here. Either way, I win, you lose, and that's just how it is. Deal with it. One way I walk out into the street a killer, one way I don't. I'd *prefer* the former," she said, using her right hand to – *finally* – slice through the rope, "but just right now I'm not too arsed either way. Because, whether I leave you alive or dead, I'm still the winner. Either way, I'm better than you, and I'll *always* be better than you, because even after all this, even after all you've put me though, I can still live in the real world. With real people." She stood up, backing away from him, but Eve/Joanna could see there was no fight left in him. They (she) could see she'd won. "And one more thing, Arthur – *fuck off.*"

She ran off into the wings then, no longer Eve/Joanna, now just Eve, and standing there, looking at her with amazement and admiration on their faces were the SM, the ASM, the curtain man, Richard and Rachael. The younger woman ran forward and threw her arms around Eve. "My God," she whispered. "My *God!*"

On stage, Hedliegh gave his last screams of "*Joanna? JOANNA!*" The SM took her eyes from Eve's and lowered her arm. The curtain man pulled the ropes and, for the faintest of seconds, silence descended.

Then the applause began. Then the cheers. And Eve Wilson, (no, she was Rogers here, Eve Rogers), knew it had all come right in the end.

If only.

*

She'd have walked back onto the stage for the calls, but it seemed like Richard and Rachael weren't going to allow that. Instead, with a silent nod, they picked her up and carried her between them. "Hey, come on," she protested, laughing, but they were having none of it. Before the curtain was raised, Hedliegh bounded to his feet and gave her the biggest hug she'd had since …well, since Carl had died, actually.

Then the curtain rose, and the swell of noise burst over them. It was deafening, a crescendo, a roar, the sound of a giant taking his meal. It pushed into them, as if it were a living thing, nearly knocking them over, and the joy on their faces was totally unfeigned. It didn't seem to end, not even after they'd bowed twice and the curtain dropped again, so the SM raised her hand and the curtain went up a second time, and the noise *increased* if anything, and the cast – unbidden and spontaneously – placed their arms around each other's shoulders, took a step forward, and bowed as one. Eve looked out – and though she couldn't make out that much detail over the lights – it seemed like the whole audience was standing, clapping, cheering, all of them, almost a thousand people.

We did this, she thought. *We made this happen, we provoked this. All of us, this team. We gave them something to remember, something to cherish, a night they'll talk about for months. Maybe even years.*

And I didn't fuck up, she suddenly found herself thinking. *I found it again. What had been lost, I found. Somehow, somewhere, it came back. I didn't let them down. I didn't let* anyone *down. Them, me, Carl …*

Tears sprang up, stinging, turning the lights into prisms, but she didn't care. She wouldn't take her arms from her colleagues' shoulders to wipe them away. She may have been crying, but they were tears of relief, tears of joy, tears of elation. *I am not broken, after all, she thought. I am still me.*

They would have gone on clapping all night, but the SM knew her showbiz law well, it seemed. She gave the signal and the curtain dropped on that storm. It dampened off eventually, and Eve knew then that the house lights were up; the audience had finally received the message. *Show's over folks. Now fuck off home, willya?*

There was a second of absolute quiet. Eve finally wiped her eyes with the heel of her hand. She gazed around at her fellow actors, all of whom were grinning from ear to ear. "Who fancies getting pissed, then?" she asked.

Turned out they all did.

Chapter Seventeen

Mike didn't even knock this time – it seemed he wasn't bothered that she was in her underwear. He simply burst into her dressing room, picked her up, and swung her around.

"Hey Mike, c'mon man, Jesus, I'm going to puke here," Eve protested, but she was laughing. It seemed she couldn't stop laughing.

"No," said Mike, and he was laughing too. 'I'm *never* going to put you down. I'm going to spin you like this forever. Puke, who cares? It's a cheap jacket." But his actions made him a liar and he did set her down. He even stopped laughing – with his mouth, anyway. His eyes kept it up. "Eve," he said, "right now I love you so much I may even turn straight for you."

"You'd have to shave first," she replied, wondering how long it'd been since she'd felt this good.

"Fuck that," he spat. "To paraphrase an old hero of mine, I'll do anything for an actress who'd just smashed it, but I won't do that." Then he started laughing again. Then she joined him. "You know that old fart who crits for *The Independent?*" he said, when he'd regained control. Eve nodded. "Crying at the curtain. Bloke from the *Mail*, ditto. *The Guardian*'s just shaken my hand so often it's damned near useless for *anything* tonight." This set her off giggling again. *Giggling, oh my. Such a long, long time since I giggled.* "We're going to be a hit, darlin'. *You're* going to be a hit. You can forget all that shit about being ill now."

"Well, look," said Eve, "let's not be too hasty, eh? One Swallow…"

"Doesn't make Anne Summers, got you. But you want to know what *I* think? I think that, if for the rest of the run, you only give me half of what you gave me tonight, it'll be a million times more than you gave me in rehearsal. Am I right, as usual?"

"You're right, as usual."

He pulled out one of her chairs and sat. "So," he said, "and don't think I'm complaining, because I'm not, but what was it, darlin'? Were you sandbagging? Did you get a visit from three ghosts? Did the Talent Pixie sprinkle you with magic dust? What?"

Eve sat opposite him. "I wasn't sandbagging, I can tell you that for a kick off. I don't know, Mike. That's the truth. I got stuck in this fucking room before curtain up, I walked out there and did not have a clue about what I should be doing – or even where I was. You want to know how scary that was?"

"I can imagine," said Mike.

"No you can't," she protested. "You *can't*. I couldn't have told the colour of orange juice out there, just after curtain up. And then Rachael came on, spoke to me …and, I don't know," she said again. "It just *happened*."

"I'll say it *just happened*, all right," he said, smiling. Then the smile dropped a little, and he put a hand over hers. "Maybe …maybe you've got someone looking out for you."

A succession of thoughts – images, really – raced through her brain at that. Photos that went, came, went then came back again, ripped. Dreams of her husband with Mike's face. *Whatever the piece is, you gotta play it.* Prompts, pushes, signposts even, leading her here, to this point, to this triumph. "Yeah," she said. "Maybe."

"If you have, then bless him, 'cause he steered you right tonight, darlin'." Then the smile was back. He clapped his hands together and stood. "Now, you gotta get dressed, Eve, before the sight of you in your undies gives even this good ole gayboy a boner. People want to see you, you know. They're gathered in the reception room – and this is going to be *some* reception, I can tell you. Sir Peter may even propose."

Eve giggled some more at that, then waved Mike out. Before wiping away the rest of her makeup and slipping on her dress, she took one final look in the mirror. *Someone looking after you.*

"Thanks Carl," she said, utterly unselfconscious. "Thanks honey."

*

The noise as she approached the reception room door – the room on the first floor reserved for backers, Producers and the like so they could party on down without interacting with the hoi polloi - was jubilant. It was a success noise, a victory noise. She'd heard it before in her professional life – but had she ever heard it like this? Had it ever been so vibrant, so alive?

Yes, Eve thought. *Always. The differences here are twofold, I think. One: you didn't expect to hear it tonight, not after the shambles of the last three weeks and the previews. Two (and this may be the most important): is that tonight you're actually hearing* properly *again.*

Eve paused before entering. *What do I mean by that?*

I mean, she went on, and for a wonder in her own Voice, not Sarah's, *that you may have finally quit your latest addiction. Yeah, you'll get cravings now and then, like you still do for the coffin nails (and the speed and the dope, don't deny it), but I think that addiction's done for. I think you've passed it. Like gas. It's over.*

What addiction? Okay, I like a drink, but ...

No, not the drink. The grief.

Eve actually blinked and shook her head at this – not in denial, it utter astonishment. *The what?*

The grief. Your grief for Carl. Don't get me wrong, I'm not criticizing you – it was right for you to grieve, it was natural. He was your husband and you loved him. And I know you kept (sort of) going, I know you kept (sort of) together, but in a quiet sort of a way, part of you actually liked *the grief, liked the way it* felt. *It's why people keep smoking even though it's killing them – it's what non smokers like Carl never understood – smoking's quite nice, really. And in a way, so's grief. It keeps you warm, like a comfy blanky. And you* want *that, you* want *the numbness that the comfy blanky brings. But, like any drug, it's dangerous. It's not the real world, you see. But now, I think, you've begun to quit it, you're back – doesn't tonight* prove *that - and your senses are sharper than they have been for over a year.* That's *why this party sounds the way it does.* That's *why the applause felt the way it did. It's all* real *again.*

She may have stood there for a long time, inwardly debating this point, but Sir Peter spied her loitering. "There she is," he boomed, stepped towards her, and took her arm. Guiding her inwards, he proclaimed, "Ladies and gentlemen – Eve Rogers!"

Eve opened her mouth to say something – something along the lines *of oh, come on Peter – everyone here knows me, don't be such an arse –*

but the round of applause that started drowned out anything that might have come to her lips. Embarrassed, she tried to wave it away, but the crowd were having none of it. The backers, the crew, her fellow actors – and was that Tom over by the window? Yes it was – applauded her, cheered her, and yes, she was embarrassed …but she was also pleased, and proud. Pleased she was back, and proud she'd done so well. Various people – some of whom she knew by sight, a lot she knew not at all – crowded around her, using words like "brilliant" and "exceptional" (Eve actually thought she heard the word "transcendent" battered around), and though she'd always done a fine (ish) job of keeping her feet on the ground, she was as prone to flattery as anyone else. It would have been a lie to say it didn't make her feel good, and though she may be many things, Eve Wilson (and she *was* Wilson again, she left Eve Rogers in the dressing room) was not a liar.

Tom sliced through the throng as Eve was mouthing "Thanks, oh thank you very much," and handed her a gin and tonic so strong it would have taken Mike Tyson right there and then. Then, with a practised palm on the small of her back, he steered her (still smiling, still miming gratitude) to the window and relative calm.

Once there, he did something he'd never done before. He kissed her on the bridge of her nose. "Well done, darling. *Well done.* You showed the bastards, didn't you?"

"Maybe," Eve agreed, sipping.

"No *maybe* about it," said Tom. "Try to get *my* client to bow out sick! I tell you, when that option comes up for renewal I'm going to screw another grand a week out of them."

"C'mon, don't get greedy."

"*Greedy,*" he nearly exploded. He dug into his pocket and pulled out a BlackBerry. "Since the interval I've taken twenty calls for interviews. Press, radio, TV. People are *begging* to talk to you, Eve. This mob couldn't *buy* the publicity your performance tonight is giving them. The box office queue tomorrow will be six deep! They'll rake in enough cash to keep them solvent until the Rapture! A grand a week? Christ, I'm letting them off lightly."

"Look, see how the week goes – see if I'm any good tomorrow night, or the night after – then do what you think is best, okay?" Eve had never had that much of a business head – that was what Tom was for, after all, and after the night she'd had she just wanted a few drinks and a bit of a gossip.

"That young boy who played opposite you," Tom went on, seemingly impervious to his client's desire, "who's representing him?"

"Oddly enough, not a topic of conversation that's ever come up."

"Hmm, he could be a prospect. I might go fishing there. And the blonde girl, might see what she's up to. She's got a look."

"Why don't you fish then," said Eve. "Go grab them while they're still young and cheap."

"Might just," said Tom, finishing his own drink and setting his glass on the sill. "See you later."

"Sure." Eve didn't watch him mingle. In fact, she turned away slightly from the room and dialled down the murmur around her. She was starting to feel tired – well, tired and a little drunk. That gin had landed (that was how Carl used to put it, as though booze was an alien invasion force). Landed, and brought reinforcements. Also, she was a little overwhelmed by the whole night – from zero to hero in less than five hours – and the adrenaline rush was subsiding. She was beginning to calculate how long she'd have to wait before she could leave diplomatically, when Jon's voice spoke from behind her. "Hey you," he said. "My friend and I wanted to say congratulations – I think you know her."

Eve turned, saw Jon first and smiled at him, glad and a little surprised he was there. He'd not mentioned it. Typical of him really, though, to turn up unannounced. Her surprise turned to astonishment, however, when Eve saw his "friend."

Her sister, Sarah.

Sarah was looking back at her, and with a look that mirrored the one Eve imagined sat on her own features; open eyes, wideish mouth …but there was another layer, too. A look of …what? *No, it couldn't be, not on Sarah's face.* In the split second before Eve ran to her sister and hugged her, hugged her hard, Eve acknowledged it for what it was …and the gratitude swelled up in her like tears.

Sarah was amazed. Sarah was *in awe.* Sarah was *proud.*

The tears fell then, as she ran to the older woman and held her. And Sarah, always clumsy when it came to emotion, held her back. *I've done it, she thought,* trying not to break down completely. *I've finally, really done it …I have received my sister's approbation.*

"Eve," said Sarah, "Jesus. What can I say? That was …that was …oh, brilliant, kid. Just *brilliant.*"

She broke the embrace then, but not the contact. She held Eve at arm's length and looked at her, just took her in. "At the end, when you were strangling him, I wanted you to do it, I wanted you to kill the bastard. And I know it's just make believe, I know it's not true, but I wanted you to *kill* him! He'd battered you and tried to rape you and he'd cut you, and I'm sat there thinking, 'it's only a game, they're just messing around,' but I was *also* thinking, 'if you touch my kid sister again, you arsehole, I'll get up there and stab you myself!' I mean ..." Sarah shook her head, bewildered, "I've seen you in stuff, I've seen you in *loads* of stuff, and it was always like ...you doing your job, yeah? Y'know, doing it well, but doing your job – like me stacking books or Steve filling out a spreadsheet – it's what you *do*. But *this* ...tonight ..." She ran out of things to say then, but Eve didn't care. That was enough, more than enough. Eve knew then that she didn't care a bit what the reviews said. She didn't care if the show closed after one night. She wouldn't have cared if the audience had hated her, just so long as her sister had said what she had just said.

"Listen," said Eve, trying to choke down her emotions, "why didn't you tell me you were coming?"

Sarah nodded at Jon. "He told me not to."

"I cannot tell a lie,' he said, smiling. "Well, I can. But I'm not. I did, indeed, swear your sister to secrecy."

"Why?" Eve asked.

"Because," said Sarah, then trailed a bit. She looked over at Jon. *Do I?* her eyes asked. *Yes,* his responded. "Because Jon rang me up last week, said he thought you were in …" Sarah trailed again, obviously wanting to avoid saying something.

"I thought you were in trouble," Jon said. It was odd, really – he and Carl may have looked alike, except for Jon being a little pudgier – but in mannerisms and styles they couldn't have been further apart. Carl had always been …well, *tighter* seemed the right word. Not mean, just more driven, really. Like her, he had ambition. Like her, Carl had focus. Jon, on the other hand, didn't appear to give much of a tuppenny hoot about anything much. He was a fair enough camera operator who worked most of the year on whatever the first shoot offered was. He'd no desire to become a Director of Photography or anything more. He was the same with his women. They kind of floated in and out of his life. Similarly money. Sometimes he had some, and sometimes he hadn't. He was relaxed, easygoing, charming …but feckless.

But when he said, *I thought you were in trouble,* that *easy come, easy go* expression vanished. His eyebrows knotted together and his eyes darkened, and he looked so much like Carl it almost hurt her heart. "You looked like you were carrying a heavy head, Eve, and I've *never* seen you carry one of those before. Mostly you glide through your work, no matter how challenging it is. And I didn't like it. You're my only link to my brother," he went on, "and I know he'd want me to look out for you. So after we'd met up for lunch the other day – and I got really concerned about you – I rang up your sister and we plotted some moral support. Of course, turns out I didn't need to …"

"But I'm glad you did," Sarah finished for him. Then, looking back at Eve, "I wouldn't have missed tonight for anything."

"You two …" Eve started to say, meaning to go on with something like *were looking out for me* or *were that concerned,* but she couldn't find the words to express exactly what it meant to have them both before her, so she just grabbed them in another hug.

Actions, they say, can speak much louder than words.

"Where are you staying?" Eve asked Sarah a few minutes later, as Jon left to refill their glasses.

"At the Travelodge near King's Cross."

"No you're not. You're checking out tonight and coming home with me."

"Oh Eve, I can't," Sarah protested. "It's after eleven, and I've put my bag in the room, and …"

"And me no 'ands'," Eve cut her off. "How long are you down for?"

"Well, Jon wasn't sure how much …" *of a state you'd be in* went unspoken, "so I booked for three days."

"Great, that's three days we can spend together. In my house. No argument, big Sarah."

"Oh …all right then. But what the bloody hell will I do of an evening?" Then sudden inspiration struck. "Hey, you still got that puzzle magazine?"

"The what now?" asked Eve, dropping into an uncanny imitation of her elder sibling's loving for hip American slang. *What's she on about?*

"The puzzle mag. The one I left behind, after the funeral? The one you were trying to do that time you rang?"

Barking Clappers? Almost! (7, 4). Yeah, the one I lied about after that dream where you ate the jigsaw with Carl's dead face on it. I remember now. You were crying. "No. I threw it away. Bastard thing was impossible."

"Ah, we can pick up some more. They'll keep me busy."

"Then we're decided?"

"Stop quoting musicals, Eve, even you think they're shit. Yeah, we're decided."

*

"Not happening," Jon was saying, half an hour later "I'm driving. Argument, end of. You are *not* getting a minicab."

"How much have you had to drink?" Sarah asked.

"Four glasses, three of which have had nothing but Coke in them – and the vodka was before curtain up. Ladies, I'm sober. A shame at a party, but sober I am. So keep any objections behind your delectable mouths and let me know when you're ready to depart."

"Oh, I'm ready," said Eve, but not before noticing the odd, frankly admiring look her sister had given Jon. With something like fright, she *really* realised Sarah was now forty-three years old. Forty-three, and looking at a man ten years her junior with …what? A little lust, maybe? How long had she and Steve been married? Eighteen years? Nineteen? Long enough for her to get too familiar with him, maybe? Long enough for – how did that cliché go? The bloom to fall from the rose? Long enough for her to know every bump and crevice of his body, long enough for her to second guess his every thought, every utterance?

And now, here she was, alone, at a (*let's not lie, Eve*) glamorous party filled with glamorous people after a glamorous First Night, and the younger man (who'd accompanied her all evening, probably talking that way for hours – what Carl had called "Jon's Roger Moore persona"- glib, articulate one liners, easy compliments, lashings of charm) had intrigued her, flattered her, supported her when she felt out of her depth ...what woman could *fail* to respond to that?

My sister's got a crush on my brother-in-law. Paging Dr Freud, paging Dr Freud ...you're needed in the West End.

Ah, so what? She found herself thinking as she excused herself and made her way over to Mike and Sir Peter, who were crowded around the buffet. *A little harmless infatuation hurt no one, did it? Let Sarah have her little crush. Little crushes hurt no one. Keep them in your head, don't let them escape into your pants, and everyone's fine.*

Yeah. Like Carl and Laura.

Eve's step faltered a little, but she kept the smile plastered to her lips. It was taking longer to get to her destination than she'd like, because people – who they were she had no idea – kept bobbing into her eyeline and mouthing "Brilliant, dear" or "So spectacular" and she had to keep shaking hands and mouthing "Thank you." But her mind was elsewhere as she gave these grace notes out.

There was nothing *between Carl and Laura.*

Sure, sure. 'Whatever,' as Sarah would say. That's why Laura left those flowers and that note on his gravestone. How did it go again? I forget.

No you don't – no I don't. It went, How? How could you do this to me? All my love forever. *And no signature.*

But you knew who it was, didn't you?

Do we need to re-cover this old ground? Richard bobbed his way through the crowd, and a more drunken man than him Eve had never witnessed. Well, vertically at any rate. He was smiling, though. "What's the deal with your agent?" He slurred, happy. "He taps Hedliegh up. He taps *Rachael* up. Then he looks at me, shakes my hand, and says, 'It was nice to meet you,' and slopes off." He tried to put on an indignant face, but it wasn't working – he wasn't really bothered. He'd be bothered in the morning all right, but not by Tom's overlooking of him. He'd be bothered by a hangover roughly the size of Wales. "I mean, what's the matter with *me?*"

Eve managed both to push her thoughts back and turn her head slightly, as the younger man's breath was two hundred per cent proof. "Confidentially, Richard – I think you're just not his type."

"Ah," said Richard. "Gotcha." He tried to tap his nose with his index finger and missed. "Eve, can I tell you again how *brilliant* you were tonight?"

"You can," she replied, "but you won't remember doing it. Go home, Richard. Drink plenty of water, sleep till noon, and then bathe in black coffee."

"Will do," he smiled. "But you *were* brilliant tonight."

"And so were you. Now go."

He smiled even wider, sketched a wobbly salute at her, and weaved his way back to Rachael, who was looking at him with a sort of glum love. The two women made eye contact. *Take care of him, won't you,* Eve asked. *Will do,* Rachael answered. *I suppose I have to.* Then, *well done.*

Thank you. And you.

Nicely distracted, she thought as she made her way back towards the buffet table. *But we were talking about crushes and how harmless they were …*

So, what d'you want me to do? Phone Laura up and say, "How you doing? Got any work I can fit around my play? Talking books, a voice over? Oh, and just by the by – were you fucking my husband?"

It'd ease your mind, wouldn't it?

I don't know if you've noticed, but my mind hasn't exactly been restless on this. Here's the deal; even if she was – even if they were – what, actually, does it matter now? He's dead, he died as my husband and I loved him and I believe – no, I know – he loved me. Whatever happened, if anything did happen, is long since dead and gone. Like him. So I'll bury it, like I buried him.

Yeah, you buried him. Didn't keep him quiet though, did it? And if you can't –

"Here's my little star," said Sir Peter, marginally more sober than Richard, but the key word was *marginally*. "*Never* have I seen a performance like it. *Never,* in all my life."

"Thank you," Eve said, though the performance she'd given on stage was as nothing to the one she was giving now. Those troubling thoughts were winning …but no one would ever know. Then, to Mike, "I'm going home now, Mike. I need my beauty sleep."

"I can think of a couple of things you *do* need – like a pay rise and a pan of stew down you – but beauty sleep? Nah." He hugged her. "You got a ride home, darlin'?"

"Yes, Carl's brother is taking me."

"Good for him. Okay, tomorrow. Let's do it all over again."

"And you're not getting that rise," Sir Peter smiled, shaking her hand. Knights of the Realm did nothing so vulgar as hug. "Goodnight, my dear."

"Goodnight, both of you." With that, she snaked her way back to Sarah and Jon, gathered them up, and got the hell out of Dodge.

Chapter Eighteen

"It might be a bit ...*unaired,* is that the word?" said Eve as she entered the living room after dropping Sarah's bag in the guest room. "But it's still cheaper than the hotel."

"Which you need to let me pay you for"' said Sarah, looking up from the rows of books she'd been examining. Nothing much there she'd like to read, by the looks of it. "And it's a good job Mum's not here. If she thought you weren't airing your rooms properly ..."

"Yeah, I'd be straight to bed with no supper and no story. She had a thing about *airing* all right."

"Airing, germs, dogs, cats, rabbits ...what <u>didn't</u> she have a thing about," smiled Sarah as she sat on the sofa and picked up her coffee mug. "Made you one – still just milk?"

"Still just milk." Eve gracelessly *flumped* on the armchair, her stage liquidity long vanished. "Thanks, big Sarah."

"Don't mention it. Though it did take me ages to find everything. Your cupboards are a mess, little Eve."

"I got a system," she replied, wondering oddly why she wasn't growing a bit pissed off. It was, after all, one in the morning and once again her sister was throwing a javelin at her.

It was usually around this time that the gloves came off, the fencing stopped, and the full-blown argument started. But right here, right now ...nothing. *Maybe I'm nice and mellow because the show went well. Maybe she can say what she likes and it won't hurt me. Maybe ...*

Maybe she doesn't mean it. Maybe it's just a bit of teasing, the way families are. Maybe you've just been far too sensitive, little Eve. Maybe you've been looking *for criticism ...perhaps because you feel a bit guilty about the fact you've escaped from the Chorlton Suburban Massive and Sarah got left behind. You think that could be the case?*

Could be a part of it, I suppose ...but another part of it is Sarah. I didn't always imagine that tone, you know. That vague mix of patronisation and disapproval. It was *there. Not always, I'll grant you some over-sensitivity on my part, but it's certainly not there tonight. She's ...softer, I suppose. What did she say after Carl's funeral? Something about how his death may bring us closer together? Well, it's been a year ...but you never know.*

"A system," prompted Sarah, and forty-three or not, the smile on her face made her beautiful.

"It's very simple. I throw everything in, slam the door on it and run like hell. Used to drive Carl mad."

"How much do you miss him?" Sarah asked, after a brief pause.

"A lot."

"Does it hurt?"

"It's a duller pain than it once was. But yeah, still hurts. It was …look, don't misunderstand this …but it was easier, I think, when he was in hospital. There was stuff going on, get me? Doctors and consultants and things – there were people to take the pressure off. Even when he died, there were people all around, funeral directors, you, Jon – always someone there. But people have their own lives to get on with. It's natural, not a problem, but eventually you get left alone, and that's hard. For a while I …you'll laugh at this."

"Doubtful."

"For a while I kept him alive in my head. Kept talking to him, imagining he was here. And you remember, big Sarah, imagining is what I was best at."

"No one could forget that."

"Then one day I realised I wasn't doing that anymore. I didn't pretend he was in the room or looking after me anymore. That's when I think I turned the corner."

There was a small pause, not much of one, but long enough for Eve to find the word to sum it up; *companionable. Here we are, she thought, for maybe the first time in our lives, no longer just sisters, but friends.*

"I hated the fact you were so far away," said Sarah eventually. "It broke my heart. I'd lie there, night after night, thinking of you being all alone down here, and there was nothing I could do about it. But you know what was worse," she continued over Eve's waving away of this, "you know the *worst* thing? The fact I'd keep reaching for the phone and then pulling my hand away. Loads of times I'd punch in the area code and then …just stop. Because I couldn't think of an excuse to hang it on. Isn't that pathetic, little Eve? I needed a reason to call you up, something to talk about. Even though all I wanted to do was ask, 'Are you okay?' I couldn't just do that. I had to try and find …what d'you call it? Just cause? Sometimes I think that's our real legacy from Mum and Dad, get me? Not the money we got from their policies or the colour of our eyes, the fact that *we just can't admit,* either of us, that we actually give a shit." She laughed at that, but there wasn't much humour in it. "See? I can't even say 'I love you.' I had to say 'give a shit' instead. I mean, they weren't *cold,* were they? Not like some Victorian parents you see on telly, they just didn't *do* that sort of thing. And neither do we. Sad, isn't it?"

"Yeah," said Eve, her mind now back in her childhood. "It is." Sarah, of course, was right. That's how their parents had been. Good, solid, practical Mancunians. Churchgoers, sensible, realistic, grafters. Love was shoes on the feet and food in the belly. It was a full fridge and central heating. No, they hadn't been aloof – they'd both known how to laugh, and they'd both told bedtime stories – but the only times their father's eyes had really shone was when City beat United (so in those days they *rarely* shone), and their mother …well … "Why do you reckon she fell into the gin, Sarah?"

"I keep asking myself that. Particularly when I'm drinking."

Eve laughed – a kind of shocked, *we share a secret* laugh. "I do that, too!"

"And I've done a bit of reading. That's the beauty of my job. Pay's rotten, but there's all the books and free Google time you want. Could be there's a genetic predisposition, as they call it – in which case we'd better watch out – but I think she was looking for some form of affection from somewhere. Affection she couldn't get from Dad or us for some reason. Some people find it in pets. She found it in the bottle. And *that's* sad, too, isn't it?"

"Yes." *Poor cow.*

"But," said Sarah, and her *I-take-no-nonsense-from*-anyone-*Sonny-Jim* voice was back, "we are not our parents. We're not each other. We're just who we are and we can make choices. So, right here and right now, in your front room, I choose to be a bit warmer than they were from now on. And if I want to phone you for no reason, I will. How's that?"

"I think that's mighty fine. As long as I can do the same."

"Hell, you can do it more often. You're richer than me." With that, Sarah drained her mug. "And one choice I choose to make is to go to bed in this unaired room." She stood. "Goodnight, little Eve."

Eve finished her coffee too. "I'll turn in as well. Long day. C'mon, big Sarah. I'll walk you up the wooden hill to Bedfordshire."

"Freak," said Sarah. But she smiled when she said it, so that was all right. As they climbed the stairs together, bringing back memories of their childhood, Sarah said, "Jon's a nice bloke, isn't he?"

And don't think I can't hear that tone in your voice, big Sarah. A bit wistful, a touch of longing, like a woman on a diet who's seen a chocolate éclair. "He's a sweetheart."

"Thinks a lot of you. Very kind, considerate …"

There are, of course, some things that siblings – new found rapprochement or not – are powerless to stop, and one of them is a little pig-tail pulling. "Careful, big Sarah. You're a married woman!"

They were at the guest bedroom door now, and Sarah turned, her cheeks a little flushed. "So?" She said and – truly, this was a day (and a bit) of miracles! She *giggled!* Sarah had *never* been a giggler – that had been Eve's prerogative – but now … "Just because I've got a ring on me finger doesn't mean I can't look in a shop window every so often. I'm not going to buy – I'm not even going to step inside – but looking never hurt anyone, did it?"

"No," said Eve. *That's exactly what I thought.* "It doesn't. But …"

"But?"

"Well, say – for instance – that Steve had an affair. Maybe not so much as that - a fling, a one night stand. Could you cope with that?"

The giggle and the blush had gone; there was something approaching fear in the older woman's face. "Why? What do you know?"

"Oh God, nothing," Eve blurted. "Nothing at all, I promise you. It's just …a question, a thought."

"So Steve hasn't been playing away?"

"No, not as far as I know." Then, realising that wasn't a complete denial, "I promise you, he wouldn't. He loves you too much. But, just if he had ...could you cope?"

Sarah scanned Eve's face for a second or two, trying to see if the younger sister was covering anything up. Seemingly satisfied, she said, "No. No, it'd kill me. And after a bit, it'd kill him too. I'd see to that."

Yeah, I bet you would. I've been on the wrong side of you far too often to doubt that. Still, she persisted. "What if you didn't know for sure? What if you just had suspicions?"

"I'd have to find out." Then she laughed again. "It'd be like a puzzle, wouldn't it? And I can't leave a puzzle unsolved." The smile died, and that look of genuine, soft concern replaced it. "Why are you asking, Eve? Is there ...do *you* have suspicions? About Carl?"

"I don't know," she lied. But then she stared at her big sister, her practical big sister who was making a choice to be less practical, and decided that lying wasn't an option. "Yes. There's a doubt."

Sarah reached out then and took Eve's hands into her own. "Okay, I won't press you. It's late and we're both tired and you've done a lot today. We'll talk more about this later. You knew Carl better than me – and so I should bloody hope – but I will say one thing that I know as truthfully as I know my middle name is Anne. He loved you. No, he worshipped you. I'm not sure if he was a romantic man – probably not, he always seemed a little too preoccupied for that sort of thing – but I could see it every time he looked at you. You just *know*, don't you? You can't disguise that look. And I saw it on his face every time you entered a room. He was a man, granted, and men make mistakes – even us girls sometimes – but if anything happened between him and another woman, then that's *all* it was, a mistake. You hear me now?"

You hear me now. Their mother's phrase. *Don't go too far on that bike, Eve, and don't go too fast. You hear me now? Put that down, you don't know where it's been. You hear me now? Don't pat that dog, it'll bite. You hear me now?* The voice of authority, the voice of reason, the voice of No Argument. "Yeah. I hear you."

"Good. Then give your big sister a hug, get some sleep, and if you want we'll talk tomorrow."

*

Fifteen minutes later, Eve was under the duvet with the lights out. *A mistake. Hear me now? Could be. Who knew? It's a puzzle. And you know me and puzzles ...*

Yeah, you have to solve them. But that's you, and I'm me. Don't get me wrong, I couldn't be happier we seem to be bridge building here – it's one of the things I've been after all my life – but because you'd do something doesn't mean I have to do it, does it? Sleeping dogs. Not that we ever had a dog, they may bite. Hear me now? But what do I do, big Sarah? What if I solve the puzzle and don't like the solution? Do I write it off as a mistake? Then again, what if I solve the puzzle and find out there's one of those perfectly innocent explanations you hear so much about behind it?

Another troubling thought. *Is this what was going through Carl's mind, night after night, as he lay beside me wondering? As he felt his body betray him? As he felt things go wrong? Did he stare into the dark like I am, weighing up his options? Did he think "Maybe it'll go away on its own"? Was he so scared of the answer a visit to the doctor's would bring that he put it off and off until it was too late? And how blind was I that I didn't notice? How self-absorbed? "You're too fucking skinny," I said, but after that, what?* Nothing, *that's what, until I came home from rehearsals and he told me he'd been to 'the Quack's' as he put it, and they were going to send him for some tests. Some wife! Some lover! Jesus Carl,* Jesus, *if I had that time over I'd do it all different, my love, all of it, I'd drag you to 'the Quack' as soon as I saw you drop an ounce! Even if you screamed all the way, I'd drag you! Drag you by the hair, if I had to! I'd change it all, because I loved you so fucking much ...*

And if he had *been banging Laura? What then? Maybe cancer was his punishment.*

But that thought, so horrible, brought a fantastically clear moment of revelation. *I wouldn't care. Not if he was still alive, I wouldn't care. I'd be hurt, and it'd cause trouble - big trouble in Little Ealing - but he'd still be* alive *to hurt me. I'd have him* alive. *Alive, we could work through it. Dead, and I've no options.*

Big Sarah, you'd be proud of me. I've solved a puzzle.

At that point, she fell asleep.

*

The house was burning down. She could feel the heat, smell the smoke, hear the sirens growing closer …but she couldn't move, nor was she coughing.

"Fire! Fire!" A voice was screaming – male or female she couldn't tell. "Fetch the engine! Fetch the engine!"

You're got that line arse about face, Eve thought. *You need more rehearsal.*

"Come on, little Eve," said Carl, emerging from the smoke. He looked old, tired, as if he'd expended great energy, like he'd been running a marathon. "Don't sit there like cheese at fourpence, *move!* I don't know how much longer I can keep the bad thing back."

"What bad thing?"

"This is no RSC workshop and I'm not running a Q&A," he sighed, then bent double, coughing. *He's affected by the smoke and I'm not. How come? Who's the ghost here anyway?* "The bad thing's coming, it's coming fast, and in the event of evacuation please leave in an orderly fashion by the doors marked EXIT." He waved an arm that seemed to weigh a ton, and there, through the flames, appeared a door with a large green EXIT sign above it, the kind seen in theatres.

But Eve couldn't move. She *wanted* to move, she just couldn't. "Were you having an affair?"

"There's a time and place," said Carl, *and oh dear God – look at him!* He was sagging, literally *sagging,* the flesh hanging from the bone. "And this is neither. I tried, little Eve, I did all I could …but you were right. You were too selfish, too self-absorbed. I wanted to stop this. But now it's inevitable." Another burst of explosive coughing. He bent double, opened his mouth, and a stream of guts and blood hit the floor.

"Were you having an affair?" She asked again, rooted. Carl's strength just evaporated then. He fell into the sickly pile he'd excreted. It coated his face. "Were you having an affair? Were you having an affair? Were …"

*

She awoke in the dark, in her own room, as if jerked from her dream on a bungee wire. For a second, so embedded in her subconscious imagery was she, Eve convinced herself she really could smell smoke. *Alarm'll hit any minute,* she thought mushily. *Got to get Sarah out.*

But the alarm didn't hit, and as the new day (four and a half hours old by the clock), grew brighter around her, Eve finally began to realise she'd just given herself a late night horror show. *Thanks for that, brain,* she scolded, trying to decide whether to just snuggle back down or plod across to the bathroom and urinate, *it was good of you. What you trying to do, balance the scales? Give me a lousy morning after a brilliant night? Is it your idea of karma? If so, stick it. It, as Sarah would doubtless say, sucks.*

She tried making herself small, a hedgehog, tiny and invisible to the workings of her mind. She just didn't try hard enough it seemed. *Nasty business, wasn't it? Fire, smoke, Carl warning you of inevitable bad things ...and then just coughing – literally – his guts up! Yuk!*

"Fuck off," she mumbled into her pillow. "I need sleep."

Yeah, sure. Fine. But Jesus – did you see the mess? Intestines, lungs, kidneys, blood ...all just flopping from his chin! No wonder the poor bastard went all saggy. I mean, there was nothing holding his skeleton together!

Eve turned over, angry, and thumped the pillow for want of something else to hit. *Knock it off, I said.*

Hey, right, got you. I'm down with that. Sleep? Best thing, you bet. I'm going to shut up now, going to leave you alone. Night, night. Sleep tight. Don't – whatever you do – think of why, when you'd thought you didn't care much anyway, all you could do was ask Carl whether or not he was shagging around behind your back. Don't give it a second thought.

Eve gave up for the time being and sat up in bed. *What do you mean?*

No listen, forget it. Don't think about that great moment of revelation you had before nodding off, the one where you thought you didn't care a fig what Carl might or might not have been doing behind your back. Hey, you were a good girl weren't you? And you had people throwing themselves at you. You could have had a hundred men! It probably stands to reason he was a good boy as well. It's an equation, like they used to have in Maths. You remember? "If one side of the equals sign is this thing, then the other side is that thing." I think that pretty much covers it. So, if you were faithful, he was faithful. And you said you were okay with it. So don't wonder why you stood – or were you sitting? – rooted to the ground in a burning house that would kill you because you just kept asking him, over and over, if he'd had an affair. Forget about it. What does it matter? You don't care, you told yourself that. Just because it pops up in your mind while you're sleeping doesn't mean *anything. Obviously. Which is why I haven't brought it up.*

Eve Wilson stared into the darkness – a darkness that in less than twenty-four hours would deepen into terror like she'd never known – and realised that, sooner or later, she would actually *have* to know what Carl had done. She *had* to find out, one way or the other. She had to discover the truth.

Even if it killed her.

Chapter Nineteen

"Morning slugabed," said Sarah, as Eve thumped into the living room at a little after half ten.

"That's only your opinion," Eve replied with as much wit as she could muster. She'd only managed to drift back into a doze at a little after six, and frankly it hadn't been much of a help. She felt wrecked. Then she blinked a bit and took in exactly what she saw.

Her sister – showered, changed, made up and looking resplendent – was sitting on the sofa surrounded by newspapers, all of which were open. She had a red pen in her hand and lots of passages were underlined. Oh, and on the coffee tables were a stack of puzzle magazines, all of which had a different sexy young girl on the front for some reason. They, however, were still *puzzle intacta.*

She still wasn't awake enough to articulate clearly, so Eve simply pointed. "I went to the shop down the road, the one that reckons it sells *Fags, Mags and Bags,*" said Sarah. "Picked up all the papers – and some stuff for me – just to see what they said." She held up the red pen, an apologetic half embarrassed smile of her face. "Yeah, well …I just thought you'd like to see the good bits first."

Two thoughts went through Eve's head, and like any good actor she filed them in the right order. "Are there any *bad* bits? And how did you get there and back?"

"No bad bits for you, or the other actors or the director. Couple for the play – not really *bad*, just a bit equivocal, I think the guy in the *Express* calls it 'piebald' – but mostly I think your lot call them 'raves'. And I let myself out and back. Seriously, leaving the keys in that pot on the sideboard? Ealing must be a shitload safer than Chorlton."

"I never did that, they must be Carl's. Had a key thing, forever losing them." But her heart wasn't in the key conversation, her heart was on the crits. Oh, she knew actors were never supposed to read their reviews – that's what they all said, anyway – but they did.

"Get reading," said Sarah, "and I'll make the coffee. Or do you want tea? I think I saw some of that sucky herbal stuff there last night."

"No, coffee's fine," Eve said, picking up the pile of papers. "As strong as you like, ta."

In the time it took Sarah to boil a kettle, find the Nescafé, retrieve the milk and bring two steaming mugs of caffeine goodness to the living room, Eve had scanned (most efficiently, thanks to her sister's red pen), the crits in *The Daily Mail, The Express, The Guardian* and *The Telegraph.* If she were to pick any of them, she'd probably have picked the *Mail,* but that was because of the headline A STAR IS RE-BORN! All four contained roughly the same words, variations on "magical," "piercing," "magnetic" or "sublime." *The Telegraph* called her "the most important dramatic actress of her generation, back where she belongs – where we all need to see her."

The others, of course, came off well. Mike's direction was "pin-point accurate," (*The Guardian*), Hedliegh was "as terrifying a creation as a thousand Dracula's," (*The Mail*), Richard and Rachael gave "credible support" (*The Telegraph*) and "were not swamped by the magic around them" (*The Guardian*).

But the final paragraph of the *Express* piece did cause Eve to frown slightly. "Mostly, though, the play itself only really transcends its horror movie hand-me-down scenario in its final moments, when – not to give anything away – some excellent, passionate writing suddenly elevates the piece to a whole new level. It is here, I suspect, that we really understand what the writer has to say. Certainly, these were the moments that brought the greatest response from the packed house."

Oh, Barry's going to love *that,* she thought, *considering that's what I bullied him into –*

She broke off then, and laid the paper on her lap. Barry. *Where was he last night? He wasn't at the party. So where* was *he? This was, after all, his Big Night. Why would he want to miss it? People were cheering for his work – standing, applauding. Why didn't he hang round to be adored?*

Perhaps more importantly, *why didn't you notice? More of your selfishness? More of your self-absorption?*

Bullshit, Eve reasoned. *So what, I didn't notice him not being there. Big deal. I'm only one woman; I can't be expected to see everything. I had my own stuff to deal with.*

But still, it was niggling. Why *wasn't* he at the party? Had he even been at the show at all? Had anyone else *mentioned* him at all – Mike, for instance. Or Sir Peter?

But at that point Sarah brought the drinks in, asked how Eve was feeling about the reviews, and all thoughts of the writer went straight out of her head.

*

They spent the rest of the morning pleasantly enough – Sarah brought Eve up to speed with what was happening in her own life (possible redundancy due to library funding cuts, Steve keeping the business afloat but was looking at making 'cost savings' – or redundancies in plain English – and dreading it), and Eve kept marvelling at the easy way they were talking. *We wasted a lot of time, me and you,* she found herself thinking. *We could have had this a lot earlier. Still, what does it matter? What matters is that we found it at all.*

It would have been even more pleasant if the phone had stopped ringing. However, from eleven onwards the calls kept coming in. Mike, asking if she'd seen the reviews, raving over what they were going to select for the plastics. Tom, asking if she'd seen the reviews, raving about the offers that were hitting his desk. ("You'll be in work until you're sixty – and rich! Oh, and I've nineteen requests for interviews …") Sir Peter, asking if she'd read the reviews, wondering already about "Capitalising on the press – maybe transferring to a bigger theatre. Maybe look at Broadway in January. There's even been an enquiry about a film adaptation." By twelve thirty, Eve simply pulled the plug. "The rest can go to voicemail. C'mon, big Sarah, let's do lunch."

"Where?"

*

They pottered up the road to the Moon on the Water, blinking a little in the strong late September sunshine, and over some pasta and a couple of Americanos they reminisced a bit about their childhood – about the bike Sarah had mangled trying to ride double with her friend Amanda, about next door's dog Russ, a Jack Russell who just wouldn't *shut the fuck up barking* (but whom Eve had loved with all her heart and wanted to kidnap), about times long gone but not forgotten. They kept away from the hurt and the anguish that had blighted most of their lives, for they both seemed to understand that their new found peace hadn't quite bedded in yet, that it would only take one wrong word to shake the foundations loose, but what mattered most to Eve was the fact they were building *something*. That was enough. It was more than she had ever expected, in fact.

But at around two in the afternoon, she felt the usual tingle start. *Show tonight,* it said. In time, that tingle would spread from her belly and all but consume her, pulling her head from the world until, by seven o'clock, she would be sat in her solo dressing room, door closed, narrowing her concentration to a laser point, just as she had been the night before. As she would be the night after. *That's the one downside to the theatre,* she'd thought often enough. *You don't just have to be brilliant. You have to be brilliant over and over again. Film, TV? Four, five takes maximum. Theatre? Months and months.* Now, of course, she had something to live up to. Raves in the papers were all well and good. Strong word of mouth was all fine and dandy. But tonight she had to get up and do it all over again, and to be at least as good as she had been the night before, lest the audience go away disgruntled.

Big deal, said Sarah Voice in her head, overriding the real Sarah sat opposite her, who was telling a story about her first boyfriend Dave, *a hundred million Red Chinese don't give a shit. You think you got it hard? Surgeons,* they *got it hard. Day after day they cut people with scalpels and try to save lives. Teachers in Salford,* they *got it hard. Day after day they try and avoid knives and stick some knowledge into smackheads' heads. Hell, the station staff at Ealing Broadway Underground have it harder than you. They do a twelve hour shift and try and keep a hundred year old network running. So you got to get up on a stage and do it again? Diddums!*

You know, you're a lot more irritating in my head than you are in the flesh, Sarah Voice. Yeah, got it, I know the whole "Doctors and nurses" speech, and I don't deny it. It's true; they work a damn site harder than I ever will. But I can only speak from my own perspective, right? And I have to keep reproducing what I did last night for a minimum of three months. It's in my contract. You can call me a spoilt bitch if you like, and I know I chose this life, but sometimes it's a colossal pain in the butt.

So thinking, she let the tingle start its spread outwards, and put the pretend Sarah Voice to bed, and concentrated on the real one, who was telling her that she'd once found Dave – and she'd *never* told anyone this before – giving his dog Mitch a reach around.

Eve just exploded with laughter at that, then laughed even harder when Sarah said, "And when I called him on it, he just looked up at me and said, 'aw c'mon, it's all a part of growing up'."

That was it for half an hour or so, conversation died, and all there could be heard was the screaming laughter of two sisters. People looked over at them – some of them disapproving – but neither Eve nor Sarah noticed. For the first and last time in their lives, they had found the same thing funny at the same time, and oh dear Lord how Eve was determined to wallow in it.

But by three-thirty, the two sisters were ready to go back. Sarah wanted to call Steve and see how he was, and Eve wanted to shower and change before leaving at about five. That would give her plenty of time.

*

"You sure you're going to be okay?" asked Eve as she gathered her bag to her and did the check. Car keys, door keys, purse ...

"I'll be fine. Got me mags, got the Spar down the road if I can't find anything in that mess of a kitchen, and I've got your telly."

"Okay then. It'll be back at eleven. Half past, latest." Then, just because of the pigtail pulling, "Hey, you want me to leave Jon's number in case you get bored?"

Sarah flicked the Vs at her. "Go fuck yourself, little Eve." Then, seriously but still smiling; "Thanks for putting me up. And for lunch."

"Nothing to it, big Sarah. See you later."

She walked into the hall, Sarah calling out, "Be brilliant," from the living room.

"I will," she said as she closed the front door. She backed the car out of the driveway and motored off to the Tube.

And the horror *really* began.

*

The play that night was a rousing success. There was, perhaps, a *slight* dip in the energy level – but it was so slight as to be imperceptible to the audience, and also only to be expected, really. Certainly, Mike wasn't bothered when he bounded into Eve's dressing room just after curtain down.

"Brilliant again, darlin'! Brilliant *again*! If applause were hard currency I could retire! Actually, I may have to retire after this – I'm not sure I can replicate this kind of buzz. Did you see the returns queue?" Eve shook her head, unable to help smiling at his ebullience. *"Went round the block!* Those poor bastards at the Royal thought it was *their* box office line! I did enjoy telling them it wasn't."

"You are mean, cruel and heartless," said Eve, not meaning it, as she took her makeup off. "And speak not of retiring. I want you to direct my next piece."

"I'll keep my diary free for you forever," he grinned back. "Listen, we're off for a drink at the Zanzibar – don't tell the coppers, I've got a lock in sorted. Coming?"

Eve felt genuine regret, but declined. "I can't, Mike. Got my sister staying with me from Manchester, she's on her own, and I said I'd be back."

"Oh well. Your loss, darlin'." He trotted to the door, but Eve called him back.

"Mike? Was Barry here tonight?"

"Didn't see him," he said, a faint frown trickling his forehead. "Maybe he's at home, jizzing into his reviews."

"Charming. Which, by the way, weren't too hot for him."

"Maybe, but he'll get noticed from them, he's caused a stir. He'll be hot now."

"He wasn't at the party either, was he?"

The frown reappeared, deeper. "No, you're right. He wasn't. I didn't even notice, either. Too wrapped up in everything else. Shame, lot of people would've wanted to meet him."

"But he saw the show?"

"Yeah. Well, I assume so – he was in the auditorium before curtain up. Didn't sit with me though. Come to think of it, I didn't see him in the bar at the Interval either." He absent-mindedly stroked his moustache, a gesture that Eve reckoned he thought made him look wise, but which actually made him resemble a pantomime villain.

"Have you spoken to him at all today?"

The frown went, replaced by a sheepish shamed dog look. "Well, I meant to …but stuff kind of kept coming up. You?"

"No," Eve replied, equally regretful. "Spent the day with my sister, gossiping. I'll call him tomorrow, see what's up with him."

"Do that. I will, too – *and* get Sir Peter to contact him as well. Right," the sorry look gone, and a much brighter one in its place, "I'm off to get pissed. Sure we can't tempt you?"

"Next time. And I'm paying."

"If you're paying, I'm there," Mike said, then left the dressing room. *Okay, that's sorted,* she thought as she stepped into her street clothes. *We'll all talk to Barry tomorrow. Find out what the deal is. Pour oil on whatever troubled water there may be.*

So thinking, she checked her face in the mirror, wandered along the corridors, said good night to everybody, and stepped out into the by now slightly chill September night.

A look at her watch told Eve it was 10.47 as she emerged from the Tube station. Fifteen minutes and she'd be back home. She hoped Sarah hadn't been too bored – but frankly there wasn't much Eve could do, even if she was. *I could invite her to the show again,* she thought as she made her way to the car, *then we could go for a meal, or a drink with the cast. She could sit with Mike, he'd entertain her. He might be a bit...well, 'camply ebullient' (if that's a phrase) for her, but you never know, it might be okay. Get her out of the house, anyway. Look, I'll suggest it and see what she says. I mean, she could invite Jon ...*

Full of these thoughts, the last one making her smile, Eve didn't much notice her surroundings. She didn't really take in the fact that Ealing Broadway car park was virtually deserted. And she certainly didn't hear the footsteps as they approached. The first she knew was when a voice said, "Miss Rogers, can I have your autograph?"

But before she could turn and meet her fan, something hard and heavy slammed into the back of her head, and there was blinding white agony. Then things went dark.

Chapter Twenty

Sarah Brown (who had once been Sarah Rogers), didn't grow worried until half past midnight. In truth, she hadn't expected Eve when she said she'd turn up. Eve and timekeeping were strangers. Well, maybe that was a bit harsh – they had a nodding acquaintance - but it had been a standing joke in the family that things would be arranged for E.T., their abbreviation for "Eve Time." "Eve Time" was the scheduled start date plus thirty minutes. "What time's the meal booked for, Mum," Sarah would ask. "Half seven, E.T." would be the reply. It was different (of course!) when it came to her job – for that, apparently, punctuality was a virtue – but when it came to the rest of her life …well, that was another story.

It may have surprised Eve to learn that Sarah, actually, wasn't that bothered. It may have surprised her further to realise that a lot of what Eve believed about her relationship with her sister was fairly bogus. No, they hadn't been close as children – nor as adolescents or even as adults, that much was true – but, really, did that *matter?* They had a tendency to rub each other up the wrong way occasionally – but what siblings didn't? Sarah, in fact, pretty much loved her sister as much as it was possible to do. She just had too much of her parents in her to admit it. No, that wasn't quite right. It was actually deeper than that. Sarah had too much of her parents in her to realise how much she loved her sister.

I thought what you did was a job, Sarah had said yesterday, and that summed up how Sarah felt about acting. It was a job like any other. Maybe not as secure as some, but who the hell had a secure job anymore? *Did* such an animal exist these days? Okay, it was a strange sort of job where people turned and applauded at the end of it, and for a while Sarah had found that hard to come to terms with (*no one applauds me when I stack the newspapers correctly on the reading desks, or Steve when he balances the figures at the end of the tax year*), but the epiphany (of sorts) had come to her during a six month appraisal meeting when the Head Librarian had given her a spotless report and said, "Well done." *Ah, I get it,* she'd thought. *The applause is Eve's version of my appraisal. Makes sense now.* The fact that Eve was good at her job was something Sarah had kind of accepted as ...*just right,* really. Why shouldn't she be? It didn't occur to her that Eve would be feeling a kind of void, a desire to prove things to her, to have her say great things ...why should she want *that?* She knew she was good, didn't she? She had her contemporaries to tell her that. What did a Chorlton librarian have to add to any of it? Why would *her* opinion make any difference?

She'd seen most of Eve's plays – not all of them – but most of them, and of course she'd been impressed; she was, after all, doing her job and doing it well. It was only watching her in *Pavlov's Bell* that she'd been actually *knocked out* by what her kid sister could do. It'd been something special all right – like watching City (before the big money arrived) beat United. It was like watching somebody *good* suddenly become somebody *great* – no, more than that. Last night was the first time she'd actually *forgotten* it was her sister, her *kid* sister up there on that stage. Last night she'd watched Joanna Playton, not Eve Rogers (or Wilson, or whatever), being tortured and brutalised and finally getting the upper hand, and that had been …well, a revelation.

So Sarah had kept herself busy while Eve had been at work. She'd rung Steve, told him how it'd gone and how much she loved him, watched a little TV, made herself a sandwich (fighting the temptation to reorganise Eve's cupboards with only the strongest effort of will) and had then buried her head in a copy of *Puzzler*. As was her way, the world faded into insignificance as she filled grids and solved clues, and before she knew much of anything it was eleven o'clock and Eve would soon be home.

What does she do when she gets in, Sarah wondered. *Drink? Eat? Both? Neither? Should I fix her something?*

Ah, she'll tell me, she thought, climbing the stairs to the toilet. *Never second guess a thespian.*

But eleven became half past, and still no Eve. *Eleven thirty at the latest, "E.T."* Sarah boiled the kettle and made herself a cup of tea. It was as she was doing this that she suddenly began to feel …well, *odd* was the best way to describe it. Almost …anxious. *I'm alone in a strange house after dark,* she found herself thinking for no reason at all. *The last time I was here was for Carl's funeral – such a shame, he was taken before his time, nice guy if a bit distant* – but she knew the place well enough, she'd been down plenty of times (well, four) and it had always seemed …well, a happy sort of place, she supposed. Okay, maybe not happy "happy", like full of parties and japes and raucous laughter, but just a *house,* just bricks and stone and glass. Nothing to give you the heebie jeebies.

And I don't have *the heebie jeebies,* she thought as she poured boiling water onto a PG Tips bag. *Tea bags! You think she'd have some Earl Grey at least!* (Was her hand shaking slightly as it replaced the kettle?) *There's no reason to have the heebie jeebies. Whatever heebie jeebies may be. I'm in my sister's perfectly ordinary house making a perfectly ordinary cup of tea which I will drink in her perfectly ordinary living room.*

All the same, she didn't turn the kitchen light out as she left it, and an observer might have thought she was scuttling back to the living room instead of walking.

By twelve thirty, when Eve still hadn't arrived, it was harder for Sarah to convince herself that she was feeling fine. She was trembling – slightly, but trembling nonetheless – and she found herself glancing apprehensively to the window that overlooked the street. Her heart was beating just a little too rapidly. She felt ill, as if she was coming down with a fever. *Come on, little Eve,* she started thinking, over and over like a mantra, *where are you? Come on, little Eve, where are you?*

By a quarter to one Sarah could stand it no longer and she pulled her mobile from her handbag. Only two bars on the battery – had she remembered to bring her charger? Never mind, there was a landline here. She scrolled through the phonebook until she found EVE MOB, then pressed CALL.

"C'mon, c'mon," she muttered, unaware. "Pick up."

The phone rang six times in her ear, then; "This is the Vodaphone Voice Messaging Service …" Sarah swore violently and waited for the beep, then said "Eve, its Sarah. You okay? It's nearly one. Call me back as soon as you pick up. Please." She clicked off and sat on the sofa, staring at the wall. *What do I do if she doesn't? What do I do then?*

*

"Miss Rogers," said a man's voice in the darkness, "I asked for your autograph."

Eve's eyes opened and she tried to turn to the sound, but two things stopped her. The first was the shocking bolt of pain that ran from the back of her head to her temples. It was electric, galvanising, white, pure agony. It drove every thought away before it.

The *second* thing that stopped her turning was the fact she appeared to be …well, she wasn't sure. Some …resistance …

"Please," said the voice, which appeared to be behind her, to her right. "I'm a big fan. Not your number one fan, no. You're only like my fifth favourite actress. But I still love your work."

The pain was – thankfully – subsiding now. That blinding awfulness was rolling back, leaving a kind of dull throbbing ache that felt like it was settling down for a long stay. It was nauseating – literally, Eve could feel her stomach tumble greasily over and over. *Fuck,* she thought, *I'm going to vom* –

She sat (*sat?*) forward (but not far forward …again, some kind of resistance), and opened her mouth, expecting a jet of crap to come spewing from her throat. But instead, all that came out was a buzzing belch, as if a as if a thousand cicada's had been let loose in an echo chamber, and a gassy cloud of acid smelling nothing.

"Oh, excuse *you*," said the voice, still behind her but now more to the left. "Little baby *pig!* And *phee-yew,* what a pong!" The voice darted to her right ear again, still behind her. "What *have* you been eating?"

I don't think this is a dream, Eve. Of course it wasn't, the pain proved that, but still it *felt* like a dream. She was muzzy, disconnected, that sodding *thump-thump* at the back of her head and the rolling nausea in her stomach made it impossible for her to concentrate. *Got to try and focus she thought. Got to try and …*

Eve flexed her right arm, meaning to rub her head – or maybe her stomach – and was utterly dumbfounded when it didn't move more than a quarter of an inch. There was a vague rustling sound …no, not a rustle. A crackle? Yes, more a crackle. Like cellophane. Behind her – *right* behind her now – she heard the man titter.

What the fuck?

She tried her left arm. The same thing happened. A little bit of give, then that …crackle?

I'm sitting down, she finally, fully realised. *I'm in a chair.*

Eve decided she didn't want to be in a chair, so she'd stand up. Since her hands wouldn't raise, she pushed down on the armrests.

With the same result. A quarter of an inch or so of movement, then that unpleasant noise and nothing. No momentum. She started to panic and kicked out her legs. Well, she would have kicked out her legs if not for …the same thing.

With a sense of horror the like of which she had never, ever felt before, Eve Wilson realised she was trapped. Trapped, with someone behind her. Someone who could do what he liked to her. And she was powerless to move.

Genuine panic set in then. She started flailing as best she could against her bonds, trying to arch her back, her head see-sawing from side to side (and every movement making that pain rise, *thump-THUMP, thump-THUMP*), trying to find some sort of *give*, a terrified high-pitched whine escaping from her throat, *screeee-eeee, screeeeee-eeeeee…*

And of course, it made no difference. Whatever was holding her held her fast. The only noise that she could hear was the chair thumping against the floor. That, and the damned faint crackle of …

Tape? *Gaffer* tape? *Masking* tape? What the Yanks call duct tape? Was that it?

Maybe, but whatever the hell it was it was strong, unyielding. Her fingers were free, but her wrists and forearms …no. They were bound to the chair arms. There was more around her stomach, she could feel it digging into her as her breath grew shallower and more frequent, and still more on her legs – from her ankles up to her knees.

Strong male hands clamped down painfully onto her shoulders, the fingers really squeezing, really digging in, and stopped her rocking. "Easy now, Miss Rogers, easy. You might fall and hurt yourself. Of course, you'll be hurt plenty before this is over, but I want the hurt to be of my choosing. I'm the boss here. I'm in control." Then, in her right ear, "I know that's not the way you feminists think, but it's the natural order." In her left ear, "You don't agree with me, I know." Right behind her, "Before this is over, though, you'll see who's in the right."

Something terrible – more terrible – and unexpected happened then. Eve burst into tears. Great floods of them – tears of desperation, of terror. "Hush, you," said the voice. It was chuckling, almost patronising. As if he'd expected it. "Don't you go upsetting yourself over stuff you can't control." It was moving, coming out from behind her, coming into her line of blurred view. "Cry if you've burned the tea, fine. Cry if you've not made the beds, fine. But cry over *this?* Waste of time."

He was in front of her now, but Eve's sobbing face was resting on her chin. A gloved hand reached out and grabbed her savagely by the cheek, forcing her to look upwards.

Black trousers. A black sweater – chunky, cable knit. And a black ski-mask with holes for eyes and mouth. They were kissing close.

"*Boo,*" said the man, and Eve fainted dead away.

Chapter Twenty-one

By two o'clock in the morning, Sarah could no longer convince herself that Eve would walk in any minute, whistling (not that she ever whistled), swinging her keys and uttering apologies along the lines of, "Sorry, got talking and forgot the time – oh, and I switched my phone off for no good reason at all."

What was worst about the whole thing was that *convincing herself* was exactly what she was trying to do. That odd, creeping sensation of …well, *wrongness* was growing and growing, closing in, seeping into her, oppressing her. She had never felt like this before, and it bewildered her utterly. It was as if there was something outside her (she really couldn't put it any better than that), whispering in her ear bad things are happening. *Bad things. REALLY bad things.*

Sarah was a Manchester girl, and Manchester girls knew all about bad things. Though she lived in Chorlton – barely a stone's throw away from the house where she and Eve had been raised – and Chorlton was reasonably affluent, reasonably calm, she worked in Stretford. Stretford may be just a five minute drive from her front door, but it was another world. The kids who came into the library …well, they'd *seen a bit of life* was Sarah's preferred way of putting it. Sixteen year old girls pushing prams. Fifteen year old lads with their hoodies and their bumfluff beards, stinking of pot. People were stabbed not far from where she lived. People were shot. Raped. Murdered. It was in the *Evening News* every day of the week, it was on the local TV updates, it was everywhere. Everywhere in Manchester. And Manchester was a lot smaller than London.

Bad things are happening, she …felt? Yes, felt. *Bad things happening to Eve, to your sister. Right now. Don't kid yourself any longer. Get help.* Then, utterly bizarrely, *solve the puzzle.*

What bloody puzzle, she thought, but that conundrum didn't stop her reaching out, picking up the phone, and for want of any other ideas, punching in three nines.

"Emergency," said the woman in her ear. "Which service do you require?"

"Police," Sarah heard herself say.

*

Was she moving?

No, Eve couldn't be moving. She was sitting on the banks of the ship canal, throwing bread for the ducks. To her right, she could see a Jack Russell terrier who she just *knew* was called Russ. Russ was barking. He wanted to chase the ducks, but he was on a tight lead. Eve was six, she was perfectly happy, and she was *not moving.*

I am, though. I'm being turned.

No she wasn't. She was utterly still, ripping up another slice from a Warburton's Toastie Loaf, and chucking it to the quacking hordes. Some of the ducks had green heads; she liked them best.

Who's turning me?

No one, because she was on her own, feeding ducks. There was no one here besides herself. And Russ. Even Russ didn't have an owner, which seemed like it might be cruel – but then again, if Russ's owner had tied him up and left him, that meant she could take him home. Oh yeah, sure, they could put posters up (FOUND! JACK RUSSELL! ANSWERS TO NAME OF RUSS! IF YOURS, CALL 0161 871 4298) but, let's face it, anyone who tied up such a *gorgeous* little dog and left it to die on a canal bank wasn't going to claim it, were they? Then she'd have a dog and she'd love it and feed it and walk it *at least* twice a day. She'd always wanted a dog.

Is that rain?

Eve looked up – nope, not a cloud in the sky. Still, she'd felt something …on her face …

"Eve," said a voice. *Who the flip's that*, thought six year old Eve, and looked around. It was Russ. He was no longer barking, he was talking. *Brilliant! A talking dog!* "Eve," he said again, and spat at her. Misty droplets covered her face, making her wince. *Dirty boy,* she thought. *Have to cure him of that or Mum will have one of her "canary fits."*

"Eve," said Russ again, "why don't you wake up now?" Then he spat in her face and Eve woke up. She was back fixed to the chair. Every muscle in her body was strained, aching. The agony at the back of her skull had abated somewhat, but she was still confused, hazy.

Also, she was starting to think she could do with a piss.

Then, jolting, the man in the dark clothes and ski mask jumped up, right in her eyeline, nose to nose. "Hiya," he called, camp falsetto, like he was talking to a baby, like he was playing peek-a-boo. There was something in his right hand, some kind of bottle.

Eve screamed – not a scream of terror, a short howl of shock. Two firsts for the price of one. First time fainting, first time screaming. The man giggled. He juggled the bottle closer to her face. Her swollen, petrified eyes took it in – some kind of spray bottle, the kind you use to water the leaves of plants with. "You were missing some of the fun," said the man, "so I had to wake you. But I played a little game. On my own, because neither you nor she were awake, but games are games nonetheless."

She?

He raised his left hand, and there was another bottle, identical to the first. She could see liquid sloshing around in its translucent innards. "It's a game called *Fifty-Fifty*. I tried selling it to Endemol some months back – y'know, they have all the big L.E. hits; *Millionaire, Weakest Link, Big Brother*. Not stuff I suppose you watch, but hey – bread and circuses, with me? They're populist, could have made me rich. But they didn't take it, bastards. *I* know it'll work though. Hey, you've got contacts, maybe you can help. Here's the rules; one bottle of water," he jiggled his right hand, "one bottle of highly concentrated sulphuric acid," he jiggled his left.

What did he just say …

"I mean, in the proposal there was a quiz thing, right? General knowledge questions. "What's the capital of Nova Scotia?' 'Who wrote the 1812 Overture,' nothing too difficult. Then, when a contestant gets an answer wrong the quiz master picks up one of the bottles – neither of them marked – and squirts the contestant *full in the face!* See? It's *Fifty-Fifty* as to which one they get! Either just a soaking or *scarred and blinded for the rest of their lives!* Imagine the *tension!* Imagine the *ratings!* It'd go through the fucking *roof!* And the stupid bastards never even acknowledged my letter! Jesus, is it any wonder no one watches TV anymore? *Is* it?"

Eve goggled at him. Too much was going on at once, too much weirdness. She couldn't process it at all. She was coming on for total sensory overload.

"Okay, okay," said the scary demon in the mask. "I know what you're thinking. It's just a joke, right, a bit of a sick joke, no one would do anything like that to another human being. But, y'know, you're wrong. I'm *very* serious about my work, Eve – hey, you don't mind if I call you Eve, do you? I feel like we're getting to know each other – I even arranged a pilot programme. Strictly non-broadcast, of course, but I needed to know if there were any kinks to be ironed out before I tried another company – Tiger Aspect, maybe. And, guess what? It's perfect. Look!"

The monster moved to one side, and behind him Eve could clearly see – much, *much* too clearly – Laura Rossi, clearly out of it and handcuffed to a radiator, with half of her pretty face burned away.

While Eve screamed again, the man in black giggled.

*

The police left by a quarter past four, having taken all the notes and descriptions they needed, and Sarah had never felt so useless.

The Emergency operator had – quite scornfully, she thought – told her in no uncertain terms that missing persons hardly constituted an emergency, but had, grudgingly, connected her with the local station. The desk guy who'd answered had listened, taken some notes, then told her some officers would be round as soon as possible. He made it sound like it wasn't a priority.

The knock on the door had come at half past three – nearly ninety minutes after making the call – but in truth, Sarah hadn't needed to hear it. She'd spent that hour and a half standing at the window, looking into the silent, dark street in front of her, hiding – no, make that *cringing* – whenever an occasional figure had loomed into view. As soon as the car had swung into the driveway she'd bolted for the front door.

She took some, but not much, reassurance from the calm way the two constables had gone about their business – what time did Eve leave here, what time would she have left the theatre, do you know if she turned up at all, what time did the show end, was she driving, what clothes was she wearing, do you have a photograph – but there was some kind of undertone about them, and it wasn't until she'd closed the door behind them, after they'd promised to put Eve's description out and check up on her movements that she realised what it was. *She's free, white and over twenty-one.* That's what they were thinking. *Also, only …what? Three, four hours overdue? And she's an actress. She'll be at some coke snorting party or having a threesome, you know what they're like. You ever seen her? Yeah, in the paper. She's a looker. Dirty sort, I reckon. Had everyone every way, filthy* bitch. And we've got a hundred stabbings and sixteen million murders to deal with – some dirty fucking whore bitch actress deciding to get her holes filled and not letting her hillbilly sister know? Well up on our priority list, I reckon. You want chips? Yeah, I'm Hank Marvin, me.*

On the way out, the smaller constable had asked, "Is there anyone else with you?"

"No, I'm all alone," Sarah had answered.

"Do you have anyone to call?"

"No," she said again, 'my husband's up in Manchester." Then, for no reason except that panic which had enfolded her, "He runs his own company."

"Good for him," said the constable. 'Well, don't worry. Ninety-five percent of the time these things are just some misunderstanding. You'll see, your sister will turn up sooner or later, all apologies."

Then they were out, walking to their car, and Sarah saw the looks on their faces and they glanced to each other, the ones that said, *and frankly, we've got much more important things to be going on with.*

Back in the living room, back on her own, Sarah began to wait. Maybe not for long – I mean, ninety-five per cent of the time these things were just some misunderstanding, weren't they? – but maybe forever.

*

The monster in black didn't attempt to stop Eve screaming, he just stood there and let his giggling fit run its course. Not that she took much notice of him. She was staring, eyes fixed at the body before her, her …*acquaintance,* really, not friend, one side of her face normal, the other side a ruin, the flesh peeled, burned away to reveal muscles, tendons, bone. Pus was leaking from these holes in slow yellow rivers. Some of it collected in the side of her mouth, and it was only the fact that these bubbled and popped that convinced Eve that Laura was still alive.

Her screams wound down, her throat burning – burning, the way Laura's face must have burned, her pretty Scots/Italian face – then she turned her neck as far as it would go. For the first time since waking up in hell, she spoke. Her voice was scratched, hurt, but she spoke. "You bastard."

"Yes," said the Devil before her. 'I am. I'm a bastard. I'm a mad bastard, to tell you the truth. I'm a total fucking psycho. I labour under no delusions, Eve. I'm as nutty as a fruitcake. I *honestly* don't know what I'll do next. I'm as likely to shit in my hat and wear it sideways as I am to poke your pretty eyes out with dressmaking scissors. Every day's an adventure. I may even decide to cut you free from that shit you're bound with and pay for a taxi ride home

– though frankly, that's unlikely." He was speeding up now, moving around her ...and with total and abject horror Eve realised *exactly* what was going on here, and the tension in her bladder ratcheted up a notch. "Eve, old Eve, you must understand – you *must* – that it's been many a long year since I was responsible for my own actions. I'm what the religious types call 'other directed.' I'm mad, barking, got toys in the attic, I'm one Jack short of a full deck, all my lights are on but no one's at home." He was darting around her, back and forth, side to side, sometimes making complete circles. "You pick a cliché for abnormal psychology and I'm its poster child. However, and *I want to make this quite clear, minister,* I'm the nutter who's in *control* of this situation. I'm the nutter who has the two of you at my mercy. And I have lots of toys in the house. Not even specialist toys – you'd be amazed at the amount of damage you can do with ordinary household objects." He stopped moving then, and addressed the air, but Eve had long since stopped listening to him. She was too immersed in the terrifying reality of her situation. "Maybe that's why so many accidents happen in the home?" He shook his head, dismissing the thought. "Well, who cares?" He put his face very close to hers then, and she could smell his breath. "All you need to know is that at any moment I could just go apeshit and hurt you very, very badly. Keep that foregrounded, Eve. Keep it uppermost in your mind."

But Eve couldn't. There was something else taking up space there. *This is the last act of the play,* she was thinking. *The last act of* Pavlov's Bell. *Only it's for real. Dear God in Heaven, it's for real.*

It's for real.

"Anyway," said the madman, "I've got to make a number one. That's what my Mummy told me to say in company. Or, very discreetly, ask where the lavatory was. But I don't need to ask here. I know where everything is. So, I'm going to make a number one. But don't worry, I wash my hands. For fifteen seconds exactly. My Mummy was very insistent on that. It keeps the germs away. Back in a tick!"

Then he was gone, off to her left, and Eve was …well, not alone, for Laura was there, but since the other woman was (unconscious? Catatonic?) Eve might as well have been. Panic was nibbling away at her – hardly surprising – and the need to flush her kidneys was growing ever more urgent, but she tried desperately to keep some control.

There'll be a way out. There has *to be a way out. All I have to do is find it.*

Yes, that was all. Simple really. *I mean, what's all the fuss about? I'll just use the knife I have up my sleeve or those superpowers I keep secret and bingo, I'm loose.*

But that was a panic thought, a thought that told her she was powerless, and Eve just wouldn't accept that. *There'll be something ...*

First up then, where was she?

Well, taped to a chair, by what felt like an entire roll of gaffer. She tried to flex her arms and legs, but there was no joy there – just that tiny amount of give, then nothing. More around her stomach, presumably wrapped around the chair back. *But no gag, nothing across my mouth. What does that mean?*

It meant this ...whoever he is ...didn't think he needed to bother keeping her quiet. There was no need for that. Wherever she was, screaming for help didn't seem to be an option.

So then, where *was* she?

She looked to her left. Three foot or so away there was a door through which the nutter had vanished to do his number one. There was something right at the periphery of her vision that she couldn't quite make out; a box like structure with a hood of some sort. She looked to her right, extending her neck as far as she could. A foot away, a sink with cupboards underneath. Above that, a window. It was dark outside.

I'm in a kitchen, she realised. *Somewhere isolated.* How much did that help? Not much at all. But there was that window above the sink. She could break that, get out, run to the police ...

Right, and it'd all end happily ever after. Maybe not for Laura, but modern medicine could do wonders these days. Skin grafts and the like. Oh, and by the way, what is she *doing here?*

Eve had no idea, and no time to wonder. She had to get out, and she had to get out while that bastard was washing his germ laden hands. Fifteen seconds …how long's he been gone? At least double that. *Got to get a move on, Eve.*

And I do that how, exactly? I don't know if you've noticed, but –

Shut up, little Eve, and there was a thing; Sarah Voice was back. *Yeah, taped to a chair, got it. Now you* may *be fixed, but is the chair?*

Eve closed her eyes – if nothing else it blotted the sight of Laura's devastated features – and concentrated, trying to remember. *When I woke up, when I "came round" or whatever, I panicked, didn't I? Hardly surprising, who wouldn't, don't blame yourself, I heard nothing but the crackle of the tape and the …*

The 'thump-thump' of the chair legs beneath me.

Well done, exclaimed Sarah Voice. *And during your dream about the dog, you felt yourself turning, didn't you? Suppose that was him, Mr Nutjob, doing that so you could get a look at Laura. Maybe you were facing the other way around before. So no, the chair isn't* fixed, *is it? Which means –*

"Which means I can get the fuck out of here," she whispered, opening her eyes. She glanced at the window. A foot and a half, maybe. Eighteen inches. *Crab the chair to the sink, smash the chair apart, use one of the legs to break the window, and run like the gingerbread man.*

Oh, there are so many holes in this plan ...

It's not a plan at all. It's nowhere near a plan. But I think it's my only chance ...

Straining every rebellious muscle in her body, Eve sat as far forward as she could, trying to generate some momentum, trying to take the weight of the chair on her ankles, hoping to crab her way sideways to the sink ...

It was, of course, hopeless. She got no further than a quarter of an inch before the tape pulled her back. There was no way she could throw weight onto her legs – and even if she could, what then? They were strapped to this fucking kitchen dining chair right up to her knees. Even if she could throw her weight (such as it was) forward, she'd simply topple over and smash her face on the floor.

The panic which had threatened before now overcame, and she started thrashing about as much as she could, weeping hopelessly. She was, it seemed, totally helpless. Helpless, and at the mercy of some crazy, mad bastard who thought it was funny to recreate a play in his kitchen and throw acid in people's faces.

To compound it all, Eve's thrashing and panic made her lose control of her bladder, which voided itself in a gush. As she felt the wetness spread, she cried harder.

Please God, she found herself thinking. *Please God, don't make it hurt too much.*

*

Sarah awoke from a thin, uneasy sleep with a start. For a second, she'd thought she'd heard a key in the lock. "Eve?" She called into the not yet light morning.

No answer. Of course, no answer. There wasn't going to be an answer, was there? Because her sister was missing.

Missing. Like people on TV, like the news reports you see. Sobbing relatives with cameras rammed in their faces, reporters pleading for people with information to contact their local police. Like those poor bastards whose daughter was snatched, never to return. Would that be her soon? Probably. Eve was, after all, famous. And what was better that a Missing Person Story? A *famous* Missing Person Story! Who *wouldn't* love that? How soon before the BBC or Sky or whoever came knocking, their cameras zooming straight into her eyes, waiting for the tears to fall?

I think you may be focusing on the wrong thing here.

Quite right, but it was – Sarah checked her watch – just after six, she was alone in her sister's house, her neck and back hurt from the time she'd spent on Eve's sofa, she was in a state of low, nipping terror, and she did not have a *clue* what to do next.

How soon should I leave it before calling Steve? It'll be an hour and a half before he wakes for work. Should I ring him now? Is it too early? Should I have rung him last night? Do I beg him to come down here and keep me company? Do I go back home to him? What do I do? What do I actually do?

What she needed to do, it seemed, was to take a leak. Then maybe shower. Grab some coffee, get her brain in gear. Then she could think about her practicalities.

She stood up too quickly having made these conclusions, and for a moment the world ran away, fading into gray, a low rumble in her ears. She felt her knees buckle and shot out a hand in reflex to steady herself. It found the coffee table and the pile of magazines she'd placed on it, which scattered to the floor. The arm that supported her jittered wildly, as if she was receiving a low voltage electric shock, but it supported her until the haze cleared and she had some confidence in the fact her legs would keep her upright. When she felt as good as she could under the circumstances, she made her way out of the room and up the stairs.

It was while Sarah was standing under the hot water spray that something suddenly occurred to her.

The smaller constable had asked, "Is there anyone with you?" She, of course, had said she was alone. Which she was. But he'd gone on to ask, "Is there anyone you can call?" She, of course, had said no, her husband was in Manchester (which he was) where he ran his own business (which he did) ...but that didn't mean she had *no one* to call, did it?

"I can give you Jon's number if you like," Eve had said (or something close to that), her mouth pulled in that naughty, impish smile. If truth be told (and at a little after six in the morning, there wasn't room at the Inn for lies), Sarah had been a little tempted. Not much, not enough to actually take Eve up on the offer, but Jon seemed a nice bloke, he was good looking, and it would be someone to pass the time with ...*I mean, everybody did a little light flirting from time to time, didn't they? Doesn't make them bad people ...*

But she hadn't needed Eve to give her Jon's number, had she? Sarah already had it. It was logged in her mobile's memory, from when he'd called a couple of days ago. "Hi, is that Sarah – Eve's sister?" He'd said. "I'm Jon. Remember me? Your brother-in-law? Listen, I think Eve's in a bit of a fix. She may need you around."

There'd been more, of course – he hadn't been as stark as that – but that was the gist. And he'd met her off the train two days later, helped her navigate the Tube, witty, charming, handsome …and concerned about a woman he wasn't blood related to.

Sarah turned the water off and rubbed herself down with a towel. *I'll call Jon. His number will be in my phone. Then I'll get him the hell over here.* Then *I'll call Steve.*

Feeling a little better now that she had a plan (of sorts), it was only as she was zipping up her jeans that a question formed in her mind.

How the hell did he get my mobile number?

*

"I smell a pissy tramp," said the madman from behind her left ear. Eve said nothing. She couldn't think of a thing to say. In truth, she just wanted to fall asleep or get knocked unconscious – anything so she didn't have to confront the reality of what was happening.

"Now, I'm not accusing anyone," said the Devil as he walked in front of her. Eve dropped her head as low as it would to avoid looking at him, but a gloved right hand reached out and tucked itself under her chin, forcing her to look upwards. A faint dawn was creeping through the kitchen window and she could make out much, much more than she wanted to see. Through the slits of the ski mask Eve saw that

Satan had dark blue eyes that flicked here and there constantly and a small, pursed mouth. *Great description. When you get out of here you can take that to the police and they'll have this guy in custody in thirty seconds flat.* "What did he look like, Ms Rogers?" "Dark blue eyes and a small, pursed mouth." "Jesus, that's Madman O'Malley! Calling all cars! Calling all cars!"

Yeah, right. It's obvious you'll get out of here, isn't it?

"I mean," Lucifer went on, more to himself than anyone else, "it could have been either of you. Yeah, the Jock Wop is out for the count, but – and here's a thing you won't learn on the Discovery Channel – just because you're unconscious don't mean you can't pee yourself. Or drop a cable. In fact, you are *more* likely to do those things in that state because you have no motor control. Your bladder and your sphincter can do pretty much what they will. And *somebody's* has."

He withdrew his hand. Eve kept her head level (even though it hurt her neck) and kept her eyes on the mad bastard as he kept talking, strutting left and right, insanely reminding her of Foghorn Leghorn from those old Warner Brothers cartoons. *Any minute now he's going to say, "Ah say, ah say – BOY!"*

"I admit and accept my culpability in this matter," he said, sometimes to Laura, sometimes to Eve, "it would be wrong of me not to. My mother always used to say, 'Son,' because she could never remember a name, 'son, when you have done wrong, and you have been caught out, you must hold your hand up and admit it.'" Then, crouching low to Laura (who didn't flicker an eyelid, so far under was she and Lord how Eve envied her), "She's not dead, by the way. She just doesn't say that anymore. Mostly because, last night, I crept into her room while she slept and sewed her lips shut with catgut." Then, with horrifying liquid speed he scooted over to Eve, face to face, and she flinched. "I'm sorry, *that was a lie!*" He screamed into her face. "I never did that *at all!* It would be *impossible* to do that to a sleeping woman!" In a more normal tone, "Not without her waking up, anyway. So no, I didn't sew her mouth up with catgut. Sorry. But I did kill her." Now he was right up close, his voice soft, seductive, and Eve couldn't take it anymore. She closed her eyes, screwed them shut. "I taped her nose and mouth closed. Not last night, I was busy with you last night, but not long ago. Not here either, at her own home. I watched. She did a very funny dance, then her face went all red, then she stopped dancing and her face went all blue. It was a fun way to pass the time.

"But," he went on, his voice receding and then growing louder as he resumed his ludicrous strut around the kitchen, "this isn't addressing the issue. The issue being, of course, *who made the smell?* The *other* issue being, of course, what do we *do* about it? Potty training, you see, is based on basic aversion therapy – both in humans and in animals. I'm very well read, aren't I? If a person or an animal makes lemonade or chocolate in the wrong place, they must be made to realise that it is bad. So you make an aversion to it. You point at the puddle or the brown Mr Whippy and you make an angry noise, or maybe give a light slap – then you place whatever made the mess where you'd *like* it to do its business in the future and make nice friendly noises. Or give it a treat. Whatever. You associate something bad with a bad time and something good with a Bonio. Eventually the whatever it is learns and you're not wandering around with a bottle of Stardrops anymore. Peace reigns. So somebody here made a smell, which means *somebody here must be punished.* Must be taught to never do it again."

Eve finally understood what the phrase "her blood ran cold" meant. She understood *exactly* what it meant. Her eyes popped open, and there he was, right in front of her. "Otherwise," he said, "we're just going to be drowning in the stuff. Aren't we, Eve?"

Nothing came out of her mouth except a thin layer of drool. She started shaking. *Please God,* she found herself thinking again, *don't make this hurt too much.*

"We'll play a game," the madman said. "Just you and I. This game is called *Truth or Consequences,* just like the one they used to have on TV. I'm going to ask you a question, and you're going to answer. Tell the truth, and you'll be okay. Tell a lie, and you won't be. Got that?"

Answer? How? I can't talk, I'm too terrified to talk!

Unable to speak, she somehow managed a nod. "Good," said the small pursed mouth behind the mask. "Let me get my prop. Can't do a show without props." He vanished from her sight, off to her right, and once more Eve was left staring at Laura's shattered face. *Poor bitch. I'm sorry, Laura. But ...what was that H.G. Wells line? Something about survivors envying the dead, or in this case the unconscious? Yeah. I envy you right now.*

Then the maniac was back, those dark eyes glittering with hectic joy. "Didn't take long, did it? I'm my own ASM, I got everything to hand. So, Eve," he went on in a gameshow host kind of voice, "round one, question one. This for one hundred pounds; who pissed themselves?"

Tell the truth and you'll be okay, they're the rules, she thought. She opened her mouth and tried to speak when the creature raised his right hand into view.

The vaguely growing morning light glinted on the kitchen knife he held.

Blind panic overtook her again. Her brain locked, only capable of repeating the words *ohgodohgodohgod* over and over in a mantra. The shakes increased. "Eve," he asked. "Have to hurry you."

He's going to stick me with that thing, ohgodohgodohgod, he's going to stab me …

"Eve? You're running out of time. Once more; who pissed themselves?"

No, she heard Sarah Voice say, but even she was scared. *He's not going to hurt you. Remember? "Tell the truth and you'll be okay. Tell a lie and you won't be."*

"Eve?" A titter. "Would you like to phone a friend?"

She barely heard him. She kept looking at the knife. He held it rock steady. She, however, was twitching like a leaf in a gale. *Eve,* said Sarah Voice again. *Just tell the truth, find the strength to say "Me," and you'll be okay. Go on, you can. You can!*

Eve's mouth dropped open a little more, another line of spittle flecking her chin. "M-m-m" she stuttered, then hitched in as much air as she could and was about to shout *ME* to the heavens, when Sarah Voice shrieked in her mind. *No, it's a trick! SHUT UP! IT'S A TRICK!*

Eve clamped down – just – on what she was about to say. "Sorry Eve," said the bad man, "Could you speak up? Didn't quite catch that on the mic."

It's a trick, a trick, shut up say nothing, just a trick, babbled Sarah Voice. *Aversion therapy. Make them associate bad things with doing their waste in the wrong place. You say "me" and he cuts you to stop you doing it again.*

"Eve," he droned, "if you don't answer I will have to accept it was you who made the pissy smell and act accordingly."

Say it was Laura. Say it was her. Get him to cut her, not you.

Almost as impossible at it seemed, Eve felt even more horror at this. *No! I can't!*

You can, said Sarah Voice. *You* can, *because it's her or you. And look at her, look at that badly tarmacked road that passes for her face now. Who'd notice one more cut? And she's off on another world, she probably won't even feel it. Whereas you ...oh yeah, you'd feel it all right. You'd feel it good.*

I can't ...I can't sit here and ...

Okay then. Tell the truth and suffer the consequences. Get your *blood spilled instead of her. Instead of the woman who won't even notice and who, by the way, almost certainly fucked your husband.*

"Five seconds, Eve. Then I must have an answer or you pay the penalty."

What you going to do, Eve? What you going to do? What you going to do?

"And your time is ...*up.* Eve, who pissed themselves?" The knife came closer, right up to her eyes. *My eyes.* The knife was everything. The knife was the world.

"Laura!" screamed Eve. 'It was Laura! Laura! *LAURA!"*

The knife was withdrawn, and a soft, reflexive look came over the dark blue eyes. "In answer to the question *who pissed themselves,* Eve Rogers, you answered – and right on the buzzer – Laura." The knife was away from her line of sight now. She was safe. She'd condemned the other woman, but she was safe. That was all that mattered. She was safe. "Do you want to change that answer?" Eve shook her head. "Are you sure?" Eve nodded. "The question was *who pissed themselves,* and you said, *Laura.* And Eve – that was *the WRONG ANSWER!"*

He flung himself at her, the knife held high in front of him. It stopped less than an inch from her left eye. In a perfect stasis of terror, Eve found she couldn't even look away. She was locked, frozen. *He's going to blind me,* she thought, almost hysterically. *He's going to blind me.* Again, she found herself praying for the pain not to be too great.

"You see," he said, but all she could see was the knife. It was at least a hundred feet long, maybe twice that wide. "I could *smell* it was you. Actually, I didn't even need that. There's a fucking big puddle around your feet. Do you think I'm *blind*, Eve? Is *that* what you think of me?"

No, but I think I'm *going to be blind any second now ...and what* then? *What do I do* then? *Please, God ...PLEASE, God ...*

"But one thing I *do* know now, which is good, every day's a school day, is that you'll do *anything* to save yourself. You'll shop *anyone* rather than take the blame. Not that it's really news, I already knew that about you – well, heavily suspected, shall we say, but now I've got evidence that will *stand up in a court of law!* You're a selfish woman, Eve. A selfish, stupid, evil woman. And what do we do to selfish, stupid evil women?" A pause, the knife retreated an inch or so, then; *"We cut them, of course! We cut them!"*

The knife came down, and Eve knew there was no stopping it this time, she knew it was over, he'd psyched himself up to the ultimate point, and that thing was going to pierce her eye, make it pop like a soap bubble. Where would it land? Would it flop onto her cheek like a grotesque party razzer? How much would it hurt?

A lot. It will hurt a lot.

But he didn't put her eye out. Instead he placed the knife along her cheekbone, held it, then pushed. A sharp, incisive pain – like a needle prick or a wasp sting – rammed home and made her hiss. She felt the knife burrow deeper, widening its point of entry, and the hiss became a cry – he was gouging her. Hot blood ran down her face. The knife hit bone, and there was a terrible squeak, almost the sound of polystyrene rubbing against tile. She cried out again.

Then he pulled downwards, literally slicing her skin. She felt tendons and nerves ripping. A lance of white hurt flashed through her, making her jerk. "Hush now," said the monster, "hush – and don't move, Eve, *don't move!* I know it hurts, but *don't move!* I may hit an artery." The creature dragged the knife down to her jawline. She could hear the patters of blood as they hit the tape around her waist. She could feel the raw, exposed skin on either side of the wound. *How deep has he cut? How deep has he cut? How much has he damaged?*

Then the Devil withdrew the knife, and held it up so they could both inspect the flecks of sinew that dangled from it. "That'll do for now," he said. "After all, it was only round one, only a hundred pound question – we've got lots more rounds to play." But that was all coming from the other side of the moon, his voice echoey and giant-like. She was going to faint again. *It took me thirty-eight years,* she thought over the hurt, *but I finally managed to faint – not once, but twice.*

But before she went under, she heard the man who now held the power of life and death over her say, "See you after the break."

Chapter Twenty-two

"Hold on, hold on," said a sleep fuzzy Jon down the phone. "Back up a bit, will you?"

Somehow Sarah kept patient. It was hard for her – Steve had said many times that she could stare at a bloody crossword for hours but if a person didn't get *exactly* what she meant at the very *second* she said it, Sarah would flip – but she managed it. *Remember it's six thirty, he's still three quarters asleep and he's hearing something he never expected to be hearing.*

"Eve didn't come back last night," she repeated. "She's still not here this morning. I called the police, they took her details, now I'm calling you."

"Right. Okay." A bit more life in him. Not much, but a bit. "Where are you?"

"At Eve's."

"Yeah. Okay" *Stop saying "okay" and do something useful, will you?* "Give me an hour - maybe an hour and a half – and I'll be there. Um …do you know if she actually did the show last night?"

"What do you mean?" asked Sarah.

"I mean, did she actually turn up? Or did she go missing before she got there?"

"I …" *Good question. Did* you *think of it?* "No idea. How would I find that out?"

"Phone the theatre. Hang on, no; there'll be no one there yet. Box office won't get in till eight or so. I'll call when I get to you." She could hear him moving about, drawers slamming. "I'm on my way. And Sarah?"

"Yes?"

"I'm not going to tell you not to worry, because you will anyway. And I'm worried too. But I am going to tell you that I'll do everything I can to find Eve. Okay?"

There he goes again. "Okay."

With a promise that he'd be there as soon as was humanly possible, Jon hung up. *Half six,* she thought. *Time to phone Steve.*

She sat on the sofa, then stood up again as she felt something under her. A copy of *The Puzzler* she'd bought the day before. Open.

She paid it no attention, flung it on the table, and scrolled through her phonebook until she saw HOME.

*

She let Jon in at a quarter to eight, perfectly fuming. Steve had listened, shocked, upset ("You should have called me the *minute* you got suspicious, Sarah,") and had then refused to get in the BMW and hightail it down there.

"You left it too late," he said. "I've got a meeting with the Cohen's about their stores. It's set for nine. I can't cancel it now."

Sarah couldn't speak for a while, so stunned was she. "Look," she said eventually, "tell them it's a family emergency. And that's no lie, is it?"

"No time. If I'm not there, someone else will get that contract. And it's huge. It's nine months money. I've *got* to go."

"But …I need you here." That, surely, would do it. In all their years together, Sarah may have uttered the phrase *I need you* maybe twice, and once had been naming an old George Harrison tune.

"No hon," he said, "you need me *here*. You need me at this meeting. You need me to make sure we've enough cash until next June. Now, I promise you, after the deal is done I'll head on down to you. I reckon I'll be out by eleven, could be with you – what? One? Two o'clockish?"

"Don't frigging *bother* yourself," she heard herself say, then hit the red DISCONNECT button, wishing she'd called on Eve's landline so she could slam the receiver down. There was something deeply unsatisfying about angrily ending a phone call without a slam.

Steve had, of course, called straight back. She, of course, had ignored it. He'd called three times after that, and she'd ignored them all. *Bastard*, she thought …but wasn't that why she loved him? No, not because he was a bastard, because he wasn't – not in the way that some other people's husbands were bastards. He was just a hard-headed, practical man, much like her father, who had a list of priorities and stuck by them.

A lot like she was herself, in fact. *Like calls to like,* she thought, as her mobile rang once more and she saw HOME CALLING in the display. *Some people say "opposites attract," but not me. I saw in Steve what I saw in my father and what I see in the mirror. Sensible, matter-of-fact, down the line thought processes. But the trouble is, Steve, something appears to have* changed. *The situation is no longer the same.*

No. Her kid sister was missing. Her only sister – her *only blood family* – was missing. That meant everything had altered, *so frig the Cohen's, and frig the money and shift your frigging arse and get down here!*

She ignored the phone and found herself wandering in circles. She found herself unable to stop until the doorbell rang.

"Sorry I'm late," said Jon as he tumbled in. He'd obviously left in a hurry – hair corkscrewed and unwashed, clothes badly matched, all out of breath. "I called in at the station, see if there was any news."

"Was there?" Insane, they'd have surely let her know, but she couldn't help her spirits rising a bit.

"No, sorry," said Jon. "Her description's out, they're reviewing the CCTV tape from around the theatre, they've spoken to the director and producer, so yes, we know Eve did do the show.

But aside from that …"

"We're nowhere," Sarah finished.

"Maybe, maybe not. There'll be *something,* won't there? Something *somebody's* missed. We've just got to find out what."

"Oh," Sarah asked, and though she hated that cranky tone in her voice she was powerless to stop it. "How, exactly?"

"Don't have a bastard clue," Jon said, either totally oblivious to her tone or choosing to ignore it. "Listen, you look wrecked. Get *any* sleep?"

"A bit."

"Go in, sit down, I'll make coffee. I need some."

He put his hands lightly on her shoulders and guided her to the living room doorway, then made his way into the kitchen. Sarah plodded to the sofa and sat, then stood up as she heard the crackle of paper. A copy of *The Puzzler* she'd picked up the day before.

She paid it no attention and flung it on the table.

Maybe he's right, she thought. *Maybe two heads are better than one.*

*

"Hard bloody work, isn't she?" Carl asked.

No, it wasn't Carl. It was a woman. And she didn't say *hard bloody work, isn't she,* she said, "Eve?"

Eve woke up ...no, Eve *came to,* and there she was, once more in the kitchen, once more strapped to the chair. Her lower back muscles were groaning, her ripped face screaming. There was more light now – enough for her to make out the peeling, water damaged wallpaper, the murky tiles. *Place must give up its five star rating soon. Really, next year I must try somewhere different.*

"That's you, isn't it?" the woman's voice said. It was cracked, awful, like someone drowning in phlegm. "Eve? Oh, Jesus ...he got you too. Jesus." Then a sob.

Eve looked straight ahead. Laura was awake ...nearly. Or as awake as it was possible for her to get. Her head was lolling on one shoulder, and when she spoke Eve could see the muscles working through the burned gaps in her olive skin. She tried not to recoil. *By the by, how good do you reckon you look?* The gouge on her left cheek blared in pain ...but there appeared to be no more bleeding. *How long do you reckon you were out for? Long enough for the blood to clot? Or did that mad fucker clean you up?*

"Laura," she said, then stopped. Her mouth was as dry as a bone, her tongue swollen. *Dehydrating. Hardly surprising. When did I last have some water? Just after curtain down last night ...what, ten, ten fifteen? And it's now* ...she couldn't make out the time, and there was no clock in her eyeline, but gauging by the light filtering in through the unwashed window it could be eight thirty, maybe nine in the morning. *Eleven hours or so without a drink. And all the adrenaline I've been pumping ...no wonder I sound like someone with cerebral palsy.*

Laura flicked her eyes up to Eve's. Then, incredibly, she tried to smile. It obviously hurt, but she tried anyway. "We got ourselves in a fix, didn't we?"

"Yeah." She swallowed hard, trying to generate some moisture. "What happened to you?"

"Dunno. Last thing I know – last thing I remember – was leaving the flat. Ages ago. A week. Maybe longer. Someone – him - hit me from behind. Then I was here." She was losing focus, fading again. Hardly surprising. *A week, maybe longer, chained to a radiator. Jesus fucking wept.*

For the first time, fear vanished, and a perfect flare of hatred for the man in the ski mask took its place. *If I get out of this I will kill him with my own bare hands.*

"Was it the same with you?" Laura asked, drifting off.

"Laura," she said as loudly as she could. The rip in her face opened wide and a small trickle of blood leaked down. She saw the other woman wince at it. "Stay awake, okay? *Stay awake!*"

Shouting was agony, more blood, but it did the trick. Laura flinched and banged her head on the door.

"Ow, *motherfucker!*"

If Laura smiling had been incredible, what happened next bordered on the miraculous. Eve laughed. It opened that ragged slit in her face even more, but she couldn't help it. Laura goggled at her, then joined in. That was clearly torture for her, but she did it anyway.

"'What do you know?" Asked Eve.

"About *him*, d'you mean?" Eve nodded. "Nothing. Apart from the fact he's mad. Apart from the fact he sprayed me with something and burned half my fucking face off." That last choked into another sob. "Is it…is it *bad*, Eve? *Is it?*"

What do I do? Tell her the truth? Lie? Oh, and when do I tell her about how I gave her up? "Yes. It's bad." Christ, her tongue was nearly suffocating her. She needed water badly, she needed it soon. To hell with that, she needed it *now.*

"Thought so. Hurts like fucking hell." Another sob. *My pretty, pretty face*, she was thinking. Eve could read it. *My pretty, pretty face that got me so much, that got me so far. Ruined.*

You want to think about your own *face*, Sarah Voice spoke up. *And about what else Mr Mad of Madtown is going to come up with, no matter what he's forgotten.*

What do you mean, forgotten?

Oh, use your eyes, little Eve.

Eve blinked that away. It wasn't what was important. What was important was that he – whoever *he* was – was somewhere else, Laura was awake, and they needed to …needed to …

Well, pool information.

"Why?" Eve asked.

"Why what?"

"Why did he do that? Your face."

"Because he's a mad fucker, that's why."

"What did he ask before he did it? Did he make you play some sort of game?"

Laura thought, and thought hard. "Yeah," she said at last. "Bogus gameshow thing, like *Millionaire*. Phone a friend shit. Kept asking if I loved him."

"You said no?"

"I fucking did *not*," Laura exclaimed. "I fucking told him I loved him with all my fucking *heart*. I told him that I loved him and I'd love him *forever!* He had *acid,* girl! I told him what I thought he wanted to hear! *He had fucking acid!* But …but it wasn't …what he …and he sprayed …and the fucking *pain* …"

She was so close to losing it. In truth, so was Eve. It wouldn't take much for this thin veneer to crack again. But it couldn't be allowed. Not yet. "I know hon, I do. Okay, yeah, he's mad, mad as a snake who's married a hosepipe, mad

mad as a box of frogs," the words were tumbling, painful in her dry mouth, but ...well, time was short, wasn't it? She didn't know how she knew that, but she knew it anyway. That mad bastard wouldn't let them alone for long. "But why *us*? Why us *together*? It can't be just coincidence, can it? *Can it?*"

She saw the look that crossed Laura's wreck of a face ...then heard *his* voice from her left. "No. I daresay it can't be."

He crossed into her field of vision, dressed just the same, a nightmare vision come to life. He stood between them, smiling. "The question is, can you guess your captor's name? You do that and I'll let you go."

Like hell you will, Eve thought ...but then stopped cold.

No matter what he's forgotten.

Eve, strapped to a chair, arms, legs and stomach bound. The Nutter, before her, between the two women. Laura, chained to the radiator. By her arms.

But not by her legs. They were free.

*

Maybe Sarah shouldn't have found it so odd, but having Jon around was sort of ...well, comforting. Even if he wasn't able to do much – and it didn't seem as if he could – just having another person there, someone who could understand, helped.

A little, anyway.

"Okay," he said again and he swilled down his third coffee in just over an hour, "this is what we have. Eve leaves the theatre after the play, at about half ten. Walks to the Tube - Tottenham Court Road's the nearest, so we'll say it's that one. After that …"

"After that, we've no idea."

"No." Then he sighed heavily and flopped back on the armchair. "Who am I kidding anyway? I'm a cameraman, not Sherlock Holmes." He rubbed his red eyes. "I'm not even a very *good* cameraman. Competent. Still, Carl always said competency was a meal ticket in this industry. Mostly he was right. You turn up, do the job, never miss a deadline …that's what people are looking for, mainly. Genius costs money."

"Fascinating," muttered Sarah, even though it wasn't. What's worse, it was so far from being germane to the issue she could scream. But she managed to keep herself under control – just – by reminding herself Jon was floundering as much as she was.

"It is if you're me. Or my bank manager." Then, with a sudden burst of energy that Sarah found alarming he jumped to his feet. "What's happened to her, Sarah? *Where is she?*"

Sarah was just about to snap well; *of course I know the answer to both of those things, obviously. I*

I just thought I'd string things out a bit. I mean, I've got a little crush on you and thought it would be nice if we could spend the day together. But again, she kept her temper. Instead, she said, "I think someone grabbed her."

There. It was out, in the open, the thought that had been festering inside her for nearly twelve hours. Jon stopped his pacing and looked at her. "What?"

"Look, what *else* is it going to be?" Sarah asked, standing and looking straight at him. "If she were to …I don't know …*die* suddenly – outside the theatre, on the Tube or whatever – she'd have been *found,* right?" It was horrible having to think these things, even worse having to say them …but didn't *somebody* have to come out with it? Didn't *somebody* have to (as they said) think the unthinkable? Jon's eyes widened as he looked at her. "But she's not been *seen* for about eleven hours. So something …unnatural happened, right? That fits the clues." She saw Jon looking around, taking in the stacks of magazines on the tables, including the one open at the top of the pile. "Yeah, that's right," she went on. "That's the sort of mind I have. If it wasn't *natural* causes that stopped her coming home, or she didn't *want* to come home – if she suddenly decided to take a plane to Amsterdam to pick tulips – then someone had to *prevent* her coming home."

"Jesus," said Jon. *Has he really not considered that? Sarah wondered. How could he exclude it?*

Because not everyone sees the world the way you do, that's why. Eve didn't – doesn't - for example. Things fit *in your world, you do the corner pieces first, then the straight edges, then supply the middle. There are white blocks you fit the letters into, across and down, and they all* fit, *nice and snug – always supposing you understood the clues.*

"Okay, I could be wrong. Maybe Eve did just decide it was time for a holiday, or she had a weird fit and just couldn't take anymore, like that guy …the one who does the quiz thing."

"Stephen Fry," Jon muttered. Then, stronger, "Doesn't fit Eve, though. Fry's got a history of depression and anxiety, and he had some bad reviews. Eve hasn't, and her reviews were off the chart."

"Yeah, I know. But you said yourself she was …how did you put it? 'In trouble.' When you rang."

"And she was. She was …disconnected, a bit anyway. Not quite Eve, if you get me. But, she'd been through a bad time with Carl dying, and she was about to go back on stage …"

"There was more to it, though. Otherwise you wouldn't have rung me." *Oh, and don't forget to ask him how he got your number. Your* mobile *number.*

"Yeah ...there was ... Jon sat down again, then lifted his left buttock, reached onto the cushion and retrieved an open copy of *Puzzler* magazine. It rested absently on his lap. "Look, it's hard to say. I went for lunch with her and ...she was sort of fine, if you get me. Chatty, smiling a lot ...but there was a kind of ...how do I put this? *Cloud,* I think. Yeah, a kind of cloud over her. She looked ...*heavy.* She'd not put on any weight, but she seemed *weighed down.* I just felt like I had to call someone, get her some support."

Hold on then, Sarah thought. *Maybe I've been following the right clues to the wrong word. The more I hear from Jon, the more the I'm-about-to-do-a-runner theory gains weight. She's "not herself." "Heavier." "A cloud." Then the First Night, and she's a sensation, toast of London, everybody wants a piece of her ...might that have had the* opposite *effect to calming her down? Suppose that was enough to tip her over the edge entirely ...*

For the first time, a horrible word emerged in Sarah's mind. She tried to suffocate it, but it just wouldn't go.

That word was *suicide.*

You've been looking at the wrong piece of the box, Sarah found herself thinking against her will. *You've been thinking someone had grabbed Eve with remarkably little evidence, because that way you thought there'd be a way of getting her back. But a complete nervous breakdown? In someone as creative as* Eve? *Don't they say the more imaginative the person, the more spectacular the collapse? And she's an actress. A lover of the dramatic. And what's* more *dramatic than suicide?* Really? *What's the biggest show-stopper of them all?*

Hey, how did *he get your mobile number?*

That last thought was so abrupt, so counter to the terrible line of thought she was pursuing, that she was just about to ask it when the landline rang.

They both stared at it without speaking. She didn't know about Jon, but her own heart told her it was bad news. It *had* to be bad news. She couldn't move. She didn't want to hear bad news.

Eventually it was Jon who walked across the room and picked up the cordless. "Hello, Jon Wilson," he said. Then he listened. "Okay. Yeah. Understood. With you in …" he checked his watch, "fifteen. Twenty at the latest. Yeah." He hung up then, and Sarah knew from the look on his face that this wasn't going to be a happy ending.

"Police," he said, trying to keep his voice level. "They've got something they want us to look at."

Chapter Twenty-three

Somehow, Eve managed not to scream, *Laura, kick the bastard in the balls!*

She wanted to, oh yes, she *very much* wanted to, she wanted to see that insane ogre hurt, hurt properly, the way he'd hurt them, but somehow she choked it down. Suppose Laura did just that, anyway? Suppose she gathered up all her strength and fetched Ski Mask a monstrous kick in the nads? What then? He'd just roll about on the floor for a bit and they'd still be helpless, and then, when his pain went away, he'd extract his revenge.

His *terrible* revenge.

Or – both best case *and* worst case scenario – suppose Laura did strike him a good one, he collapsed, hit his head on the floor and died? Yeah, that'd be great. Eve found she was very able to get on board with the concept of him dying ...but what would happen to *them* as they sat, immobile, in a kitchen with his corpse? Slowly starve to death while they chatted over old times? Would she finally get to ask Laura about her relationship – if any - with Carl?

No, she told herself. *I've got to keep this a secret. It's something he's forgotten – he's mad, after all – and there just may be a way to use it. All I have to do is figure out how.*

Yeah, that was all.

A strange sort of barking laugh came out of her throat at that, and Ski Mask looked sharply at her. "Eve? Something you'd like to share?"

Then something else – not fully formed, but there regardless – almost danced in front of Eve's vision. It skipped away before she could reach it …but not far, just out of arm's reach. Something about this murky daylight. *Something different …no, not different. Just something I can see. Or* nearly *see.* "No,£ she said. "Just a cough. Thirsty."

"Yeah, yeah," said their captor dismissively. "Everyone's thirsty. So, what would you like? Evian? A nice, cold bottle of something you can get from a tap for free that'll cost you £2.50 from Spar? You want a runner to get it for you?" He took a step towards her, and Eve thought she could make something out about him – something familiar - that she couldn't quite place. "That's what you do, isn't it? Send someone for your posh water? Get someone to hold a brolly over you when it rains on location. A driver to ferry you from trailer to set even when they're only *three yards apart!* What do you do when you have a shit, Eve? Get some poor bastard on work experience to wipe your arse for you?" He turned, staring down at Laura. "And *you?* You don't even look at the miserable wretch who gives you what you demand. You just put your hand out and *expect* it to be there! But you can't do that now, can you? I've seen to that, yessiree Bob, I've sorted that little *Countdown* conundrum good and proper. That's what I do," he ranted on, a thin line of spittle flying from his lips, "I fix things, I sort them out. I'm what they call an 'unsung hero,' an invisible puppeteer, a manipulator, a prestidigitator – I can get you looking at the object, not where my hands are! I *misdirect!*" He took a step backwards, now addressing them both, "But here, now, is where I get credit. Here, now, with you both as my audience, I step forward from the dark and *finally take my bow!*"

Of course, that's just what he did, being insane. He bent forward from the waist, flourishing his arms to the side like some badly crucified heretic. It took everything Eve still had left to stop from screaming, *Laura, now! Kick him! Kick him in the face!*

"Anyway, where was I?" He asked, straightening up. "Oh yeah, in the kitchen with Dinah. Dinah Sheridan. Now there was a talent, Eve. You ever work with her?" Eve slowly shook her head. "Great actress – oh, sorry actor. Or is it actress again? Terms go in and out of fashion so quickly these days, don't they? I tell you the one

Whore. Hey – don't misunderstand, not in the sexual sense," then with a growl of distaste to Laura, "Well …" and back to Eve; "but the whole role play thing, with me? Be a different person on different nights, different costume, different wig, different voice – that's pretty much what a whore does. And, of course, you *both get paid for it!* I had an idea once," he kept darting in and out of her sight, meaning she could finally look at Laura. The other woman was drifting off again, her eyes glassy. Eve frowned at her. Laura didn't respond. Eve coughed slightly, and Laura's dazed head swung to her. Keeping silent, Eve looked down at Laura's legs. The other woman didn't respond. Eve did it again with as much of a jerk of her head as she dared. Nothing came back, no cognition at all. *She's out for the count.*

Then Ski Mask was back between then, dragging a kitchen chair. He reversed it and sat astride, cowboy style. "Living theatre, my idea was. We'd take a troupe of actors to Amsterdam and set 'em up in a shop window in the red light area, and we'd get punters in for – I don't know, twenty euros a pop maybe – and the punters would make the actors do *anything* they wanted." His dark blue eyes darted from woman to woman. "Now, don't you think that'd be magic? No one's thought of that, it's genius, it's brilliant, it's up there with the inventor of sliced bread looking down at a loaf and thinking, *hmmm, I can't be arsed cutting that myself.*" Then, with a low, confidential voice, he said, "I am a visionary, and visionaries are often overlooked in their own lifetime." More brashly, "Of course, no one saw the value of that idea, but I'm sure you knew that, didn't you? You saw that coming, both of you, you recognised the developing theme, you understand, I know, when *subtext* becomes *text*. There will be lots of this while we live together, lots of great ideas that are ahead of their time. So, as leader of this workshop – and I thank you all for coming, great to see you all – I invite questions from the floor."

Eve couldn't think of one. She was too busy hearing the words *while we live together* roll around her head. *How long is this horror show going to last? On top of that, he's kept Laura here for maybe two weeks. This show could be in for a long run.*

Laura, however, proved herself more in the world that Eve had thought by saying, slowly and indistinctly, "Why don't you just fuck off and die, you cunt?"

With that terrifying, liquid grace and speed, Ski Mask leaned forward and punched Laura flat in the face. There was a hideous crunching squelch, and as the Scots/Italian screamed in agony, Eve thought, *her nose. Fucker's broke her nose.*

"This is a family show,' said Satan, perfectly calmly, "and there's no smut before the watershed. Of course, *after* the watershed it's all going to be different, but for now …" He trailed off again, and more horrors flooded Eve's head. *Oh dear God, we're powerless …he can do anything he wants to us …*

On top of *that,* Eve saw that Laura was starting to thrash about. She was rattling those chains like an S&M Jacob Marley. But worse, she was staring to twitch her legs. If that madman noticed them …noticed what he'd forgotten …

"I've a question," she said, as loudly as her rasping throat would allow.

The Ski Mask turned full on to her. "Yes, Eve?"

"May we both have some water, please?"

"*JESUS!*" He exploded, standing, thrusting his head to hers. *Here it comes,* she thought. *It's time for my nose to shatter.* "It's all me, me, me, isn't it? I give you a home, I put a roof over your heads, and what do I get? What do *I* get? Any thanks and praise? *No!* Is that right and fitting? *No!* All I get is *GIVE ME MY FUCKING EVIAN!*" Then, abruptly, he calmed down again. "Well …no one goes away empty handed, do they. Okay. For playing, for being great contestants, you get some water. It's your consolation prize."

Ski Mask moved off to the sink, to Eve's right, allowing her a really good look at her fellow hostage's face. Laura was fading now, back into oblivion. *Thank God,* Eve thought. *At least she'll be spared the pain. And she'll stop thrashing those legs around.*

Water was running from the tap, but Eve couldn't see that far. She could only see Laura, and the after image of Ski Mask's mad eyes, like flashburn on her retinas.

Except he's not mad.

Again, she had to suppress a start. Any kind of sudden movement was a Very Bad Idea. *Of course he's mad. Who else but a madman would do what he's done?*

His eyes, think of his eyes. Manic. Darting.

Yeah, the eyes of a madman.

No, Eve. Think. Think! Not the eyes of a madman, the eyes of someone you've seen before …no, maybe not someone, but some tone you've seen before, some expression …

Then it came to her, and the horror was almost exquisite, almost orgasmic in its totality. His eyes …mad, flicking from here to there, focused …unfocused …but *in control.*

No. He's not mad. He's totally sane.

He's just acting mad. He knows every move in advance, he knows all his lines, he's properly rehearsed. He's one hundred percent in the moment.

He's an actor.

That was what she recognised about him. She'd been the same as Desdemona all those years ago, a pinwheel apparently spiralling where she would, nor' nor' west, but behind her affected mania there was control. In her mad eyes had been sanity. She'd made the whole thing up, she'd acted a part, and while to the audience she'd just been a loonie throwing rose petals around, to her fellow professionals she'd been just an actor doing a job.

And oh dear God, that is so much worse. A madman, yeah, that's bad …but someone who is so sane he can pretend *to be a madman …oh Lord, oh save my soul Lord, that's as bad as it gets.*

As if to confirm this, Eve heard two separate smashes of glass. The Ski Mask bounded before her, holding out a tumbler – no, a third of a tumbler, all that was left after he'd broken it against the sink. Jagged, lethal shards glinted feebly as they were tipped towards her.

"Ooops, daisies," the man said, and she looked very carefully at him, and yes, Eve was right. There was no madness there. Just the illusion of it. "I'm afraid I've been clumsy, I'm a butterfingers, I've made a boo-boo. Anyway, here's your water. Just be very, very careful as you drink it. I'll be careful too …but, you see,

I'm very nervous. I've never been this close to a star before." He made his hand shake crazily, as if he was electrocuted. "I'd hate to cut your pretty face even more than I have …at least by mistake." He giggled, making the glass judder even more. It was less than an inch from her mouth. "So …for two hundred pounds and the non-stick pans, how thirsty are you, Eve?"

She couldn't speak; not just was her throat suddenly drier than ever, but what little breath there was in her lungs just wouldn't expel. Instead she jerked her head spasmodically from side to side.

"I'm sorry," said the Not Mad at all Madman, "are you saying you're *not* thirsty?"

Eve's head jerked up and down.

"But," he went on regretfully – but not really regretfully – "I'm afraid I have to take your first answer. Those are the rules of the game, I'm afraid."

So saying, he ground the shattered tumbler into her mouth, ripping her lips, her gums and her chin to shreds. Fresh agony blighted her sight, and the world turned pure white.

Through it all, through the torture, she kept her mouth shut and her eyes open, fixed on Ski Mask's. There was no expression on his face. None at all. It was as dead as death itself, as dead as Carl's face had been when the monitors had finally flatlined. As dead as hers would undoubtedly soon be.

She didn't pass out. She stayed awake as the grinding broken glass frayed her face, she felt everything, saw everything. She stayed awake, in terrible hurt.

She stayed awake, and wished she were dead.

*

Right up until the Inspector (what was his name? Allen? Alby? Atlee?) slotted the disc into the player, Sarah was convinced she was going to have to formally identify her sister's body.

All through the silent drive from Eve's house to the police station (only ten minutes – fifteen at the outside – but to Sarah it seemed like forever), Sarah found herself repeating these words in her head; *yes sir, that's Eve. Yes sir, that's my sister.* She heard various officers saying, *we found her in the Thames this morning, a definite suicide* or, *she jumped off a motorway bridge* or, *she was in an alley with her wrists slashed; we found this note about her person.* She'd even seen the note, wrapped in one of those plastic wallets they used on TV to keep fingerprints off. It read, *I'm sorry, the pressure was just too much. At least I will be with Carl now. Please forgive me.*

Jon, to his credit, said nothing, made no attempt to comfort her, to reassure her. He didn't patronise or cajole her along. He let her fret as he concentrated (almost too hard) on driving safely. He was well under the speed limit, he left lots of room for other traffic, he didn't accelerate until the lights turned green. *He has something to concentrate his mind,* Sarah thought. *And so have I. I have to know exactly what I'll say when they pull that sheet back. Yes sir, that's Eve. That's my sister. I'm rehearsing, just like Eve.*

After that? Well, who knew? Something, anyway. Inquests, post mortems, funeral …then life going on again, she supposed.

They'd pulled into the station car park, and as Sarah had climbed out of Jon's Volvo she felt the world spin on its axis. The daylight grew brighter, then appeared to cloud over. *I'm going to faint,* she thought. *How interesting.*

But then Jon's hand was under her elbow, and she sagged onto him, unable even to clutch at him for support. "It's okay," she heard him say, and even though intellectually she knew he was whispering, his voice boomed and rolled like that of God Himself. "I've got you."

He held her until the world was right again – almost, it still seemed a little too bright to her – and, after she nodded that she could go on, he led her up the ramp and through the doors. After he gave their names to the officer on the desk, they were escorted into a small room by the Inspector whose name she just didn't quite catch. With Jon's help she managed to sit.

Any second now, she thought. *Any second now, he'll say "I'm afraid I have some very bad news for you, Mrs Brown. A body matching your sister's description has been found, almost certainly suicide, and we'd like you to formally identify it."* At which point she'd be taken down a long, lime green corridor where a cadaver lay on a slab, covered in a sheet (which this Inspector Who would turn back), and she would say, *yes sir, that's my sister. That's Eve,* just like she'd rehearsed.

Instead, he held up what appeared to be a DVD.

What the hell, Sarah thought. *Has he got a copy of that Film Four thing Eve did? Does he want me to sign it?*

"We got this from our CCTV control room a couple of hours ago," Inspector Uncertain Name said. "We believe it shows your sister being abducted. We'll be going public with an appeal for information at noon – though we'll hold back this footage for the time being. I want to show it to you in case you recognise anything, but before I do, I must warn you that it is unpleasant. If you feel like you don't want to see it, I understand completely. However, you may be able to make out something that we can't. Do you think you're able to watch this disc, Mrs Brown?"

Sarah felt them both – Jon and Inspector No Name – looking at her, but she was unable to speak. *Abducted? Did he say* abducted?

Then, *she may be alive!* Then, *I was right the first time!*

"Sarah," said Jon, "did you hear?"

"Yes," she said – or thought she said, her voice was so tiny. "I heard." Then, to the Inspector With No Name, "Please. Put it on."

It was footage the like of which Sarah had seen a hundred times on shows like *Crimewatch* or *World's Most Violent.* It was grainy, jumpy and almost impossible to watch.

The screen showed a high shot of an open air car park, apparently at the back of a Tube station, illuminated by orange streetlights. Maybe five people made their way from the station entrance and found their cars, drove off. Then last, and on her own, Eve. Despite the quality of the tape, Sarah recognised her immediately – that straight backed, determined walk, the one no one else on Earth possessed.

Little Grainy Jumpy Eve zig-zagged through the rows and found her Focus. She was pulling the keys from her bag when …

Sarah caught her breath and sat forward. Another figure, a man, A Grainy Jumpy Man, approached Eve from behind. Maybe he said something, because she half turned to him. Then he smashed his laced fists into the back on her sister's head and Eve fell to the ground.

"Jesus," someone in the room said, and after a second Sarah realised it was her.

Grainy Jumpy Man then dropped, pulled something from Eve's bag (keys?), picked her up, and propped her against the car door. *Anyone watching would think she was pissed,* Sarah thought. Then the man opened the car's driver side door and pulled the seat back. He bundled Eve onto the back seat, climbed in himself, and drove off.

The Inspector switched the monitor off. "I'm sorry," he said. "But was there anything you recognised?"

For a second, Sarah felt like saying, *How? There was barely enough definition to make out what actually happened.* "No."

"Are you sure? I appreciate how distressing this must be for you, but *anything,* anything at all would help."

Tears appeared to be pricking the corners of Sarah's eyes. "I'm sorry. No. But …Jesus, that *bastard.*"

The Inspector looked like he was about to say something else, but Jon interrupted. "Eve was targeted, wasn't she? This wasn't random."

"It appears not," said the Inspector, reluctantly. "We're working on the theory that it was someone who knew her, if not necessarily someone *she* knew. Miss Rogers is, after all, an actress, and that profession has been known to attract …well, *stalkers* to use the popular term."

Popular, Sarah thought. *What an odd way to describe it.*

"That man," said Jon, "that *bastard*, must've known where Eve parked up, must've known what time she'd get back from the theatre."

"It seems likely, yes," the policeman said. "He may have been tracking her movements for some time. From what we have from …" he shuffled some papers in front of him, "Mr Hughes, her director, she'd been making that journey for over a week now. He may have seen her in the play she was doing and followed her – more than once – before …well …"

"But to be so …" muttered Sarah, then the word she wanted escaped her, so she had to make do with another, much less fitting, "*brazen* about it …in a big, open space …with cameras …"

"He's confident," Jon said, before the Inspector could open his mouth. "Practised. He's probably done a million dry runs in his head before …" Then he looked away, staring at the ceiling. "I hope the fucker gets cancer. I hope he gets cancer and I'm in charge of the morphine."

"Between you and me and these four walls," the policeman said, "I agree with you, Mr Wilson. Right here, right now, I'd hang the little scrote myself and swing on his ankles. And if you repeat that, I'll deny it. But that's not what we should be discussing. The timecode on that put the abduction at 10.35 p.m.. It's now ten past eleven. Just over twelve hours since it happened. The car turned east out of the station, and we've got a team scanning the traffic cameras for a Ford Focus of that number travelling in that direction at that time. We'll find it, but it'll take time, and time may well be something we don't have a lot of. So," he continued, sitting forward, "if there *is* anything, Mrs Brown, anything *at all* you can help us with, we'd be very grateful."

"I didn't …there was nothing …" muttered Sarah.

"Would it help if I ran the disc again?"

No, not a bit. But what else can I do? What use *am I?*

"I'll give it a try," Sarah said, and the Inspector whose name she would never, ever be able to recall pressed PLAY.

*

Let me die, Eve thought over and over after the tumbler had been placed back on the sink, back out of her vision. *Let me die. I can't take this pain any longer.*

But she didn't die. She sat, strapped to her chair, very much alive as fresh blood dripped onto her lap, mixing with the maroon spots that had been left by her earlier mutilation.

How much damage, she thought again, as bitterly she reconciled herself to still breathing –

ragged, agonising breaths, but breaths nonetheless. *Bastard's ripped my mouth and chin apart ...are there any arteries there? Will I bleed to death? Please, let me bleed to death. Let me slide into the dark, like Carl. Maybe I'll even see him again.*

But there were no arteries where she was cut, she knew that, of course she did. And that not-mad-at-all fucker had been careful. Oh she was cut, she was bleeding, she was almost blind with pain ...but he'd been careful. He'd stopped just before the blood would *really* begin to spout, just as he had with the knife. Cut ...and cut deep, seemed to be his motto, but don't cut mortally. Yet.

Where was he? She didn't know. He'd gone off somewhere again, the way he seemed to between ...well, fits of torturing people. She and Laura were alone, and Laura didn't seem to be talking.

Where does he go? Eve wondered, deliberately giving herself a problem, a concrete question to concentrate on in some effort to ignore the pain ...not that it seemed to be working much, as there was quite a considerable amount of it. In addition to the fresh, sharp, stinging cuts in her mouth and chin, there was an uncomfortable burning sensation in the flap he'd cut down her cheek. Some sort of infection starting there, possibly. *I mean, I don't reckon he sterilised that ...that knife. Nor did he swab the wound down afterwards, did he? His hygiene leaves a little something to be desired. I mean, Christ, it's like a bad NHS hospital in here, germs flying around in packs like the Luftwaffe. So, to add to the ripped mouth and cheeks I could well be incubating tetanus or MRSA, like a little bonus prize.*

I wouldn't bother worrying about that, Sarah Voice said. *You'll most likely be dead before they get a chance to breed properly. Unless, of course, you work out a way to get out of here.*

Cheers for that, Eve answered through the low waves of suffering that rolled over her. *I could always rely on you to ...OOOOWWWWWWWWWW!*

A new problem presented itself. A stab of cramp, as intense as the glass or the knife that had shredded her features, rammed into her lower back. She arched herself as far forward as she could (which wasn't, of course, very far ...the tape saw to that), and clenched her teeth together to stop the scream escaping.

This was a bad idea, as her mangled teeth and gums shot out a lance of pain of their own at this, leaving Eve wracked with what appeared to be bright white steel bolts attacking her from her coccyx to her jaw. She jittered and jived, tears leaking down her cheeks, tears of hurt, tears of misery and angst, until some endless time later, her back decided to unlock.

Her face fell forward in relief, fresh droplets of blood spattering the shiny grey tape around her waist. *Oh God Jesus please thank You please Jesus no more Jesus God Mary please* ...Then, so savage and sudden that it almost made her laugh, *I would* kill *for a cigarette right now.* She tried to raise her head, and found it almost impossible; her neck muscles seemed to have no strength whatsoever. *Go on, Jesus, if You're looking on and fancy working a miracle, how's about it? Nothing fancy, nothing expensive, I'll take a Pall Mall, really. That'd be fine. Just lit and in my mouth ...I mean, what harm can it do me here? I got a bad case of dem ole no chin blues, might be incubating a nice little infection somewhere, my body's going into spasm, I've had nothing to eat or drink in quite a while and I've lost more blood (blood! Who'd have thought the old actress had so much blood in her?!) than I care to consider, so c'mon, what do You say? Just one lousy cig? Do You seriously think lung cancer's a concern of mine right now? It just might help me relax a little, to focus ...*

And that's just what you need to do, said Carl from the back of her mind. *Focus.*

As sudden and unexpected as the laugh (and that phantom craving, which seemed to never go away, just hide in the shadows and pop up every now and then, much like the mad bastard who had inflicted all this damage on her), Eve felt something else. *Rage.* Pure, unadulterated *venom,* anger like she'd never known before – even during the time when she'd imagined pummelling Carl into a pulp for leaving her. This was fury at its most potent, most clean, most terrifying.

You can go and fuck yourself back to whatever hole you climbed out of, you vicious cunt! You *did this to me! You're the one who led me to this place! You and your fucking clues …'whatever the piece is, do it', remember? Well I did, I took your fucking advice, the advice of my loving and caring husband! I* did *the fucker! And look what happened!* LOOK WHAT HAPPENED!

No, I - spoke up her long dead husband, but she cut over him.

If I'd followed my own *instincts I'd be at home now, at home with a full face, not taped to a fucking chair smelling of my own piss with most of my features lying in little clumps on my lap. If you had just the* fucking decency *to* stay dead *like any other corpse I wouldn't be in the worst pain of my life …if you hadn't …*

She stopped thinking such vile thoughts as what felt very much like a slap – not a hard slap, but a shocking one nonetheless – stung her right cheek.

I'm sorry, I'm sorry, said Carl, *I didn't want to, I didn't, I'd never hit you, but you were losing it, hon. I had to.*

She'd *felt* the slap. Eve *had* felt it. It was as real a pain as any on her face, any in her body. She started trembling …she felt cold. Oh, so cold.

I didn't get you here, Carl went on. *Please Eve, please, believe me. I did everything I could to stop you, everything I was capable of. I tried everything. There was nothing left I could do, and it wasn't enough. I tried and tried but I just couldn't make it clear. I knew, hon, I knew what was going to happen …*

You …knew …?

Yes, sort of.

Eve was still hunched forward in her chair, the chair that now seemed so much like her last resting place, the chair that was numbing her muscles and forcing the blood to sit in the wrong place for too long, and if Laura had awoken from her semi-catatonic state, she'd have been convinced the other woman was dead. Eve's eyes glazed, her skin (what was left of it above the jawline, anyway) was slack and doughy, a thin line of drool ran from her mouth. The only sign of life was that slight tremble of her muscles, the faint thrum of a circuit almost driven to overload.

In truth, Eve had gone inward, away from the room. Not like a dream, not like the one she'd had of the canal bank and the quacking ducks, she had simply withdrawn into a dark space, an unlit stage in an empty theatre (almost certainly the Dagmar, but who really knew?). She was standing, and that felt wonderful. Her face was intact, and that felt better.

But she was talking to Carl, and that felt best of all.

Chapter Twenty-four

"I always hated this theatre," said Carl. He was in his favourite casual gear; jeans, cheap trainers and a baggy Bart Simpson t-shirt. Bart was imploring people not to have a cow.

He looked incredible. Fit, well, handsome and young …just as he had on that night when she'd met him all those years ago. The cancer had yet to leave its mark, his hair was full and his eyes were strong. That incredible charisma washed over her again, and Eve felt that terrible, unadulterated rage blow away like the seeds of a dandelion clock.

"I know you did," said Eve, and the joy that sprang up in her at really being able to talk to him again nearly caused her tongue to lock in her throat.

"Its bad luck," Carl went on, "*always* bad luck. All that stress, all that worry – and for what? So a few idiot people could spend a few idiot nights away from their idiot TV. One thing I have to say, Eve, being dead gives you a hell of a perspective on your life."

"You did a good show," Eve protested. "You always did."

"Yeah, I suppose." He said, pacing around a bit. "And I *also* suppose perspective depends on where you stand. If you look down on a rock pool and see all the little creatures swimming about it all looks a bit pointless, doesn't it? But, to them it's the world. Still," he went on, rubbing his hands together, "none of this is getting the dog washed, is it?"

This made Eve laugh. That had been one of his favourite phrases.

"I tried to stop you doing that play," he continued. "Any way I could, which wasn't much. There's only so much I can do, physically, which is a bugger to be honest, but I tried my best. I messed up the computer, tried to stop the car, turned the TV on to some crap old sci-fi movie. I tried ringing you once. Got so frustrated I kicked the bedroom door shut. Even had a go at trapping you in the dressing room. I did *everything I could* to warn you, to stop you. And nothing I could do would *work*." Anger and frustration creased his face, that face she just wanted to cover in kisses again. "You're just so *stubborn,* Eve. You just *will not* let go, will you? I mean, I love you and I always will, but sometimes I'd just wish you'd say, 'Fair enough, I can't do this,' and just bloody *quit!*"

"I quit the fags," Eve found herself protesting, "and the drugs – the speed, the dope. I've quit lots of things."

"Oh, only stuff you didn't need," Carl dismissed. "Stuff you never really wanted in the first place. Face it, hon, if you really wanted it you'd have kept going. They were just things you *thought* you wanted. But when it comes to acting …oh, you're just a terrier with a rag."

"Did you …interfere with my performance in rehearsals? Did you make me shit?"

For a moment, Carl looked so sheepish she was convinced he was about to say, *well …yes,* but instead he said, "No. Sorry, wish I had. But honestly? You were just floundering, first time in your life. And you know something? I was glad. I was dancing with joy! Because I thought they'd just kick you out and never mind all the money they'd invested …but, again, that bloody *stubbornness!* You just had to go and give the performance of a lifetime! And yeah, I saw it, I saw it all, and even though I was terrified …I was just a little bit proud as well."

Oddly, Eve felt a little deflated. *Okay, I get an explanation of why all that strange shit was going on – it was my dead husband playing about, which makes perfect sense when you think about it – but I'm responsible for being inept during those three weeks? Bummer, as they used to say back at RADA.*

"But look," Carl said, 'please let me speak, don't distract me. I'm using up a lot of energy here and there's other stuff I have to get on with – *please,* Eve," he went on as she opened her mouth, "trust me, whatever other mistakes I have made don't count right now, there's time to deal with those I hope, but for now *trust me!* I've got better perspective than you, I'm looking from a higher place, but I *can't see the whole picture!* I don't know how this thing ends, and I'm working my dead arse off to make sure it ends with you safe and well, but I just don't *know!* So please, *work with me!* This man – this man who's doing these things – is dropping clues like mad, I know you've heard them, put them together, get him to reveal himself – he will, I'm sure, he's an egotist, he wants that – *stall him that way if you can!* Buy me time; because that bloody sister of yours is *such* hard work, I need that! Promise me, Eve! *Promise me!*"

"Yes, I ..." she started to say, startled at this desperate pleading. He was almost in tears.

"And *trust* me! *Believe me!* I made a mistake once, and I will never do it again. I love you with all my heart and soul, Eve, and *I'll never let you down again!* Everything I have ever done is to keep you safe, that's what you do when you love someone, and everything I will *ever* do is to keep you safe – but *I don't know if I win!* So remember the clues, piece them together, remember the mistakes he's made – you've found one, and there's another – keep yourself alive as long as possible! *Promise me! Promise me!*"

"I promise," she said, crying herself now, "I promise."

*

"Promise," she muttered, as she came back into the real world, back in the dirty kitchen with the grimy windows and the chained up body of an old acquaintance (who should *never* be forgot!) in front of her.

Pisser, she thought. *I was enjoying that.*

Never mind ...was it real?

No, of course not. It couldn't have been. Carl's dead. Dead people don't talk. They burn or lie in the ground and rot, that's all they do. That was my head, somehow, trying to sort things out.

Okay then, I'll take that. So what have you noticed that needed arranging like that?

Clues. He's been dropping clues; that's what my mind made Carl say. And he has, hasn't he?

Realisation like a bucket of cold water made her sit up as straight as she could (once more, a low growl of pain came from the bottom of her spine). *Yeah, clues.* Except he hadn't been dropping them so much as planting sixty foot neon signs in her way. "I had this idea once ...sent it to *Tiger Aspect* ..." an independent production company. "I had an idea once ...hire a troupe of actors ...take them to Amsterdam ..."

Jesus, how could I have been so blind? But of course, there was a very good reason for her being so blind. She'd been beaten up and abducted and woken up tied to a chair ...

No, not tied, taped ...

Yeah, whatever. Anyway ...

No, not anyway. *It's important.*
No it isn't, this *is. I think I know who it is. And the thing that confirms it …the thing that confirms it is …*

Eve looked straight ahead. Of course.

The thing that confirmed it was Laura.

*

"What are you going to do, Sarah?" asked Eve, deep in the dream. "Stay here, watch a bit of TV, maybe solve a puzzle."

Sarah was dozing on the sofa in Eve's front room; lightly, but dozing. She wasn't fully asleep; it was as if there was a thin curtain between her and the real world, a veil like the one she'd worn at her wedding. She could hear the faint drone of the traffic from outside. She could hear Jon pottering around somewhere (the kitchen? Upstairs? Somewhere close anyway), she could hear the world, the world around her, the world where everybody else's sister was safe and no one was suffering this awful, creeping terror but her.

But still, she dozed. Her body was tired; hell, her *mind* was tired. She'd watched that disc not once but twice more in that stuffy, airless police interview room while the Inspector whose name she would never be able to recall if she lived to be a hundred stared at her, waiting for her expression to change, waiting for her to exclaim "Of course! The butler!" or somesuch.

Which, naturally, she hadn't. There'd been no clue at all, not to her, not to Jon. Just Grainy Jumpy Man hitting her sister from behind time after time and bundling her into the back of the car, then driving off. Eventually, the Inspector had just given up, let them go (once again reminding them he'd be going public with the story at around midday – what time was it now? – and should they have any sudden revelations they were to get in touch straightaway), and they'd driven back to Eve's house in a desperate silence, Sarah thinking that the disc had both given and taken away hope at the same time. *Eve's not dead – at least she wasn't then – she didn't commit suicide, she didn't have a breakdown – but someone, some lunatic, has her – I was right at the start – what will he do to her ...*

As soon as she'd entered the living room, she felt the grey wash over her vision again. Once more, Jon reached out his arm and caught her elbow, leading her to the sofa, overriding her protestations that she was fine, just fine, and he'd encouraged her to lie down, rest her eyes, take it easy while he (made something to eat? Built a box girder bridge?) went off and did something, and Sarah said no, even as her eyes were closing, she couldn't rest, she had to be alert in case ...in case ...

"What are you going to do all day, Sarah?"
"Watch TV, solve a puzzle."

Except she *couldn't* solve this puzzle, could she? The puzzle was Who's Got Your Sister? And Sarah didn't have a frigging clue. How *could* she? She knew no one down here, did she? Just Eve, and Eve was gone. Just Carl; and Carl was gone. Just Jon, and she didn't *really* know Jon did she? He was just her brother-in-law, occasional birthdays, some parties and the odd funeral.

"What are you going to do, Sarah?" "Solve the puzzle."

You could only solve a puzzle with clues. If you had no clues you couldn't solve anything. Jigsaws had a boxtop; crosswords had (*Barking Clappers? Almost!*) riddles. Every puzzle had a way in, a crack, a chink ...*something*. Except this one.

I'm a hick from Chorlton. That's where I've lived all my life. I've holidayed, oh yeah, been abroad...been to Spain, Italy, France ...even America ...but I'm a hick from Chorlton, all the same. Holidayed but never travelled, if you get me. I speak like a Manc (a posh Manc, but a Manc all the same) and I think like a Manc. Don't like London much. Don't like the Tube or the way people push you aside on the street, don't like the way you don't get a smile in the shops from the man who sells you Puzzler *and* Crossword Weekly, *don't much like the dirt or the smell down here, don't like it, not at home, don't know anyone, don't fit in, can't see the boxtop, so how can I solve this puzzle?*

By thinking really, really hard.

Well, that was great, wasn't it? Really useful. "By thinking really, really hard." *About what? C'mon, give me a frigging break, throw me a frigging bone, just give me some help …*

Are you lying comfortably, Sarah? Then I'll begin.

Actually, she *wasn't* lying comfortably now she came to think about it. There was something sticking into the small of her back. Rolling over (and without so much as opening her eyes), Sarah plucked the thing that was disturbing her rest – such as it was – and flung it to the floor, where it flopped with the sound of turning pages. *Right, that's that gone …*

Gone? Yeah, maybe. But it'll turn up again, won't it? It keeps *turning up again.*

That made no sense to her, so once again that image of Eve looking at her rose up in the paper thin pall between her inner eyelids and the world. "What are you going to do," Eve asked, but before Sarah could answer, Eve stole her line. "Solve the puzzle?"

You just will not *let me have the last word, will you? Besides, I can't. I keep telling you that!*

No, said Eve, *I'm the one who can't solve puzzles, remember? You're brilliant at them. And you've got clues; you just can't see 'em for looking, as Mum used to say.*

No I frigging haven't.

Yeah you have. Clues which are questions. One you keep forgetting to ask, one you've only just thought of. So get that logical head in gear, big Sarah, and do it quick. Because you never know how much time you've got left, do you, not in the real world. On Countdown *there's that big clock in the background with the annoying jingle that ticks off the thirty second time limit. Here there's nothing. No hint at all. So may I humbly suggest that every second counts and you* get on with it?

"Sarah," whispered a voice from the real world. She rolled back, eyes opened, and there was Jon. He had a sandwich (cheese?) in one hand and a coffee in the other. "Sorry," he said. "Didn't mean to wake you."

"It's okay," she mumbled thickly, "I wasn't really asleep." Sarah sat up and felt her feet collide with something on the floor. A magazine. She picked it up without glancing at it and placed it on the table.

"I don't know if you want these," Jon said, placing the items next to that copy of *Puzzler*, "but it might be an idea if you try to force something down."

"I'll use the coffee, but the sarnie …no, I'd throw it up." She reached forward and sipped. Strong, sweet, gorgeous. *Oh,* said the naughty Eve in her head, the *coffee or the guy who brought it?*

The coffee, you witch, Sarah smiled back in that new, somehow easy way that they'd found only in the past couple of days. *I'm a happily married woman, remember?*

But still, window shopping, that was allowed, wasn't it? Even when your sister was …well, you could still be thankful that he was around, couldn't you?

Now that's *the question you keep forgetting to ask.*

God! Of course it was! "Jon, how did you get my number? My mobile number, I mean?"

Jon had sat in the armchair, gazing straight ahead (looking pretty much worn out himself), but at the question something – some form of light – came back into his eyes. "It was in my phone," he said. "I had lunch with Eve, saw something wasn't right, came home and rang you."

Hang on … "My number was in your phone?"

"Yeah," he replied. "Look." He dug into his jeans pocket and pulled out a Samsung. He entered his pin number, scrolled though to PHONEBOOK, ran his finger down it and held it for Sarah to see. SARAH MOBILE, it said. "There you go."

"Right," she said, even though there wasn't anything right about that at all. "And when did I give you that? At Carl's funeral? That was the last time I saw you, wasn't it?"

Jon shrugged. "Yeah, guess so. And that must've been it. Can't really remember."

"Jon," she persisted, and there was a feeling of *slide* now, a feeling that things which had been wrong for a while now were growing somehow *wronger*. "I didn't give you my number. Why would I? No offence, but *why*? And if I would, why *that* number? Why not the landline?"

"I …" Jon started to say, but then she saw it hit him, too. "Yeah …you're right …you wouldn't. In fact …no, you *didn't*, did you?"

"Was it Eve? Or Carl? Did they give it to you?" *No, of course they didn't. But it's there.*

"I …" he said again. He licked his lips, as if his mouth had gone dry. "Pass me some of that coffee, will you please?" She did so, somehow resisting the urge to shake him. He took a huge swallow, then passed it back. His hand was shaking. "No. I don't think they did. You're right; why would they? Why would I *ask*?"

"It was just *there*." Sarah said, more to herself than anyone.

"Yeah," Jon said, eyes huge, wide like saucers.

"You were worried about Eve, decided to call me, and the number was just *there*. In your phone. And you didn't think anything about it."

"No."

"*And neither did I!* Until this morning, I never gave it a thought! Why not? What's the *matter* with me? Why wasn't the first thing I said 'Hello Jon, how's things, by the way how did you get this number?'"

"I've no idea," he said, his voice flat.

"Me neither, which is odd, don't you think? I wasn't curious *at all*, not until this morning. And I've been meaning to ask you, but it kept slipping my memory."

"Yeah, fine ...but is it, well ...important?"

"*I've no frigging idea,*" she roared, standing (swaying a little), and moving around the room like (as her Mum *also* used to say) the Mad Woman of Shiloh. Jon flinched. "But it's *wrong,* it's wrong, it doesn't fit, and that makes me frigging *insane!*"

Jon stood, tried to catch her. "C'mon Sarah, just calm down."

She could have killed him, there and then. "What? *Calm down?* When Eve's having God knows what done to her by some madman and my number just magically appears in your phone?" She managed to turn from him before something escaped from inside her. 'How? How do you suggest I do that, Jon?" She stormed about the room. "Herbal tea? Yoga? What ever else kind of shite you types practise? C'mon. I bet you get all sorts of great tips with that shower of friggers you hang out with!" She turned in a tight half circle and banged her ankle on the coffee table. A magazine fell to the floor. Almost insane with fear and bewilderment, she picked it up, meaning to shred it into a thousand pieces and dance on them. "What *use* am I?" she screamed. "She's my little sister and I can't help her, I can't do *anything,* and you tell me to *calm down!*"

She held the magazine in front of her, her hands dug deep into the pages, ready, ready to turn it to confetti, when one of the clues – it was, of course, an issue of *Puzzler* - leapt out at her.

It said, "Progenitor of the Piece (6)."

Sarah stopped, ran down, shut up completely. "What are you going to do, Sarah?" "Solve the puzzle."

Well, there was a puzzle right in front of her wasn't there? "Progenitor of the Piece (6)." Five down, it was. Merging with nine along, "Night and Day? No, both (10)." *Those* blocks she'd filled in. "Terminator." Obvious. Which meant the penultimate letter of five down was O. "Progenitor of the Piece (6)." *Blank, blank, blank, blank, O, blank.*

Blank. Like her mind.

"What are you going to do?" "Solve the puzzle."

Yes, but this puzzle? Why this puzzle?

Because it keeps turning up. Everywhere you sit, it keeps turning up. Even though you pull it from underneath you and place it on the coffee table, it keeps turning up. Even under Jon.

No, that's …

Ridiculous? Yeah, maybe. As ridiculous as your sister being abducted in a Tube station car park? That happened, you saw the evidence yourself. As ridiculous as your mobile number somehow being in Jon's phonebook? That happened, you saw the evidence yourself. And this magazine …which just keeps turning up… that's ridiculous too. But it happened. You saw the evidence yourself. And what are you, *Sarah? What's your place in the family? Eve's the imaginative one, the one who thought she could reach Narnia through the wardrobe, the one who thought dogs could speak when no one was looking, so what are* you? *The logical one, the sensible one, the one who knew what two and two made and that the moon was made of rock and not green cheese and that the only sounds dogs made were barks and growls. So these things present themselves to you, and you see the evidence yourself, so what do you do? What do you do? What do you do?*

"I solve the puzzle," she heard herself mutter.

"What was that," Jon asked, but she didn't hear him.

"Progenitor of the Piece (6)." Penultimate letter O. *Progenitor …creator …father …maker …instigator.* Instigator? No, too many letters. And "piece"? What kind of piece? Piece of cake? Piece of eight? Piece of piss?

"I will solve it," she said. "I'll *solve* this …"

"What is it," asked Jon, "what are you looking at?" He crossed to her, stood behind her, close.

Sarah stabbed her finger at the clue. "That," she said, still taking no real notice of him. "What does that mean?"

"I've no idea," said his voice right behind her ear …but a million miles away.

I'll solve it. I will. I will.

And with a flash of insight so sudden it made her gasp, she did.

Chapter Twenty-five

Where does he go? Eve had no idea, and she'd a feeling it was very, very important. She tried to figure out what time it was, how long she'd been here. *I think its late morning,* she reasoned, craning her head as far to the right as it'd go, straining to see as much of the dismal sunlight that managed to struggle through the disgusting, greasy window. *Maybe elevenish, maybe later.* So she'd been here – what? Twelve hours, thirteen? Something like that; a little more, a little less maybe, but twelve or thirteen hours taped to a chair seemed a reasonable working estimate.

Where is he now? Is he right behind me?

Could be. How would she know? She couldn't turn around, couldn't move (*well, yes you can*), so for all she knew, the Man in the Cloth (Ski) Mask could be crouched down back there, breathing low through his mouth, ready to pop up with a scream and hands full of knives or cut throat razors or anything else that could cut and rip

I will not panic, I will not panic

or maybe worse, maybe his hands would be empty and they'd just bring themselves down on her breasts and rub and squeeze and pinch

I will not panic, I will not panic, I refuse to panic

and how could she stop him, how could she stop him as he rubbed and squeezed and pummelled, what could she do, she was helpless

I refuse to panic, I will not panic, I REFUSE TO

and if he decided to cut her blouse open, her filthy blood spattered blouse that had once cost her £100 from Karen Millen (money, what was money when you were a success, why shouldn't it buy you a blouse if you wanted it, why not?) and then the bra underneath it (nothing fancy, but these days her bras were there strictly to keep things pointing north, these days there was no one around to admire her taste), what could she do? If he decided to get down and play the Lappy Cat, licking from one to the other, what could she do? If he decided to roll them about as if he was testing for weight, what could she do? If he decided to unzip himself and indulge in a little Sausage Valley, what could she do? Spit on him?

I WILL NOT FUCKING PANIC!

To prove this, she bit down on her destroyed bottom lip as hard as she dared – in truth, not very hard at all – and the lance of pain (not to mention the thin dribble of blood) that accompanied this move brought her as close to her senses as she was likely to get.

Okay, right, got it, got control. Now hold it, just for a while anyway, while I try and work some stuff out ...

Like where he went, for instance. Off for a nap, somewhere. Maybe upstairs, maybe in one of the other rooms down here. *I mean, it's a house, this is a kitchen, so it stands to reason there are bedrooms and lounges and – for all I know – what Gran used to call a "parlour", so okay, he's off doing stuff. Or sleeping. If I'm right about who he is, he's probably got lots of other things to keep him occupied, I know those kinds of people, they've always got lots of projects on the go.*

You've known no one like him, little Eve.

Fair point, big Sarah, with you on that, but useless right now. So, he goes away from time to time – to recharge his Mad Batteries, if you like – somewhere else. Probably not upstairs, he'd want to be close …a quick power nap on the lounge sofa? Yeah, let's reason that. He's less than a minute away.

She looked as far to her left as she could, the sheer effort of just keeping her head upright pure agony, never mind actually turning it. She could hear the tendons creak. A doorway. With a closed door. *Could lead through the hallway. Could lead to the way out.*

Yeah, *could*. On the periphery of her vision, that odd, protruding hood, that metal sort of triangle she'd noticed earlier.

Jesus, that's an eye-level grill!

Well, maybe. It certainly looked like one – like the one they'd had back in Chorlton when she was little – but how could she be sure? I mean, who had eye level grills anymore? They were as dead as Cathode Ray TVs, as dead as VCRs, as dead as …well, as dead as she would soon be if she didn't get out of here. And what good would it do her anyway? She was rooted to the spot …

No, you're rooted to the chair. And not rooted, taped.

At this, Eve grew very still. Yeah, he'd moved her, hadn't he, swung her around so she could face the still catatonic Laura, the piece that had unlocked his identity. The chair was free standing, even if she was (ho ho) neither.

Could I hop, somehow? Drag it maybe?

Possibly, but she was weak, tired, and in such a lot of pain. She'd last eaten – what, almost twenty-four hours ago, with Sarah at the pub. She'd taken her last drink at the theatre, just after curtain down. Factor in the blood loss and the cramps, and she was in much less than top physical shape. Anyway, suppose she *could* somehow turn this fucking prison of a chair round, what then? What good would it actually *do* to confirm or deny her supposition that there was an old cooker on her left? She was tied down, remember?

Oh, how many more times? You're not tied down, you're taped. Gaffer tape, duct tape, whatever you want to call it, but tape. And tape's strong, yeah, tape keeps things in place –

that's why riggers use it to stop people tripping over their cables – but what about at the end of the shoot, Eve? What happens when they de-rig? Why, they just pull that stuff off the floor! Just give it a good hard yank and rrriiiiiii-iiiiiiiiiip, there it is, wrapped up in a ball and kicked into a bin! Because tape gives. That's what someone like him doesn't understand, he isn't a techie, is he? Tape gives.

Yes. It did. After a while, it did. All those posters she'd had on her bedroom wall as a girl – Simon Le Bon, Adam Ant …even Boy George, much to her father's horror ("Is that a boy or a girl?"). They'd all fallen down after a while, first one corner, then another …because *tape gives*.

That led to another memory, to the movie she'd made for *Film Four,* years back. They'd been shooting on location, a house exterior, and the Director and the cameraman were setting up a tracking shot. It was a damp, drizzly day in March, the sky was overcast and leaden, and lighting the thing was a bitch for the DP. No matter what he tried, there wasn't enough natural light to bounce onto her face. He'd tried to talk the Director into doing a static single of the scene, but no; the camera track was hired by the day and on that budget there'd be no wastage. They'd paid for it, they were going to by-God use it. With much huffing and puffing, the DP had agreed to set up the lights high and wide, which meant running more cable to the generator, which meant riggers with gaffer tape, and that meant lots of cries of "it won't fucking stick, it's too wet."

They'd got the shot in the end, after much cursing and sweat and a row between the Director and the DP which had never really healed, but so what? What of *that?* An idiot shot in an idiot film that distracted a lot of idiot people, who cared?

What mattered was that tape *gave.* And it *rarely* did well with moisture. Moisture like …well, sweat. Not that she did anything so uncouth as *sweat,* exactly …nor did she even *perspire. Pigs sweat,* her Mum had said on many occasion, *men perspire, women glow.* And with all that she'd been through, Eve was glowing like a hundred watt lightbulb.

Eve sat forward as far as she could. Half an inch? Maybe …but that was further than before. That was the nature of tape, wasn't it? It didn't bounce back exactly. It *settled,* didn't it? No matter how hard you wrapped it – and this was wrapped very, very hard indeed - if you worked at it long enough, if you worried it long enough, it'd *give.*

The question was, how long did she have?

Not long at all, she didn't think. Eve was, after all, Someone. She wasn't a superstar, she wasn't Cameron Diaz or Scarlett Johansson, but she *was* Someone. She wasn't a homeless tramp, she *was* Known. And when you're Known, people notice, people make a special effort, people …

Yeah, tell that to Jill Dando, will you? Chances are you'll be bumping into her soon.

Exactly. Exactly my point. That poor bitch was dead and gone in seconds, because she was Known, she was Someone, and when you're those things people have to put you away quickly.

Hey, come on – think about Laura. She's been here a couple of weeks.

Or so she reckons. You think she can track the passage of time? Anyway, Laura's unknown. She's a director, like Carl. directors are invisible. Who's she actually got in her life to miss her? No husband, no family she's ever spoken of. She can stay missing for years. You, Eve old Eve, are truly that Norse of a different colour.

Okay then, she didn't have long left. She'd probably only stayed alive this long because (if her guess about her captor's identity was right) there was a whole lesson in this he felt she needed to learn, and she hadn't had that yet.

So what little time I've got left, I've got to use. Somehow I've got to work loose. And then I've got to get through to Laura, get her to realise he's fucked up with her as well. Maybe then we'll have a chance.

Eve strained forward as far as she could go, then relaxed. Did she get further that time, or was it just wishful thinking? She flexed her right wrist as far as she could, then her left. Then her right ankle. Then her left. Then she leaned forward again.

Just wait a little longer, you sane motherfucking bastard. You just wait. Because if this works, I'm going to surprise the shit out of you.

Waist forward, right wrist, left wrist, right ankle, left ankle. The more she exerted, the more she *glowed.*

At each rotation, there was just a little more give.

*

They were in the car, driving – but slowly, so slowly.

London's bastard traffic, Sarah thought savagely. She looked once more at the dashboard clock. 13.10. Too long, it's taking too long.

"Are you *sure,*" Jon had asked, after Sarah had told him what that clue meant.

"Of *course* I'm sure, what else could it mean?"

He'd taken the magazine from her, frowning, chewing on his bottom lip. "I dunno, Sarah. It seems pretty random."

Somehow she managed not to punch him – just. "This is the guy who's got Eve, I know it Jon! I *just do!* How can we find out where he lives?"

Jon had actually rubbed his forehead at that. "Jesus, I dunno …I mean, shouldn't we go to the Police?"

"And say what? 'Hey, Inspector What's-Your-Name, we found out who it is by some random crossword clue that just wouldn't frigging *leave me alone,* yeah, guess I *am* psychic, anyway, I'm sitting here now telling you you've got to mount a raid on this guy's house!' You think that'd go down well, do you?" She snatched the copy of *Puzzler* back from him and – just about – held it in her hand instead of swatting him about the face with it. "*This* is why you called me, *this* is what I was supposed to do, do you understand me? Am I clear? *Your* job was to get me here, *my* job was to solve this bastard thing, and I have, I have, so tell me how we get to him *before Eve dies!*" *If she hasn't already.*

Jon continued to gape at her for a minute, and though she so very dearly wanted to throttle him, she could understand why. After all, she was talking lunacy. Utter madness.

Sarah Brown, (once Sarah Rogers), the sensible sister, the one who saw the world properly, was suggesting that she and Jon had been used as guided missiles, set in motion so that they would be in this place to make this conclusion.

You've sailed off the edge of the world, Sarah, little Eve's Voice spoke in her head. *You're as mad as I am. Possibly your anxiety, possibly lack of sleep, maybe the menopause – who knows? How does it feel?*

Oddly, it felt right. After all, what had Sherlock Holmes, that great puzzle solver himself once said? Something about the impossible and the highly improbable?

Yeah, but see – you're kind of along the impossible *axis here. And don't forget that Conan Doyle believed in fairies and mediums, so what, actually,* did *he know? The fucking nutter.*

"Jon," she said, keeping her voice as level as she could, "*trust* me. Please. I'm right on this. I know I am. And look, even if I'm wrong, what would it matter? Really? The police are doing all they can, we can't help them. We're not going to cloud what they're up to. And they're going to go public in," she checked her watch, "well, about ten minutes ago, and how long before we're under siege here? Cameras and reporters and all that crap? You want to sit here, surrounded by all that? Okay, so maybe I'm off the deep end here …but *so what?* At least we'd be doing *something,* at least we'd be moving …and it may well save Eve's life!"

It took Jon less than a minute to make up his mind, but that minute took forever in Sarah's head. "Okay. Right. Let me make some calls."

*

He switched off his mobile ten minutes later, having achieved precisely nothing. "The bastard's at the theatre, some emergency rehearsal, and he's not to be disturbed, apparently."

"Didn't you tell them who you were? Didn't you tell them what it was *about?*"

Of course I did, you know I did, you were in the same room as me, remember, his look said. But he kept his voice even and said, "Yeah, but there's a crisis – as far as they're concerned – and they're working like shit on the understudy for tonight, and unless it's police they won't knock on the door."

"So what do we do?" She was nearly hopping with frustration. A look at the watch. 12.20, which meant that the news had broken and camera vans would be on their way ...

Jon stood up. "We drive down there. And kick the door in if necessary."

*

An hour later, stuck in London traffic. An hour, stuck there, crawling, a mile a week. *How long before we get there? How long before we get to see him? How long before we get that information out of him?*

How long?

With a terrible, sickening feeling, Sarah knew it would be too long.

*

"Eve," said the scratched Scots/Italian voice, "the fuck're y'doin'?"

Quiet Laura, she tried to whisper, but the damage inflicted on her mouth was so severe that all she could manage was some kind of nonsense, the kind of gibberish cruel schoolchildren uttered when poking fun at a mentally challenged fellow pupil. It sounded something like *blighet Borah. Christ,* she thought, *if I do get out of this I'm screwed for voiceover work.*

Forward, back. Right wrist, left wrist, left ankle, right ankle …and yes, there *was* more give, each time, just a little more, just a bit …but enough for hope.

"The fuck're y'doin'?" Laura persisted. Eve glanced over, trying to make her understand by simple force of expression that *absolute quiet* was the order of the day here, but the other woman just wasn't tracking at all. Her eyes were bleary, bloodshot, rheumy, the eyes of someone who's had much too much Special Brew, the eyes of a pure space cadet. *What else has she had to put up with, the poor bitch? What else, beside acid sprayed on her face? What has he done to her? I promise you, kiddo, I promise you that if I can just manage this I will make him pay, and pay big, for this, for all of this, but please, just please keep your gob shut.*

Whatever face acting Eve had once been good for appeared to have abandoned her now. "Hey, Eve," she just *bloody well went on,* "the fuck're y'doin'?" Christ on a bike, she's sounding like Billy Connolly now. "Eh? Eve? Eh?" *She's snapped, she's fucking snapped …*

Or has she?

That almost caused her to stop, but she didn't, she kept up her flex/relax rotation.

She's loud, and getting louder …why? Because she's mad, because whatever's happened here has caused her to slip her gears? Or …is she like him, *playing a game? Is she part of the set decoration? Is she on his side, for Christ's sake? Is she faking it all? Can she see me starting to work my way out – slowly, pitifully slowly – and is trying to warn him? Is she? And if she is, what can I do about it?*

Waist, wrists, ankles …just a little quicker than before. Faster. More urgent.

*No, she can't be …*look *at her, look at her* face, *look at what he's done to her, there's holes there, holes burning into her flesh. I mean, Jesus, I think I can make out bone! What do you think that is? Makeup?*

Yeah, and you thought the bastard who put you here was insane, didn't you? But you know better now. Maybe it is *makeup, maybe it's one superb prosthetic – you've seen what they can do with latex and collodean these days, that stuff can stand up to a 70mm lens in close up. But look hard Eve, look* hard, *and you'll see the join. There's always a join.*

Eve did, still wriggling, still flexing and relaxing, flexing and relaxing (there *was* more give, there *was*) she stared hard at Laura's face, looking for any hint, any mismatch, any bump, any incorrect colouring …

Of course, she found none. She found none because this *wasn't* a makeup job, no five hours spent in a trailer while a team of the country's finest SFX appliance people worked on her. No, she was just used up and scarred, scarred badly and for life (however long that life may be). That Eve had even *thought* such a thing was an indication of how badly that masked bastard had got into her head, how twisted his game had made her.

But still …

"Eve, y'listenin'? Are y'? The fuck're y'*doin'*?"

She's going to call him, accomplice or not. He'll hear. He'll …

"Shhh," she managed to splutter, and once more fine drops of rain splattered from her chin.

"What?" Asked Laura. *"What?"*

God in Heaven, please, please get her to shut the fuck up, okay? Because if she doesn't …

Sure enough, behind the closed door, Eve heard a man say, "Oh? Who's that talking in my kitchen?"

*

It was 13.38.

They finally pulled in at the side of the road, ignoring the double yellow line, and just leaped out of the car, Sarah narrowly missing being mown down by a passing Bentley. She started to run for the Box Office doors, but Jon called her back.

"Stage door," he yelled, "down this way."

He led her down what appeared to be an alley, and – magically – he found a small door set into the wall. It was, of course, closed.

Jon rattled the handle. Nothing. Above it was a code entry thing – useless to them - but above that was a call button. Jon leant on it. While he was doing that, Sarah battered on the wood with every ounce of force she could muster.

Buzzzzzzzzzzzzz. Bangbangbang!

Nothing. Nothing for hours, nothing for eternity, then – hallelujah! – a distorted Cockney voice. "What the hell do you want?"

Jon opened his mouth, but Sarah spoke – well, shouted. "I'm Eve's sister, Sarah! I know you know what's going on, and you need to know I have to see the director of this play *now!*"

There was a pause, and at any second they'd hear the hum of an electric lock being thrown. Then they'd race in and throttle some answers out of somebody.

Instead they heard, "Prove it."

Sarah literally couldn't speak. Jon, however, could, though all he could manage was, "What?"

"Prove it," said the buzzing voice, like the world's biggest Cockney wasp. "How do I know you're not press? Story's just broke; they've been on the phone every five seconds. How do I know you are who you say you are?"

Sarah just made some weird noise, a high keening whistle of aggravation, but Jon kept his temper. "You know what, mate? We can't, we really can't. I'm Carl Wilson, Eve's brother-in-law, that's Sarah Brown, Eve's married sister, we were both here for the opening night, something's happened, you know that, and we need to speak to Mike Hughes, *now*, because he just might be able to help us."

"Mr Hughes is in an …"

"I know, I know," Jon interrupted, "emergency rehearsal, understudy, with you, got that, not to be disturbed. But you have to go and get him *now*, he can identify us, because every second we stand here *could see Eve die!*" He was screaming now, screaming, spittle flying everywhere. "You want that? You want her to die? Because if she does, my friend, I'll go to every arsehole with a microphone and tell them *WHO WAS RESPONSIBLE!*"

Another pause, another endless pause. Then, "Wait there a minute."

It was a minute that lasted a million years.

*

Eve stopped her flexing at the very second the Man in the Cloth Ski Mask entered the room. She caught the quickest glimpse of what lay beyond the door before he closed it; she'd been right. A hallway and what looked like a glass front door.

"Heigh ho," he said cheerfully, like a man well feasted and rested, "it seems my two lady friends are awake, and nattering away like hens in a battery shed. And what merry topics have you found to amuse yourselves? Shampoo? Health spa treatments? Periods?"

They kept silent. Eve because she didn't really have much choice, the way this bastard had messed up her mouth, Laura because she just didn't seem to know where she was anymore. She looked like she was dreaming awake.

"Isn't it always the way," he continued with sing song intonation and a drop of his masked head. "As soon as the men enter the room, the women fall silent." Then, all big eyes and massive startled shoulder jerk, "Why, have you been talking about *me?* Oh, I'm flattered, so flattered! But it is, of course, understandable. You two are, after all, only human. And like me or loathe me, I'm the only boy in town. So," he went on, clapping those gloved hands together and rubbing them with a disgusting whispering noise, "Who's up for another game?" He turned to Eve, and those eyes she knew only too well bored straight into her, "Only this time I think we should up the stakes, don't you? See, the thing is, I've got two contestants, right? Which means it's time to play the head to head. On most shows, of course, the loser goes home with a trophy. Here, the loser doesn't go home at all.

"We're talking Sudden Death. Got me?"

Eve just nodded, slowly, up and down. Was she scared? Oh yeah, scared plenty. Surprised? No, not anymore. Nothing would surprise her ever again, she thought. She'd used up her ration of surprise, drank it dry.

But maybe *she* could surprise *him.* If she could speak. If she could *just clearly speak.*

She gathered up all her will, all her strength, and tried.

*

It was, in fact, *ten* minutes before Mike Hughes flung open the stage door. He looked wretched, old, tired, manic. *Pretty much how we look ourselves,* Sarah thought.

"What is it," he asked. "Have you heard anything?"

"No," said Sarah, "but we think we've an idea."

"We need your help," butted in Jon.

"Yeah, sure, anything," spluttered Mike. "But is she …is she okay?"

"*We don't have time,*" shouted Sarah, "we just need an address. Do you have it?"

"I don't know, whose is it?"

Sarah told him, and she saw the confusion on Mike's face. "Yeah, it'll be inside somewhere. Why?"

"Because it's *him*," she said. "*He's* the bastard who's got Eve."

A second's silence, no more, then Mike said, "Follow me."

*

"Bye blow hooo foo far," said Eve.

"I see," said Ski Mask. "No I don't, never mind. You're not making a lot of sense, Eve. Cat got your tongue? Unlikely, since I no longer have a cat. I had one, but it died. Well, I say died, actually I killed it, because that's how we serial killers *start*, with animals, cats, dogs, horses, elephants, llamas, then humans. It's a classic pattern."

Eve wasn't listening, mainly because she guessed all of that was just bullshit, something he'd gleaned from old crime shows or (worse) the internet, but she was also concentrating so hard on getting her mouth to work right.

"Eye know hooo you far," she managed, and it worked. It stopped him dead, stone cold.

But only for a second. Then he just roared with laughter, a great belly laugh, a *gutbuster* as they'd said when she was young. "Yeah, you do, don't you? Well done, Eve, *well done!* Give you ten bonus points for that. Yeah, I was hoping you'd work it out – you ain't thick, you ain't *never* been thick – but, credit where it's due, I'm surprised you got it so early. Does that mean I can take this mask off now? Tell you the truth, it itches like hell."

Once more, Eve gave the slow nod. And his gloved hands reached up to the neck of the ski mask and pulled.

*

The paper chugged out of Mike's printer, and Sarah snatched it up. "This is it? You're sure?"

"The only one we've got on file, yeah," said Mike. "But come on …it *can't* be …"

Sarah wasn't listening, she was running out of the tiny office and heading down the stairs, back to the car, Jon close behind her, Mike tailing.

"Look, maybe I should call the police …" Mike was saying.

"Do that," she heard Jon call, but Sarah didn't speak. They had the frigger's address in her hands now, and soon those hands would be round his throat for daring to lay a finger on her sister.

The progenitor of the piece, six letters, fifth letter O. The author.

*

"Hi, Eve," said Barry Mackie. "Want to change some of *these* lines?"

Chapter Twenty-six

"How far's Acton?" Sarah asked.

"Not that far. The way this bloody traffic is, though ..." Jon trailed off, not bothering to finish.

Christ, thought Sarah, *what is it with this bloody city? Do people just never get off the roads?* Aloud, she said, "Is it east of Ealing?"

"It's right next bloody *door* to Ealing," Jon muttered, trying to thread his car through a gap at the mind numbing speed of twenty-eight miles an hour. "Bastard was close, Sarah. We could've *walked* to his place from Eve's!" Then, as he put his foot down and they shot to an amazing thirty-five, "I just hope ..."

"Hope what?" *Hope Eve's okay, hope Mike phoned the police, hope we can deal with what we find.*

"Nothing," said Jon, not taking his eyes off the road. "I just hope."

*

"I don't suppose it's come as much of a surprise," said Barry, as he dropped his mask to the floor. "Dramatically, I feel it may lack something. The *reveal* is, after all, supposed to elicit gasps from the audience. There's supposed to be a whole line up of suspects, each more likely than the other. Then the final, theatrical flourish when the bad guy is made known to one and all. 'Goodness,' say the audience, 'I never saw *that* coming, did you? What a twist!' But hey, I'm an iconoclast as a writer. Show me a rule, and I'll break it. Same as a kid. No running in the corridor? Why? Who says? So I ran. The nuns hated me."

He started strutting about the place again, all the time keeping away from Laura's unfettered legs …but what good were they now? Laura was looking up all right, tracking his movement, but her eyes reflected light like a teddy bear's. She wasn't following this at all. Even if Eve called her to action, Laura would just stare back, vacant.

"Also," he continued, looking towards Laura, "I'm a bloody good engineer." Back to Eve, "After all, I made you sound better than you *ever* did. That's the way of the world in the first quarter of the twenty-first century though, isn't it? Multi-talents. Keeps the wolf from the door, as the old cliché has it, if you can bounce from one job to the other." He dropped down to his haunches in front of Eve. "Unless you're *special,* unless you can get by on your *uniqueness,* like you. *You* never had to learn anything else, did you? *You* never had to learn how to cue a reel or tweak the e.q. or study structure and pacing, did you? No, all your work was done for you. Face it, Eve, all you *ever had to do* was read aloud and follow the moves someone else gave you. Stand here, sit there, frown a bit on *this* line, laugh a bit

But you couldn't even do *that*, could you? You *had* to mess around."

I really do think I'm going to die, thought Eve, the panic was darting around her now, pinching her with sharp witch's fingers. *He's taken that mask off; he's let me see his face …yep. I'm going to die. There's no way he'll let me live now.*

Perhaps surprisingly, perhaps not, a sudden well of anger spilled over inside her. To die like *this*, taped to a chair, her own piss dried to her thighs, her own blood caked to the gouged mess of her once pretty face, to die in a grotty shit hole of a kitchen, to die because some random person you hardly knew has *decided* that you'll die, just woke up one day and looked at his To Do list and, under BUY MILK had written TORTURE AND KILL EVE ROGERS, to die for *that reason and no other*, to die in that condition, *outraged* her momentarily. She drew up as much moisture in her mouth as she could and spat in Barry's face.

The dry, sardonic humour vanished from his face in an instant. His *true* face – the one she'd seen towards the end of rehearsals, the one he'd formed as he snarled "Happy now?" - took its place; cold, weak, hateful. He slapped her across the mouth, hard, causing the half closed wounds to open, blood to trickle weakly down her chin for the sixteenth millionth time, and tears to spring from her eyes.

"Watch that," said Barry. "We've still got a game to play, remember?"

"Go fuck yourself," Eve managed to say.

"Apt, if vulgar," he said, standing. He was smiling again, once more a happy chappy. He crossed over to her right, and once more she heard the jingle of cutlery from past the periphery of her vision.

Eve stared straight ahead, trying to fix Laura's gaze, trying to get the other woman to just bloody *focus. Okay, so maybe we can't just get up and run, but maybe …just maybe …if she kicks him hard enough it might knock him out, maybe even kill him, and then if I can keep flexing and relaxing, maybe I can work loose before we die of dehydration. Or maybe I can hop this fucking chair to a phone. Maybe.*

She stopped thinking this when Barry came back into view. Once more he was smiling. "Ready to play?" He looked at both women, then nodded. "Here goes. Good luck to you both. Let's play Sudden Death!"

In his right hand was a meat cleaver.

*

They pulled into Lulworth Place at just after half two in the afternoon, and as luck would have it, Lulworth Place was a Bellway Estate, every tiny little Close or Grove or Avenue just a clone of the other, tiny boxes, like hideous three dimensional photocopies.

"What's the street name?" Asked Jon as he began circling the repulsive site.

Sarah didn't hear him. She'd seen something in the rear-view mirror. "Jon. Look."

He glanced up, then looked over his shoulder. "Bless you, Mike."

Three police cars, lights flashing but sirens off, were less than a mile back. As she watched, the lights went out one by one. *I hope we're in time, please God let her be okay, please God let me be right, please God.*

"The street name, Sarah," Jon repeated.

"Ashton Grove," she read from the sweaty, multiple folded printout. The address on his initial submission, the return for *Pavlov's Bell,* the piece he was the progenitor of.

"Okay, got it. You look left, I'll look right." Then, under his breath, "Watch out, you mad fuck. Here come the good guys."

*

"The rules of Sudden Death are very simple," said Barry, standing between them, just slightly to Eve's left. "I'm going to ask a question. If you both answer honestly, nobody gets killed and we go on to the *next* question. *If* one of you lies, I kill the liar and make the other one watch. If *both* of you lie, I kill you both. Understand? Good. So, here we go, the first question. Laura? Did you fuck me?"

Oh dear God, thought Eve, *the poor bitch has no idea what's going on …she's just going to sit there until he calls "time's up" and then he'll …he'll …*

"Laura, have to hurry you," said Barry. "Did you fuck me?"

The bastard was actually *raising his hand* when, mercifully, Laura nodded. "So, in answer to the question, 'Did you fuck me,' your answer is 'yes'?"

Once more, a nod. Just enough. *Okay, good, she's following* something. *In that case …*

"*That's the right answer!*" Barry screamed. "You did, indeed, fuck me all the time while we were producing Eve's Talking Books session. Twice nightly for five nights. Then you dropped me like a stone when the gig was over." Back straight ahead. "Question two, for Eve this time." He turned to her. "Eve …did *you* fuck me?"

Emphatically, she shook her head.

"Are you sure of that?"

Eve nodded, hard, fast.

"Are you saying you *are* sure of that, or that you wish to change your mind? Because I have to accept your first answer."

What do I do, what do I do, Christ that cleaver …

"I'll repeat the question. Eve, did you fuck me?"

She shook her head.

"Once again, the right answer. So, with the scores tied, we go into the second round."

That cleaver. Eve couldn't take her eyes off it. *That cleaver. The damage that could do.*

*

"There!" Sarah pointed. "There it is, Ashton Grove!" A quick look at the paper. "Number Twenty."

Jon stopped the car, unclipped his seatbelt and climbed out. He stood, facing away from the road.

"What are you *doing*," Sarah panted, as she slammed the door behind her. "We've got to get *in* there!"

"Not us, Sarah. Them," he pointed at the three police cars, then waved them towards him. "They know what they're doing. We have to leave it to them."

"You can, you coward," she snapped, staring to run. "I'm going to …"

He caught her above the left elbow with surprising speed, and surprising gentleness. "No. What'll we *do?* They're trained for this." He brought her round, held her, turned her to where four officers were disembarking from each car, stab vests present and correct, CS gas in holsters, and what looked suspiciously like Tasers dangling from hips. "Look at them. *They'll* catch that bastard."

Despite everything he said, despite the logic of it, Sarah still wanted to run to that house, to Number Twenty, and to kick the door off its frigging hinges good and proper.

She just had a feeling. A feeling that time was very, very short.

*

"Round two then," Barry went on. "Back to Laura. Laura – and remember this is Sudden Death, where a lie can cost you your life – did you fuck Eve's husband?"

*

"May I ask who you are, sir?" asked the middle-aged sergeant as he sauntered up to them, hands lightly out from his sides like the gunslinger in a Wild West movie.

"Jon Wilson, this is Sarah Brown. I'm Eve Wilson's brother-in-law, this is her sister."

"I see," the sergeant said, obviously not caring. "I'm afraid you'll have to vacate this area." Then, to Sarah, "We have information your sister may be being held in one of those buildings and we have to put a cordon in place."

"I'm not going anywhere," Sarah said, but the sergeant had stopped looking at her. He was looking at Jon, at the man, because that was how these things worked.

"If you'll take this lady to the estate entrance, sir, we'll let you know as soon as we have any news."

"Fuck you," said Sarah, "that's my *sister* …"

"I understand your anxiety, Miss," the sergeant interrupted, obviously not understanding anything, "but if you stay here you may interfere with the operation we have to carry out, and I'm sure you appreciate that the situation may be time critical." Once more, to Jon, "Move her, please sir." Then he was off, to his men.

Sarah started to struggle, but Jon kept a tight hold. "No, c'mon, we have to do as he says." He started to drag her away, away from Eve, away from anything practical she could do, and try as she might, she wasn't strong enough to stop him. All the time he was crooning, "It's okay, it's okay, leave it to them, they know what they're doing, it's all right now, everything's all right now."

That should have been enough, it should have been reassuring – after all the police were here, Authority was here, the Good Guys had arrived with body armour and debilitating weapons, the Good Guys were going to catch the Bad Guy, and that was *right,* wasn't it? That was how it *should* end, shouldn't it?

So why did Sarah feel like nothing was going to work out right after all?

*

Eve saw that in her final moments, Laura was well and truly back.

Something had got through, broken that terrible catatonia – maybe the sight of that cleaver, maybe the implacable cheeriness of Barry's voice – but *something*. The light came back on, her dark eyes widened, she knew, she *understood!*

And she was going to lie.

Every line of her body language screamed it; the sudden tension of the shoulders, the way she looked up and to her right, a general shiftiness – she knew what she'd been asked, she knew who was in the room, and regardless of the man with the weapon, she was going to lie.

A total brain freeze struck Eve then, a chilling realisation of the inevitable consequences of what the other woman was about to say. Eve was locked between two thoughts, both screaming at her, both imperative, both clamouring for attention, and neither backed down.

On one track, she screamed, *kick him! Kick the bastard! KICK HIM HARD!* She actually *saw* this, saw it happen, saw Laura draw up her legs and punt Barry right in the balls, with every ounce of strength she still possessed. She saw Barry double over she saw him whack his head on the floor, she saw blood welling from the wound, she saw herself somehow break free of this fucking tape and drag Laura to safety.

On the other track, she heard herself scream, *it doesn't matter, I don't care, it's over, DON'T LIE!* And Laura heard her, accepted it, nodded, and told the truth. "Yes, I did fuck Eve's husband," and that was okay, sort of, because it meant they got to live.

"LAURA," she screamed, "IT DOESN'T MATTER! I DON'T ..."

She got no further, as Barry almost absently punched her in the face. Not hard enough to break anything, but enough to shut her up. "No help from the audience, please," said Barry. "Once more Laura - did you fuck Eve's husband?"

"N-no," stuttered Laura. "*No.* No I didn't. Eve, I didn't!"

Eve went frantic, literally frantic. She shook and rocked in her chair, hooting and bellowing nonsense. Barry looked at her, coldly, then smiled at her. *If I get out of this I will dance on your grave, you bastard.* "I said, no help from the audience." Back to Laura. "Your question was, 'did you fuck Eve's husband.' And your answer was ...?"

"No," she said again, louder, and oh God, it sounded more like a lie than ever. "*No, I did not!*"

In tones of great regret, Barry said, "Laura, I'm sorry. *That's the WRONG ANSWER!*"

He raised the cleaver.

*

It was nearly three o'clock, and Sarah and Jon had stood at the entrance to that soulless, awful estate for the longest half hour ever. Maybe three hundred yards away they could see the lines of police officers cordoning off the street, and by standing on her tiptoes she could make out a band of them at the front door. Presumably there were more round the back as well.

"Jesus Christ, what's going *on?*" she moaned.

Jon was just about to answer – probably something as illuminating as *I dunno* - when all of a sudden they heard a door being smashed in, and a faint cry of "Police! Stay where you are!" rolled back through the air.

Sarah gripped Jon's arm, and became aware she was praying.

*

The meat cleaver struck Laura above the bridge of her nose with a sound like splintering wood. Bone, cartilage and greyish pink messy stuff shot everywhere, immediately afterwards followed by a gout of clotted black-red blood that sprayed like a fountain onto the lino.

She didn't make a sound. That last light died from her eyes forever and she slumped forward, the mess of her once beautiful head sagging on her shoulders, gore beyond belief dripping onto her lap with the sound of a rain shower. *Blip, drip, flip, bib.*

Laura didn't make a sound, but Eve did. An inarticulate call of outrage, of horror that ripped her vocal chords to pieces, a desperate cry against the brutality she saw before her.

Barry took no notice. He simply tried to pull the cleaver from Laura's head. He couldn't, it was stuck in there, so he put his foot on Laura's shoulder for leverage. He yanked with all his might and with a grunt of exertion he pulled it clear. The stuff dripping from the blade was thick, viscous and rank. Eve felt her stomach roll as she looked at it.

Barry looked down at the woman he had murdered, shrugged, then raised the cleaver and hacked at her again. And again. And again.

A sound like meaty wet thumps followed Eve down as she fainted, and she had never been so grateful for oblivion in her life.

*

Time had no meaning for Sarah anymore, none. Time no longer moved, time was frozen in that one minute. It seemed she didn't breath, didn't blink, didn't so much as twitch. All she did was grip Jon's arm and pray. *Oh God, please God, let her be okay, please, she did no harm to You, please God, let her be okay.*

Eventually she became aware of a policeman walking towards her – the same sergeant who had patronised her earlier. He was walking slowly. Heavily. And on his own.

Sarah barely tipped the scales at nine stone – like all the Rogers women, she was tiny of frame – but when she saw that lone man approach, when she saw the helpless look on his face, she suddenly weighed a million tons, she was literally unable to support herself. She sagged, grateful Jon was there to keep her upright. *God, You bastard, You let her die! You fucking shit, God, You let her die!*

At first that thought hammered far too loudly in her head to hear what the sergeant actually said to her. Jon must have had the same problem. "Sorry," he said. "What was that?"

"Nothing," said the sergeant. "No one there at all. Totally empty house."

What the frig do we do now, Sarah found herself thinking.

Chapter Twenty-seven

She was in her kitchen – no, *they* were in *their* kitchen – except they weren't in their kitchen at all. They were back on stage at the Dagmar, and this was a set constructed to look exactly like their (*theirs*, not *hers*) kitchen. They'd done a wonderful job, Eve noticed – even down to that handprint on the wall by the fridge she'd (*they'd*) never quite got round to doing something about. Even the dressing was spot on; same mugs, same glasses, same cutlery, same kettle.

Really, it's only the fact this place has got three walls and no ceiling that's the giveaway. Ignore that, and we could be at home.

They were at the breakfast table – slightly unusual, as they'd very rarely sat down to breakfast together, but hey, dreams were dreams – opposite each other. Carl had the *Guardian* open, a plate that bore the remnants of a full English fry up on it, and a fresh, steaming mug of coffee. He looked well settled for a morning's slobbing about.

Eve, however, was dressed in a blood splattered blouse and jeans that stank of her own piss. Still, her face seemed in one piece and – joy of joys – in front of her was an unshattered glass of water. Just one look at it made her latent thirst roar to the forefront of her mind, and she grabbed at it, throwing it back.

Then, puzzled, "Nothing. I don't taste anything."

"I know," said Carl, barely looking up. "Swizz, isn't it? Still, that's dreams for you."

"And that's what this is? A dream?"

"Yeah, sort of. Well, it's not reality, is it?" He folded the paper and put it to one side. "I hate this theatre," he said again. "It's a spook. Bad things happen here."

"You kept a show on for six months here," said Eve. "I had two really good nights …"

"And then look what happened. Listen, hon, this guy's clever. Cleverer than I thought. Bastard sold me a dummy and I went for it."

"Don't get you."

"I know, and it's hard to explain, but – look, you're *in* the valley, right, and I'm a little bit up the hill."

"What valley?" *The valley of the shadow, maybe?*

"Just the valley, okay? Long metaphysical arguments we don't have time for. But you're down there and I'm – well, up here. Only it's one big mother of a hill and I've hardly gone fifty feet yet. I can see a bit further than you can, just not all the way to the horizon. Maybe I never will," he went on, eyes clouded, but then he smiled, and oh Lord, how she'd missed that smile. "But who cares? The fact is, Eve, I screwed up because I couldn't see far enough. I thought, what with being dead and all, I was pretty much onto the *I can do just about anything* trip. Turns out my influence is pretty limited."

"No, that's not true," said Eve, not just because she wanted clarification, but also because she wanted him to stay. She knew Carl. He had that getting down to business before I go to work expression on his face, and if he left she'd be back in that kitchen with …with …

With Laura.

Yes, with Laura, the poor dead bitch. Eve wanted to delay that return as long as possible, thank you very much. "You got me that job with …the Talking Books job …you could influence that."

"No," he said, and his face was so sad she just wanted to leap across the table and kiss him. Kiss him, then mount him. Just one last time.

Because this *was* the last time, wasn't it? There was something in the air that screamed it. Something in the set of his body, in the look in his eyes.

"That was nothing to do with me," he said. "All of that was just coincidence. It happens all the time, apparently. People so desperate for comfort that they ascribe all sorts of things to …well, the supernatural, I suppose. Laura," and what *was* that look on his face, "Laura just rang when you needed a job, that was all. Nothing special about it at all."

"But the photo …"

"Fell out of the album, simple as. You know what tape does, Eve. It gives."

"But it was back, back in the room the next day!"

"You'd found it while looking, you just didn't *see* it, you were so wound up. You'd gone to bed with it there, on the carpet. Next day, when you *weren't* looking, you spotted it straight away."

Eve frowned, well aware she had that pouty little girl look on her face, the one Carl always laughed at. "But then ...it was ripped ..."

"Again, you. You were more asleep than awake when you did it, but it was you. You ...well, you knew, didn't you? Deep down. You knew about us."

Dream or not, oh Christ it hurt. "Were you having an affair?"

"Not an affair. We slept together once, while you were on tour. And I'm sorry. *I'm so sorry.* I was *always* sorry. I hated myself for it for the rest of my life. I was disgusted with myself. Press do at the Arcadia for the upcoming season; I was there, she was there, just the wrong amount to drink, just enough for a bad idea to seem good ...and she was *full on,* you remember? She got what she wanted. Always. That night she got me. And until I died I crucified myself with it. I loved you, dear *God* how I loved you, but I betrayed you."

Rage like a panther leapt into her dreaming heart. "You *bastard!*"

"Yes. I know. And I never knew what to do, whether to tell you or not. Bravely I kept quiet. Sometimes I wonder if getting cancer was some kind of payback. It's a bitch, they say."

"I never so much as *looked* at anyone else! And you …"

"But you did, Eve, you did. You *looked*. You just didn't touch."

"Don't you *dare* make this about me!"

"Eve, it's *all* about you, don't you see that? It's been about you from the start! This mad fucker's fixated on you, has been since the recording. I made a mistake – no, more than one. I slept around behind your back – *once* – and I never, ever forgave myself. *But that's not the story here.* The *important* mistake is that I misdirected her."

Her, thought Eve? *Who? Laura?*

"I swear to you once again," said Carl, as intense as he'd ever been, "I will not let you die. If it is within my power, *I will not let you die!* If that means that …she …has to take your place *then that's just what has to happen.* I let you down once. Never, ever again."

"Carl, just …"

Carl talked over her. "This is a hard time. And what do hard times do? They pass, right? That's the only thing I know for certain, it's the only thing I've *ever* known for certain. Hard times pass, remember?" She tried to shout him down, but he just talked over her. "Like what's happening to you now, in the world, it's a hard time, but *it will pass!* I just don't know *how!* That bastard's tricked me somehow, but I will find a way to put it right. *I just need time!* I need you to stall him. Get him talking, get him singing, get him to do a fucking tap dance – *anything!*"

"Oh yeah? How?" Oh, she didn't want to be angry, not if it was the last time she would ever see him again, but she seemed unable to stop it. He'd cheated on her after all.

"Find a way, focus, Eve – *you have to!* We could be almost out of options here. *Just do it!* And remember what you thought when I kicked the bedroom door shut. After I was dead. *Remember that!*"

Gradually she became aware she was back in the kitchen. She'd sagged forward during her (faint?) and all of her weight (what there was of it) was resting on the tape that bound her across the waist. There was a thin puddle of drool (mixed with a fair amount of blood …how much damage had he done to her mouth exactly?) pooled in her lap.

Laura, she thought, and somehow managed to raise her heavy head.

There she was in front of Eve, the terrible horror that had once been a (friend? colleague? betrayer?), a woman no longer, just a cadaver. Her head was hacked into slices, like a loaf, the remains of her features matted with blackish blood, bone, brain.

And the worst of it all? The first thing Eve thought was, *good*.

That's what you get, you bitch. That's what you get for fucking my husband.

It took two to tango, the dead face seemed to say back. *It was him as well as me, I didn't force him you know. Yeah, I might have worked on him a bit, got a bit close, a bit over friendly maybe, I might have whispered in his ear or "accidentally" brushed up against him, but guess what? I was single and a bit pissed. I can flirt – well,* could *– with anybody. I can't be held responsible for how they reacted, can they? Fish gotta swim, birds gotta fly, I gotta try and fuck people. It's the way I was made, like being left handed. Can't go against your nature, can you?*

Maybe that was true – well no, it *was* true – but did that make it any better? No. People weren't animals, Eve had always believed that, people could transcend their natures. Otherwise they'd behave like dogs, sniffing the arse of anyone they met or shitting in the gutters. So Laura was someone who liked to screw around? *Fine. But pick on people who were single, for Christ's sake, don't pick on anyone just because you can!*

Are you sure you're concentrating on the right problem, Sarah Voice asked.

What's it to you, anyway? You're okay, aren't you? Your husband didn't cheat on you – as far as you know. Let's face it, he wouldn't dare.

Insults won't help you know, little Eve. Remember what I told you? Even if Carl did sleep with someone else – and, yeah, it seems he did, sorry – he would have regretted it, it would have been a mistake. And from what he said, he did and it was.

Bollocks, thought Eve. *He was presented with an opportunity and he took it.*

Yeah, he did. No argument. And were either party still alive there'd be some discussion to be had, wouldn't there? But they're not, *so put this to one side and concentrate on* getting out of that chair. *I mean, every second that passes makes you a little bit weaker, wrecks your muscles, makes you hungrier, thirstier, reduces your capacity for reason. Look through the window. See the light? Starting to fade, turn golden. You want to spend the night here?*

Hey Sarah, has anyone ever told you you're a pain in the – OWWWWWW!

She'd tried to sit up, and once more a cramp attacked her – only this one ran from the balls of Eve's feet through to her calves. She hissed pain through her teeth and the sharp air stabbed at the cuts to her gums. She jittered again, tensing every muscle against the pain, the sheer thumping *pain* of it, she spasmed uncontrollably, straining against the bonds that held her.

And heard a rip.

Chapter Twenty-nine

Sarah lay on the bed in Eve's guest room, half asleep but very much awake, and had no idea of what to do next.

After all, why should she? She was just a librarian from Chorlton, Manchester, no great shakes in the world, nothing special, someone who could organise some things, someone with a certain logical sense, a woman with a hidden sense of humour who was sometimes irrational and irritable. She was a childless forty-three year old who could (on a good day) pass for thirty-five, who went to the gym twice a week and did yoga in front of her instructional DVD. Who was she, really, to decide what should happen next? She wasn't a detective, she was no Sherlock Holmes – she was, let's face it, a bit of a washout in that department.

She'd been so sure, so *sure,* and she'd been wrong. That house had been empty, after all, not a single person in it. Looked like it hadn't been occupied for a while, the sergeant with the patronising (and pissed off about his wasted time) voice had said. Spotless, no doubt. Immaculate – maybe just a little bit of dust because no one had been round with the Pledge – but no Eve, and no Barry Mackie. Oh sure, the sergeant said, they had his description out and they'd be doing house to house around the estate and *blah* and *blah blah frigging blah,* and they'd be in touch as soon as they had any information, any at all, but now she was back at Eve's and Jon was downstairs and she was lying on this bed again as the light from outside grew dim and old, and she was aware she was beginning to resign herself to never seeing her sister alive again.

Eve, she half thought, half dreamed, *ah God, Eve. This just doesn't happen, does it, not in the real world, not to people we know, not to us. Those poor bastards who lost their daughter in Portugal, yeah, I know …the Dowler family …those little kids in Soham, that was stuff you saw on the* news, *not lived through. Oh dear Lord, how did they cope? How did they frigging* cope, *because I already think I'm going mad and it's not even been a whole day …*

There was a ring of the doorbell, and Sarah sat up, her heart hammering through her ribcage. *This is it, this is the Bad News Fairy come to tell me my little sister's been gobbled up by trolls …*

But it wasn't, it was Steve. She could tell by his big, rumbling voice. For a second she was utterly baffled – what the hell was he doing here? – but then she remembered. Driving down after his meeting. His big, important meeting. John Wayne finally showed up in Dodge, ready to clean up the town. Yippee-kay-eye.

There was some sort of conversation below her – *where is she, what's gone on, she's upstairs, trying to get some rest* – and then she heard his tread on the risers, coming to see her.

With a sudden, terrible anger that made remarkable sense to her, Sarah decided she just didn't want to speak to him. Not then. Maybe never again.

She curled herself into a ball, rolled away from the door and closed her eyes, trying to make her breathing slow and regular. *Should I fake a snore*, she thought, and almost giggled – which would have ruined the effect somewhat.

She heard the door open, and Steve's voice whispered, "Sarah? Are you asleep?"

Again, she had to fight a giggle – insane, yes, but wasn't *everything* insane now? It was like the Thursday nights when he'd come back from Rugby, just a little drunk, and tried to have sex with her. Oh, she loved Steve all right, loved him good and proper, but after an evening of battering heads on the pitch and a couple of Stella's the last thing she wanted was his hands on her – or in her – so she just pretended to be asleep. Sooner or later, he got the message.

Marriages keep many secrets, she thought, *it's how you ignore those secrets that counts.*

"Sarah," he asked again, but then she heard the door close behind him and his steps – comically soft – descending, back into the living room, to talk to Jon, with whom (no doubt) Steve would have a lot in common. After all, how many times had they met? Twice? At the wedding and Carl's funeral? And they were, of course, remarkably similar types. Jon, tall and a little excitable, Steve stocky, muscular and (like Sarah), extremely level-headed.

Yes, the last time they met was at Carl's funeral. Did they say much to each other? Probably not.

But was Sarah as level-headed as she thought? Apparently not. She'd found an odd facility in herself, a touch of Eve's imagination perhaps – hardly surprising, that stuff just didn't appear out of thin air, they were sisters after all, they were bound to share *some* characteristics – but where, ultimately, had that led? To an empty house. A random clue from a random page in a random magazine, a meaningless event she'd ascribed meaning to, so desperate was she. Maybe that's why she'd spent so much of her life ignoring that side of her nature; maybe she'd known all along it was useless.

Astonishingly, she let out a jaw-cracking yawn. Yeah, Carl's funeral. Odd, it had been. Well, no; not odd, normal, and that was what was in itself odd about it. *Y'know, it was a normal, Protestant funeral, nothing arty-farty, nothing ethereal, no one in floating robes except the Vicar, no chanting except for the prayers, just the man in the front reading about his father's mansion, like any other funeral.*

Another yawn, every bit as big as the last, then – once more – a stifled giggle. Sarah realised she'd somewhere along the line imagined Eve and Carl's friends as some sort of witches, or at the very least the sort of hippies who hugged trees and said "Yeah, man" whilst smoking a joint the size of the Etihad Stadium. *Hey, why* shouldn't *I? What do* I *know? I know how to alphabetise and file by subject – what the hell do I know about how actors or directors worship? Or* who they worship?

But there it had been; a perfectly ordinary funeral. Readings from the Bible (the usual sort about death being not proud, about the number of rooms in my Father's mansion, about a sure and certain hope – although Sarah had a feeling *a certain hope* was a contradiction in terms), some remembrances from his friends, all of them positive – one or two of them actually quite funny – and then all of that about rooms and mansions and her fragile sister at her side –

Rooms and mansions. You're thinking that a lot, aren't you?

Well, yeah little Eve. That's what they say at funerals – they said it at Mum's, at Dad's, they said it at Carl's. Y'know, the one about how "I've not died, I've gone into another room, for my Father's mansion has many rooms." You know the song, join in on the second chorus, if you like.

Yeah, chorus. Apt, that – because that phrase has been chorusing around your head for a while, hasn't it?

Couple of minutes, tops. Hey, I'm just free-associating – is that what they call it? – pay it no nevermind, as Mum used to say. Bizarrely, I do think I'm actually on the verge of nodding off here, and everybody knows the amount of shite that runs through a person's head when the Nod-Nod train gets ready to pull out for Sleepyland.

Yep, big Sarah, with you on that. All sorts go through your head. Like rooms and mansions. Many rooms, many mansions. Many places, many houses. That metaphor they use – I've just nipped into the kitchen, be back soon – doesn't it sound like the deceased is hiding, mucking about? Playing Hide and Seek? In his many mansions?

Well, I suppose, if you put it that way ...anyway, he doesn't have many mansions, *he has many* rooms. *One mansion, just a big one, with east and west wings. And servants' quarters, probably.*

Oh come on, if he's that rich he'll have more than one mansion, won't he? Lots of mansions, lots of rooms, lots of places to hide ...

Sarah sat up suddenly, no longer tired. *Many mansions ...or houses ...places to hide ...*

Who the hell said Barry Mackie only had one address?

*

It was a small rip, but to Eve it was the finest sound she'd heard since ...well, since Carl had rung her up out of the blue all those years ago.

It was the sound of hope.

She looked down at her right wrist. The tape had *definitely* frayed there. All that thrashing about, that flexing, relaxing, that final devastating cramp burst had done it. Not much, not enough, but it was a start. Like finding your way into a part, really. There was always a way. Even when she'd thought there wasn't, there had been. There was always a crack, a chink.

Always.

So Eve put all thoughts of Laura and Carl behind her (a struggle, but they went), and concentrated on flexing and relaxing once more, back in rotation, and every time she flexed her right wrist, that *riii-ip* grew just a touch louder.

*

Sarah crept from the spare room into Eve's "office" on cat feet, desperately trying not to disturb the men downstairs. After all, what would she say to them? *Hey guys, just got another mad notion which is clinically insane! Want to join in?*

Had she ever been in this room before? Not that she could remember – and why the hell would she have been? This wasn't her space. This was private.

Sarah looked around the posters and the pictures on the walls in the radiant light given off by the monitor screen, and her heart broke a little. Eve and Carl, younger, together, the things they'd done, the places they'd seen …

Why is the computer on? How long has it been on for?

That stopped her cold. Had Eve been in here yesterday, checking her emails? Possibly, but could Sarah remember that? She could not. No reason at all why Eve would have told her, of course …but it didn't feel *right.*

Somehow, it felt righter to believe this computer had just …well, switched itself on a second or two before she entered the room.

Drifting, almost as if she was still half asleep, Sarah sat down at the keyboard and double clicked the funny swirly 'e' that would open Google. And when that appeared, she typed BARRY MACKIE LONDON ADRESSES into the dialog box.

Please God he's not registered under any aliases …please God …

A link to the Electoral Register site. A savage, bitter smile plastered itself on Sarah's face. She was, after all, a librarian. She needed access to a site like this. She was already registered.

She entered her username and password, then sat back and waited.

*

Eve's right wrist wasn't free – it was, in fact, a country mile from free – but it *was* loose. It grew looser with every flex and relax. The fact that flexing and relaxing became harder at each rotation was, of course, hugely irritating – but who would expect anything else after God knows how many hours strapped to a chair without food or water? And how much energy had she expended on simple shock? High emotional states like that – not to mention pure terror – wore the body out like nobody's business. That's why people had hot drinks loaded with sugar, to replenish the stock. She'd had nothing. So each flex and relax became just that little bit weaker, just a little bit feebler …but no matter, not really, because that rip was *growing*, and sooner or later her right wrist would just pop free like a bullet from a gun.

Oh, Eve wished she had a gun. To stand up, free from that hateful chair, to see Barry's face drop in astonishment, to pull the gun from behind her back, to shoot the bastard right between the eyes …

Ah, that'd be nice. Oh, and maybe George Clooney could turn up to rescue me. Dressed as a fireman …

She flexed her right wrist again, and the *riii-ip* was much louder now, a *rrriiiiii-IIIIP*, and her jittering, spasming fist made it to almost an inch – inch and a half, maybe – above the arm rest. Looking down, she could see the tape splitting and fracturing. Just a bit more …just a little …

Footsteps approaching from the hallway. Eve dropped her head forward, and looked as beaten as she could – not difficult. But she didn't relax completely. Every ounce of strength she possessed went into keeping her body as tensed as possible without *looking* as if she was as tensed as possible.

Eve knew she didn't have long. With a cold wash so reminiscent of the moment when the doctors had told her that they were going to make Carl "as comfortable as possible," she knew she was entering the final stages of whatever sick psychodrama she'd stumbled into.

"Beginners on stage please," she muttered, then followed it with, "I'm not a beginner, I've done this before." *Yeah, she thought. Only this time you're doing it for real.*

The hallway door opened.

*

Got you, you son of a frigging whore, thought Sarah as she hunched over the monitor.

There was Barry Mackie's Acton address, all present and correct, but underneath that was another; 76, Little Street, Tottenham. And the postcode. *My father's mansion has many houses.* Of course it did, he'd need one to live in and another to take people he kidnapped – it was obvious, really, if you thought about it. *How long had he been planning this? What kind of sick puppy is he?* She hunted around and found a pen in the desk drawer, then pulled a sheet of paper from the printer and jotted it down.

Of course, I could just hit control and 'P.' So why aren't I?

The answer seemed to be that would make a noise, and that seemed perfectly sensible, so she just folded the paper up and stuck it into her jeans pocket, then switched off the monitor.

Sick, yeah. But clever, cunning. Clever and cunning enough to know – or suspect – that he may somehow enter the suspect list, clever enough to know he needed a bolthole ...but he's also monumentally stupid. He takes a second property ...and registers it in his own name?

Of course, he'd need identity if he was renting – and he'd have to be renting, you don't take a mortgage out on some kind of holding pen – but surely false papers weren't that difficult to fake? Not if you were clever, not if you were dealing with an unscrupulous landlord (and weren't there plenty of those around?) ...so what does that lead you to, Sarah?

Well, he's either so arrogant, so sure of his own cleverness that he doesn't think anyone else would go looking for a second address ...or he just doesn't care. And if he just doesn't care, that makes him even more dangerous than I thought. If he just doesn't care, he could do anything ...and you can't frighten someone who just doesn't care.

A minute of terrible immobility struck her at that. What, exactly, was she supposed to do next? Phone the police? Yes, of course, that would make sense – but why would they listen? Hadn't they already been led on a wild goose chase by her once today? Anyway, if they were as on the ball as all the TV shows and books she'd read then surely they'd be onto this already? After all, Sarah was just a Chorlton librarian, and *she'd* found a second address – surely all those Hendon graduates with their degrees and training would have checked this out? Of course they would. They were doubtless on their way already.

Should she then go downstairs and tell Jon and Steve what she'd discovered? Yes, of course, that would also make sense. Then the three of them could saddle up like one of those awful John Wayne Westerns that Steve liked to watch and they'd charge to the rescue. Just like they'd done before – well, two of them had, anyway. *Oh by the way, how did that go?*

Not so well, actually. He – this Barry Mackie – was one jump ahead of us.

Well, fine then. Do it all over again, then. And what if he's two *jumps ahead of you, what then? How foolish would you look in their eyes?*

Not, of course, that it mattered, what mattered was Eve – obviously – but still …drag them out, drag them to Tottenham (wherever the hell *that* was), pump them up with macho fantasies about sorting the whole mess out and then …nothing, all over again. How would they look at her, those men? Scornfully? Or worse, would they just patronise her, tickle her under the chin, and tell her not to worry, she'd done her best?

Are you seriously putting your pride above Eve's safety?

No. Sarah actually shook her head in negation as she very quietly stood and opened the "office" door. *I'm just making sure. I'm just going to take a quick trip to Tottenham and see what's going on. If nothing, if the bastard's* really *so clever he could lay a third false trail, then so what? But if I find what I'm looking for, I'll be on the phone so quickly I won't have time to blink.*

She crept down the stairs, listening as Steve's bass rumble of a voice grew louder, tiptoeing like a little girl desperate to eavesdrop on a grownups' party. *Of course, there's the small matter of actually getting there. What do I do, hail a cab?*

Don't be stupid, you take the Beamer. The one Steve drove down in, the one with the satnav. The family car for the family you never quite got round to having. The one you have keys to in your bag.

Good point, thought Sarah as she opened the front door – oh so carefully – without stopping to consider that the voice that had spoken in her head had, in fact, sounded suspiciously alien.

Had sounded quite a lot like her dead brother-in-law, to be completely accurate.

*

"So," said Barry merrily as he stood in front of her (mercifully blocking her view of Laura's cracked head), "we find ourselves in the final round of today's competition. Eve Rogers, you've successfully manoeuvred your way here, managed to avoid all the pitfalls and traps, and you've proven yourself a worthy finalist. So, are you ready to play – The Last Round?"

Keep him talking, Carl had said in that dream that didn't really feel like a dream, *stall him.* And then, *remember what you thought after I kicked the bedroom door in.*

As she'd prepared to walk up the stairs – so brave! - she'd thought, *I'm no fucking victim.*

Except I am, she thought. *That's what he's made me. That's what he's reduced me to. A fucking victim. Yeah, he hit me from behind and taped me down to stop me fighting back, but he made me into a victim.*

And I hate *being a victim.*

Gathering as much control over her destroyed mouth as possible, she said, "No. Fuck off."

*

Sarah had a moment's terrible panic when she couldn't see the car. Of course, it wasn't parked in the drive – it couldn't be, Jon's Volvo took up the space – but as she walked out onto the street, she couldn't spot it anywhere. *Maybe he didn't bring the car,* she thought. *Maybe he didn't drive at all; maybe he took the train …or the coach …*

A brittle bark of a laugh escaped her then. *Steve? On a coach? And pigs will have pilot's licences.* Steve could no more let someone else take the responsibility for his journey than he climb up a wall like Spider-Man. *Hell, that's why he hates flying. He's not scared of heights, he just hates handing over control to somebody else.*

So he drove, of course he did. Question was though, where did he park?

Why don't you point the key, press the button and see where the lights flash?

That was a good idea (once again, Sarah didn't give the fact it came from an alien voice a second thought), so she followed it. About twelve feet to her right she heard the musical squeaks that gave its location away.

Thanks, God, she thought, and ran to it.

*

"What did you say to me?" asked Barry, utterly unperturbed, still smiling – and why shouldn't he? He held all the cards here, he was in control, he was in power; why shouldn't he smile?

Speaking slowly, carefully, Eve said, "I said no, fuckface. No more games. This time *I'm* going to ask some questions."

The tape gave just a little bit more on her right wrist; it seemed to leap upwards an inch or two. *Careful, got to keep track of that. Got to rein it in. Got to be ready to use it.*

That was going to be difficult, though. The tension in her body was thrumming through her like a low voltage electric shock. *Got to keep him looking at me, at my eyes, got to distract him.*

"Eve," Barry said, in an unctuous tone that made her think of Uriah Heep, "you've got it arse about face again. You just don't understand your role in all this, do you? Though that shouldn't surprise me overmuch, not after what we went through recently. But let me do what that weak brew of a director didn't; remind you of your place. You victim, me sadistic torturer with personality disorder. You scream, I mutilate and act all weird. Got it?"

"No. I refuse."

"Eve, oh dear, sweet, little, old Eve, you just don't *get* it, do you? *I'm* the boss here, I call the shots," then suddenly, he barked out, 'Vodka! Sambuca! Tequila!" Then he turned to the window, arms outstretched, as if to an imaginary audience, "Calling the shots! Get it? Oh, please yourselves!"

"Knock it off," Eve enunciated precisely, "there's just you and I here. I'm immune to the lunatic act. Want to know why you're a writer? Because you're a lousy actor."

Barry punched her hard in the stomach, his face flat and unexpressioned. A great hiss of air escaped her, and an involuntary spasm nearly tore her hand free. Even under this fresh assault, part of her brain chanted, *watch it, watch it, keep that secret!*

Somehow, she managed it.

"Fair comment," she heard him say through the shock, "but still; no one likes a critic. But yeah, it's valid. I *am* a lousy actor. However, I'm a *genius* writer. I mean, look at this scenario! It's *brilliant!* I get two women to this place and I get to cut them with knives and glasses and cleavers! It'd make a hell of a movie. Cheap, too. One set, three actors – bit of a bugger for the director, making sure he keeps it interesting – but that's his problem, not mine.

"Granted, yes, my performances are a bit broad – but when you come to think about it, what's so great about being an actor anyway? I mean, what do you actually do, beyond parrot other people's ideas? I mean, you're all vampires, really. What do you bring to any creative endeavour? Nothing, because you don't create. You're *interpreters,* that's all. You say what I tell you to say, think what I tell you to think. Is that a talent? Is that a skill? Jesus, you could train *chimps* to do what you do, if you could only stop them wanking all the time or throwing shit at each other – actually, no, don't bother, who'd notice? Your lot don't behave any differently. You jump into bed with each other like they were going to outlaw sex tomorrow, you snort all the coke you can get your grubby little paws on, you generally have the morals of the Sodomites. And the poor bastards who make you who you are, the galley slaves who give you all these wonderful thrills, what do *we* get?

Ignored. Poor wages. Inadequate living conditions. An Invisibility Coat for Christmas. And *no fucking gratitude* from the whores we turn into stars! What do we get from them? "I can't say this line,' 'My character wouldn't do that,' or the simply spellbinding, *'Change the last scene, make it* my *scene, rewrite the fucking thing from top to bottom and I JUST MIGHT CONSIDER IT!'"

I'll say this, Eve thought as she struggled to regain her breath, *I'm discovering more and more about the world these days. I thought he was* pretending *to be mad. And, in a way, he was. But under that pretend madness lay a pretend sanity. He's a goner; he's truly,* truly *mad.*

And another thing; did I think I was scared before? I've hit a Brand New and Improved level of terror. Because –

"Are you saying …" she gasped out, desperately struggling for breath, desperately trying to be understood, "that you did …all *this* …just because I asked you to change your bloody *play*?"

"Well, *d'uh!*" Barry exclaimed, mimicking her thick-tongued voice. "Why else?"

It was almost one madness too many for Eve. She could feel her tenuous grasp on this situation spinning away from her. Bad enough what had happened to her, bad enough what had happened to Laura …but to discover that it was all for a reason so *stupid*, so *pointless*, nearly sent her over the edge.

"See," Barry went on, "I'm God. *All* writers are God. We sit down at whatever we sit down at – computers, notebooks, maybe even still typewriters, who knows? – and we do what God did. We *create*. Okay, He did it in a week and it'll take me roughly a year, but He's bigger than me, and more experienced. But other than that, we're pretty much the same, me and Him. We give the people the *illusion* of free will – we don't let them know that they're running along our railroad tracks – but we guide them through every move they make. We create hoops and make our people jump through them. And when *one* of then – one *stinking little bitch crack whore* – sets herself against us, we *smack them down!* And that's what *you* did, Eve old Eve. You set yourself against me. You looked upon my works and you didn't despair, you said, 'Oh, that's not good enough for *me*, I'm so much *better* than that; but if you create your world in *my* image *I might just condescend to join in!*' That's when the face of God looks wrathful upon His creations. Seriously, look what happened to Lucifer when he wanted to sit in the Big Chair for a bit."

He actually believes *this*. Eve could see it in his eyes; no artifice there now, no games. *Did I think I was in trouble before? Did I?*

"So you make your idiotic demands," he went on. "You give your ultimatum. And those weedy directors and producers say, 'Yes Miss Rogers, no Miss Rogers, three bags *full*, Miss Rogers,' and my play, my *world*, ends up as a piece of shit! A joyless, feminist rant about how great women are and how powerless men are. Now, I ask you," he continued, bending low, face to face, "who's got the power now, you great big titted *slut*? I can do what I like to you. I could rape you to death. I could cut your head off and jizz down the hole. So *who's* got the power, Eve? Who's got the fucking *power*?"

She said nothing. She was too terrified to say anything.

"So they bow to you," said Barry, straightening up, back to his semi-jocular tone, "and I work my arse off to make sure you're satisfied. And you are – oh, and did you ever thank me? You did *not*, did you? You asked that queer of a *director* to thank me, but could you get off that whore's arse of yours and actually do it *yourself*? No, not our Queen! That would be too fucking *much* to ask! But, you know something? You were shit. All through rehearsals, you were shit. And how I *laughed*! How I karmically *laughed*! All I had to do was bide my time, let you die on stage, and wait till they replaced you! Then, when some new whore came in, I could get my *real* script – my real *world* – back."

The humour ran out of his voice, and his face once more became a void. "But you even had to fuck that up, didn't you, bitch? You had to go out there and be brilliant! You had to have the audience stand and cheer at the end of that abortion! And they'd never let me change it back then! *Never!*"

"So you decided to make your world real, did you?" Eve wheezed out. She wasn't sure if it was a good idea to speak, but she couldn't stop herself.

"No, my world *was* real, *always* real. I just decided to take it out of the theatre, that's all. Ever since that reading, that Talking Book gig, ever since I made you sound better than you've ever sounded before, ever since I saw you sat in that chair behind that glass …that's when I knew. That's when I knew one way or another I'd knock that arrogance out of you."

"And her …Laura? Where does she fit in?"

He shrugged. "Synthesis of ideas, I suppose. Oh, one way or another she was going to get punished for picking me up and dropping me like that. But then, in the usual flash of inspiration that only writers know about, I realised I could – excuse me – kill two birds with one stone. Get her here alongside you, get her to admit to your face that she'd fucked your husband. Oh, and Eve – I gotta tell you, she'd lie next to me, night after night, my jizz still on her lips, and boast about how she fucked your old man. About how *guilty* he'd been afterwards …but how frantic he'd been *during*. About how much he loved it. I bet he would've, too. That Laura knew some tricks, all right."

He's trying to hurt you; he wants to see you cry. And I know he's succeeded, but don't give him the satisfaction. "You kept her here, tortured her … for weeks …just because …she blew you off after an affair? Just because you wanted me to hear what she did?"

"Yeah, pretty much," the nutter reflected, gazing at the ceiling. "Some people might think it's not strong enough as a motivation, but fuck 'em, I'm the writer, this is my world, I can do what I want." Then he looked straight back at her. "But she wasn't that important. Truth be told, her biggest contribution to the plot was to write that note on the flowers. The ones I put on Carly-Warly's gravey-wave. And she only did that because she thought I'd let her go if she did. Stupid cow. I bet *that* got in your head, didn't it? I saw you, you know. I was there, watching. You didn't see me, but I saw you. I saw you pick that note up and frown." He darted a little closer, and why not? He could do anything he wanted after all. "Bet it got in your head, didn't it? Bet it burrowed there, like cancer."

Yeah, you little prick, it did. Well done, round of applause, have a Bonio. It hurt. Hurt then, hurts now. But I swear to God not as much as you will hurt if I get out of this chair. Because I'm no fucking victim.

"Now then, Eve. Anything else? Only this is a live show, and we don't want to hold back the news."

Okay Carl, thought Eve, *I've kept him talking. Even though it's hurt me on so many levels, I've kept him talking. Thing is, I'm running out of things to say. So, if that dream I had about you really was more than a dream, I've kept my end of the deal. What about you?*

*

Sarah drove through the unfamiliar streets as calmly as she could, directed by the woman's voice, trying to keep to the speed limit (well, almost), unwilling to be pulled over by some idiot traffic cop.

Had they noticed she was missing yet? Had one or other of them gone upstairs to check on her to find an empty bed? If they had, they hadn't called. Her phone was on the passenger seat, silent.

A sign on her left. LONDON BOROUGH OF TOTTENHAM, it said. *Okay,* she prayed again. *C'mon God, let's get it right this time, eh?*

The woman on the satnav told her to turn right, so she did. The red arrow in the centre of the screen kept scrolling. *How much farther have I got to go?*

That was the problem with London, she was beginning to find. It just didn't appear to frigging end.

*

"So Laura was a whore, and she ended up with many a twat in her head. You're a mouthy whore who just can't keep it buttoned, so you end up with a little broken glass surgery. You see what I'm doing, right? I'm taking control of my world again, taking it from *you.* I've pointed out your foibles and faults – and I don't care if you accept them at all, it's all about what the *audience* realise, not the characters - but the question remains; what do we do for the Big Finish? How do we dramatically *resolve* all of this? Well, I'm sure by now you've realised I'm not going to let you go, you're not going to survive. You've seen my face, haven't you? You could blab to any Mr Plod you like. And I'm sure even a thick bitch like you has spotted my predilection for sharp objects – there's many a Freudian interpretation for those, I daresay – but have you considered *my* place in all this? Of course you haven't, you're an actress, one step up from those worms that hang around vent holes at the bottom of the ocean. You only think of *yourselves.* See, the great existential angst of a writer is this; *how do you top your last work?* You have to keep going *on,* you have to keep *creating,* but oh, the more you do, the harder it gets. Tennessee Williams couldn't get produced in the Sixties, he'd burned himself out. Arthur Miller likewise in the Seventies. It happens – maybe there's only so many stories in the well, only so many worlds one God can create. In a sense, my job is harder than His; He only had to do it once, I've got to do it *again and again.* But this," he gestured around him, "is just so grand, so stunning, so *perfect,* that I've decided to take the Hemmingway out." Down to her again, eye to eye, "Get it, Eve? The Hemming Way out? Jesus, you thick bitch. Anyway," he said, moving away to her left, back to the hallway door, "the fact is, I can't top this. It's just brilliant, and anything else I do will just be second rate. And I *won't* create a second rate Universe. So, here's the plan."

He held up the knife again, of course the knife, always knives and broken glass, these things hurt the most. "I slit your throat from ear to ear. You never speak again. And I dip my finger in your blood and write the last thing I will ever write on the wall. It will say THE END. Then I'll stick this knife in my left eye and ram it home with my right fist. It will pierce my brain. And I will die in seconds. Smiling."

Chapter Thirty

Even before the woman told her she'd reached her destination, Sarah knew. It sang to her heart, it called to her. *If I was going to kidnap someone,* she thought, *this is where I'd bring them.*

Little Street was marked for demolition. The majority of semi-detached houses were boarded with what looked like reinforced plastic over their windows and doors. Messages scrawled across walls read GAS OFF and ELECTRIC OFF. Half torn signs in windows told her EVERYTHING OF VALUE HAS BEEN REMOVED FROM THIS PROPERTY.

It was as depressing as hell, even the streetlights were out, the almost gone sun casting huge opaque shadows across the rotting hulks. *What kind of landlord would rent out a place like this?*

As soon as she asked herself that, she realised the truth. The other place, the Acton house, was his rental. *This* was his, his *real* place. *Of course. He'd want to feel safe, wouldn't he? Where safer than a house where you know every creaky floorboard and every loose piece of stair carpet.*

She dropped the car into first and crawled along, then switched off the headlights. Thick gloom enveloped her as she scanned for number 76. *Over there, on the right …*

Sarah Brown pulled up, pulled the keys from the ignition and very gently opened the Beamer's door. Unlike the other houses in this desolate hole, 76 hadn't been boarded up, nor did it possess any messages on its brickwork. 76, Little Street, Tottenham was a holdout. *What's he after, more money from the Council? Or does he claim squatter's rights? Or is he just a festering rat, refusing to be gassed from his bolthole?*

Oh, and one more question. What the frig do I do now?

She stood outside the house, just to the left so she could avoid being seen through the living room bay windows, and chewed her lip in terrible indecision. Kick the front door down? Slide down the chimney like Father Christmas? What?

Then it came to her. First, she had to make sure she had the right place, didn't she? Crouching low, she scuttled to the living room window and peered in through the filthy net curtains. Nothing to see – almost literally, in fact. No TV, no bookcases, no fireplace – just a three piece suite that looked as if it had been bought around the time John Major was Prime Minister.

Well, if Eve was *here, he wouldn't keep her in plain sight, would he? She'd be hidden away, round the back. Maybe upstairs.*

Pondering just for a second as to who, exactly, would be looking around a street like this when it seemed everyone had been re-homed, Sarah made her way round to the back door, to see if there was a way of climbing over the fence into the garden.

*

"You're really going to stab yourself in the eye?" Eve gasped, trying to keep him talking. Oh, her wrist was so nearly free …not that she knew exactly what she was going to do with it, but she'd be damned if she was going out without a fight. She never had done. Ever. She'd gone her own way, made her own destiny, made her own career – even that last play, *Pavlov's Bell* (and it almost certainly would be her last play, she knew that now), she'd taken control of at the last minute, she'd steered into that skid all right, and she'd keep doing that right to the end. Which looks like it'll be in about five minutes time.

She gave up any pretence of trying to hide what she was doing. Her death was very close now, and the time for subtlety and subterfuge was over.

"Sure am," said Barry. "And wriggle about all you want, I like seeing your titties bounce. Yeah, I know, dramatically – because I'm a writer – I should hack my hands off or something, but that's a really crap way to commit suicide. The whole knife in the eye thing looks so much better to me." Then he giggled. "Well, would look so much better if I didn't have a knife in my eye."

Frantically, Eve risked a glance down, and to her right. There was just a fraction of tape left holding her arm down – a sliver, maybe half an inch thick. *A minute, please. Just a minute.*

*

There was a wheelie bin stacked up in the dark, and (giving thanks for those twice weekly gym sessions), Sarah used it to boost herself onto the fence. She lowered herself down gently into the – well, yard, not a garden. Clumps of weeds shot through the cracks in the flags. A shed held up by woodworm holes nestled by the door to the alleyway beyond. *In there,* Sarah thought, *I bet she's in there!*

Try the house first, said the calm voice in her head. Without a pause, she did. First window opened up a view of another room – what her mother would have called "the lounge." Flock wallpaper and another tatty suite, but aside from that, absolutely nothing. But beyond that window was another, and if she had any sense of geography, that should be the kitchen.

Bent almost double, Sarah inched towards it, taking care to be as quiet as a mouse. Her heart banged in her ribcage as her foot struck a loose brick (*what the frig's that doing here?*), making her stumble …but she didn't fall, and kept on.

*

God oh please just a minute please oh God so nearly.

He stood before her, knife in hand. "Time to take a final bow, Eve."

He brought it down in an arc, aiming for her throat …

And her hand broke free and caught his wrist!

*

Sarah raised her head and looked through the kitchen window. For a second her shock was so complete she couldn't even think. Eve, her sister, *little Eve,* tied to a chair with what looked like tape, one wrist free, a man, dressed in black, holding a knife to her …Eve struggling to hold him back …but losing.

*

There was a perfect second as Barry's face simply fell apart with shock. "What the fuck you *doing,* you whore?" He screamed.

All I can, Eve realised. *This is it, I can only delay the inevitable. And for how long? Seconds, maybe. He's bigger, stronger, he's got all his limbs in motion …this is it, my entire defence.* And then, her mind gabbling, *My God, I'm sorry for all I've done that has offended You. I've been a bitch sometimes and I'm sorry. I don't even think I really believed in You, and I'm sorry. But if you can, forgive my sins. Please.*

Then, as she heard Barry laugh and felt him increase the pressure on the knife, as it edged ever closer to her jugular, she thought, *Carl, hope you saved me a seat. I'll be along in a minute.*

Then things went a bit mad.

*

Hey, what about that brick, the calm male voice said to her. *Hell of a way to get someone's attention.*

Good plan, Carl, Sarah thought without really thinking at all. She knelt down, felt for it, picked it up, then stood. They were still locked together, Eve and the man she was sure was Barry Mackie, only the knife was almost at her throat.

Avon calling, arsehole, she thought. She pulled her right arm back and threw with all her strength.

*

Something smashed through the kitchen window with a sound like the end of the world. Before either of them had a chance to look, something hard and heavy hit Barry on the temple and a wonderful spurt of blood erupted from a gouge that magically appeared there. He continued to gape at her for a second, then his eyes glazed, rolled upwards, and he hit the floor with a most satisfying *smack.*

Eve just sat there for longer than she would ever know, goggling. *Why aren't I dead? I should be dead.* Then she heard a voice calling from her right. "Eve," and this was just impossible, it sounded like Sarah. "Eve, can you get up?"

Eve turned to the voice, and God, it *was* Sarah, her big sister ...and she'd saved her life.

*

As Eve turned to face her, Sarah recoiled in horror. *What has that bastard* done *to you?*

The lower half of Eve's face, from the mouth down, appeared to be missing entirely. A great, ragged hole ran down her left cheek. *I'll dance on that frigger's grave, I swear to that.*

I'm afraid not, said the calm voice in her head ...and did he seem sad? Maybe, but that was just one more piece of lunacy in this whole lunatic day. *What you have to do now is phone the police. And don't for one second think this is over.*

Sarah pulled out her phone and hit three nines.

*

How the hell did she find me? "No, I can't, not yet," she said, as clearly as she could. She saw Sarah nod as she spoke into her phone. *But I will in a minute. If I have that long.*

A quick glance to her left. Barry was lying where he fell, inert. How badly was he hurt? Could he even be dead? Could that be true? Could whatever Sarah had pitched through the glass *really* have killed him?

Don't know, but I seriously doubt it. I've seen enough thrillers to know that the bad guy never stays down for long. And I fucking hate *thrillers.*

She started working on the tape that bound her left wrist.

*

"My name is Sarah Brown, I'm Eve Wilson's sister, and she is being held captive at 76 Little Street Tottenham. I'm there now. I have ...well, temporarily rendered the bastard incapable, I think you'd call it, but you have to get here *now*, right this *second*, got me?"

The jobsworth on the other end tried to hold her on the line for more details (probably), but Sarah couldn't hang around. She looked through the shattered pane as Eve tried to free herself. "Hang on, I'll get through the kitchen door."

"You can't," Eve said. "There's …" a hitch in Little Eve's voice, like she was trying not to cry. "Something blocking it. Can you try the front?"

Sarah nodded. "Don't worry, Eve. The police are on their way." *And the bastards had better get here quick. Because if I've not killed that frigger already, I will do when I get inside.*

Sarah took one last looked at the fallen body, satisfied herself it wasn't moving, then got running.

*

Sarah, if I – if we – get out of this, I will never, ever let you out of my sight. The wrapping started to unravel from her left wrist. It was uncomfortable leaning over like that, but compared to what she'd been through over the last few hours it was no more than a mild headache. *I mean it, Big Sarah, I will follow you around like a puppy, I will sit at your feet and wag my tail every time you speak.*

The last wrap of tape unravelled, and Eve sat there, holding both hands in front of her, rubbing her wrists, trying to get the circulation flowing. *Okay, just a minute, then get to work on my feet.*

Which was, of course, when Barry rolled over onto his back.

*

There was no wheelie bin to help in the yard, so hoisting herself onto the fence was a much more painful and protracted business this time around. Sarah stood at five foot four, the fence was six foot at least – it took two jumps even to reach the top, then a third to hold on.

Frantically she scrabbled her feet against the wood for purchase – and wouldn't you know it? The wood was rotten to frig. Clumps of it crumbled to powder under her fingers. *One word, arsehole. Cuprinol.*

Still, no matter. She'd either get over the thing or it would collapse from under her. Either way, she didn't mind. One thing she *did* know – by hook or by crook, she was getting into that house.

Hey Sarah, said the male voice. *Why don't you try that other window round the back? The lounge window? I mean, why make it hard for yourself?*

Good thinking, Batman, she thought, then dropped back down. *Sorry, wasn't thinking straight.*

Oh, and get a shift on. This isn't over yet.

*

"The fuck was *that*?" Barry asked thickly.

To hell with the circulation, Eve thought, and bent as far forward at the tape around her stomach would let her, blindly feeling for the join of the gaffer around her right calf. From somewhere close, she heard a crashing of glass. *Way to go, Sarah.*

At the very periphery of her vision, Barry sat upright, rubbing his left temple, gazing curiously at the blood on his fingers, wincing at the pain. "Jesus, that hurt. Did you do that, Eve?" Then he turned to look at her, saw that she was almost half free, and a look of fright that made her want to sing exploded on his face. "Don't you fucking *dare*," he raged, and scrambled to his feet. "I mean it, whore, *don't you dare!*" He ran towards her – only three steps and he'd be onto her – but he tripped over the unfettered legs of Laura, and fell to the ground again.

Nice one, you cheating dead bitch, thought Eve …as she grasped the edge of the tape around her right leg and began to pull.

*

Sarah looked about her, couldn't find any more bricks just lying about, so with an almost cheerful thought of *frig it,* she removed her jacket, wrapped it round her arm, and hit the lounge window as hard as she could. *Thank you God for making this an old, unloved house. Double glazing would have really ruined my evening.*

It shattered. Remembering the many crime dramas she'd watched, Sarah battered the shards loose as well, then boosted herself onto the windowsill. *Why can't I hear sirens yet? Where the fuck are they?*

*

He wasn't down for long – people like Barry never really were. He jumped back upright like a massive ungainly spider. He looked at the floor, spotted what he was after and sprang for it.

That knife. That fucking *knife.*

Eve worked faster at the tape, unravelling it …then her right leg was free.

Just her left leg and her stomach bound now. Just them. She had to work fast. Very fast.

Praying it would be fast enough, she felt for the tape on her left leg.

*

Just as she dropped into the lounge, Sarah heard him roar, calling her sister a whore. *Jesus Christ almighty,* she thought in panic, and ran to the door.

*

She nearly made it. Nearly had that left leg free.

But Barry picked the knife up and stood, looking at her as if *she* was the dangerous one.

Yeah. Give me two more minutes and I'll show you how right you are, fuckface.

But it seemed her time was up. Barry advanced on her, knife outstretched, then stopped. "No," he said. "Not from the front, Not with both your arms free. From behind. That's how you whores like it best, isn't it? Up the dirtbox."

He stepped out of her view, circling her, and it just didn't matter anymore did it? *So close, so bastard close ...*

His hands on her hair, pulling her head back. The knife at her throat. His breath in her ear. "Going to slaughter you like a pig, bitch."

*

The door led through to the hallway, and to her left Sarah saw the bastard circling behind Eve, ready to slit her throat. Six, maybe ten feet away that was all. But it was too far.

It will be if you just stand there looking, the male voice (Carl? Did it sound like Carl? Could it?) spoke up, only this time it wasn't calm. *Run, you stupid cow!*

Even though she hated being spoken to like that, she ran. And as she ran, she screamed, *"ARMED POLICE, STAY WHERE YOU ARE!"*

She'd seen *that* on the television, too.

Sarah barely weighed nine stone, but she'd been going to the gym twice weekly for quite a few years now. She had muscle tone all over her body. She could move when she needed to. She could put on a spurt. Man or not, if she hit him hard enough and fast enough, she reckoned she could take him down. And she'd frigging well laugh as she did it.

The man she damned well knew was Barry Mackie turned at her scream, eyes bulging with surprise and frustration, and he took the knife from Eve's throat. He held it in front of him.

Sarah tried to put the brakes on, but it was no good. She'd built up too great a speed. Her flat shoes skidded on the greasy linoleum floor. Not enough friction. She was heading straight for the knife. Straight for the knife and the frigger who held it. The *smiling* frigger.

Strangely, the last thought in her head wasn't hers. It was a male voice saying it was so very sorry.

She hit the knife full on. It pierced right through her chest. The pain was brilliant, bright and total. Then she felt that frigger thrust it deeper, and she didn't feel anything at all.

Chapter Forty-one

All this happened behind Eve, she had no idea what was going on. All she knew was that knife wasn't at her throat any longer, that Sarah had screamed something hysterically funny, and there was some kind of fight going on behind her – she heard Barry give a low grunt. *Nice one, Big Sarah. Hope you gave him a good kick in the balls.*

But the Lord helped those who helped themselves, so Eve leaned forward and ripped the last of the tape from her left calf. *Now keep him occupied – but keep safe – while I get this shit off my stomach.*

As she thought this, the very dead body of her sister fell into her view. Big Sarah hit the floor, with a hideous meaty thump. A gouged hole had been ripped into her chest. Blood was pumping everywhere ...but slowly, because her heart was no longer beating.

Eve stared at this, disbelieving, then howled in anguish and despair. *No, no, NO! God, you bastard! You fucking BASTARD, God! How dare you? HOW FUCKING DARE YOU?*

Sarah's glazed, fixed eyes looked back at her. *Hey, little Eve – how did I wind up dead?*

Jesus oh dear Jesus sis Sarah sis oh Jesus how could You oh my sister how could You, You fucker?

Then Barry whispered in her ear, low and soft, but she hardly heard him. "Sorry about that," he said. "Unexpected interruption from persons unknown. And now, back to the action."

The hand on her hair again, pulling it back.

Eve didn't even care. She was still looking at her dead sister. *You were so brave, big Sarah. And for what? Whatever you did to get here, you did for nothing, and died. Like we all do. All for nothing. Then death. With you in a minute, big Sarah.*

A tear ran down Eve's cheek, and she wiped it absently with her left hand. *I was so near. So near to escaping. So near to being free.*

She felt the cold twinge of metal at her throat. *Not all stories have happy endings.*

She felt the knife start to dig in.

Please don't make it hurt too much.

More tears fell ...tears for her sister, for her husband. For her.

Tears she could wipe. If she wanted to. Because, after all, her hands were free. And her legs.

And the chair, of course, was freestanding.

I made him rewrite his ending once, she thought. *And I'll do it again. Because -*

"I'M NO FUCKING VICTIM," she screamed.

She grabbed hold of the chair seat with both hands. She pushed down with her feet. *C'mon, let me be strong enough. Please.*

She was. Even after nearly twenty-four hours without food and water, even after fairly serious blood loss, she *was* strong enough. Eve was a stubborn old cow, after all.

For the first time in what seemed like forever, Eve Wilson stood up.

Not completely up,of course. She was, after all, still taped to a chair. She was bent forward from the waist, chair spilling out behind her, ready to damage anything at her rear.

Like a fucking psycho with a knife, for instance.

She heard his inarticulate whistle of rage as she stood. She felt the knife gently caress first her breasts, then her stomach. *Jesus, another two pound of pressure and I'd be –*

She choked that off. She *wasn't* ...that was all that mattered now. That, and showing this fucker just *who* was boss. That *no one* messed with her.

Her, or her sister.

Eve felt the pressure of carrying the chair, of standing like a crab, bite into her lower back and her calves. *I don't have long,* she thought. *Not long at all. He can reach forward at any time. Press home your advantage, Evie.*

So she pivoted her hips to her left, and brought the chair legs smashing into Barry Mackie's thighs. He screamed. Eve heard the distant clatter as the knife went flying. She pivoted her hips to her right (*and oh listen here, boys and girls – do I hear the faint rip of the last of this fucking tape?*), and once more battered wooden legs into real ones. Another scream, (and another rip, tape was never really designed to keep a chair attached to a standing, fighting woman), then she heard him stumble and fall, hitting the deck heavily.

But he'll be up soon enough, he's been down before and just will not lie still, so turn and beat the bastard into a pulp. Don't walk away with a beady eye on him, don't leave him screaming your name hoarsely, do what Sarah wanted you to do on that First Night.

Kill the bastard.

He was tangled up on the floor, legs under each other, looking at her with a *how the fuck did this happen* expression on his face.

Mindful of the aches in her muscles – which were growing worse with each second – and the very pressing need to *get this done,* she cut away her glance from him for a second, looking for the knife.

It was lying in Sarah's outstretched left hand. As if she'd caught it. Caught it, and was holding it out.

She saw Barry follow her gaze, and he tensed, ready to jump. "Stay where you are," she said, panting, sounding a lot less threatening than she wanted to. Her muscles were jumping and jiving now, her back and claves screaming an aria or two.

"Or what, whore?"

Keeping her eyes firmly on him, she took a step to her sister. Her sister who this fucker had murdered. "You know something," she said, seeing how this would go down now, visualising it in her head the way Carl had visualised his plays, "people who abuse women are queers."

His face was suddenly livid with rage. "Shut the fuck *up*, bitch."

Another step. He was wary of her, oh yeah …but he was a writer. And, after actors, nobody had bigger egos than writers. "Fact. Read it in *Cosmo*. Queers. Dirty fucking homos," another step, "who got fucked by the bigger boys in school." Another step. His eyes were bugging, his face redder than a stop sign. "Filthy limpdick mother-fixated Nancy boys." One final step. Keeping her eyes on his, she managed to squat down, ignoring the pain that threatened to lock her back in place once and for all. She reached blindly out and touched Sarah's still warm hand …and in it, the cold of the knife.

She ran her fingers along it until she reached the handle, not bothering if she cut herself. *What's another pint of blood, more or less, amongst all this mess?*

Faintly, from somewhere outside, there came the sound of sirens. Police sirens. Growing closer.

No you don't, she thought. *You don't cheat me out of my final scene.*

"And you know something, my maggot dicked queerboy friend? Your play fucking SUCKED!"

If anything was going to do it, it would be that.

Bellowing, Barry Mackie shot to his feet and ran at her, all arms and legs, insane, truly insane, a monster, vermin that had learned to walk and talk.

Eve Wilson stood as tall as she could, and thrust the knife forwards. Either by luck or judgement, it slid easily into Barry's left eye. Despite everything that had happened to her – and possibly for the final time in her life - Eve started laughing. She laughed at his scream of pain and shock. She laughed as his eyeball popped like a balloon, shrivelled and dropped back into its socket. She laughed at the squeak of metal on bone and she gouged the blade deeper and deeper. She laughed as she felt some resistance, pushed forward and was rewarded by a sudden spurt of blood that coated her wrist. *Is that his brain,* she thought, laughing harder as the police sirens grew louder ...louder ...*have I punctured his brain?*

Maybe she had, for Barry Mackie slumped then, and Eve found herself holding his entire weight with her right hand. It was too much for her, and, still laughing, she let him drop. He hit the lino with a wet slap.

Eve fell to her knees, still laughing, and the sirens outside were accompanied by loud banging on the door and men shouting "Police! Open up!"

Eve Wilson knelt in blood and gore, looked at the three dead bodies around her, and still laughed. Well, maybe she was crying.

Fade lights to blackout, she thought. *And CURTAIN.*

After

She sits in her chair, no longer caring that it's her *chair and not* their *chair, and gazes out of the bedroom window onto the street below. She does that a lot now, and has no idea why. Maybe it's because from here she can see the door. Eve likes to be in sight of doors now. She has a feeling she'll be like that forever. Even at Sarah's funeral, she kept glancing behind her, needing to see the doors. Still, that's unsurprising really. She looks out of her bedroom window and thinks* hard times pass.

The doctors and the district nurses come to her often – at least once a day – and they assure her that she's recovering well. Maybe she even is. One doctor tries to talk about "reconstructive surgery," but the thought of having anyone come near her with a knife or scalpel is just too much to bear, so she turns it down. And when he brings it up again, Eve screams at him until he goes away. She'll go to her grave with a ruined face. That's it.

She doesn't sleep well, but that's hardly surprising either and she pays it no nevermind. What sleep she does get is broken and haunted – the pain, the fear, his face in the dark – but it goes away soon enough after she wakes. They're only dreams, after all, and who cares about dreams? They come and they go. They pass.

The police don't come around anymore. She told them her story over and over again in the first few weeks, all of it, the truth, the whole truth and nothing the truth. And they nodded, made her go over it again, and nodded some more.

Well …maybe she edited some of the story. Maybe she left out the bit where she goaded the bastard into running at her. Maybe she thought they didn't need to know that.

She misses Sarah, misses her like hell – of course she does – and the tears she cries for her seem endless, but Eve knows they're not. They'll pass too.

The dreams will pass, the latent pain she feels will pass, the fear will pass, the tears will pass. One way or another, they'll pass. Everything passes eventually – like the craving for cigarettes. It either happens in life or it happens in death. Why fret about anything? It'll all pass.

When that happens, when Eve Wilson finally passes and all this is left behind, then one way or another she'll have the answer to the only thing that really bugs her still.

Carl.

Was he there or wasn't he? Was he *ever* there, or was it just her grief, her terrible, overwhelming grief? Was he nothing more than a figment of her distraught imagination right from the start – the picture from the album, the dreams, that last conversation on the surreal dream stage of their kitchen? Did that **actually** happen? Or did she just conjure him up because she needed him so badly? Did she project her desire to see him again on a whole series on random coincidences? Did she just use his face and voice as a sounding board?

She hopes so. Because if he was actually real, if he was genuinely *there in some way after his death, then she thinks he murdered her sister. What had he said – or what did she think he'd said?* I will not let you die. And if that means she has to take your place, then …

Is that what he did? Load her up and fire her like a bullet? Did he lead Sarah to her own death so Eve could live? Ah, that was such an awful thing to think. Awful. The pain that she and Steve were enduring. The grief. Once more, the grief. Was that all Carl's doing? Was it? And if so …how could she ever forgive him? How?

Were such things even possible? Could *the dead really influence the living?*

There's really no way of knowing. Yet.

But one day there will be. One day when Eve Wilson (known to some as Rogers) finally exits stage right for good, she'll know for sure. And if they somehow meet up again – Eve and Carl and Sarah - in the great hereafter, if she gets proof, then finally she will have the answers.

And if there's nothing – no Heaven or Hell - then she won't know because it'll all be black and she won't care.

That's enough, Eve thinks as she gazes at the street below. That's good enough. On top of that, for the millionth time that day, hard times pass.

Hard times pass.

The End

June 2009 – April 2013

Printed in Great Britain
by Amazon